THE WIND
IN HIS HEART

Other books by Charles de Lint

Riding Shotgun
Newford Stories: Crow Girls
Paperjack
Where Desert Spirits Crowd the
    Night
Out of This World
Jodi and the Witch of Bodbury
Seven Wild Sisters
Over My Head
The Cats of Tanglewood Forest
Under My Skin
Eyes Like Leaves
The Painted Boy
Muse and Reverie
The Mystery of Grace
Woods & Waters Wild
What the Mouse Found
Dingo
Promises to Keep
Little (Grrl) Lost
Triskell Tales 2
Widdershins
The Hour Before Dawn
Quicksilver & Shadow
The Blue Girl
Medicine Road
Spirits In the Wires
A Handful of Coppers
Tapping the Dream Tree
Waifs and Strays
The Onion Girl
The Road to Lisdoonvarna
Triskell Tales: 22 Years of Chapbooks
Forests of the Heart
The Newford Stories
Moonlight and Vines
Someplace to Be Flying
Trader
Jack of Kinrowan
The Ivory and the Horn
Memory and Dream
The Wild Wood
Dreams Underfoot

Spiritwalk
Hedgework and Guessery
I'll Be Watching You (as Samuel M.
    Key)
From a Whisper to a Scream (as
    Samuel M. Key)
Ghostwood
The Dreaming Place
The Little Country
Into the Green
Svaha
Angel of Darkness (as Samuel M.
    Key)
Drink Down the Moon
Wolf Moon
Greenmantle
Jack, the Giant-Killer
Yarrow
Mulengro
The Harp of the Grey Rose
Moonheart
The Riddle Of The Wren

THE WIND IN HIS HEART

CHARLES DE LINT

TRISKELL
PRESS

TRISKELL PRESS
P.O. Box 9480
Ottawa, ON
Canada K1G 3V2
www.triskellpress.com

Cover design by MaryAnn Harris.

ISBN: 0920623787

ISBN-13: 978-0920623787

The quote from Steve Earle's "Over Yonder (Jonathan's Song)" first appeared on his Transcendental Blues album (E-Squared Records, 2000). Used by permission of the artist. For more information on Steve Earle go to www.steveearle.com

Also thanks to Sandra Kasturi for the use of the lines from her poem "Speaking Crow," which originally appeared in Come Late to the Love of Birds (Tightrope Books, November 2012). Used by permission of the author.

This is a work of fiction. Names, places, businesses, characters and incidents are either the product of the author's imagination or are used in a fictitious manner. Any resemblance to actual persons living or dead, actual events or locales is purely coincidental.

for MaryAnn
and our Johnny boy.

Nearly everything that matters is a challenge,
and everything matters.
—Rilke

Some things have to be believed to be seen.
—Madeleine L'Engle

I am going over yonder
Where no ghost can follow me
There's another place beyond here
Where I'll be free I believe
—Steve Earle, "Over Yonder (Jonathan's Song)"

THE THROWAWAY CHILD

1

THOMAS CORN EYES

Those days, the prickly pear boys hung around the Little Tree Trading Post during the day, drowsing in the desert heat mostly, but still seeing and hearing everything that took place between the old adobe building and the two-lane road that ran up into the rez from the highway. They weren't seen, themselves—or at least not *as* themselves. Nobody gave a second glance to the small grove of cacti crowded up against the base of one saguaro or another. Nobody even noticed that they were rarely in exactly the same place from one morning to the next.

But Thomas Corn Eyes did. He worked at the trading post and noted their different position every morning when he arrived for work.

No one in Thomas's family had ever had eyes the colour of corn, either the green leaves of the tall midsummer growths or the yellow of the kernels. They got their name back when the federal government insisted a surname was required for everybody, without exception. On the rez they had a lot of fun coming up with names the whites thought were pregnant with traditional meaning. Johnny Squash Mother. Agnes White Deer. Robert Twin Dogs.

No, Thomas had brown eyes, the same as everyone else in the tribe. The difference was he could also see a little deeper into the invis-

ible world of the spirits than most people could, but that wasn't something he would ever talk about. He didn't want to risk gaining the
attention of the tribal shaman, Ramon Morago. For the past decade
Morago had been searching for an apprentice, and working with him
was the last thing Thomas wanted.

It wasn't that he was ashamed of his Kikimi heritage, or even that
he didn't consider himself a spiritual person. But he was only eighteen
and he didn't want to spend the rest of his life living on the rez, orga-
nizing sweats. He didn't want to be making medicine bags for the
aunties, taking Reuben's dog boys out on their spirit quests, or any of
the hundred-and-one other things a shaman did.

But no matter what he wanted or didn't, he still saw into the spiritworld, and the spirits knew it.

Thomas was studying the cacti through the windows, trying to
catch one of the prickly pear moving, when the long black Caddy
pulled into the parking lot. It was a '56 or '57, a real classic and in
perfect shape, the glossy black paint job so deep it seemed to swallow
light. He couldn't see a speck of dust on it, which, considering the
roads around here, had to be a bit of a miracle. The tinted windows
didn't let him see the driver, but man, you'd have to feel like the king
of the world behind the wheel of a car like that.

He straightened up behind the counter when the driver's door
opened and a striking older woman stepped out. He wasn't sure what
made him think she was older. Her features were youthful and she
moved with the easy grace of a dancer. She was tall and colt-thin with
a wave of thick black hair that was almost as glossy as the car's paint
job. He figured her for a model, maybe even an actress, but neither
explained what she was doing driving herself out here in the sticks
except that she looked Native—not Kikimi, but definitely Indian.
Then he caught a glimpse of her aura—the ghostly shape of a raven's
head on her shoulders—and he figured she was going into the rez to
meet with Morago or the Aunts.

She glanced in the direction of the trading post and caught him staring. Thomas looked away, but not before he saw her smile.

So much for maintaining his cool.

When she came inside she should have seemed out of place in her tight designer jeans, strapped sandals, and the midriff-baring T-shirt that probably cost more than everything he had in his closet put together. Her skin was the hue of the shadows in a red rock canyon and her eyes so dark they seemed all pupil. The eyes, he decided, were what had made him think she was older.

The trading post was like an old general store, the shelves stuffed with everything from groceries and toiletries to clothing and tools, with a cast iron stove up against one adobe wall around which Reuben's friends would sit in the afternoon to gossip and drink coffee or tea. But oddly enough, the woman appeared to fit her present surroundings as comfortably as she might a runway or some fancy restaurant. Odder still, her raven aura didn't rest passively on her shoulders. It looked around the trading post as though it had a mind of its own.

He'd never seen anything like that before. He wasn't a stranger to the auras themselves—his awareness of them was an element of his being able to see into the spiritworld. Not everybody had an aura. It was only those with the closest ties to their *ma'inawo* blood. Those who carried an animal spirit as well as a human one inside them. But he'd never seen an aura that acted independently the way this one did.

"*Ohla*," he said. "Welcome to the Painted Lands."

The woman smiled and pointed to the cooler at the far end of the counter. "Do you have any bottled Coke in there?"

"Yes, ma'am."

His response seemed to amuse her, and Thomas felt a flush creep up from under his shirt collar. To cover his embarrassment, he went over to the cooler. He took a bottle out of the icy water, wiped it down with a terrycloth towel, and popped the cap. Returning to his place behind the counter, he set it down in front of her.

"How much?" she asked.

"A dollar."

Her perfectly shaped eyebrows went up.

Thomas shrugged. "People around here don't have a lot of money. Reuben, my boss, doesn't like to gouge them."

She pulled a twenty-dollar bill out of the front pocket of her jeans and handed it to him. Thomas didn't think there'd been room for even a bill in that pocket.

"Keep the change," she said.

Do I really look like that much of a charity case? Thomas thought, but he only nodded and put the money in the till. A woman like her? She could afford to help out Reuben's bottom line.

"And how much for a map?" she asked.

"Of the rez or the National Park?"

"I'm going to the casino."

Of course she was.

"You're on the wrong side of the rez," he told her.

"There's a right and a wrong side?"

"No. Though I guess that might depend on who you're talking to. What I mean is, this isn't the fancy side with the casino. That's south of here, on the other side of the Vulture Ridge Trailhead."

"The what?"

"That's just the part of the National Park that divides the two sides of the rez. All you need to do is keep going south when you get to the trailhead. There's plenty of signs, so you don't need a map."

He gave her directions that would take her back down Jacinta to Zahra Road where a south turn would take her straight to the casino. She barely seemed to be paying attention, but her raven aura fixed him with an unwavering gaze as he spoke. It was as if it was more than simply an aura and was memorizing his words for her as well as itself. Thomas focused on the woman's face, trying to ignore the ghostly presence of the bird.

"Just remember," he said, "that Zahra changes names at the crossroads and becomes Redondo Drive when it continues south."

"I will. Thank you."

He watched her start for the door, the head of the raven aura revolving so that it continued to face him. She paused just before stepping outside and turned back to look at him.

"You've been so helpful," she said, "that I feel I should share some direction with you."

Thomas had no idea what she was talking about.

"That's okay," he said. "I'm pretty sure I know where I am."

"Are you?"

Thomas shrugged. "I've lived here all my life."

"But do you know *who* you are?" she asked.

The raven aura cocked its head when she spoke. Thomas had really never seen anything like it before. He'd never seen a woman like the one at the door, either. She could as easily have stepped right out of the pages of a magazine, or from a movie screen, as from that long black Caddy she was driving.

"I don't really think it matters who I am," he said.

"That might be the saddest thing I've heard all day," she told him.

That was because she didn't live on this side of the rez, he thought, but all he did was give her another shrug.

"It should matter to you," she added. "You should learn about yourself. Embrace all the aspects of who you are."

Thomas couldn't stop himself. "Says the woman in designer clothes on the way to the casino in a vintage Cadillac."

Her dark gaze held his for a long moment.

"Not everything is what it appears to be on the surface," she said.

Then the door was closing behind her.

He tracked her through the window as she returned to her car. She never looked back, but the raven aura watched him until the closing car door cut them both from view.

Well, that wasn't weird.

He stood looking out the window long after the dust kicked up by her tires had settled.

2

STEVE COLE

I'm camped on a ridge overlooking Zahra Road, the highway that
follows the foothills of the Hierro Maderas Mountains, when I
hear the car. It's been a perfect night. Crisp, cool air, with a
moon close enough to full that it casts long shadows on the desert
floor below. It's the kind of night where you can imagine you're the
only person in the world. It's just you and the desert. Sure, there are
coyotes talking from time to time off in the distance. An owl hooting
from the top of a saguaro this past hour or so. Mice scurrying about in
the brush closer to hand. But no people. No hikers. Nobody joyriding
on their ATVs. Not even any Kikimi whose land this is.

Until the car.

The stars tell me it's not yet midnight. I step over to where the
ground drops off and watch the headlights as they come down the
otherwise deserted two-lane blacktop below.

A few hundred yards past my camp, the car pulls over. The
passenger door opens and a figure stumbles out onto the packed dirt
on the side of the road. I make it to be a woman or a girl, with that
head of hair, though I've known my share of long-haired guys. But she
doesn't move like a guy.

Once she gets her balance, she lunges back toward the car but the door slams shut. The driver stomps on the gas, spitting gravel. The figure runs a little ways after the car, only stopping when she sees she doesn't have a hope in hell of catching up. She stands there for a long moment, shoulders drooping, arms hanging at her sides in defeat. Then she sinks to the ground and sits there hugging her knees.

The coyotes howl again, closer than the last time I heard them. I'm not worried, but the woman below jerks her head.

Coyote attacks are rare. She doesn't know that. Or maybe she's smart to be nervous because, bottom line, you can't trust anything you meet out here in the desert. Not the thorns, the heat, the mountains, the animals, the people. Maybe especially not the people.

Possum Jones, the old desert rat who took me under his wing way back in the eighties, told me his number one rule was, don't get involved. You see somebody, best walk in the other direction.

"Most times," he said in that drawl of his, "you'll get more sympathy from a hungry mountain lion."

Of course, this was while he was setting my broken leg after he found me at the bottom of a canyon, so I took what he had to say with a grain of salt. Until that moment, we'd never met. But the fact of the matter is, up in the mountains, out in the desert, most times he's right.

That girl down there, she could be in trouble. Or could be she had a little spat with her boyfriend and he's already on his way back. He catches me with his girl, he could pull out a 12-gauge and teach me the difference between buckshot and gut shot. Let me give you a hint. The first causes the pain. The second is the pain.

"Goddamn," I mutter as I turn back to my camp.

I pack up my gear and throw dirt on the fire, then make my way down to the highway. It's a roundabout route, so it takes me a good fifteen minutes before I'm standing on the blacktop. I'm a quarter of a mile south of the woman. I don't know which I'm hoping for more—that she'll be there, or she'll be gone—but when the highway takes me around the headland, I see the small figure still huddled on the side of the road.

I start to whistle an old cowboy tune as I get closer, to give her some warning. The first few bars of "Streets of Laredo" work just fine.

Her head lifts like it did when the coyotes called, but she doesn't do anything more than look over her shoulder in my direction.

I sigh. She's just a kid—I doubt she's even sixteen—and too damn trusting. Meeting a stranger out here, she should have been smart and taken to the scrub till she could figure out what's up. I'm at least three times her age and twice her size. But all she does is sit there, still hugging her knees, watching me come.

I stop ten feet away, lower my pack to the dirt and hunch down to reduce the appearance of my size, resting my weight on my ankles.

She's wearing jeans and a hoodie, sneakers with no socks. She looks cold, and I don't blame her. Once the sun goes down in the mountains, the temperature drops with it. I'm wearing a sweater under my jean jacket and I can still feel the chill in the air.

"Hey," I say.

She just looks at me.

I dig a bottle of water from my pack and offer it to her. "You thirsty?"

"Fuck off."

Nice.

"Your mama kiss that mouth of yours?" I ask.

"The only part of her that ever touched my mouth is the back of her hand."

Okay.

"Was that her who pushed you out of the car?"

"What are you—stalking me?"

"I was camped up there." I jerk a thumb up to the top of the ridge. "It's more like you brought your drama into my living room."

"You live out here?"

"Most of the time."

She scoots around so that she's no longer looking at me over her shoulder.

"What do you do?" she asks.

"Commune with nature?"

"I bet you run drugs. You got any weed in your bag? Maybe some uppers?"

I sigh, but I don't answer. "Who pushed you out of the car?"

"Why do you care?"

I want to be charitable. I really do. But I've never had the patience for this kind of crap.

"Not so much, I guess," I say and stand up. "Not enough to have to work at it, that's for damn sure. I'll leave you the water—you'll need it when the sun comes up. You have yourself a good day."

"Hey!" she calls when I start to walk away. "You can't just leave me here."

"Watch me," I reply without turning.

"It was my dad—okay? That's who dumped me here."

This time I stop and turn to look back at her. She's standing up, hands stuffed deep into the pockets of her hoodie, a challenging look in her eyes.

I have no idea how to respond.

"Jesus," I finally say. "Why would he do that?"

"To make room for a new foster kid."

"So he's your foster father."

She shakes her head. "But he gets money for each foster kid they take in. He's up to three now, but if he gets rid of me, there's room for one more."

This is why I live in the mountains and desert. They insulate you from the crap people do to each other.

"Seems to me you've got three choices," I tell her. I count them off on my fingers. "You can wait here. Come morning, you might be able to hitch a ride to wherever you need to go.

"Or you can come back to my camp and wait while I go find somebody that can help you.

"Or you can take the hike with me."

"Why don't you just call somebody?" she asks.

"Don't have a phone."

She gives me a look. "Everybody's got a phone."

"Okay. So where's yours?"

"I use Reggie's, and seeing how things played out today, I guess I won't be borrowing it again."

"And he's...?"

"My loser dad."

Everywhere this conversation goes, it takes me to a story I don't want to hear.

"Three choices," I tell her. "Which is it going to be?"

"Can we go to your camp and take the hike in the morning? I don't want to go walking into a cactus."

There's still hours before the moon sets, but I guess she's a city kid and doesn't see the way I can out here. Hell, I can make my way through this land in the dark of the moon.

"Sure. We can do that."

TWENTY MINUTES later we're back on the bluff from which I first spotted her. I get the fire started again and she sits up close to it, my spare blanket wrapped around her shoulders while she stares into the flames. I boil some water and make tea.

"Here," I tell her as I hand her a tin mug. "Sorry, I don't have sugar or milk."

"'Sokay."

"You hungry?"

She shakes her head.

I settle across the fire from her. "I'm Steve. What's your name?"

"Sadie."

"Huh."

She looks up, that challenge back in her eyes. "I know it's a loser name. I didn't pick it."

"It's not that. My grandmother's name was Sadie."

I guess she sees something in my face because she asks, "What happened to her?"

"She got the death penalty for killing her husband. This was back in Texas, where the family's from. She might have gotten off, or only had to serve some time, but instead of shooting him when he was hitting her, she waited until he was drunk and asleep, and then shot him in the face."

She doesn't say anything for a long moment, and I wonder what the hell made me tell her that. I walked the desert with Possum Jones for twenty years and it never came up once.

Her head lifts and she looks at me from across the fire. The firelight makes the glint in her eyes look fierce. "I can relate to that," she says.

"I like to believe that we can be better than that, myself," I tell her, "but honestly? Knowing what a piece of work my grandfather was? I can relate to it, too. I still miss her."

"Must be nice, having family you can miss."

"So you've got nobody else you can stay with? Friends? Kin?"

She shakes her head. "Reggie didn't like us making friends outside the house."

"Sounds like Reggie's a real piece of work."

She shrugs and takes a sip of her tea, pulling a face at the bitter taste.

"So what do you want to do?" I ask.

She gives me a puzzled look.

"With your life," I say. "Where do you want to go? What do you want to do with your life?"

"I don't know. I don't wanna go anywhere. There's no place to go anyway."

"What did you think was going to happen when you came up here to my camp?"

"I thought maybe you'd fuck me and then give me some money."

"*What?*"

"Except I guess you don't think I'm pretty enough."

I shake my head. "You've got this all wrong."

"You wouldn't have to look at my face while you're doing it."

"For Christ's sake—you could be my granddaughter."

"But—"

"It's never going to happen, kid."

Confusion returns to her face. "Reggie says old guys all like to fuck young girls."

"Yeah, well, Reggie needs his face rearranged."

"That's not all he needs rearranged. He can't get it up anymore, and that pisses him off."

"Listen kid, you shouldn't even know that shit."

She shrugs. "It's just what it is. So what?"

"Jesus. You're young and you've got your whole life ahead of you. Focus on getting an education. Make something of yourself. You ever hear the expression 'success is the best revenge'?"

She shakes her head.

"You make something of yourself and that just shows losers like Reggie you're better than them."

"But I'm not."

"Don't say that," I tell her.

She fiddles with the cuffs of the hoodie, pulls them down over her knuckles. She won't look at me.

"I wouldn't even know where to start," she says.

"I know people who can help you."

"Why would they?"

"Because it's what they do. You should get some rest. It's a bit of hike in the morning."

She nods. "You don't sound much like a Texan," she says.

"How would you know what we sound like?"

"You think I've never seen a movie or a TV show? They all talk funny."

"Maybe when I left home I made a point of learning to talk like a Yankee."

"Why would you do that?" she asks.

I shrug. "Kids get embarrassed about the stupidest things. If I had to do it over, I wouldn't. But now this is just the way I talk. The only time you'll hear me drawl these days is when I'm putting it on."

"Why would you do *that*?"

"Why don't you get yourself some rest."

She has another sip of her tea and grimaces again before she sets it down in the sand by the fire.

"You need to get some normal tea," she says as she lies down. "That tastes like a dog pissed in it."

"Goodnight to you, too," I tell her.

I finish my own tea. It's not my best batch, but it beats buying it from a store. I wait until her breathing evens out, then stand up and stretch. I walk away from the camp and take a leak. When I get back, Calico's sitting on a rock, a big grin on her face.

I don't know why she's attached herself to me, but it's not like I got any choice in the matter. She just showed up a few years ago, not long after Possum died, and has been hanging around ever since. Not that I mind—her smarts and beauty are off the chart.

"Didn't think I'd see you tonight," I say. "I thought you said you were off leading the dog boys on a chase."

She shrugs. "I took them up through Devil's Canyon and wore them right out. Those boys are not in good shape." She nods to the sleeping girl. "Didn't take you for the nurturing type."

"I'm not. But she needs help."

"Yeah, I overheard. I was feeling horny before I got here, but listening to her story pretty much put a damper on that."

That's Calico in a nutshell: full of innuendo and mischief.

"I'm taking her to Morago—see if he can help."

"But she's not Kikimi."

"Neither's the money they got for their center."

Calico cocks her head. "Except I thought it came to them with no strings attached."

"It did. Same as Sadie's coming to them. They can help or not, but I'm hoping they'll help. It's pretty damn obvious her own people are useless."

She nods. "Call me if you decide to go break this Reggie's head. But remember, it's not the Wild West anymore. They come after you for stuff like that now, doesn't matter how justified."

"Call you?" I say with a laugh. "How am I supposed to do that? Neither of us even has a—"

But she's already gone.

"Who was that woman that came by last night?" Sadie asks me in the morning.

I'm in the middle of pouring myself a second cup of coffee and almost drop the pot.

"You *saw* her?"

"Well, yeah. Was I not supposed to? You could've told me you already have a girlfriend."

I stop, mid-pour. I was sure the kid was dead asleep. It's a good thing Calico and I didn't get into anything amorous.

"You really saw her?" I repeat.

"Have you been into the weed? That's what I just said. And what's with the furry deal? Is that your kink?"

I don't know what to say. My girlfriend's a—for lack of a better term—foxalope. Part antelope, part fox. You should see the look on Calico's face when I use the word. She looks to be in her mid-thirties, with a shock of fox-red hair that she usually wears loose, and a pair of small antelope horns push up from the top of her brow. Some days, she's also got fox ears and a big bushy tail. She calls herself a *ma'inawo*, which is Kikimi for "cousin."

We keep our relationship on the down-low, so this is weird, and I don't know how to explain it.

"Furry?" I manage. "That's a thing?"

She nods. "Yeah, you know. People who put on costumes, pretending they're some kind of animal. It's how they get it up."

"Sure," I say. "Let's go with that."

"And that's what turns you on?"

"No, she's—look, we should get going."

I turn away and start packing my gear, covering the fire.

"God, I hope I never grow old," she says. "If you've got a kink, so what? Own it."

I don't bother answering.

THREE HOURS later a gaggle of rez dogs welcomes us into Abigail White Horse's yard. They run circles around us, barking, tails wagging. Sadie shrinks away from them and moves closer to me.

"It's okay," I tell her. "They're friendly."

"Yeah, tell that to the last guy they ate."

Aggie's place is high up in the foothills at the end of a couple of miles of winding dirt road. It's a long low adobe building with a lean-to and corral made of saguaro ribs on the south. A pair of those big cacti dominate one side of the yard, with a stand of raggedy mesquite and palo verde on the other. There's the remains of a fire pit out past the corral. Farther up the hill is a little adobe casita that serves as the old woman's studio.

She comes out of the little building now, drawn by the dogs' welcome. Someone once told me she's got to be in her eighties or more, but she looks more like she's in her late sixties. Out hiking, she's got staying power long past anything I can muster, and I can jog for a couple of hours under the hot summer sun. She's sturdily built, with an open brown face and grey-white hair pulled back into a long braid.

"I thought you were Old Man Puma," she says, "coming down off the mountain the way you did. Pretty sure you gave the dogs a heart attack."

"We were up on the ridge trail."

She nods. Her gaze shifts to Sadie.

"Who's your friend?" she asks.

"Says her name is Sadie. I found her up north on Zahra Road."

"Found her? Was there a wreck?"

I shake my head. "She got tossed from a car."

Aggie frowns.

"It wasn't moving," I add.

"And that makes it better?"

"I didn't say that."

She focuses her attention back to Sadie.

"How are you holding up, child?" she asks.

Sadie fiddles with the cuffs of her hoodie and shrugs. "I'm fine," she says.

Aggie studies her until the girl finally looks up. Sadie shifts from foot to foot, but she doesn't look away. Aggie has that effect on people.

"So you're looking for a safe place for her?" Aggie asks me.

I nod.

"Whoa," Sadie says. "I'm not staying out here in the middle of nowhere."

"It'll just be for a day or so," I tell her. "I need to talk to this guy named Ramon Morago, figure out a few legalities. But you should be able to move to the dorm in a few days."

"What dorm?"

"You want to finish high school, right? We talked about it on the way here."

"We didn't talk about no dorm. I want to go with you and live in the desert."

I shake my head.

"Don't worry," she says. "I won't cramp your style with your furry girlfriend."

"Girlfriend?" Aggie says, her brows rising.

"Yeah," Sadie says helpfully, "the one with the furry fetish."

"Forget it," I tell her.

But Aggie isn't about to let it go.

"What does that mean?" she asks Sadie. "What's a furry fetish?"

"You know. She likes to dress up and pretend she's an animal. Big fox tail and ears, little deer horns."

Aggie's lip twitches.

"And how long has this been going on?" she asks me.

I sigh. I like my privacy and don't want to talk about the relationship, especially in front of a kid, but Aggie's waiting for an answer.

"She showed up after Possum died."

"Possum?" Sadie says. "Are *all* your friends into this animal thing?"

"No," I tell her. "It's just his name—I don't know how he got it. He never told me and I never asked."

"John Little Tree gave it to him," Aggie says. "Back in the day. Because he was playing dead back then."

"I don't get it," I say.

She shrugs. "He lived in the desert while the rest of the world thought he was dead."

Now it's my gaze she holds. I know what those dark eyes of hers are saying: We might as well call you Possum, too.

"So it was like, his Indian name," Sadie says.

Aggie nods, her gaze still holding mine. "And what's the name of your friend?" she asks.

"Calico."

"I know her. I'd say be careful. Fox girls are tricksters, but antelope are loyal. So you're probably okay."

Sadie's following our exchange with big eyes.

"She visits you?" I ask.

Aggie shrugs. "Cousins. They stop around from time to time."

"So you know Calico? Does anyone else?"

"Ask Reuben Little Tree about her visits. She seems to have made it her life's work to tease him and those dog boys of his."

I pinch the bridge of my nose, trying to make sense of what she's saying. Calico does have a thing about running dogs, but this business about Reuben is giving me a headache.

"When you say 'dog boys,'" Sadie asks Aggie, "are they really part dog?"

"No," I say, eyeing the kid.

"Yes," Aggie says at the same time.

I sigh, but Sadie doesn't seem to have any problem with it. That's clear from the bright interest in her eyes.

"I'd like to stay here," she says to Aggie. "If it's still okay."

"Of course," Aggie says. "I'll get a poultice for those injuries of yours."

Sadie's eyes go big. Me, I'm in the dark.

"What injuries?" I ask.

Neither of them responds for a long moment. Then Sadie pulls down the zipper of her hoodie and takes it off. She drops it in the dirt and stands there in a sleeveless T-shirt. Her forearms are covered with dozens of tiny scars and cuts that cross each other in a bewildering pattern. They look like they were made with a razor or a really sharp knife. Some look infected.

Then she lifts the T-shirt up to the bottom of her breasts. Her whole torso is a mess of bruises. Yellow and green. Purple and blue.

"The fuck?" pops out of my mouth. My hands are clenched in fists at my side. "Who did that to you?"

But I already know.

"He only hits me where it doesn't show," she says.

"And did he cut you, too?"

When she doesn't answer, I realize she did it to herself.

"Maybe," Aggie says, "it's a way to take back ownership of your body?"

Sadie shakes her head.

"It's okay," Aggie says. "You don't have to talk about it. And you can stay here as long as you need to."

She nods and picks up her hoodie, but she doesn't put it on. I can't take my gaze from all those crisscrossing cuts on her arms. Why the hell would anybody do that to themselves?

"You go on ahead inside and make yourself comfortable," Aggie says. "I'll be right in."

She nods again, but she doesn't move.

"Is there something else you need to tell us?" Aggie asks.

Sadie looks at me. "You're not going after him, are you?"

"Who? Reggie?"

"Yeah."

"Why would you want to protect him?"

"I don't," she says. "But I don't want you to get into trouble and I don't want him taking anything out on the foster kids."

"You've got a good heart," Aggie says.

"Do I?" Sadie asks. "Then why's my life such crap?"

Aggie shakes her head. "We'll see what we can do to make it better."

Sadie turns her attention back to me. "Am I going to see you again?"

"Sure. I come by here all the time."

She doesn't say anything else, but she keeps looking at me, waiting.

"Okay," I say. "Reggie's off limits. For now. I can't promise forever."

She mouths the word "thanks" and walks toward the house. One of the dogs steps close to her and bumps its head against her leg. I expect Sadie to freak, but she just drops a hand and absently strokes Ruby's head. It's like Aggie's words changed something inside her and she's no longer afraid of the dogs. She goes inside the house, the dog with her, and the door closes behind them.

I turn to Aggie. "Calico and I—we've been keeping this private."

"So I see. I thought you were alone most of the time out there, by choice."

"I am, just not always. But solitude doesn't bother me. And crap like Sadie's life—that's why I'm done with the world beyond these mountains. I'm not running away from anything. I just don't like the way people live their lives out there."

"I understand," Aggie says. "But when it comes to the world right here, maybe it's time you realized some of the other people you meet out in these hills aren't necessarily human."

"Like who?"

"That doesn't matter right now. What matters is that you keep your heart open. Speaking of which, why did you help the girl? Why didn't you just walk away?"

A lot of things go running through my mind. The way Sadie was just sitting there on the side of the road, arms wrapped around her knees. Possum shooting a coyote caught in a trap, the festering of its infected forepaw having already crawled up into its torso, swelling its chest to twice its normal size. Reuben catching packrats nesting around the kids' dormitory and taking them clear across the mountain before letting them go, whereas somebody else would have just shot them.

"The hell would I know?" I finally say. "I'm going to talk to Morago."

I head off before she can ask me something else I can't answer.

3

SADIE HIGGINS

Sadie didn't know what to expect inside the old woman's house. If she was lucky, maybe she could find something she could pocket and pawn if she ever made it back to town. But it didn't look like she'd find much in here. The back door she came through led her into a large open-concept space sparsely furnished with chunky wooden furniture that looked handmade. There were patterned rugs everywhere—on the floor, hanging on the walls, draped over the back of the couch. They were like the kind you'd see in the Indian Market on Mission Street, except these ones were all old and faded. Everything here seemed old and faded. And a little weird. There was what looked like a whole field of dried plants hanging in bundles from the rafters of the kitchen area. Who did that? There weren't any normal glasses or plates—except for finely-woven baskets, everything seemed to be made of pottery.

And then there were all the paintings hanging on the walls, perched on surfaces, or on the floor leaning against the walls. They reminded Sadie of the woman who had visited Steve at the camp last night. Like her, all the people in them had animal and plant parts. A man with a coyote's head. A stand of prickly pear with a hundred little faces. A rabbit with human arms. An owl with a woman's face. See-through saguaro, with people sleeping inside them.

The figures were stylized, but at the same time appeared too realistic for her comfort. There was something creepy about them. She wanted to ignore them but she couldn't seem to look away, either. The background colours seemed all off as well. Brown skies and blue desert floor. Purple and pink mesas with yellow and blue cacti. They made the figures pop out, but that only made their own oddities harder to ignore.

After she'd walked around and looked at all the paintings on the walls, she started going through the ones on the floor. They were three to four deep in places. She didn't know why she was doing it. She didn't even want to look at all these strange creatures in the first place.

Finally she came across a couple of stacks of portraits of ordinary people. They were still a little creepy—just because of the way Aggie painted, she supposed—but at least they were normal. She figured they were folks who lived on the rez. She didn't know any of them.

Then she stopped. There was Steve.

Sadie sat back on her heels and studied this one. Because she knew what he actually looked like, this was the first time she could appreciate that maybe the old lady wasn't a complete loser. The figure in the painting didn't only look like Steve. It *felt* like him, too.

And it didn't creep her out as much as the animal people did.

After a few moments she let the other paintings in the stack fall back in front and got up to finish looking around.

The red dog that followed her inside had dropped to the floor and stretched out as they came in. Its eyes followed Sadie as she roamed around the room. The only modern convenience she could spot was a laptop computer on a table in one corner. Even the phone was an old black rotary model.

She lifted the receiver and listened to the dial tone for a moment before she laid it back in its cradle. There was no one she could call. Nobody who'd want to hear from her except for maybe Aylissa, the oldest of the foster kids her parents had taken in. But she couldn't call her because just like Sadie herself, Aylissa didn't have her own phone.

The only people allowed to answer the house phone were Reggie and her mother, Tina.

The dog lifted its head and Sadie turned to see Aggie come in.

The old woman was interesting, but she was kind of creepy weird, too. Just like her house. How had Aggie known she was a cutter?

"Did you do these paintings?" she asked.

Aggie nodded.

"And people buy them?"

Aggie smiled. "Not to your taste?"

Sadie realized she'd better dial it back. She didn't want to offend the old lady and get thrown out on her ass.

"I've just never seen anything like them before," she said.

"You're not alone," Aggie told her. "They make other people uncomfortable too. But it doesn't matter one way or the other. They're not for sale. Each one is a little piece of the subject rendered in the portrait, and how could one sell pieces of one's friends?"

Sadie remembered the conversation outside.

"So these are, like, people you know? And they look like this?"

"When they wish to," Aggie said.

"And they're not wearing costumes?"

"No. Now come sit here," Aggie said, motioning toward a chair at the kitchen table. "I want to look at those cuts. Stretch your arms out on the table."

Sadie hesitated, suddenly feeling embarrassed and shy.

"I don't make judgments," the old lady said. "I don't agree with what you're doing to yourself, but only you can decide whether to keep on doing it or to stop."

Sadie put her hands in the pockets of her jeans. Her fingers closed around the handle of the little utility knife she carried everywhere.

"I can't seem to stop," she found herself admitting.

"Maybe it will become easier now that you're away from the bad situation you were in. And if you concentrate on something else."

"You mean like schoolwork?"

"Or whatever else you can find to distract you."

"A joint would seriously help."

"Except for that," the old woman said.

Of course she'd think that, Sadie thought. God, old people.

"I'm not so sure about this whole 'going back to high school' deal," she said. "I only agreed so Steve would shut up. The whole morning he kept going on about how things were different back in his day. How a kid didn't have to finish high school, but they could still get a decent job and do well. But now even a degree doesn't promise anybody anything. But without it, you've got nothing."

Aggie went to the long table by the sink while Sadie sat down.

"Did you promise Steve you'd do it?" Aggie asked.

"No. I just said I'd think about it."

"Good."

"Good what? That I'll think about it, or that I didn't promise him?"

"Both, really. It's important to be an honourable person. The oppressors can take everything else away from us. Our freedom, our hope, our dignity. But they can't take our honour. So when you give your word, be sure you keep it. And make sure you only promise what you can deliver."

"What's that supposed to mean?"

Aggie regarded her for a long moment. "Let's say your best friend is dying of cancer. You could say to her that you promise she'll get better, but you both know that's not a promise you can keep. But if you say that you promise to stay with her until the very end, *that* has meaning. It lets them know they won't die alone, and that means more than any empty promise."

"Okay. I kind of see that."

"Good."

Aggie fussed with a few things at the long table where she stood, then finally brought back a clay bowl filled with some kind of thick green-brown paste.

"What's that?" Sadie asked, grimacing.

"Medicine. It'll fight the infection and itchiness, and help the cuts and bruises to heal more quickly. It'll sting a bit when it's first applied, but you should find some immediate relief. Try to think of something else while I put it on."

How was she supposed to do that? Sadie wondered. All she could do was anticipate the coming pain.

She winced when the old woman began to spread the paste on her cuts.

"Talk to me," Aggie said. "Don't think about this."

Okay. But crap, that really stung.

Sadie had to blink back tears. She tried to think of something to say.

"So, Steve's girlfriend," she finally said. "She's not wearing a costume either?"

Aggie shook her head.

"Weird. I guess he's got a kink or something."

"Or maybe he doesn't see the difference."

"What's that supposed to mean?"

"Steve's one of those people who sees a person for what they are inside, not what they show to the world."

Sadie shivered. "God, he must think I'm a total freak. No wonder he didn't want to fu—I mean, you know. Sleep with me."

"I think that has more to do with your age, and that you were in a vulnerable position when he found you."

Sadie didn't get that.

"So what's his deal, anyway?" she asked the old woman. "Does he really just live out in the desert?"

Aggie nodded. "Has for probably thirty, forty years now."

"What's he running from?"

"You'll have to ask him."

"You don't have a guess?"

"I don't go poking into other people's stories. It's not polite."

"I'm just curious," Sadie said. "I don't mean anything by it."

"I know. And there we are—all done."

Sadie realized she'd completely forgotten what the old woman was doing. And she'd been right. The itchiness was completely gone. And so was the pain.

"If you feel chilled," Aggie said, "go out and sit in the sun. We should try to keep your hoodie from chaffing against the skin until the medicine has done its work. You can rinse it off in an hour or so."

"Okay. Um. Thanks."

"Now I want to go back to the piece I'm working on. Will you be okay here on your own?"

Trusting much? Sadie thought. But she just nodded. Until she figured a few things out, she had nowhere else to go.

"Are you hungry? Or thirsty? I should have asked you sooner."

"No, Steve gave me all kinds of crap from that backpack of his. The thing must weigh a ton."

"He's a strong man in more ways than one."

"I guess," Sadie said. Then she had a thought. "Is it okay if I use your computer?"

"Go ahead. It's on dial-up, so it'll probably seem like it runs on molasses compared to what you had at home."

"Reggie doesn't let anybody use his computer except for him. I used the ones at school or the library."

Aggie gave her a look Sadie didn't recognize. She thought maybe Aggie felt sorry for her, but there was no way to tell. Nobody had ever felt sorry for her before. Not even her teachers. The school was so rough, they all looked exhausted most of the time.

Aggie started to reach out a hand to her, then seemed to reconsider and let it fall to her side.

"Well, you can use this one as much as you like," was all she said. "Make yourself at home," she added, then she stepped out the back door and Sadie was alone again in the old woman's house.

Except for the dog. Ruby, Steve said her name was.

"So are you a real dog?" Sadie asked. "Or are you like the guys in the paintings?"

Ruby looked at her but didn't even bother to lift her head.

Sadie walked over to the computer. She wondered how far it was to civilization. Maybe she could take off, sell the computer to somebody for a quick few bucks... Oh, who was she kidding? Even if she got back to the city, she had nowhere to go. She was stuck out here in the middle of the sticks until she could figure out more than just running away. Because the problem with running was, you needed to have somewhere to run to.

All she knew for sure was she wouldn't be going home again. Who knew where the hell Reggie would dump her the next time.

She sat down and opened the computer. Once it woke up, she called up a browser.

Yeah, she was stuck here. But until she came up with a way out, she could at least find out who Steve really was and why he was hiding out in the mountains. She knew just where to start.

She typed a string of words into the browser's search bar: Sadie. Texas. Death penalty.

4

THOMAS

Working at Little Tree Trading Post, there was no way Thomas would ever be able to save enough money to get away from the rez. His boss, Reuben Little Tree, couldn't afford to pay much, but the little Thomas did earn had to cover living expenses for the whole Corn Eyes family. Mom and Auntie. Two sisters. A little brother.

He had no other jobs except for the one at the school, but that was volunteer work since he didn't have a degree. But he liked kids, so he did it anyway. He couldn't move to the city because even if he could get a job, there'd still be nobody here to take care of the family.

Which meant Thomas was never getting out of this place.

He leaned on the counter now and stared out the window. He did that a lot. The prickly pear had shifted again since the woman had driven off in her Caddy. That made him think of her raven aura, and *that* made him think about this ability he had to see into the spiritworld.

Maybe he should go talk to Ramon Morago. For all he knew, a shaman's apprentice got a salary. Though if he committed to studying with the shaman, he knew he'd *really* never get out of here.

The doves and quail out in the parking lot scattered suddenly as

Reuben's pickup pulled in, dragging a cloud of dust behind it. It was early October and the rains would be coming soon, but right now the land was bone dry. You couldn't even walk without kicking up dust.

Thomas went out to help Reuben unload.

"What are you doing this weekend?" Reuben asked as they brought the last load of dry goods and dairy inside.

Thomas shrugged. "I promised my sisters I'd take them to some thrift shops in the city, if Ben will lend me his truck."

"You can borrow mine if he's using his."

Thomas's spirits lifted a little. He loved driving Reuben's pickup. Taking it all the way to Santo del Vado Viejo would be a fun adventure for a change.

"Thanks."

They busied themselves restocking the shelves and cooler.

"There's going to be a sweat on Saturday," Reuben said. "Over by Aggie's place. You should come."

Thomas shook his head. "You know I don't do stuff like that."

Reuben regarded him for a long moment, then just shook his head. "Sometimes I can't figure you out," he said.

"What's that supposed to mean?"

"You come from one of the most traditional families on the rez— you know your Aunt Lucy was Morago's spiritual advisor, right?"

Thomas shook his head. Lucy was Auntie's sister. They were both his mother's aunts, not his, and he didn't know much about her since she'd died when he was still a little kid. He knew her sister Leila— whom everybody just called Auntie—better, but not by much. Leila had turned ninety-eight this past summer, and spent her days sitting on the porch looking at the mountains. She told stories and handed out advice whether it was asked for or not, but she never talked about herself.

"I didn't think women could be shamans," he said.

"They don't have to be. Women's magic is more powerful in our people—always has been."

Thomas just looked at him.

"You're a good kid," Reuben said. "You're responsible, you take care of your family, you help out at the school. But sometimes I get the feeling you're embarrassed about being a Kikimi."

"You think I should be running out in the desert with your dog boys."

Reuben waved that off. "I get it's not for everybody. Some of us run in a pack, some are lone wolves. Whatever turns your crank. I'm just curious as to why you don't want anything to do with our traditions." He held up a hand before Thomas could even think about how to respond. "But if you want to tell me to mind my own business, that's fine. No hard feelings."

Thomas sighed. "You wouldn't understand."

"Try me."

Thomas put a last bag of sugar on the shelf and stood up. He looked out the window to the dusty parking lot, the scrub brush on the other side of the road, the foothills, the mountains rising up behind them. Finally he turned back to Reuben. "I feel trapped here," he said. "There's more to the world than these dry hills and dust, but I feel like I'm never going to see it."

"Because you have to take care of your family."

Thomas nodded. "That. And no offense, because I appreciate this job, but there's no way I can put enough aside working here to get a travelling stake. I'm stuck in this place."

Reuben laughed, but he stopped right away when Thomas began to bristle.

"You think you're the only one to feel that way?" Reuben asked. "I left the rez when I was sixteen and spent the next ten years seeing the world until I realized the thing I was looking for was right here."

"You? But you're—"

"Yeah, yeah. Warrior Society. Out beating the drum for all our traditions to anyone who'll listen. But once upon a time I was a punk whose only dream was to get as far away as I could from here."

Thomas didn't know what to say.

"I wouldn't even be telling you all of this," Reuben went on, "except I know you're not like a lot of kids. You've got something—in here." He brought a closed fist up against his chest. "A connection to this place. To the spirits. And I guess I just want to tell you that you don't have to be afraid of it. Embrace that connection, even just to try it on for size. You could surprise yourself. You could fall in love with this place, the same as me. And if nothing happens, or you don't like what you're feeling..." He shrugged. "Well, you can still just walk away from it all."

Thomas returned his gaze to the stark landscape beyond the windowpane. It was weird how Reuben's words echoed those of the woman with the raven aura.

"Except I don't want to be a shaman," he said. He glanced at Reuben, who raised his eyebrows.

"Who says you have to be?" Reuben asked when Thomas didn't go on.

Thomas cleared his throat. "You see those cacti out there?"

"The prickly pear?"

Thomas nodded. "Every morning when I come here, they're in a different position."

"Yeah," Reuben said. "Those prickly pear boys don't try all that hard to go unnoticed."

"Seriously?" Thomas said. "That's all you've got to say?"

"What am I supposed to say? I know you see things other people don't. I watch your eyes track things only people like you and I see."

"Exactly."

Reuben gave him a puzzled look. "I'm not following. What's your point?"

"Kikimi who see stuff like that end up as shaman. Or one of your dog boys."

Reuben smiled. "Well, at least you don't go through life in denial like Steve Cole."

"The old desert rat?"

"He's not that old."

"Come on. He might be even older than you."

Reuben's smile widened and he shook his head. "Some parts of being eighteen, I forget."

"Okay," Thomas asked. "So neither of you is old. But what about Cole?"

"He's been living outside of the world for the past forty years and he doesn't even know it."

"You mean he sees stuff too?"

"You bet. But mostly, he just takes it in and carries on as though everything's normal. He doesn't even realize how special that spot is, where he's camped.

"But he's not even Kikimi."

"You don't have to be Kikimi to see spirits or to walk in their lands."

"I didn't know that."

"Sounds like there's a lot you don't know."

"I..."

Thomas's voice trailed off. He took a steadying breath.

"So what time does this sweat start?" he finally asked.

5

STEVE

I think about my conversation with Aggie as I follow the ridge trail from her place down into the rez and finally to the Painted Lands Community Center, which also houses both the school and Morago's office. The whole time I'm walking, I can't get one comment out of my head.

Be careful. Fox girls are tricksters.

What the hell's *that* supposed to mean? I can't see any reason why Aggie'd go warning me about Calico. It throws me a bit, then I remember she added that antelope are loyal, so I'm probably okay. I hope she's right.

I have to admit that when Calico first showed up, I thought I was having some crazy LSD flashback. Even having heard plenty of campfire stories on the rez about *ma'inawo*, or 'cousins,' it took me a while to accept not only Calico's presence, but how she took such a personal interest in me. Personal is an understatement. That girl-friend of mine's horny as a jackrabbit and not the least bit shy to let you know about it. She's another piece of the beauty in this wild land, and I love it all the more for her part in it. I just wanted to hold on to our privacy. Sadie spouted off to Aggie, but I hope it doesn't go any further. Like any small place, people on the rez love nothing more than to toss around some juicy gossip, so it travels fast.

THE COMMUNITY CENTER is a long low adobe building. It looks like every time they needed more space, they just added another few rooms on, which is exactly the case. Mesquite and palo verde cluster near the walls, with one old uncle saguaro and the usual mess of prickly pear and brush.

I pause at the glass front doors and try to clear my head before I go inside.

Janet's at the front desk, looking at something on her computer screen.

"*Ohla*, Steve," she says.

"Hey, Janet. Is Morago in?"

"Are you kidding?" she says. "Sometimes I think he lives in that office of his. There's nobody with him right now."

"Thanks."

I can hear kids playing in the gym as I follow the hall to Morago's office. He's the tribal shaman, but he also runs the whole center and the dorm down the road, where the kids who don't have homes live. It's mostly other tribes in the dorm—Yaqui, Apache, Tohono O'odham—with a handful of Mexican kids who lost their parents crossing the desert and don't have families on this side of the border. They're supposed to be sent back, but Morago's got a way of bending the rules if it's better for the kid.

He's on the phone when I step into his office, and he waves me to a chair. The furniture's all mission style, solid and dependable, softened with pillows and rugs in bright Kikimi patterns. It feels more like a traditional home than an office, if you ignore the modern gear. Computer, printer, fancy phone.

Morago's pureblooded Kikimi, but he doesn't look it. Where most of the tribe members have wide faces and carry some weight, he's lean, with piercing amber eyes and narrow chiseled features, and his hair is a deep russet colour. I remember asking him about it once and he said he thought a few generations back one of his ancestors was probably a red-tailed hawk.

I laughed at the time. Now, thinking about Aggie's comment about cousins stopping in for a visit, and I'm not so sure anymore.

Morago finishes up his conversation with an "*Ohla*" and hangs up. In Kikimi, *ohla* means both 'hello' and 'goodbye.'

I get an "*Ohla*" too, then he asks, "And how are you today, He Who Walks With the Moonlight?"

"Feeling stupid. And stop trying to give me one of your phony made-up Indian names."

Every time I see him he's got a new one for me. My favourite is Pisses Like a Horse. Is it my fault I've got a big bladder?

"Feeling stupid's a good way to start a journey into wisdom," he says.

"No, it's just because of something Aggie told me: that some of the people I meet out in the hills aren't necessarily human."

Morago smiles. "And you're only figuring that out now?"

"Jesus. Don't you start."

Morago spreads his hands. "The world is what it is." He waits a beat before adding, "Is that what you came to talk to me about?"

I shake my head.

"Then it must be about the white girl you left at Aggie's place."

"How the hell could you know that?"

He nods to the window. On the other side of the glass, a couple of crows are perched on a low-hanging branch of a mesquite tree that's almost touching the pane.

"The crows were gossiping about it," he says.

Aggie's got me so rattled that I can't tell if he's joking or not. He's always coming out with crap like that. The difference now is, I'm actually wondering if it's true.

I decide to ignore it and tell him what I know about Sadie.

"You sure it's a good idea?" he asks when I'm done. "The kids are all getting along right now, but they still hang out with their own tribe or race. She'll be the only white kid."

"Aggie says it's okay for Sadie to stay at her place for now."

"Okay. And you're sure she's serious about studying? We've only just gotten Olivia to stop acting out. I don't know that we need another source of disruption right now."

"Maybe you could have a talk with her—judge the situation for yourself? I mean, she's got nothing to go back to."

"Yeah, but is anybody going to come looking for her?" he asks.

"What do *you* think? Her old man threw her away like garbage."

Morago sighs. "The problem is, lots of people throw things away and then decide later they want to keep them after all."

"Sadie's a person, not a thing."

"I know that. It's just that the Indian and Mexican kids—we can be sure nobody's coming for them. Their parents are dead, or in jail, or meth heads who can't string a couple of thoughts together. Sadie's father sounds like a monster, but he's still in the picture, as it were. Trouble starts with her, it could blow back on everybody."

"Just tell me you'll talk to her and think about it. That's all I ask."

"Of course I'll talk to her. Hell, if you really want her in, just say the word."

I shake my head. "When we started this I said no strings attached. You're the guy in charge."

"Sure, but—"

"We can't go down that road," I tell him. "She either gets in on her own merit and your say-so, or I start looking for other options." I stand up. "And I'll know if you're bullshitting me."

"You always do. You heading home? Aunt Nora puts on a great spread for the kids. You could eat with us."

"No, I need to get back to my place and think about all of this."

I'm about to turn away, except Morago's holding my gaze and I find I can't look away.

"Don't look at this new knowledge as something that's going to mess up your life. Look at it as finding a deeper understanding of the worlds you're living in."

"What's that supposed to mean?"

Instead of answering, he asks, "You're going home by the ridge trail?"

I nod.

"Do me a favour when you get back to the trailer. Pull out a map and measure the distance from here to Painted Cloud Canyon."

"I know how far it is. I've walked it a thousand times. It takes me about an hour."

He nods. "I know. But humour me. Look at a map when you get back."

"You don't have to do the cryptic shaman crap with me."

"I'm not. But if you have any questions later, you know where to find me."

I am so not enjoying this day.

"Fine," I tell him.

He smiles. "*Ohla*, brother."

He's got a smile you can't resist. No matter what's going on—how pissed off you might be about something, or how bummed—you can't help but respond.

I'm still grinning when I give Janet a goodbye wave and head out the front door of the community center.

ONCE I'M CLIMBING up into the foothills behind the rez, I decide to time myself. I get a reading from the sun and start walking. It's steep going until I reach the ridge trail. The sky is cloudless and the sun is unrelenting. I pick up a trio of turkey buzzards once I'm on the trail, all three drifting in lazy circles high above me as I head north. I wish I were up there with them. The heat bouncing off the rocks and dirt makes it twice as hot down here as where they are.

We didn't have our usual furnace of a summer, but the fall's been making up for it with day after day of unseasonably hot weather. Usually the rains have come by now, cooling everything down, but we haven't had any water since the spring monsoons.

I keep to a steady pace. It gives me plenty of time to think.

I don't know what Morago's game is. Possum showed me this trail back when we first met, and like I told Morago, I've been walking it ever since. I know every foot of it, every view. I don't see how tracing it out on a map is going to tell me something I don't already know. But

Morago's always been there for me—for me and Possum. He's seen us through a lot of crap. Hell, I've probably known him longer than I have anybody else I can think of, on or off the rez, because we go back to long before I got to the Painted Hills. So I'll give him the benefit of the doubt and accept that he's got a good reason for his strange request.

When I get to the turnoff to my place, the position of the sun tells me it's taken me an hour and a bit, more or less. Just as it always does.

The new trail winds between walls of rock until it deposits me into the hollow behind my trailer. From where I stand, there's just a short cave-length to the ledge where the trailer sits.

This hollow's an odd little place, no bigger than a decent-sized backyard, and it doesn't matter how hot or cold it is in the canyon itself or out on the mountain ridge trails, the temperature in here always seems moderate. It's like it has its own little microclimate.

There's a spring-fed pool at one end, shaded by a pair of sycamores. The other end gets all the sun and that's where Possum set up the garden I still maintain. I've got corn growing there, carrots, peas, peppers, beans, all kinds of squash. On a raised bed to one side there's a selection of herbs.

Behind the trees, and between the pool and the rock face, is a tall gap in the rock that gives an overview of the valley. Years back, before I knew him, Possum set up a wooden bench there to watch the sunset, and I still come up to do the same thing. I like to watch the moonlight too—full moon, especially, when the shadows grow across the desert floor and it feels like you're looking out on some whole other world.

I'd like to settle down on the bench for a while right now, but I'm too curious about Morago's mysterious request, so I leave the hollow to walk down a short, natural stone stairway, past the cistern and into the cave. A few moments later I emerge on the ledge where the trailer sits.

Damned if I know how Possum got it up here. He'd have to have had it hoisted up with a crane because the bottom of the canyon's a good ten feet down from the lip of the ledge and the trailer's a full-size Airstream. An overhang keeps the worst of the sun off of it and there's room between the trailer and edge for a picnic table and fire pit. Everything in the trailer runs on propane. When I need a new tank, Reuben

Little Tree delivers it by ATV, though we have to haul it up by hand from the canyon floor.

But the damnedest thing of all is how people climbing up the canyon just never notice the trailer. I can be sitting on the picnic table playing my guitar and they don't even look once in my direction. When I asked Possum about it he just shrugged and said something about how sound doesn't always carry the way you'd think it would in these mountains, and the trailer was just at the wrong angle to be seen from below. Except I've been down there looking up and had no trouble spotting it. Truth is, I'd be hard pressed to ignore that big shiny tube on wheels sitting on a ledge where it has no godly right to be.

I go into the Airstream and grab a bottled water from the fridge, then pull out a roll of maps from where they're wedged in between the bookcase and the wall. Outside, I find the one I'm looking for and spread it open on the picnic table, holding the corners down with stones. I use my finger to trace the distance from the rez to the trail that took me into the hollow.

Son of a bitch. That can't be right.

Frowning, I retrace the route, but even careful measurement doesn't change a damn thing.

I decide to change tack. I find the spot where Sadie's father dumped her in the desert and follow the route we hiked to the ride trail into the rez. We walked about three hours, and that's pretty much what the map tells me it should have taken. So what gives with my route back to the trailer?

If the map's to be believed, it should also have taken me three hours to get here. Three times as long as it actually did.

Somebody's messing with me. I'd blame it on the map, except I bought it myself and I know it's accurate. I just never traced this particular route on it before. So that leaves Morago. But why the hell would he trick me?

"Whatcha doing?"

I almost drop my water bottle at the sound of Calico's voice. She saunters from the cave and drops down on the bench across from me.

A bushy tail swishes behind her, stirring up dust. She's got a teasing smile that reaches all the way up to her eyes.

"So I guess I'm not all that bright," I say.

She cocks an eyebrow.

"I mean, Aggie tells me some of the other people I've met out here are *ma'inawo*, like you."

"That's true," she says, "but why would it bother you?"

"How do I even know what's real and what isn't?"

"Do you want a practical answer or a philosophical one?"

I sigh. "Just one I can understand."

"And when you put it like that," she says, "do you really mean you want to understand, or that you want to believe?"

"Both, I suppose."

"That's not easy. For forty-some years you've already proved yourself pretty obstinate about ignoring what's right in front of your face."

I rub my face. "Maybe I'm having a flashback."

"See? There you go again. That's what you thought I was until I did some pretty convincing things to prove otherwise." She gives me a knowing smile.

I reach across the table and run a finger down the short curve of one of her horns like I have a hundred times before. No, I've never been imagining her. But I've never questioned the mystery of her, either.

"So what are you?" I ask.

"What did I tell you the first time we met?"

"You said you were *ma'inawo*. That your mother's deer, father's fox."

"That's still true."

"But *ma'inawo's* not a tribal name. It's Kikimi for cousin."

"Still true," she says. "That's what the animal tribes call each other. Cousins."

"So...what? A deer and a fox made out and had a little girl they called Calico?"

"Pretty much."

"How's that even physically possible?"

She laughs. "Well, they weren't in their animal shapes, that's for sure."

"So your parents can look like humans or animals?"

She nods.

"And you look the way you do because your parents were different kinds of animals?"

"You mean this?" she says, touching a horn, then an ear.

I nod.

She laughs again. "No, I just look like this to mess with you. I figured sooner or later you'd realize that what you see is really what you get. But it turned out to be a lot later than I ever thought."

My throat's way too dry and I'm feeling a touch of vertigo. "So..." I pause to clear my throat, then gulp a slug of water. "What do you really look like?"

"Like this," she says. "What you see. Or like this."

Suddenly, instead of the foxalope girl leaning toward me with her elbows on the picnic table, she becomes a pointy-faced fox, dark-eyed gaze fixed on mine. Then the fox is gone and a small antelope stands on the table top and seat, like she's perched on the red rocks of the canyon. "Or like this," she says. Finally, she's Calico again, except now she looks completely human. No horns, no fox ears, no tail.

I close my eyes and lay my head on the table, my cheek pressed into the map. "I'm losing my fucking mind."

"What makes you say that?" she asks.

"Well, it's either that, or I've been living a lie," I say.

"None of it's a lie. Cousins can't lie, so I'm telling you the truth. You need to take the world out of the box you put it in and accept it for what it is, not what you want it to be."

I open an eye to look at her. "Really?" I say. "My life goes batshit and that's your advice?"

She looks puzzled. "Batshit?"

I sit up and jab a finger on the map. "What about this?" I ask. "The fact that it takes me an hour and a bit to walk what should be a three-hour hike if you go by the map."

"Oh, this place. That's another story. A long one."

"I've got the time."

She cocks her head. "You know, Possum took all of this a lot better than you."

"Was he your lover before me?"

She smiles. "No. He hooked up with my aunt—on my mother's side. The antelope side."

I lay my head back down on the map and let out a groan.

"Okay," she says, brushing her hand along my cheek for a moment. "Apparently you're not. Taking it well, I mean."

She rests her chin on her hands so that our faces are only inches apart.

"Possum first showed up here in the early 1900s," she says. "I guess he must have been in his early twenties."

The rational part of my brain does the math, but I don't call her on how impossibly old that would have made him. I just let her words wash over me and try as hard as I can to keep an open mind.

6

SADIE

Sadie sat and stared at Aggie's computer screen, trying to process what she'd discovered.

It hadn't been hard to find news stories about Steve's grandmother. She hadn't even needed the woman's surname because there'd never exactly been a rash of women named Sadie in Texas who'd gotten the death penalty for murdering their husbands. What she hadn't expected was how easy it would be to find out Steve's full name and why he was hiding out here in the mountains.

Make that Steve's *real* name.

Jackson Cole. Steven was only his middle name.

The big news was that he just happened to have been the lead singer of the Diesel Rats, as well as their principal songwriter and guitarist.

Who died in a plane crash over the Atlantic twenty years ago, but his body had never been recovered.

Of course it wouldn't have been recovered, Sadie thought. Because he'd never died. Instead, he was living here in the middle of nowhere. Add on a few years, and the pictures she found online looked exactly like younger versions of the man she'd met after Reggie booted her out of his car.

Why would he hide his identity? Better yet, what the hell was he doing here? If he needed to get away, shouldn't he be kicking it back on some tropical beach? If she had his kind of money she'd be living high on the hog. She'd have the best of everything. Mansions and a private jet and fabulous clothes and jewellery—all the things that super rich people had.

And he had to have been rich, because the Diesel Rats were mega huge in their day. Still were, even if their singer had "died" and they hadn't made a new recording in forty years. They'd sold hundreds of millions of records worldwide—like Michael Jackson numbers. Even she'd heard their music before, and not just the famously sampled riff from "Burning Heart" that helped DJ Krash take his "Dontcha Mess with Me" to number one last year. You couldn't turn on an oldies station without hearing something by the Rats over the course of a couple of hours. "Gimme, Gimme, Gimme." "Jenny Don't You Cry." "Stars Are Falling." And every Christmas there seemed to be a couple of new covers of "Peace Will Come (We Can Make It Happen)."

Maybe he took off because the press at the time wouldn't let go of the fact his grandmother was a murderer. That she was one of only five women who'd been executed in Texas since the seventies. But really? How big an impact would something like that have made on his life in those days? They didn't even have the Internet, so it wasn't like it could go viral. Though, if back then was anything like now, she supposed the press would still have been all over him, especially since that hadn't been the only thing to go wrong.

Not long after Cole's grandmother was executed, Sully—full name, Frank Sullivan, according to Wikipedia—Steve's best friend since childhood and the bass player in the band, was found dead of an overdose in his hotel room. Before the autopsy report could be delivered, Cole and his drummer Martin Getty had a huge falling out over whether or not the band should get a new bass player and continue. Cole wanted some time; Getty insisted they should finish the twenty dates left on their tour.

Getty had stormed out of the hotel where they were staying and died in a car crash an hour later, speeding on the Interstate.

Cole's longtime girlfriend, Toni Shaw, chose that same period of time to walk out on him, citing that their relationship had become toxic. Later, she tried suing him for division of property, claiming she'd supported him through the hard times when the band was just getting started. It went to court, where it was revealed she'd been having an affair with the band's business manager.

Cole went from rock 'n' roll megastar to poster boy for tragedy, especially after he "died" as well.

Sadie found link after link to articles about the band and their music, and the mystery death of Jackson Cole. It was music-nerd city out there in the blogosphere. It was stupid, how much was still being written about the band.

Which, she realized, probably meant that proof he was still alive would be worth big bucks to somebody. God, how much? Ten grand? Twenty? Lots, she was sure.

Except who could you trust? One of the gossip sites? Or maybe a tabloid? But who was to say they wouldn't stiff you?

There were lots of books on the band as well, and one name kept popping up in the reviews about them: Leah Hardin. She'd apparently written the definitive biography on Cole, as well as a whole bunch of other books on the band, their humble beginnings, how they handled fame, their influence. She even had a book that chronicled every recording session they'd ever done, which just seemed like overkill, as well as one that reviewed every bootleg.

And if that wasn't enough, she also had a blog named after the band's third album, *Rats on the Run*, which she seemed to update at least every week. She'd written about other bands, politics and all kinds of crap, but she kept coming back to the Rats.

Hello, Leah. Get a life or what?

What could possibly be left to say?

But that very fanaticism of hers might make her the best person to contact. The woman would at least get another book out of it. Hell, with the amount of words she seemed able to churn out on every stupid detail of the band's life, she could probably get three or four.

There was an email contact link on the blog. Sadie clicked on it and composed her message. She thought for a moment before sending it, then used the camera on the laptop to take a picture of Aggie's painting of Steve. She attached it to the email before pressing send.

Clearing the browser cache, she shut down the laptop.

When she stood up, the red dog got up as well.

"I'm going to be rich, Ruby," she told it. "What do you think about that?"

The dog just stared at her.

Sadie had too much of a buzz on to stay cooped up inside. She went out to walk around Aggie's property, the dog following on her heels.

7

THOMAS

It was just past closing time, and Thomas was giving the store a final sweep when Reuben clapped him on the shoulder. "Hey, Thomas," he said. "Can you make some deliveries on your way home?"

"I guess."

"Great. You can just keep the truck until I see you at Aggie's tomorrow night."

Thomas grinned. Getting to keep the truck the whole next day would make the extra time worth it.

Reuben helped him load the deliveries. Thomas groaned when he saw the tall propane cylinder already strapped to the trading post's ATV, which was tied in place in the back of the pickup. He'd never made a delivery to Steve Cole's place. Reuben usually handled that.

"Really?" he said. "You want me to drive all the way out to Painted Cloud Canyon?"

Reuben smiled. "What's it going to take? Forty minutes each way if you don't speed too much. Another twenty to unload and get up to Cole's place."

"I don't even know where Cole's trailer is in the canyon."

"Trust me. You can't miss it. And I know how you love to drive my truck."

It was a sweet ride, no question. A '56 Chevy with a rebuilt engine that rumbled like a big old bear. The shocks were so good you barely felt the washboard bumps on the rez's worst roads. And it had pickup to spare.

"Just don't get a ticket," Reuben added.

"Like the cops are ever out on Zahra Road."

Reuben gave him a look.

"Okay," Thomas assured him. "I won't speed. Much."

"That's what I wanted to hear." Reuben got into the passenger's side. "You can drop me off at the community center on your way to Auntie Susan's."

Thomas looked at the list Reuben had given him. Susan Many Deer's name was at the top of the list.

"No problem."

ON HIS WAY back to the highway after making all the deliveries in the rez, Thomas spotted his sister Santana sitting on a fence with a couple of her friends. He slowed down and honked at her. The girls started to give him the finger until they saw who it was, then Santana waved him down. When he came to a stop, she trotted over and leaned her forearms in the window on the passenger's side.

"Are we taking Reuben's truck to town tomorrow?" she asked.

He nodded.

"Sweet. Where are you going now?"

"Out Zahra Road to Painted Cloud."

"Can I come?"

"So long as you call Mom first to tell her where you're going."

Santana grinned. She waved to her friends, got in and thumbed their home number on her phone.

"Hey, Naya," she said to their sister when the connection was made. "Can you tell Mom I'm making a delivery with Thomas and we'll both be back when it's done?"

"Seatbelt," Thomas said.

Santana stuck out her tongue, but she used her free hand to buckle up.

"Mom wants to know how long we'll be," she said.

"Under two hours, but not by much."

"Two hours," she said into the phone. "We're going to Painted Cloud." She listened for a moment then rolled her eyes. "Mom says to be careful," she told Thomas, "because that's a place where the deer women like to pick up unsuspecting suitors."

Thomas sighed. "Tell her we'll be careful."

"Thomas says he doesn't believe in deer women," she said into the phone.

"Santana."

"But we'll be especially careful all the same."

She laughed at something Naya said, then hung up.

"Why do you have to wind Mom up?" Thomas said.

"Because we're not living in the 1800s anymore."

She leaned back and stretched out her arms along the back of the seat.

"God, I love this truck," she said. "Someday I'm going to have one just like it. I'll pull up at the powwows and the boys will all say 'Isn't she fine?' And they'll like the truck, too."

Thomas laughed. Powwows were the one thing he'd really miss about the rez if he ever got away. Both Santana and Naya were jingle dancers, and he never missed a chance to see them perform. Powwows were also the only time that everybody got along—the traditionalists *and* the casino crowd. He'd thought of going to talk to Sammy Swift Grass at the casino and try to get a job where he could make some real money, but Auntie and his mother would have disowned him.

He wasn't the only one who enjoyed seeing the girls dance at the powwows. He'd heard more than one guy already say "Isn't she fine?" while they watched Santana. She was seventeen, almost a woman, so he made a big brother note of who they were for future reference, and let it slide. But no one got to talk that way about Naya. She was only fifteen, with a lot of growing still to do, and he was here to make sure she wouldn't have anyone hassling her.

Listening to the wheels hum on the asphalt, he had to agree with Santana about liking the truck. The interior of the Chev had been restored with the same painstaking care as the rest of it. Reuben and his nephew Jack Young Deer had done most of the work. What they hadn't been able to handle themselves, Reuben had gotten done in town at Sanchez Motorworks. Thomas could still remember the big grin on Reuben's face when he finally sold off his jeep and the Chev became his main ride. Of course, now he was already working on another old junker.

"If you think this truck looks good," he told his sister, "you just try driving it."

She sat up and gave him an eager look. "Can I?"

"Only if the deer women steal me away."

She collapsed back against her seat. "Now I'm actually hoping they do show up and take you with them."

They drove on for a while without talking. Thomas enjoyed the feel of the ride while Santana fiddled with the radio dial until she came up with some music she liked. Naturally, she chose Mexican rap. Not his favourite, but he found himself bobbing his head along with the beat all the same.

Halfway to Painted Cloud Canyon, Santana turned the radio down.

"Do you believe any of that stuff Auntie and Mom talk about?" she asked.

He thought about the conversation he'd had earlier with Reuben. This seemed to be the day for it.

"Yeah, I guess I do. I've seen things."

There. It was out.

He glanced at Santana to find her looking relieved.

"*Really?* Because you know, sometimes I think I see things that aren't really there—or at least nobody else seems to see them. I never talk about it because I don't want people to think I'm crazy."

"It runs in our family, apparently," he said. "Reuben told me today that our Aunt Lucy is the one who taught Ramon Morago to be a shaman."

"Shut up. Are you bullshitting me?"

He shook his head.

"So how come you don't talk about it?" she asked. "Auntie and Mom would love it."

"You just answered your own question. I've already had to argue with them about not joining the dog boys."

"I like the dog boys."

"You would."

She elbowed him in the side, but laughed.

"If they knew about this," he went on, "they'd probably force me to go to Morago as an apprentice."

"Would that be so bad?"

"I want to get away. Not today, but maybe someday. If I sign on with Morago, I can't even pretend that'll ever happen."

Santana nodded. "Yeah, I wonder all the time what it'd be like to live like the rest of the world does."

They were coming up on the parking lot for the Painted Cloud Canyon trailhead. Thomas pulled in, maneuvering the truck so the tailgate was pointing at the trail. He turned the engine off and they got out.

"Have you been out here before?" Santana asked.

Thomas shook his head. "Reuben just told me to go up the canyon and I wouldn't miss it."

"Huh. We're off the rez now, right?"

"Yeah, this is all National Park land."

"I didn't think people could live on National Park land."

"I don't know what the story is," Thomas said.

Santana helped him get the ramp on and he drove the ATV off the truck. Once he had it on the ground, he checked to make sure the big propane tank was securely strapped in place. Satisfied, he turned to his sister.

"You want to come or wait here?" he asked.

"You're kidding, right?"

He grinned. "Hop on."

8

SADIE

Sadie found Aggie sitting on a bench outside her studio. The handful of dogs sleeping around her feet roused when Sadie and Ruby approached. Sadie froze as the pack surrounded her, sniffing and pushing their shoulders up against her legs.

"Leave her be," Aggie said in a mild voice. "She lives here now."

The dogs immediately lost interest in Sadie and went back to sprawling in the dirt or on the porch where Aggie was sitting.

"I thought you were painting," Sadie said as she took a seat beside the old woman.

"I am. Right now I'm considering colours. I usually do it on my palette, but sometimes I like to sit out here and do it in my head instead."

Sadie nodded as if she understood.

Aggie waved a hand to take in the view. "And of course having all of this for inspiration doesn't hurt. There's a reason our ancestors called this the Painted Lands."

Sadie looked out across the foothills. Santo del Vado Viejo was a hazy smudge in the distance, hard to see because of the lowering sun. She didn't see any painted lands. All she saw was dull scrub and desert.

"I've never spent much time outdoors," Sadie said. "I mean, in a place like this."

"I've never spent much time in the city," Aggie told her, "so I can't really compare the two, but I'm pretty sure I know which one I prefer."

Sadie did too, and she knew Aggie's choice wouldn't be her own. If she could get some money out of that Leah Hardin woman, she'd be so out of here.

"I found out why Steve's been living here on the down-low," she said. "I know all about who he was."

Aggie regarded her for a moment, then returned her attention to the view.

"Don't you want to hear what I found out?" Sadie asked.

Aggie shook her head. "Just because you know who someone was, doesn't make any difference in terms of who they are now."

"What's that supposed to mean?"

"It means I know everything about Steve that I need to know."

Sadie thought about how pretty much all you wanted to know about anything was available with only a few clicks of a mouse. "The world doesn't work like that anymore," she said.

"Mine does."

Sadie resisted a retort. Aggie hadn't used the tone that Reggie did, meaning one more wrong word and you'd get a smack across the head. She didn't even think Aggie would ever smack somebody across the head. But there was a finality in her tone that made it clear the conversation was over.

Be like that, Sadie thought. If I make any money, I won't share it with you.

"You need to understand," Aggie finally said. "You're underage. We shouldn't be letting you stay here. If your parents come after you, we could be in a lot of trouble."

"My parents won't come after me. My old man threw me out —remember?"

Aggie nodded. "It's just...Steve did you a favour. He's still doing you a favour, setting you up at the school and all. Don't repay him by digging into his past. If he wants you to know about it, he'll tell you."

"Okay," Sadie said. "I get it."

The old woman stood up. "It's time we fed the dogs and made ourselves some dinner. Do you want to help?"

"I don't know anything about cooking."

"Then I'll teach you."

Sadie bit back another retort and found a smile to put on her face. The old woman was right about some things. She did owe Aggie and Steve for helping her out. And she didn't have anywhere to go.

She stood up as well.

"I'd like that," she lied.

9

THOMAS

The trail was broad, with plenty of room for the ATV. From the trailhead, their route took a wide series of switchbacks through the desert, straightening when it reached the canyon. The red limestone rose taller on each side of them. In only a few minutes of driving they'd become cliffs, and Santana tapped Thomas on the shoulder, pointing. Thomas nodded. He'd already seen it. A big silver trailer up on a ledge, gleaming in the light of the lowering sun. How the *hell* had anybody gotten something that big up there?

He killed the engine of the ATV and the two of them got off. In the sudden silence they could hear a couple of guitars playing. One played a droning rhythm that sounded like the drum beat of a powwow round dance, while the other played the chorus of voices that would normally have added to the drums.

Santana smiled. "That is so cool," she said.

Thomas nodded, but he was more concerned about how they were going to get the tank up the narrow little path that he could see going up to the ledge. Reuben hadn't mentioned anything like this.

He turned to his sister. "Let's go see if somebody up there knows how we can make this delivery without killing ourselves."

Santana nodded. "And check out the musicians."

But when they got up onto the ledge, they discovered it was only Steve up there playing both parts on the guitar. He seemed so lost in the music that he didn't notice their arrival, so they stood and listened until he suddenly became aware of their presence.

"Thomas," Steve said. He looked a little startled. "What are you doing here?"

"*Ohla*. Bringing you your propane."

"And you could see… Well, obviously you could see the trailer."

"Kind of hard to miss."

Steve nodded. "Except most people don't see it because apparently it only exists in magic land."

Thomas shrugged. He didn't know Steve Cole all that well—Reuben usually dealt with him—but even with the little he knew of him, he thought the man was acting a bit strange. How could he possibly think that anybody wouldn't notice that big Airstream impossibly set way up on this ledge? And what was 'magic land'?

"This is my sister, Santana," he said.

Steve lifted a hand in greeting.

"*Ohla*," Santana said. "I loved what you were doing with that round dance. It sounded like a couple of guitars playing instead of just one."

He shrugged. "It's just an open tuning," he said, as though that explained everything.

Thomas looked around. This was a pretty sweet spot, with a great view going down the canyon and out onto the desert floor. The overhang above the trailer would protect it from the worst of the sun, though it didn't feel particularly hot, even where he and Santana were standing. There seemed to be a cave opening beside the trailer, but from the light coming through, he figured it must be an arch. The landscape in this area was riddled with them.

"How'd this trailer get up here?" he asked.

"Damned if I know," Steve said. "This was Possum's place originally, and the secret died with him." He set the guitar aside. "I guess we need to wrestle that tank up. You want to take the empty down first?"

Thomas regarded him for a moment. Steve was fit, especially considering his age, but Thomas didn't see how the two of them were going to get the tank up that narrow trail. He wondered how Steve and Reuben had ever managed it in the past. It had been hard enough when he and Reuben had been wrestling the tank onto the back of the ATV earlier today.

"Sure," he finally said. "I guess."

But before they could move, a new voice said, "I can do it."

The newcomer was a slender woman in her mid-thirties with tanned skin and long red hair, dressed in denim cut-offs and a sleeveless white T-shirt. She was standing by the end of the trailer, undoing the hose that was connected to the old tank.

Right, Thomas thought. Sure you can. Even empty, a tank that size was a fair weight and awkward to carry.

"Yeah, I don't think you should…" Thomas began.

His voice trailed off as the woman hefted the tank easily onto her shoulder.

"I'm Calico, by the way," she said as she went by him.

"*Ohla*," Thomas said automatically.

He and Santana watched her go down the trail, managing the tank as though it didn't weigh much of anything.

"Show off," Steve said.

Thomas turned to him.

"She's a *ma'inawo*." Steve said. "You know—they're stronger than us."

"Us?"

"You know, humans."

"A deer woman," Santana muttered. "You're so screwed, Thomas."

Steve laughed. "Don't worry. She's not a deer woman. She's a foxalope."

They regarded him with blank looks.

"Part fox, part antelope."

"Oh-kay."

"What's he been telling you?" Calico asked.

Thomas felt his mouth fall open. She was already back, carrying the full tank with the same ease as she'd dealt with the empty one.

"That you're...you're a spirit," Santana said.

Calico shook her head. "Just a cousin."

She continued past them, set the tank down, and began to hook it up to the hose from the trailer. Thomas couldn't stop staring.

"Stay for a beer?" Steve asked. His gaze went from Thomas to Santana. "I've also got juice, or tea."

"A beer would be good, thanks," Thomas said.

"Me too," his sister added.

Steve glanced at Thomas, waiting for his nod before going into the trailer. He came back with four beer bottles and set them on the picnic table. Calico finished hooking up the new tank and joined them.

Steve lifted his bottle and clinked its neck against theirs before he took a swig.

"So you're the reluctant Indian," he said to Thomas, setting his bottle on the table. "We've never really had a chance to talk."

Thomas flushed. "Why'd you call me that?"

"Sorry. Reuben talks about you and your itchy feet. Says you remind him of himself when he was your age, only you're smarter."

Thomas could have gotten upset, but there was no point. Reuben talked with everyone about everything—it was just his way.

"So, if you could go away," Steve went on, "what would you do?"

"There's no real point in talking about it," Thomas said. "I've got my family to look out for."

"Yeah, but if their expenses were covered and you could do whatever you wanted?"

Thomas shrugged. "I guess I never really thought past wanting to get into a truck and just start driving."

"That's a way to do it," Steve said. "Very organic."

"Why are you so interested in me?"

"I'm interested in everybody. It's good to know about your neighbours, see if you can lend a helping hand. But mostly I'm just making conversation."

According to Reuben, Steve helped a lot of people out. He'd show up at a place when there was some work that needed to be done, then afterward just drift away. The more Thomas thought about it, pretty much everybody he knew had a story about Steve Cole. Even his mom.

"You think I should just up and go?" he asked.

"If you can get your family set up for while you're gone? Sure. The way I see it, the sooner you get it out of your system, the sooner you can figure out who it is you want to be. Maybe the world outside of the rez is just what you're looking for. Maybe it's not. But you won't know unless you go and find out for yourself."

This was the day for it, wasn't it? Designer woman in her Caddy, Reuben back at the trading post, and now Steve. Was there something in the air today?

"I'm not embarrassed about being Kikimi," Thomas said.

"No reason you should be, and I don't think that."

"It's just some of the traditions make me feel a little uncomfortable, like we're living too much in the past."

"But I hear you're going to the sweat at Aggie's," Calico said.

Santana looked up in surprise.

"How would you know that?" Thomas asked.

Calico shrugged. "Some little cousin told me. The animals couldn't care less, but the cousins live to gossip about anything, including you five-fingered beings."

Santana looked down at one of her hands. She flexed her fingers and smiled.

"Reuben kind of talked me into it," Thomas said.

"You might like it," Steve told him.

Thomas nodded, but he wasn't so sure. "You're so close to the tribe," he said. "How come you never take part in any of the traditional ceremonies?"

"The Kikimi are my friends," Steve said, "but I'm not some white guy who thinks he can walk the Red Road just because he hangs out with you and feels all spiritual. You're who you are, and I'm who I am, and we meet at the edges."

He glanced at Calico. "And I guess I've got my own traditions."

"But what do you do out here?" Santana asked. "Don't you get bored?"

Steve shook his head. "You might say I'm a student of the desert and the mountains. I can spend a whole afternoon watching a red-tailed hawk build its nest in a saguaro, or the colours change on a wolf spider as it crosses different kinds of terrain, and never consider the time misspent."

Calico smiled. "Sounds like somebody's feeling a little spiritual."

"Sure," Steve said. "It's partly that. It's partly appreciating the beauty on a very simple and basic level—you know, the small day-to-day changes around me, as well as the big picture events like a sunset, or the nightly show the stars put on. But it's mostly paying close attention to a lot of interesting things and learning not to try to impose my will on any of it. Does that make sense?"

Thomas nodded, though he wasn't sure he understood completely. It took Santana to voice part of what he felt.

"Sounds kind of boring," she said.

"One man's poison..." Steve said with a shrug.

"I'm more interested in the spirits and *ma'inawo*. The cousins. What's it like living with them every day?"

"I'll tell you truth. I didn't even know that much about them until today."

Thomas saw his own surprise mirrored on the face of his sister.

"What he means," Calico said, "is that until today, he didn't realize the dreamworld is real and he's awake in it."

"The dreamworld," Santana repeated. "Auntie tells stories about it. What's it like?"

"You tell me," Steve said. "That's where you've been for this past half hour or so."

Thomas and his sister exchanged glances. Magic land, he thought.

10

LEAH HARDIN

It was pretty noisy in the courtyard of the Katharine Mully Memorial Arts Court; the sound of kids' conversations and their music rose in skittering waves to bounce back down from the high ceiling and around the interior. Leah Hardin barely noticed. All of her attention was focused on the screen of her laptop. She was sitting off to one side of the main courtyard area at one of the tables near the pay-as-you-can café, availing herself of the building's free WiFi. Her dark hair curtained her face, green eyes gleaming with an electronic blue tint from the light cast by the screen.

She'd just finished two back-to-back volunteer shifts, the first in the Arts Court office sorting electronic invoices because nobody else liked the job, followed by a shift as a barista at the café. She'd decided to make herself an Americano before she went home, and was sipping at it while she went through her email.

Nothing could have prepared her for one of the messages in her inbox. She didn't know at the time that the message had come to her from halfway across the continent before reaching her here in Newford.

She'd read it through a half-dozen times, but the content hadn't changed.

It had to be a joke.

She looked at the sender's name again: sadinsan@gmail.com. She didn't recognize it, but it wasn't exactly hard to open a Gmail account. It could be anybody—as benign as a friend playing a prank, or as nasty as one of the trolls she had to keep blocking from her blog's comments —thinking she'd be gullible enough to believe anything so outlandish.

But she couldn't shake the funny feeling the email had woken in her.

"Hey, Leah."

Leah looked up from her laptop to find Alan Grant standing at her table with a coffee in one hand and a muffin in the other.

She and Alan both volunteered here at the Arts Court, helping street kids get in touch with their creativity. The truth was, a lot of the kids just came to hang out, drink free coffee, charge their phones, or use the bathrooms and WiFi. But that was okay. Part of the Arts Court mandate was to provide a safe space for kids who didn't have anywhere else to go. Tools were provided if they wanted to express themselves: art and writing supplies, musical instruments, even access to computer workstations with word processing, art and music programs. And some of the kids actually took advantage of what was offered.

There was no instruction unless they specifically asked for it. Various artists, musicians and writers in the Newford arts community made themselves available on a regular basis, helping in whichever way they could. They did office work and maintenance, and helped out at the café when they weren't mentoring the kids.

Alan sat on the Arts Court board and was also publisher of a small press, but he was more likely to be found down here with the kids than dealing with his administrative duties.

"Hey, yourself," she told him. "How's Marisa?"

"She's good," he said as he sat down at her table. "Right now she's back at the East Street office doing some actual work so I can goof off here."

"Like you know the meaning of the words 'goof off.'"

Alan grinned. "Says the workaholic." He nodded at her computer. "Did I interrupt your writing?"

She turned her laptop around so that Alan could look at the screen.

"Wow," he said. "That's an amazing painting."

"I know. Even though it's just shot with a webcam on somebody's laptop."

"Who's the artist?"

"I haven't a clue. There's a signature, but I can't make it out."

Alan peered more closely at the image. "Yeah, me neither. Who sent it to you?"

"I don't know that either."

Alan's brows went up. "Well, that's mysterious enough." He gave the image another scrutiny. "The subject looks really familiar."

"It's supposed to be Jackson Cole—the way he looks today."

Alan gave her a smile. "Well, now I know how come this showed up in your inbox. It's actually a pretty good fantasy likeness, isn't it? You could see Cole having grown into this guy."

"It's supposed to be what he *really* looks like—now."

"Wait a minute..."

"The person who sent this claims to have met him. They say that he's alive."

"But that's—"

"Impossible. I know."

Alan returned his attention to the image. He had an expression on his face she couldn't read.

"Are they saying that he never died," Alan began, "or..."

"Or what?" Leah asked when his voice trailed off.

Alan seemed to give himself a mental headshake. "Nothing. What *did* they say?"

Leah told him what the sender had written about being abandoned by a highway in the middle of nowhere and then found by a man that he or she later realized was Jackson Cole. How, for a price, Leah could be told where he might be found.

"How much?" Alan asked.

"The person doesn't say."

He lifted his gaze from the image to study Leah for a moment.

"You're not dismissing this," he said.

She shook her head. "I want to think it's just somebody's bad idea of a joke."

"But you don't. Why not?"

"Just a gut feeling."

"Look, I know Cole's body was never recovered, but a painting doesn't prove anything. Hell, these days a photo wouldn't prove anything."

"I know. But that's an amazing painting—you said so yourself. Even with this poor resolution, you can tell it's the work of a really good artist. Why would anybody with that much talent bother running a scam like this?"

"So let's find out who the artist is," Alan said. "Do an image search."

He stood and turned the computer back toward her, then took a chair next to her so they could both look at the screen.

Leah grabbed the image from her downloads folder and dropped it into the browser's search box. Moments later, dozens of possible matches popped up on the screen. They scrutinized each of the thumbnails, but the painting didn't show up in any of them.

"Wait a sec," Alan said as Leah sat back. "Click on that one."

The image Alan was pointing at looked nothing like the painting. It depicted a half man/half wolf or coyote figure in some kind of ceremonial Native American garb. But when it expanded on the screen she could see what had caught his attention. The style was similar to the painting that had been sent to her. It had the same brushwork, the same riot of colour in its background.

The picture of the man/wolf came from the website of an online arts magazine based in Arizona. When they clicked on the link to the magazine, an article popped up about a Native artist named Abigail White Horse. There was a photo of her, showing a broad-faced older woman dressed in a plain blouse and a long skirt, her grey hair plaited in a thick braid. She had her hand on the head of a tall rez dog that leaned heavily against her, its tongue lolling from the corner of its mouth. Two more paintings similar to the one of the man/wolf were also included in the article.

"It says she doesn't sell her work," Alan said, "and only rarely does shows. You know what that means?"

Leah shook her head.

"Either she sent you that email herself, or it was sent by someone who has access to her studio and her art. A friend or a family member."

"What are you? A detective?"

"I think I'm doing pretty well here."

Leah nodded. "Yeah, I guess you are." She went back to the article. "She lives in southern Arizona, on the Painted Lands Kikimi rez in the Hierro Maderas Mountains outside of Santo del Vado Viejo."

"With a little more digging we should be able to get a phone number for her."

"I'd rather confront her in person."

Alan couldn't hide his surprise.

"Oh, I know I can't," Leah said. "I mean it's ridiculous. It would cost a fortune, which I don't have. But it's a lot harder to blow somebody off when they're standing right in front of you and you can't just hang up on them."

Alan leaned back in his chair and turned to look at her.

"What?" Leah said.

"This would make a good story," he said. "Obviously, you're not going to actually find Cole, but the journey itself could be really interesting, given the way you write. There's this opportunity to tie in to all the things that first drew you to the Rats, and how writing about them changed you—a more personal journey to complement what you've already written about Cole and the band."

Leah wasn't sure she liked the idea, but she could understand its appeal. She knew she wasn't alone when it came to the impact the Rats had had on her life. The fans on her blog loved to talk about that sort of thing. She'd only ever touched on it lightly herself because she wanted to maintain a more professional, objective profile. Mostly. But she had other, more personal, reasons not to talk about it.

"Maybe," she said. "But I can't just jump on a plane and fly down. The ad revenue from my blog's okay, but it wouldn't come close to covering these kinds of expenses."

"But I could," Alan said. "If I can get a book out of you for the investment. And if that painting is there, and the artist is willing, it would make a great cover."

Leah just stared at him.

"I'm serious."

"You don't do non-fiction."

Alan laughed. "Don't tell Christy that."

Christy Riddell was one of Alan's authors whose East Street Press works were divided between collections of short stories and books exploring the folklore and mythology of Newford. Without apology, he always presented the latter as fact.

"I don't know if there's a whole book in this," she said.

"Depends on what you find out when you get there."

"You're serious?"

"Absolutely," Alan said. "Flights to Vegas are dirt cheap. You could rent a car from there and then drive down. You do drive, right?"

Leah shook her head. "City girl. They make public transport for people like me."

"That could be a problem, except you know what? I'll bet Marisa would be up for a road trip without much coaxing. I owe her a break, and she loves to drive. Besides, she's a Rats fan too."

11

THOMAS

"How could you live in the otherworld for as long as Steve has," Santana said as they were driving back home, "and not know it? How can you hang around with spirits—"

"Cousins," Thomas interrupted. "And he's the one who told us she was *ma'inawo*. He just seems to be learning more about them now, and about where he's been living."

"Whatever. It was weird how she could take the shape of a fox or an antelope, and more often, she was something in between," she said.

Thomas had also had trouble wrapping his head around the rapid transformations. Fox to antelope to the strange hybrid of woman and both animals she'd become at the end, sitting right across the table from them with a cocky grin and her eyes glittering in the setting sun.

"And how could he live there and not know it was the otherworld?" Santana added.

Thomas shrugged. "Well, we didn't know it was the dreamlands either, until he told us."

"Yeah, only we just got there. We have an excuse. He's been living there for ages."

"You heard what Steve told us. He never really thought about it, even though he's been living there for forty years."

"Forty years!" Santana said.

"I know, but—"

"There's coasting, and then there's sticking your head in the sand. Does he ever look in the mirror? He looks way young for a guy who's got to be pushing seventy."

Thomas made a noncommittal sound. If Steve really had been deliberately trying to ignore what was around him, Thomas could empathize with the man. He knew from experience that pretending something wasn't real, or at least not talking about it with anybody, was the easier route to take.

"You're taking this really well," Santana said.

"Hm?"

"For a guy who wants nothing to do with the old traditions."

Thomas sighed. "Why does everybody have to harp on that?"

"Because it's true?"

She tilted her head and gave him a sweet smile, eyebrows lifted.

"You forget," he said. "Just like you, I can see things other people can't. It's happened my whole life. So why should this surprise me?"

Santana shrugged. She sat there in the shotgun seat, feet up, arms wrapped around her knees.

"Mom always warns us to be careful around spirits," she said, "but Calico didn't seem particularly dangerous."

"We don't really know much about her. And that doesn't mean the other spirits aren't."

"I suppose that's true."

Thomas thought that might be the end of it, that she'd turn the radio back on again. Which would suit him because all of this had given him a lot to think about.

"What kinds of things have you seen?" she asked instead.

He thought about that for a moment.

"Nothing like today," he told her. "It's usually more subtle— catching something out of the corner of my eye, or how the prickly pear by the trading post are always in different positions every morning."

"You mean, like they moved during the night?"

He nodded.

"Cool."

He smiled. "And you?"

"All kinds of stuff," she said. "Sometimes when I'm sunning with Naya out on the rocks behind the house I hear voices, but there's no one around. And she doesn't hear them. When we're dancing it can feel like there are other—invisible—dancers moving in time with us. Or I might just be walking around the rez and I'll see somebody with a kind of animal aura. Not like Calico, actually changing into something else—more like the ghostly impression of a lizard or a bird's head just floating above their heads, or maybe nested in their hair."

Thomas gave another nod. He'd experienced all of that and more. He thought about the ghost raven from this morning—how strangely independent it had been of its host—but decided not to mention it.

"What are we going to tell Mom," Santana asked, "about today?"

Thomas shot her a defeated glance. "You ever had any luck lying to her?"

Santana sighed. She dropped her feet to the floor and slumped in her seat.

"So we tell her everything," she said.

"Don't see as we have much choice."

Santana sighed again. "Why did I know you were going to say that?"

THE DEATH OF DEREK TWO TREES

12

STEVE

"Is there anything else I should know?" I ask Calico as we walk the ridge trail heading for Aggie's house.

The twilight's thickening into night, but I can still see the amused look she throws my way. Except for the little bit of showing off she did when Thomas and Santana were at the trailer, she's looked human all day now.

"Like what?" she asks.

"How would I know? So far, I've found out I'm friends with people who aren't people, but I didn't know it—and I've been living the past forty years of my life in fairyland without a clue. Plus there's this magical otherworld passage from the trailer to the rez."

"Well," she says, "there's a benefit to spending as much time as you have in the otherworld. You don't get sick and you're going to live a lot longer."

I never thought about it before, but I haven't had a cold even once since I came here. I thought it was just the desert air.

"Great," I tell her. "I've already made a mess of my life and now you're telling me I can look forward to years more of it."

Calico stops, so I do too. A frown creases her brow.

"I thought you liked living here," she says. "And what do you mean, mess of your life? Thanks a lot."

I shake my head. "No. You don't get it. I love being with you, and living in the desert and mountains. But being me? Not so much. I'm only here because once upon a time, I let way too much go wrong on my watch. I figure if I keep mostly to myself, nobody else will get hurt."

"Possum didn't die because of you."

"I'm talking about *before* Possum saved my sorry ass."

"What do you mean?" she asks.

I wave a hand. "Nothing. It all happened a long time ago..."

My voice trails off and she doesn't say anything. She just stands there looking at me, the stars wheeling slowly above us, the desert night deep on the foothills.

"So you being here," she finally says, "is some kind of penance?"

"Maybe it was at the start, but I gave up that idea a long time ago. My living here is all about staying out of my own head and appreciating what's around me without leaving too much of an impact on it. I can't make up for what happened before I came here, but now I can at least do my best to interact with people on a positive level, and hopefully leave them better than they were before they ran into me, instead of worse."

"So you *do* think you're doing penance for your sins. You're an asshole."

"Hey, you don't know the first thing about what—"

"I know you're an asshole. I don't need to know anything else. You're who you are *now*, not whoever you once were, or thought you were. Yeah, you keep to yourself, but ask anybody on the rez—they all like you, Steve. You, here and now. They don't care who you were before, just like I don't."

"You make it sound so simple."

"That's because it is simple."

"Except you're not in my head," I tell her. "I let people down. Some of them died."

"And I haven't got enough fingers to count the number of people you've helped around here over the years."

"It doesn't feel like it's enough."

"I'm going to let you in on a secret," she says. "It's never enough. Nothing any of us does is ever enough. We just do what we can every day. That's all anybody should ask of someone, right?"

"I guess."

"Then why ask more of yourself?"

She starts walking again and I fall into step beside her.

I love a desert night. It's quiet and full of sound at the same time. All the critters are going about their business, and we're just two more of them as we continue along the trail.

As we near Aggie's studio, Calico puts out an arm and stops me in my tracks. I think she's got something more to say, except a moment later I hear someone rise from the bench on the studio's little porch. I'm trying to figure out what's up, but then Morago comes around the side of the building. So much for keeping our relationship secret.

"*Ohla*, Calico," he says. He turns to me and nods. "Walks Where the Wolves Run."

"Seriously?" I say. "I *know* you've tried that one before."

"I prefer Beans for Brains," Calico says and gives me an innocent smile when I turn in her direction.

Morago laughs, but then his features become serious. There's been some trouble," he says.

I glance past him at Aggie's house. "With Sadie?"

Morago shakes his head. "No, but I knew you'd be coming to check on her, so I figured I'd wait here and save myself a trip out to the canyon."

"So what's up?"

"It's Derek Two Trees. Sammy Swift Grass took some hunters up into the mountains to bag a bighorn and they got one, too. The trouble is, it was Derek in his bighorn shape."

Calico's hand goes to her mouth.

Crap. I liked Derek. He was a guy you could count on. Didn't know he was a bighorn cousin, but life's just full of surprises all of a sudden.

"So can everybody around here change into animals?" I finally say.

"No," Morago tells me, "but most of us have cousin blood to some degree, or can talk to the spirits. Like you can, for instance," he adds, raising an eyebrow and glancing back and forth between me and Calico.

I see where he's going with this, but I change tack. "And you were going to explain this cousin stuff to me...when?"

Morago looks at me. "Seems to me, you're the one who's been keeping secrets," he says. "As far as I knew, you never seemed to want—"

"Forget it," I say. "You said you came looking for me. What do you need?"

"Sammy's hunters are planning to bring their trophy home," Morago says, "so Reuben's gathered up a pack of his dog boys to go and stop that from happening."

"Doesn't Sammy realize his mistake?" Calico asks. "He's got to understand why the hunters can't take Derek's body away."

Morago shakes his head. "Sammy doesn't believe in the animal spirits."

"I thought all you guys believed," I say.

"The traditionalists do, but you could change shape right in front of Sammy or any of his supporters, and they'll find a hundred explanations for what they've just seen—anything but what actually happened."

"I'll help if I can," I tell him, "but I don't understand what you want from me. Do you want me to talk to Sammy?" Which I can't see helping because I only know him to see him, and why the hell would he listen to me?

Morago shakes his head. "I need you to talk to Reuben."

"Like he's going to take my advice."

"He respects you."

I don't know how to respond to that.

"Right now," Morago goes on, "he's on his way to Sammy's hunting lodge with a pack of his dog boys. He says he's going to take the head of the man who killed Derek and put it on his own wall as a trophy."

"Jesus."

"You're the impartial third party," Morago says.

"I don't know about that."

Except if I think about it, I can see how it might seem that way.

WHEN I FIRST GOT HERE, the rez wasn't divided the way it is now. But then Sammy Swift Grass came back from university full of big plans and, depending on how you looked at it, you either thought the good times had finally arrived, or everything went to hell.

The Kikimi are a matriarchal society. The Women's Council, whom everybody calls the Aunts, runs things and they're pretty traditional. They could have put a stop to Sammy's plans for a casino/hotel, the ski slopes and the hunting lodge up in the mountains, but I guess they saw how the issue was dividing the tribe to the point where family members weren't talking to one another. Instead of pushing to have their own way, they came up with a set of compromises.

So now the south part of the rez is Sammy's little Disneyland, with a ridge of National Park mountains dividing it from the north side, where people stick to their traditional ways. The National Park also bookends the rez on either side, with the unclaimed heights of the Hierro Maderas marching off into the east.

When all these divisive arguments first started up, Possum's advice was to stay out of it, and that's what we did. We didn't take a side in the argument and treated everybody the same. That got easier after the business complex was built, and anyway, nobody in the casino crowd wanted anything to do with a pair of desert rats.

Now, almost ten years on, it's just the way things are. Sammy's business ventures pay a tithe to the tribe's coffers, the traditionalists and casino crowd mostly ignore each other, and things are usually relatively calm.

Until something like this comes up.

But honestly? Twenty-four hours ago I would never have seen

tensions flare up because of an incident like this. If anything of the sort has happened before, I haven't been privy to it.

Except for Calico, I've barely thought about *ma'inawo*, and now I know that I've deliberately skirted the subject. Mostly, I've only known them as part of a story that the old aunts and uncles talk about around a campfire, like the stories they tell about Jimmy Cholla, the Kikimi trickster. Finding out Derek was a cousin is further proof I've been living in my own narrow idea of the world, and I'm not proud of how obtuse I've been.

I shake my head. "I don't know what I can do," I tell Morago, "but I'll talk to Reuben."

"Be persuasive," he says.

"You say he's already on his way to the lodge?"

Morago nods.

"I know a shortcut," Calico says.

I take a deep breath. "Of course you do."

I turn to Morago, "We'll do what we can."

"Thank you," Morago says. "*Ohla.*"

Calico says something to him in Kikimi. His lip twitches before he heads for the jeep parked in Aggie's driveway.

"What did you say to him?" I ask Calico.

"What do you think I said?"

"If I knew, would I be asking?"

"I told him everybody is a dancer, but some of us need to learn the steps."

"What's that—"

"It's not important. Come on." She catches my hand. "We've got work to do."

She takes a step. I follow suit without really thinking about it, and my stomach lurches into my throat. The next thing I know, we're high on a ridge overlooking the Swift Grass Corporation's hunting lodge, and I'm trying to regain my equilibrium.

"What the fu—"

"Shhh," she says.

She's staring down at the forested slopes surrounding the lodge. I've only been up here a couple of times, but I always find it weird how you can be hiking up from the desert and then, just a few hours later, you're in an evergreen forest.

"There," she says, pointing.

I follow the direction of her finger. It takes me a moment to see them. A pack of dogs moving up through the forest. They're hard to see with the forest canopy, but every time they come into view for a few moments, it's clear where they're headed.

Straight for the lodge.

"I see dogs," I tell her.

She nods. "And I see Reuben and his dog boys. Come on."

She reaches for my hand again.

"Do we have to travel like this?" I ask.

"We do if we want to get down there in time to stop them."

13

SADIE

Sadie had never cooked before. Back home, everything they ate either came from a can or was takeout. The neighbourhood taquería was cheap, so they ate a lot of Mexican, but Sadie liked nothing better than the special occasions when Reggie would come home with a bag of burgers and fries from McDonald's, or a deep dish pie from Pedro's Pizza, smothered in cheese.

It didn't make sense to her that anyone would spend so much time making a meal when you could just open a can or have your food delivered.

But she didn't say anything like that to Aggie as they chopped squash, celery, carrots and peppers for a vegetable and bean stew. But she had to speak up when Aggie kept telling her all these stories about bean boys and squash girls, and the feud between the spirits of the chilies and the jalapeños.

"I'm not a little kid," she finally said, putting her paring knife down on the counter.

Aggie's eyebrows went up.

"You know," Sadie continued. "You don't have to tell me little kid stories while we're doing this."

"Is that what you think they are?"

"Aren't they?"

Aggie shook her head. "We have a tradition in my family that when we prepare a meal we tell the stories of the spirits that have gifted us with their bounty. It's a way of celebrating the sacrifice they make so that we are nourished."

"Get real." The words popped out of Sadie's mouth before she could stop them.

But Aggie ignored them. "It's my reality," she said, "if not yours."

"Okay, I get that," Sadie said. "And I didn't mean to diss you, but it's kind of hard to believe. And it doesn't even make sense. If vegetables really had spirits, why would they want us to eat them?"

"Because that is their position on the wheel of life."

"Man, they got the lousy deal."

"I think the opposite is true," Aggie told her. "They are the very foundation of life. Without them, the plant eaters would starve. Without the plant eaters, the predators would have no sustenance. Without them, the wheel is unbalanced, and who knows how the world would be?"

"So they offer themselves up to be eaten, you say thanks, and then everything's okay?"

"It's a matter of respect."

"If you say so."

"I do."

And then she started telling Sadie a story related to the beans that had been soaking in water all day.

Sadie stifled a sigh, picked up the knife, and went back to chopping carrots.

THE STEW, served with flatbread on the side, was actually pretty good, and Sadie told Aggie so. It was spicy and full of flavours she didn't recognize. She had two bowls full, and didn't even miss having meat.

After they'd cleaned up, Aggie sat down with a mug of tea and a book. Sadie asked for permission to use the laptop again, then checked her email. No response from Leah Hardin. Sadie thought the woman would be jumping all over it, but no. Nada. Still, Sadie wasn't ready to give up. Hardin probably just hadn't checked her email yet.

She surfed the Net for a while, but it was hard to focus on anything. She went back to her email. This time there was a message from Aylissa, one of the foster kids her parents had taken in.

R u ok? Reggie says u ran away but I saw him take u somewhere in the car + he came back alone. Worried for u.

Like Sadie, Aylissa had a Gmail account she only checked at school or the library, so it would be safe to tell her the big news. Sadie wrote back:

Reggie took me out to the desert and dumped me, but it's cool. I ended up at the rez and I'm going to come into a shitload of money. Can't give you the deets right now but it's seriously sweet.

She thought for a moment, then added:

Let me know if you want out of that place and I'll swing by and pick you up when I get out of this town for good.

If she had someone with her, it wouldn't feel so much like she was running away. Maybe they could both get emancipated and then nobody could tell them what to do anymore.

She pressed "Send." There was still no response from Leah Hardin, so she opened a search engine, but before she could enter a single word into the search bar there was a knock at the door.

A tall Native man waltzed in without waiting for Aggie to open the door. He had a different look from the Native people Sadie knew—the ones who came to town from the rez, or attended her school. For one thing, he seemed to be all angles, and his hair had a dark reddish tinge, and his eyes were different, too—a pale amber rather than brown. They seemed to be filled with light. She wondered if he had some other race in him along with Kikimi.

"*Ohla*, Aggie," he said, then he looked in her direction. "*Ohla*. You must be Sadie. I'm Ramon Morago."

Sadie nodded. She wanted to turn away, but he held her gaze and she couldn't break the lock his eyes had on her. It was so creepy. He seemed to look right into her head as though he knew everything she was thinking, everything she'd ever done.

"*Ohla*," Aggie said, and the man finally looked away. "There's stew cooling on the stove. Do you want me to warm up a bowl for you?"

"No, thanks. I already ate. Can I talk to you outside for a moment?" He gave Sadie a shrug that she assumed was supposed to be apologetic. "Tribal business," he said.

She gave him a casual wave of her hand. Like she cared about old people's drama.

They weren't gone long, but when the door opened again, only Aggie came in.

"So who's he?" Sadie asked.

"A friend. Steve went to see him about you—he's the one that'll decide if you can go to the school at the community center." She waited a beat, then added, "And he's the tribal shaman."

"Like, a for real shaman?"

"Of course."

Crap. He probably *could* read her mind. Worse, he was Steve's friend.

"So, uh, what kinds of powers does he have?" she asked.

Aggie smiled. "Powers? He is the tribe's intermediary to the spirits. Is that what you mean?"

"Well, like, can he fly, or is he super strong, or can he, you know, read minds?"

"You play too many video games," Aggie said. "He's a spiritual leader."

While they had video games in her house, only Reggie was allowed to play them. But Sadie didn't bother to correct her.

"Okay then," she said. "That's cool. So he's like a priest or some-thing—not a, you know, wizard."

Aggie gave her an exasperated look.

"If you're lucky enough to get into the tribal school," she said, "make sure to take a course in Kikimi traditions and history."

Sadie didn't expect to be here that long, but she nodded in agreement.

"Sure," she said.

14

LEAH

It wasn't until they left the bright neon of Las Vegas behind and the rental car was heading south through the city's outlying suburbs that Leah was finally able to relax. She was a city girl, but the Vegas Strip was like mainlining all the worst excesses of downtown anywhere, without even a hint of actual culture. A full-tilt carnival without respite. They hadn't even meant to go downtown, but they'd gotten turned around leaving the airport and it had seemed to take forever to get back on track.

Leah was just happy she didn't drive because even being a passenger had her completely on edge.

Finally they caught the 95, which would take them to the junction with the 93. From there they'd bypass Boulder City and then be on their way to the Hoover Dam, with badlands and mountains on either side of the highway and an eight-hour drive ahead of them.

"This is fun," Marisa said. "When was the last time we had a real road trip together?"

Even after the long flight, and then navigating the puzzle of downtown Las Vegas, she was as perky as ever.

"I don't know," Leah said. "Probably going out to Isabelle's place on Wren Island."

"That doesn't count. A road trip requires an overnight stay."

"We did stay overnight. We stayed the whole weekend."

Marisa smiled. "True. But it still doesn't count. It was only a couple of hours to get there."

"Well, I remember our *first* road trip together. Spring break, our final year at Butler U."

"Oh God. Daytona Beach. I was there with George."

"And I was there with some loser who dumped me for a girl a couple of breast sizes larger than mine, who was happy to show them off at the drop of a hat."

"Don't you mean the lift of a T-shirt?"

"Yeah, she was the definition of a girl gone wild."

They both giggled.

"I had such bad taste in boyfriends back then," Leah said.

"Well, at least you didn't marry yours."

"But you're happy now with Alan, while I'm an old maid."

Marisa shot her a quick sidelong glance.

"Oh, don't worry," Leah said. "I'm not getting maudlin."

"You'd better not. We've still got hours together in this car."

"Do you want to listen to some music?" Leah asked.

"Do you have any Diesel Rats with you?"

"Now you're just humouring me."

"No, they're great driving music."

"Well," Leah said. "If you insist."

She'd noticed the rental had a USB interface to plug in her phone. She dug around in her purse for her cable to make the connection.

"I still can't believe Alan is putting up the money for all of this," she said as she plugged in her phone and started scrolling through the artists list on her music app. "I'm not nearly as convinced as he is that we're actually going to find Jackson Cole out here in the middle of nowhere."

"He's not," Marisa told her. "And neither am I. But we believe in you. And we believe there's a good book here, even when this all turns out to be some elaborate prank."

"How do you figure that? Without finding Jackson and proving he's still alive, the book doesn't have a satisfying ending. Nobody's going to care."

Marisa shook her head. "You're selling yourself short. It's like what Alan said. Fans of the band are going to connect with all the ways that the music and your writing about it have enriched your life. Sure, if Jackson Cole were alive, we'd have a bestseller. If he's not, we'll still have an interesting autobiography with a unique take on it. Tons of people grew up with the band's music. You're going to articulate what they felt, except on a personal level, and that, in turn, will have a universal appeal."

Leah shook her head. The story wasn't so simple and pretty as either Alan or Marisa imagined. "You should write East Street Press's cover copy," she said.

Marisa laughed. "Who do you think already does that? But I'm serious about this. You've had a three-dimensional life because of the Rats. All you have to do is figure out how to put on paper what you feel inside, and you've already proven you can do that with other subjects you've written about."

Leah had pushed shuffle on her phone's Diesel Rats playlist and "Dig Deep (Look Inside Yourself)" burst out of the car's speakers. The two women looked at each other and laughed.

15

STEVE

I stumble and start to fall forward when the step Calico took lands us on a slope just below the hunting lodge. Calico's still holding my hand and tugs me back before I completely lose my balance.

If I were fourteen years old, this would probably be the coolest thing ever. Teleportation. Beam me up, Scotty. But I'm not fourteen. I like my feet firmly planted on the ground.

"Jesus," I say to Calico. "Could you give a guy a little warning before you—"

She cuts me off. "The pack's almost here. I'm going to lead them off while you deal with Reuben."

"Maybe I bit off more than I can chew here. How am I supposed to do that?"

"I don't know. Like Morago said, talk to him. Dial it down. Keep him engaged. The pack's connected and they can talk to each other in their heads. I need Reuben to be too busy to give orders to his dog boys so I can draw them away while you reason with him. Without his control we should be able to pull this off."

Pull what off? I wonder. Obviously, I didn't think any of this through. But before I can protest, Calico shifts like she did when the kids were at my trailer, and an antelope goes springing down the slope.

The pack comes bursting out from under the trees and she charges right for them, veering aside when she's just a few lengths away. The pack goes crazy. They surge after her, all except for the dog in the front. He comes to an abrupt stop, turning in the direction of the pack, which is now in full pursuit of Calico. I realize this dog must be Reuben.

The pack's connected and they can talk to each other in their heads, Calico said.

"Reuben!" I yell and go running down the slope toward him.

It's enough to distract him and get him looking in my direction. Hopefully, it's also enough to stop him from communicating with the pack through whatever link they have in their heads. But the distraction only lasts a moment. He sees it's just me and starts to turn away again. But by now I'm right on him, and then I do either the stupidest or the bravest thing I've ever done. I leap onto his back.

It's like trying to ride a small tornado.

He shakes and snarls, canines flashing, so I punch him in the side of the head. I don't think this is exactly what Calico meant about keeping him engaged or dialing it down, but what else am I supposed to do? Let him take a chunk out of me?

Except delivering the punch makes me lose my grip and we fall apart. By the time I scramble to my feet, Reuben's already standing in human form.

"What the fuck?" he says, rubbing his temple.

"Hey, I was just trying to—"

He's not listening. He takes a swing at me. I duck the blow and move in close so all we can do is grapple.

"Can we please talk about this?" I say as I struggle to keep him from getting the advantage.

"I'm done with talking."

"Fair enough."

I give him a head butt and he stumbles back, dazed. I'm seeing a few stars myself from the blow, but I'll bet he's seeing a galaxy. When he takes an unsteady step forward, trying to bring up a fist, I give him a push and he goes down.

"Don't get up," I tell him.

For a moment, I think he's going to have another go at me, but then he sighs.

"Didn't know you were so hard-ass," he says.

"I'm not. I'm just trying to stop you from making a mistake. You go on the warpath and it's just going to divide the rez again."

"Did Morago send you?"

I shrug.

"You don't understand," he says, "and Morago doesn't want to."

"Seems pretty clear to me."

He shakes his head. "Walk away. This is tribal business."

"Derek Two Trees was my friend, too."

"This isn't just about Derek."

"I get it. It's tribal business. And maybe it is, in part. But it's also about you finally sticking it to Sammy."

He flashes me an angry look.

"Don't pretend it isn't," I say.

"What if it is? Look what he's done. The lodge, the hotel, that fucking casino. We were doing just fine before he decided we had to be modernized. Except nothing's really changed, has it? We're still the second class citizens, except this time he's made us into card dealers and dancers, busboys and hunting guides for the white man."

He spits in the dirt. "No offense," he adds.

"Yeah. None taken."

Neither of us says anything for a moment. I don't know what he's thinking, but I'm worrying about Calico keeping ahead of that pack of dogs.

"So," Reuben finally says. "You're saying we should just let that fat banker or stock broker or whatever the hell he is take Derek's head home and hang it on his wall?"

"Nope. I'm going to get it back so Derek can have a proper burial."

I don't know where that comes from, but I know it's right.

"And I'm going to do it," I go on, "in a way that doesn't wind everybody up and start the old feuds picking away at each other again."

"It's something that's got to be settled once and for all."

"I agree. But not now. Not like this."

He gives a slow nod. "So instead, you're going to do it. Your way."

"I will."

I don't have to give my word. Among the Kikimi, a person's measure is taken by how he follows through, not by what he says.

"Okay," he says.

I offer him a hand. He takes it and I haul him to his feet. He cocks his head and sighs. "I called off the boys," he says. "Not that she needed me to. They were never going to catch her."

"Yeah, I get the sense she's good at that."

"Huh."

He studies me for a moment.

"What?" I say.

"So, you and Calico?"

"I didn't see it being anyone else's business. Still don't."

He shrugs. "Your call. Make sure you deal with Sammy before Derek's head goes missing." Then he turns, changes, and it's a dog that runs off into the forest.

I watch him go, then look up the slope to where the lights of the lodge are peeping through the trees.

Was it only a couple of nights ago that my life was pretty much solitary, private and simple? First that kid gets dumped, and now every damn thing I thought was real has been turned on its head. How the hell did any of this happen?

I blame Possum. He could have told me a long time ago about our camp being on some other astral plane, and how I might meet up with *ma'inawo* out there, but instead he let the years go by, leaving me in the dark. It's a little embarrassing that the whole rez knew and was waiting for me to finally twig to what's been right in front of my face all of this time.

Calico comes soft-stepping out of the woods and slips her arms around me. She tilts her head back for a kiss and I oblige.

"I don't know about the fisticuffs," she says, "but that was a good job you did distracting Reuben."

I step back to look at her.

She grins. "So are you ready to get this thing done?"

"How do you know what I told Reuben? I thought you were off being chased by his dog boys."

"Can't a girl be in two places at the same time?"

"Apparently."

"Oh, don't be sulky. Come on."

She reaches for my hand but I take a step back.

"It's not so far that we can't walk there on our own two feet," I say.

"Baby."

She grabs my hand, moving so fast I can't avoid her, but when she takes a step up the slope we don't make some instant transition to the front door of the lodge. We're just walking through the forest.

"You know, not everything's magic," she says after we've been hiking under the pines for a while. "I didn't hear your conversation with Reuben. I just figured it out, what with you standing there looking up at the lodge and him long gone."

I glance in her direction and she gives me a wink. "Or maybe I did."

I don't bother to reply.

16

THOMAS

Auntie was sitting on the porch when Thomas pulled Reuben's pickup into their yard. Santana hopped out of the cab. She slammed the car door closed and three large black birds perched on the banister near Auntie Leila's chair flew off into the evening air. In the poor light Thomas couldn't tell if they were ravens or Yellowrock Canyon crows. Santana didn't seem to notice them. She stopped long enough to give Auntie a kiss and a hug, then went inside. Thomas followed at a slower pace.

"*Ohla*, Auntie," he said. "Talking to the birds again?"

When he bent down to give her a kiss, she sniffed at him.

"Huh," she said. "At least you didn't run off with her."

Thomas straightened up. "Run off with who?"

"The *ma'inawo* girl you've been stepping out with."

"I'm not stepping out with anybody."

"Then how come you have the smell of the otherworld on you?"

There was a smell? Thomas thought.

"We were delivering a propane tank to Steve and his girlfriend Calico," he said.

"Ah, Calico. You be careful around that girl."

"She seemed nice."

"She probably is. It's her friends that can be trouble. Deer women and jackrabbit girls. Be especially careful around them."

"I will, Auntie."

He started to go into the house, but she caught his arm. "Will you do an old lady a favour?" she asked.

Thomas had to smile. Auntie only ever referred to herself as old when she wanted you to do something for her that you probably didn't want to do.

"What's that?" he asked, keeping his tone noncommittal.

Auntie glanced toward the house then beckoned him to bend down closer. "You're a good man," she said, "taking care of your family when you'd rather be a thousand miles away from the rez."

"It's no burden."

She waved that off. "You and I both know what's true. And we know you like to keep your distance from the traditions of your people."

"I'm going to the sweat tomorrow," he said, not sure why he felt the need to say that. "At Aggie's."

It was enough to distract Auntie. "Have you met some girl? What's her family?"

"Why would you think that?"

"Why else would you be going to a sweat?"

"Reuben asked me. He thought I should go."

"Huh. It's because of Reuben I have to ask you this favour. Did you hear about Derek Two Trees?"

Thomas shook his head.

"One of Sammy's white man hunters shot him, up in the mountains."

"Is he—is he okay?"

Auntie shook her head. "He's dead. They cut off his head as a trophy and brought it back to the lodge."

"*What?*"

Thomas rocked back on his heels and put a hand on the railing to keep his balance.

"They didn't know it was Derek," Auntie said. "He was in his bighorn shape."

"I never knew..." Thomas began, but then he thought of the bighorn aura he always saw settled over Derek's shoulders like a plains tribe chief's headdress.

"That's terrible."

Auntie nodded in agreement. "And now Reuben's heading up to the lodge with a gang of his dog boys to take the trophy away from them. You know what that means. It doesn't matter which way it goes, Sammy will be down at the center to confront Morago before the sun rises."

Thomas tried to take this all in. "What favour do you want from me?" he asked.

"Your mother wouldn't want me to ask you this," she said, "but I was hoping you'd go down the center to stand by Morago as a sign of solidarity. If Sammy comes down with a gang, Morago will need his own show of force."

"You think there'll be fighting?"

"I hope not. But that's why you'll be there. If Morago has enough men with him, Sammy won't want to start anything."

"And you think Mom won't want me to—"

Auntie didn't let him finish. "This younger Women's Council needs to grow a backbone. If they had, Sammy would never have been able to build his casino and everything that came with it. And we wouldn't have this problem that we have now."

Thomas didn't know what to say.

"I understand how you feel about our traditions," Auntie went on. "I'm only asking you to stand with Morago tonight. What he doesn't need supporting him is a gang of dog boy hotheads."

"Auntie, I don't disrespect the traditions," Thomas told her. "I'm not ashamed of the tribe or who I am."

"You just want to see some of the world."

Thomas nodded. Did everybody know? He thought he'd kept this pretty well to himself.

"All young men need the chance to run in other deserts, not just the one in which they were born. You'll get your chance. But tonight I ask you to stand with Morago."

"Of course," Thomas said. He straightened up. "I'll just grab something to eat and—"

Auntie reached beside her chair and offered him a fat tube covered in foil.

"A burrito…for the drive," she said. "It should still be a little warm."

"But Mom—"

"Will only ask you not to go. If you go without seeing her, you won't have to decide between the wishes of your mother and this old woman."

Thomas hid a smile. "Of course, Auntie," he said. He took the burrito and returned to the pickup.

"I knew I could count on you," Auntie called after him.

Thomas gave her a wave and got back into the truck. As he was pulling out onto the road he looked in his rearview mirror to see his mother step out onto the porch.

He gave the truck a little more gas, but slowed down as soon as the house was out of sight. He was in no hurry to reach the community center.

It was a little ironic. He'd spent forever trying to stay off Morago's radar, and now here he was, on his way to visit the shaman. At Auntie's request, true enough, but that didn't change anything.

But it probably didn't matter, not the way this day was going. The shaman probably knew everything about him, the same way everybody else seemed to. And if he did, then maybe Morago also knew this Corn Eyes boy was the worst candidate to be an apprentice that he would ever find.

Which didn't make pulling into the dirt parking lot of the community center any easier.

There was already a fire burning, with at least a dozen lawn chairs set around it. Around half were occupied. Other men stood near a silent powwow drum. Rez dogs sprawled in the dirt. All heads turned in his direction as he killed the engine and stepped out of the pickup.

Morago moved away from the group of standing men and walked toward him. He clasped Thomas's forearms and gave them a squeeze. "One thing the People know," Morago said, "is that in a time of need, they can always count on the men of the Corn Eyes Clan. Welcome, brother. *Ohla*."

Thomas had spent half his life trying to figure out a way to get out of the rez, but at this moment, he didn't know why. An unfamiliar pride filled him. He squared his shoulders and stood straighter.

Morago smiled and stepped back. "Come," he said. "We have tea by the fire."

Thomas knew all the men here, but tonight it seemed as though they looked at him differently. They smiled and clapped his back as he followed Morago to the fire. Charlie Green—related to Thomas's mother through marriage to a cousin—sat in the closest lawn chair and handed him a metal cup. The scent of herbal tea wafted up from the warm liquid.

"*Ohla*, Thomas," Charlie said.

Thomas nodded his thanks. "*Ohla*. It's been a while."

Charlie shrugged. He dug into his pocket and came up with a pack of cigarettes. Thomas didn't smoke, but he accepted one anyway, bent down for the light Charlie offered and took a drag. He held the smoke in for a moment, then exhaled and offered the cigarette back to Charlie.

"A terrible business, this," somebody behind him said.

It was William Strong Bow. Settled on William's shoulders, super-imposed over his own features, was the vague outline of a bighorn's head. Thomas hadn't realized the man was kin to Derek.

"It makes no sense," Thomas agreed. "I'm sorry to hear about Derek."

William just shook his head and stared at the ground.

Thomas took an empty chair beside Charlie and sipped his tea while Charlie smoked. One by one, the other men came to the fire and stood or sat around it, the firelight flickering on their faces. The only one who didn't join them was Jerry Five Hawks, the deputy on duty from the rez's tribal police. He stood by the community center, leaning against a wall of the building, arms folded across his chest. Thomas supposed he couldn't appear to take sides, but it was good to know he was present in case of trouble.

There were none of the jokes and kidding around that usually accompanied a gathering on the rez. The men spoke quietly or kept their own counsel, as Morago did. The shaman stared into the flames, his thoughts unreadable. Thomas amused himself by searching each of the men for their animal aura. A few had them—he marked bighorn, bobcat, packrat, rattler, cactus wren—and some didn't. The only one he couldn't read was Morago's.

After a while, Petey Jojoba took his chair over to the powwow drum. Petey was a weaver who lived down the road from Aggie White Horse's place, but he was also a hoop dancer, storyteller and drummer. He knew over a hundred stories about the Kikimi trickster Jimmy Cholla—always a favourite around the fires—but tonight when Petey woke a soft heartbeat from the drum, he began to tell of the time Hummingbird tricked the magpie girls into giving him all of their collected treasures.

The men fell silent, nodding their heads as they listened. Like the rest, Thomas had heard this story before. He'd grown up on stories like this, first hearing them from Auntie and his mother. But tonight it felt as though he was hearing it for the first time. Tonight he could almost see the cocky hummingbird swaggering around with his pockets full of rings and trinkets.

He wasn't sure what was different. He was older, so he should have found it harder to immerse himself so completely in its well-worn telling. Maybe it was the night, or the unusual company. Or just the situation. He had no idea. The only thing he knew for sure was that everyone here felt the same, listening to Petey's voice and the soft heartbeat of his mallet tapping the big powwow drum. Even the dogs lay with ears twitching, their eyes open and fixed on Petey as he spoke.

And they weren't alone, the men and dogs, Thomas realized. As the story unfolded he became aware of animals gathering at the edges of the parking lot, half hidden in the cacti and brush. Jackrabbits. A bobcat. A pair of owls. Innumerable mice and packrats. Many of the cacti seemed to be closer to the parking lot than they had been when he'd first arrived. All of them following the rise and fall of Petey's voice.

Petey had just reached the part where the magpie girls were getting their revenge, when something disturbed the animals and they melted back into the brush. The dogs stood up, turning their muzzles to the west. The story stopped and Petey's drum went still. His gaze followed those of the dogs. When Thomas looked himself, he saw headlights coming up the road from the highway.

"Who's that?" Charlie said. "It seems too early for Sammy to be on the warpath."

One of the other men nodded. "And Thomas has Reuben's truck."

The mystery was solved a few moments later when a Kikimi County Sheriff's cruiser pulled into the parking lot followed by an unmarked car. The men by the fire had to shield their eyes against the glare of the headlights. The driver of the cruiser shut off his engine, but left the headlights on as he stepped out of his car.

Nobody got up from their chairs, but Jerry pushed away from the wall where he'd been leaning. He adjusted his holster and walked across the parking lot to meet the other police officer.

"Looks like Sammy called the cops on us," William murmured. "Coward."

The door of the unmarked car opened and a white man got out. Thomas didn't recognize him, but he knew the deputy from the sheriff's office. Bob Hernandez. He came into the trading post from time to time to talk to Reuben.

"Hey, Bob," Jerry said to the deputy. "What brings you out this way tonight?"

Bob jerked a thumb behind him. "Mr. Higgins here says his daughter's been kidnapped and that she's being held here on the rez. You think anybody here knows anything about it?"

Thomas and the other men exchanged glances. This was serious.

"You have anything more to go on?" Jerry asked. "What she looks like? When she went missing?"

"Her name's Sadie. She's sixteen, white, dark-haired, about yay high."

Bob put out a hand to indicate a girl of about five-two or three.

"How long has she been missing?" Jerry asked.

"Twenty-four hours or so."

"Do you have a picture?"

"I'll have the office email one to you."

Jerry nodded. "Good. I'll get the word out and see what we can find."

"Appreciate it," Bob said.

He started to turn away, but Higgins pushed forward.

"That's *it*?" Higgins said.

Both officers simply looked at him.

"You're just leaving?" Higgins went on. "My little girl could be in any kind of trouble. For all we know, they could have her all doped up and be whoring her out. Hell, they could've sold her to some wetbacks in Mexico by now. You need to be busting down doors, putting the fear of God into them."

"Those are some pretty serious accusations, Mr. Higgins," Bob said. "You really need to dial it down."

That was the polite way to put it, Thomas thought. All around him he could feel the other men bristling.

"If you're telling me I need to shut up," Higgins said, "I'm telling you hell no."

"What makes you think she's on the rez?" Jerry asked.

Higgins rolled his eyes. "I saw some big Indian grab her and throw her in a white van. Where else would he go to?"

"Can you give us a description of the abductor?"

"What kind of question is that? He looked like you." Higgins nodded to the fire. "He looked like those bucks. How the hell am I supposed to know the difference?"

"That's enough," Bob said.

"Enough of what? Higgins asked. "You need to start *doing* something."

The deputy shook his head. "If you don't shut up," he told Higgins, "I'm going to cuff you and throw you in the back of my car."

"You can't talk to me like that. I pay taxes. The sheriff's going to hear about this—don't think he won't. You should be getting the Bureau of Indian Affairs on this. You should have the FBI in here right now, going door-to-door. You need choppers in the air. Let these Indians know they can't get away with shit like this."

Bob took a step in the man's direction and Higgins scuttled back out of reach.

"I'm sorry about this," Bob told Jerry.

"I'll tell you who's going to be sorry," Higgins began.

Before he could finish, the deputy had him up against the side of his car. It took him only a moment to cuff Higgins and put him in the back of the cruiser.

"What're you going to do with him?" Jerry asked.

The deputy shrugged. "Damned if I know. There's something hinky about this whole business, but Higgins strikes me as a guy who knows how to work the system. I don't think this is going away in any kind of a hurry."

"We'll do what we can here," Jerry assured him.

"I know you will. Okay if I leave his car here overnight? I'll get somebody to come by and get it tomorrow."

"Not a problem."

The deputy moved Higgins' car to the far end of the parking lot, then drove away in his own vehicle. Once they were gone, Jerry regarded the men by the fire. "You don't know anything about this, right?"

He asked the men in general, but his gaze was on Morago. Everybody knew the dorm held a half-dozen or so undocumented kids from Mexico. Kids with no family to call their own. And Morago ran the dorm as well as the school.

"There's no white girl in the dorm," the shaman said. "Not a kidnapped girl or a runaway."

"If that was my old man," somebody said, "I'd *pay* somebody to take me away."

The men chuckled.

Jerry nodded. "Maybe Petey could finish his story."

He returned to his position by the community center, leaning against the wall. Petey glanced at Morago. When the shaman nodded, he woke the heartbeat on the powwow drum once again, the padded mallet tapping the big drum's skin.

"Now where was I?" he said.

Thomas smiled. As though Petey didn't know.

"The magpie girls were about to give Hummingbird the what for," William said.

Petey smiled. "So they were."

He went back to the story, but this time Thomas had trouble concentrating. He kept glancing at Morago. The shaman stared into the coals of the fire, just as he had before. It was as though the interruption had never happened and all he was interested in was hearing the end of Petey's story. But Thomas had the sense Morago knew more about this missing girl than he'd admitted to Jerry.

He was pretty sure he didn't want to know what Morago was up to. It wasn't his business. It was breaking some serious laws. But the truth was, now that his curiosity had been woken, he couldn't not find out.

The only thing he knew for certain was he'd probably regret it.

17

STEVE

It doesn't take us long to climb the slope to the clearing where the hunting lodge stands. We pause under the heavy boughs of the pines that grow at the edge of the forest, and study the building. The place is a lot bigger than I expected. Two floors, maybe fifteen hundred square feet per floor. There's no road through the forest, only a trail. Parked on the lawn are half a dozen ATVs. I know they also fly 'copters up here, so I figure the helipad must be on the other side of the building, out of sight from our position.

"I don't see any guards," I say.

Calico punches me lightly on the bicep.

"What was that for?"

"Why would there be guards? This is a lodge. A fancy, fake-rustic hotel for mighty white hunters who like to take their prey down from a distance and then leave their bodies to rot where they fall. You think they're worried about being robbed? With all their big guns? People only come up here on Sammy's say-so."

"Except for us."

The grin she gives me is feral. "Except for us," she says. "So what's the plan? Are we going to have a conversation with Sammy, or do we just steal Derek's head?"

"Where would they even keep something like that?"

"My guess? In a freezer. There's probably one in the basement."

I nod.

She gives me an expectant look. "So which is it going to be?"

"Why can't it be both? I'll go talk to Sammy while you steal the head."

Her feral grin returns. Her hand strokes the part of my arm she punched just a moment ago.

"Now you're talking," she says. "I'll come back and get you after I'm done. Try to stay out of trouble until then—or at least don't start anything you can't finish."

"Since when did I ever—" I start, but she's already gone, vanished from my sight and leaving only a soft *whufft* of displaced air behind.

I cross the lawn and aim for the big front door. I don't bother to knock. This is like a hotel, right? I could be a guest. So I go straight inside and find myself standing in a huge room dominated in the middle by a stone fireplace that disappears into a high ceiling of pine tongue-and-groove. Large pieces of rustic furniture dot the area: chairs, sofas and end tables all clustered together in small islands. There's a front desk to my right, with nobody behind it. To my left is a broad staircase going up to the second floor.

I think I'm alone until the quiet murmur of conversation draws my attention toward the far end of the room. A couple of white men are sitting in a far corner, legs up on the table between them, drinks in hand. They're in their forties, short-haired and clean-shaven, slightly paunchy, outfitted in chinos and crisp flannel shirts that I doubt have ever been worn before this trip.

I'm debating whether to go over and ask them if they know where Sammy is, when I hear a footstep. Turning, I find Dave Running Dog is now on the other side of the counter.

"Can I help—" he starts, but then he recognizes me. "*Ohla*, Steve. What the hell brings you up here?"

"Maybe I'm thinking of taking up big game hunting."

Dave laughs. "Oh yeah. Next you'll be telling me Morago's planning to drop by the casino to play the slots."

"Could happen."

"Sure. Soon as Sammy goes on a spirit quest."

I smile, then say, "Actually, I'm here to see Sammy."

Dave can't hide his surprise. I guess it's understandable. What's an old desert rat like me got in common with a guy like Sammy? Dave probably thought I'd come up to see him.

I first met Dave a few years ago when I came across him on the narrow dirt track that runs from his mother's place down to Zahra Road. His truck was broken down, his mama in the shotgun seat with what turned out to be appendicitis. Dave didn't know the first thing about car engines, but mechanics had been a hobby of mine as a kid. I can't do a damn thing with the new cars since they're all fancy computers and crap now, but give me an old engine and I'm golden. I soon had that old truck of his running again and they got to the hospital in time.

After that, we've run into each other here and there, but I haven't seen much of him since he started to work for Sammy. The two sides of the rez pretty much keep to themselves these days, and I've never had any reason to go to the casino side.

Dave looks at me like I'm a little nuts. "You came all the way up *here* to see him?"

One of the complaints from the traditional side about the casino is that it makes the people lazy. Anyone who comes over to this side drives. Used to be, folks didn't think twice about walking from one end of the rez to the other. They hunted, put in crops, looked after their sheep and goats. It was all about keeping their connection to the land. To them, the casino means easy money and a big disconnect from tradition.

"It's about Derek Two Trees," I say.

Dave has to think about that for a moment before he says, "I'm pretty sure Sammy doesn't know him. Sammy doesn't keep up with any of the old school traditional crowd."

"That's okay. Just tell me where he is," I say.

Dave waits a beat, then nods and motions me to come around behind the counter. We walk down a short hall with doors on either side, and stop dead center at the end, in front of a carved, double wooden door depicting various desert animals. Dave knocks and somebody inside tells us to come in.

Sammy's office is just what I expected. Big and rustic, like the rest of the lodge, but it's also a power exec's man cave. Native artifacts hang from the walls, including a full chief's headdress, which is kind of funny since the Kikimi have never worn that kind of thing. A stuffed grizzly stands in the corner, and I find myself wondering if it was like Derek—both man and animal. A big flat screen on the wall and a laptop on his massive desk bring us right up to modern day technology.

Sammy Swift Grass is in his mid-thirties, a heavyset man with the broad features of the Kikimi, his long hair pulled back in a sleek ponytail. He wheels his leather chair back from his desk. I see he's wearing a casino logo denim shirt with a fancy bolo tie and crisp chinos. A beaded belt with a big turquoise buckle completes the look.

He gives me a once over, then turns to Dave with a raised questioning eyebrow.

"This is Steve," Dave explains. "Steve Cole. Says he want to talk to you about Derek Two Trees."

"I don't know any Derek Two Trees."

"That's what I told him."

Sammy finally addresses me directly. "What's this about, Mr. Cole?"

"One of your clients shot Derek this afternoon," I tell him. "People on the other side of the rez are upset."

I can tell he doesn't have a clue what I'm talking about. He gives Dave another puzzled look before he returns his attention to me. I elaborate. "After your client shot Derek, your people cut off his head and brought it back here."

"Hold on," Dave says. "Are you talking about the bighorn Armstrong bagged this afternoon?"

Sammy shakes his head. "You've got to be kidding me. Now they're giving the wild animals *names*?"

"He wasn't an animal," I say. "He was a *ma'inawo*."

"Yeah, and I'm the president of the USA. Look, if the traditionalists think I'll let their crazy bullshit screw up my business, they're going to get schooled on how things work in the *real* world. I'm betting Morago sent you, so you go back and tell him that if he tries to run with this woo-woo shaman story, he's going to be talking to my lawyers. See how far he gets in a court of law. And remind him that *all* of the tribe benefits from my business—unless he's pocketing the money we send over to him."

"You know he'd never do that," I start, but he cuts me off.

"I couldn't give a crap." He nods to Dave. "Get this asshole out of here."

Dave gives me an apologetic look.

"They just want the head back so they can give Derek a proper burial," I say before he can start to usher me out.

Sammy gives me a hard look and thrusts his index finger in my direction. "My client paid good money to go home with a trophy and that's how it's going to play out. We've got all the proper paperwork. He shot an animal, not some mumbo jumbo Indian spirit. Tell Morago to save that crap for the tourists, like we do."

I wonder if Calico's had enough time to snatch the head, because this isn't going well. I don't know why I thought it would.

"Now, either you let Dave walk you out," Sammy says, "or we throw you out with a few broken bones. The choice is yours."

18

THOMAS

After Petey finished his story, the men all gathered closer to the fire, talking about Sammy and this new business with the crazy white dude and his daughter. If Jerry Five Hawks wasn't still leaning against the side of the community center, Thomas wouldn't have been surprised to see the white man's car mysteriously catch fire. As it was, the men could only fantasize about various ways to repay Higgins for his racist views.

Morago didn't add to the conversation, but he stayed in his lawn chair in the middle of it all, and Thomas didn't see how he could get a private word with him.

A sudden commotion in the desert scrub just past the far end of the parking lot negated any chance of talking to the shaman. His boss Reuben and a half-dozen of his dog boys came jogging in, kicking up dust. They slowed down when they neared the fire.

None were in dog shape, but Thomas could see their animal spirits floating above their shoulders like headdresses.

The men all greeted each other, punching shoulders and whooping. Reuben's brows went up when he caught sight of Thomas. He grinned proudly and slapped a closed fist against his chest.

"Is Sammy on his way?" Morago asked when the hubbub died down.

Thomas noticed that while Jerry never shifted position, he seemed to be leaning a little closer to hear the answer.

"I don't know," Reuben replied. "I never saw him. Steve came along and said he'd handle things."

"What, that old desert rat?" someone asked.

"The spirits favour him," Morago said.

"Yeah," Petey added with a grin, "and some of them favour him a *lot*."

The men laughed, not unkindly. Though everyone grew up with warnings about the dangers of becoming involved with *ma'inawo* and spirits, they also knew that luck followed those favoured by their cousin neighbours. Just as bad luck followed those who spoke ill of either the *ma'inawo* or their chosen.

"Do we still keep vigil?" William asked.

The subtle reminder of Derek brought a silence to the group.

Morago nodded. "Steve's not part of the tribe," the shaman said. "But just because it's him instead of one of us going after justice for Derek, doesn't mean Sammy won't still take it into his head to come down here with a show of force."

More chairs were brought out from the community center. The fire was built up and thermoses of tea were shared around with the newcomers.

Amid speculation of what Steve would do, Reuben draped an arm over Thomas's shoulders and led him away from the fire. "I was surprised to see you here," he said. "Pleased, but surprised."

"Auntie sent me."

Reuben nodded. "Because she knows Corn Eyes men have always stood with the tribe."

"I guess."

"No guessing involved, Thomas. I'm still not trying to say you shouldn't see what the world outside the rez might hold for you, but it's good to remember that you always have a place here. People who will stand beside you if the need comes."

"I know that. I appreciate the job and everything. The loan of the truck—it's cool."

Reuben clapped him on the back then let his gaze range down the slope of the hill. His nose twitched and Thomas wondered what he was seeing, or smelling, with his canine senses.

Thomas had always avoided asking his boss anything about the mystical aspects of tribal culture, but given his experiences today, his curiosity won out. "Can I ask you something?" he said.

"Anything," Reuben told him.

"A lot of the tribe carry *ma'inawo* aspects—does that mean they're all shape-shifters?"

"First of all," Reuben said, "none of us are shape-shifters—not the way people throw the word around. We are beings with more than one body—one five-fingered, one not. We don't change from one to the other, except physically." He tapped his chest. "Inside, we're always both at the same time."

"Okay..."

"The blood runs stronger in some than it does in others," Reuben went on, "but there aren't many among us anymore who can change their shapes. When you see somebody's cousin aspect floating above their head like an aura, it just means the blood is stronger in them, not necessarily that they can change."

"But some can."

"Oh, sure."

"Well, that clears everything up," Thomas said, the tone of his voice saying it had done anything but.

Reuben laughed. "You want some real training, talk to Morago. Or your Aunt Leila."

19

SADIE

Until last night Sadie had never crashed outside—and for sure never in the middle of the desert like she had at Steve's campsite. What a crazy night. First the screaming match with Reggie; then getting thrown into the car and tossed out in middle of nowhere, only to be picked up by this weird old do-gooder with the furry kink on the side.

She was surprised she'd even managed to fall asleep, but she ended up so tired that eventually she just dropped off. Not even the creepy silence broken by the distant cries of the coyotes had been able to keep her awake.

Tonight was a different story.

First off, she wasn't really tired. Bored? Yeah, big time. It was hard to even think of going to sleep, though she did try. She changed into the oversized T-shirt Aggie had given her and stretched out on the bed, did the whole deal. But then just lay there staring at the ceiling.

She figured it was because Aggie's guest room wasn't a whole lot different from being outside, and who in their right mind lived with this kind of quiet? Aggie or Steve'd probably hate the city, but she was used to the sound of traffic wafting in through her windows, snatches of drunken conversation from a few houses over, distant sirens. There was something comforting about hearing life go on even while you were in your bed. It made you feel less alone.

Here, there was only the silence and the deep dark of the night lying thick over everything. She was also starting to feel a little trapped in this small room in the middle of nowhere. The paintings of all the weird animal/human hybrids didn't help. She couldn't see them in the dark, but she knew they were there. Watching her.

Okay, she wasn't a little kid. She knew there was nothing about the paintings that could hurt her. They weren't real. Just like Aggie's stories about dog boys and the spirits of vegetables and crap weren't real, though they at least had seemed a little cool until they went on and on. But the paintings still made her nervous. The longer she lay here, the tighter her chest got.

Her knife usually relieved her anxiety. She got up and pulled it out of her jeans pocket. Taking the woven Indian blanket from the bed, she wrapped it around her shoulders and quietly opened her door.

Ruby lay on the floor outside, head lifting. The dog had wanted to come in but Sadie hadn't let her. Sure, she seemed nice enough, but what was to stop Ruby from suddenly deciding to tear out her throat in the middle of the night?

Aggie said the dog had taken a liking to her. Sadie just figured Ruby was keeping tabs on her, though why the dog would want to do that was anybody's guess. Still, it made more sense than a dog she'd only just met liking her for no good reason. She knew from experience that everybody wanted something from you. That was the way the world worked, and she didn't suppose dogs were any different.

"Is there any point in telling you not to follow me?" she whispered to the dog.

Ruby sat up and cocked her head.

"Yeah, I didn't think so."

Tiptoeing across the tiled floor, Sadie pulled the blanket more tightly around her and went out the front door. Ruby slipped out before Sadie could stop her, brushing against her legs. Nails clicking on the tiles.

Sadie wasn't sure what she was doing outside in her bare feet. For one thing, she knew there were more dogs somewhere out here in the darkness. There'd also be thorns, rattlesnakes, spiders and scorpions. Coyotes. Mountain lions. Pretty much a million things that would just love to have a piece of her.

She looked up.

And that sky. How did the sky get so big?

She shivered as much from the chill in the night air as from the immensity of what stretched over her head and the darkness that went on forever around her. Coming out here was dumb. It just made her feel more displaced and alone.

Looking for someplace hidden where she just could go make a quick little cut, she caught a flicker of light from the corner of her eye. It was a campfire, she realized. She looked more closely and saw there were figures sitting around it.

She remembered Aggie saying something about people coming over for a sweat tomorrow night. Tonight, actually, she supposed, since it was long past midnight. She wasn't entirely clear on what a sweat was, but she hadn't wanted to ask since it would've meant listening to yet another long story, and she'd heard more than enough of them for one day.

She got it already. Everything has a spirit. Thank the beans and corn for letting you eat them. Don't throw stones at the little birds because they've got just as much right to be here as you do.

That's probably what was going on over there. People sitting around telling endless stories to thank the wood for letting itself be burned up in their fire. Maybe a shout-out to the clothes they were wearing.

Just do what you came to do and go back inside, she told herself. You don't need any more stories, and whatever's going on over there is none of your business.

All true, but she still stepped off the porch to walk in the direction of the fire, her bare feet scuffling in the cool dirt, Ruby padding silently at her side.

Sadie didn't have anything to worry about. The fire cast dark shadows beyond its circle of light, and that same darkness would hide her from the people at the fire. And maybe Ruby really was looking out for her.

She'd just get close enough to see what they were up to. She sure wasn't going to go skulking around in the brush off the path, where everything had a thorn.

She could see the people a little better now. They wore blankets like the one she'd borrowed from the guest room, except they were pulled up over their heads like hoodies. A murmur of conversation came to her, not clear enough to make out the words yet, but they were obviously talking to one another, not telling long stories.

A coyote cried out in the darkness and Sadie started. It sounded so close. But then one of the figures lifted an arm as though in greeting to the wild dog's call. The blanket fell away from where it was shadowing his features. Sadie sucked in a quick breath and put her hand over her mouth before the scream inside her could burst out.

A bird's head was on the man's shoulders. He was like Aggie's paintings.

She must have made some kind of noise because they all turned in her direction, animal features showing under their blankets. Dogs, deer, a lizard, a rabbit.

Sadie ran as fast as she could back to Aggie's house.

20

STEVE

Dave's still looking apologetic, but I don't doubt for a moment that he's going to physically toss me out if I don't figure out some way to stall him. Because I can't go yet. I know Calico's going to grab Derek's head, but that only solves the immediate problem. There's a bigger issue at stake here. I have to make Sammy realize that some of these animals his clients are hunting are cousins. That the *ma'inawo* are real. And I guess there's only one way to do that.

"Calico!" I yell, hoping she can hear me from wherever she is. "I need you right now!"

My shouting startles Dave enough that he takes a step back. Sammy shoots him a withering look. "Who's this Calico?" he asks. "How many of them are there?"

Dave looks confused. "He's the only one I saw," he says.

"Calico!" I yell again.

"Shut the fuck up," Sammy tells me, rising out of his chair.

All I can come up with is a juvenile response as I try to buy some time.

"Make me," I tell him.

"*Make* you? Do you think we're in kindergarten, asshole?"

But then Calico steps out of nowhere to stand at my side. She's holding Derek's head by a horn, dripping blood and gore all over Sammy's fancy pine floors.

"Yeah, make him," she says.

I think Dave might have pissed his pants when she just appeared out of nowhere. But while Sammy's eyes widen, he takes it in better stride. He slides open a drawer and pulls out a handgun. Before he can lift it to fire at us, Calico drops Derek's head and leaps on top of Sammy's desk, scattering papers and shoving his laptop to the edge, where it balances precariously. She bats the gun out of his hand and he's suddenly looking into the face of a seriously pissed off fox, its head sitting on the shoulders of a woman, open jaws mere inches from his face.

When he tries to back away she grabs his shirt and pulls him right up to those jaws. There's no use in him trying to break her grip—I know how strong she is—but that doesn't stop him from trying.

I clear my throat. "So this is Calico," I tell Sammy. "One of those *ma'inawo* you say don't exist."

Calico's face returns to her human features, but now she's got antelope prongs lifting from her brow.

"And I don't like you," she tells him.

She shoves him back into his chair, but stays crouched there on his desk. His gaze slides to where the gun landed, then back again.

"Oh, please," Calico says. "Make a try for it."

He lifts his hands, palms out. "I don't want any trouble."

"Too bad. You already started this party." She glances over at me. "Can I kill him?"

I'm pretty sure she's not serious, but whether she is or not, the words have their desired effect.

"Wait, wait!" Sammy says, all his bravado gone. I might not be sure of her actual intentions, but it's plain he thinks his life is hanging from a very slender thread.

"Tell me what you want," he adds. "Tell me what I can do to make this right."

Dave shifts his position and Calico's gaze lands on him like a pair of lasers. He holds up his hands like Sammy did.

"I just…I just…" he says. "Can I sit down?"

I look at the wet stain on his chinos. Damn, the poor bastard's bladder really did let him down.

Calico waves a hand, a casual gesture that says both, *what do I care?* and *don't try anything.* She frowns at Sammy.

"You can start with not killing any more *ma'inawo*. And beyond that, have some respect for the poor animals you idiots feel you have to shoot. But I'm telling you, the next time you, or *any* of your clients, kill a cousin? That same night it's going to be *your* head dripping here on the floor of your office."

He looks to me for help, but I keep my face impassive.

"How am I supposed to tell the difference?" he asks Calico.

"That's not my problem," she says. "This is your piece-of-shit commerce."

She hops down from the desk and picks up his gun. Ejecting the clip, she lets it fall onto the desk where it makes a dent in the previously unblemished surface. Then she points the empty gun at Sammy.

"Bang," she says.

She grins when he flinches. He swallows, licks his lip.

"Look—" he starts.

"Ask Morago," Calico says. "Maybe he'll teach you."

"Morago?"

He says the name like it leaves a bad taste in his mouth. Calico pretends not to notice.

"You know. The woo-woo shaman guy who lives in the past and is deluded enough to think that *ma'inawo* like me actually exist. But I can see why you wouldn't want to get advice from him since he's not a modern Indian like you."

"It's not like—"

She cuts him off with a wave of her hand and drops the gun down on the desk. That's got to have made another nasty scratch in its perfect finish.

"Just remember," she tells him. "We. Bite. Back."

Then she hops down from her perch on the desk. Picking up Derek's head again by a horn, she takes my hand and steps us away.

21

LEAH

The moon had set a long time ago, but the stars seemed to go on forever, even looking at them from here on the edge of town.

After the long drive, Leah and Marisa had rented a room at the Silver Spur Motel, a long adobe building that had obviously seen better days, but the rooms were surprisingly clean and there was even free WiFi. There were about a dozen units, a third of which had vehicles parked in front. Most were so rusted and beat up they made their own economy rental look like a showroom car.

Marisa hadn't even bothered to look around the room. As soon as they'd brought their bags in from the car, she'd commandeered one of the twin beds, stripped to a T-shirt, and crawled under the sheets, asleep almost before her head hit the pillow.

Leah wasn't that tired since she'd grabbed a few catnaps on the drive down. When they'd first set out, she kept trying to force herself to stay awake until Marisa had finally noticed and told her to stop fighting it.

"Remember, I slept on the plane," Marisa had said.

It was true. Leah had envied the way Marisa just dropped off, not waking until the pilot's announcement came over the intercom, welcoming them to Las Vegas.

"But it's such a long drive," Leah had argued. "It seems unfair that you shouldn't at least have someone to talk to."

"You're the one that needs to be alert in the morning," Marisa'd told her. "I'm only the chauffeur."

So the next time Leah had felt her eyelids drooping, she'd let sleep come.

Now it was Marisa's turn to be dead to the world while Leah was wide awake.

She sent Alan a text to tell him they'd arrived. She gave him the name of the motel and said that Marisa was sleeping, so she'd call him in the morning. Then, taking a pen and one of her spiral-bound note-books from her luggage, she went outside and sat at a little rusted metal table and chair beside the door. There was enough illumination from the light over the threshold, so she thought she'd write up some notes about the trip thus far. Half an hour later, all she'd done was gaze at the stars and listen to the desert night.

It was so different here from back home, dissimilar in every way. The plants were alien, the smells unfamiliar. Even the night sky looked all wrong. She felt as though she were on another planet, or in some badlands version of fairyland.

But the odd thing was, she didn't feel out of place. On the drive down from Vegas, with the headlights picking out unusual land forma-tions and the even less familiar plant life, she'd felt welcomed. She couldn't wait for the sun to rise so she could really see her surround-ings properly.

Their motel was on the southwest side of Santo del Vado Viejo, at the edge of town. There was a lot of desert scrub around the motel—some of it just undeveloped land, and some ranches, but it still felt like they were driving through the desert. The Kikimi rez was to the west in the Hierro Maderas Mountains, surrounded by a national park. She'd already taken a walk around the building to get a glimpse of the mountains, but they were only a dark shape on the western horizon.

Right now, she had to make do with the tall saguaro that towered not far from where she sat, and some raggedy prickly pear clustered against the side of the building.

If Jackson Cole really was alive and had chosen this area to disappear into, she was beginning to understand why. Even in the dark there was something primal, yet spiritually uplifting about her surroundings, and she found herself wishing she didn't have a flight back in a couple of days. Now that she was here, she itched to get out and explore the area in depth.

Maybe with the advance she was getting from Alan she could afford to stay out here to work on the book. Speaking of which...

She pulled her notebook closer to her and picked up the pen again. But instead of writing about the trip or her surroundings, or even the email that had brought her here, she found herself writing down an all too familiar name:

Aimee Leigh.

She supposed it wasn't so surprising that Aimee would be on her mind, considering the reason she'd come out here, all these miles from home. But it made her stop and consider the wisdom of writing the book that Alan wanted from her.

There's this opportunity to tie in to all the things that first drew you to the Rats, and how writing about them changed you—a more personal journey to complement what you've already written about Cole and the band.

Did she really want to go there?

Every time someone asked her when she'd gotten into the Diesel Rats, she always told them that she'd loved the band for as long as she could remember. That even though the music was already fifteen or so years old when she was a kid, it spoke to her in a way that her own era of music—the eighties—didn't.

But that wasn't quite true, or at least it wasn't her truth. It was Aimee's. The only reason Leah had tolerated the Rats back then was because Aimee was her best friend, and Aimee had adored the band.

Though Leah had secretly preferred the music of their time—all those synthesized keyboards and horribly produced drums she couldn't listen to now—it hadn't mattered because in those days, Aimee's passion for the Rats had somehow trumped everything.

Sure, the Rats had glorious harmonies, great upbeat songs, and hooks that you just couldn't forget. But their music belonged to her parents' generation, like The Beatles or Elvis Presley. So, as Leah yearned for music she could claim as her own, she groaned inwardly every time Aimee pulled out one of the Rats' albums, or worse, one of their dodgy bootlegs with the bad sound and worse covers made up of faded Xeroxed collages.

THAT ALL CHANGED when Aimee died.

All these years later, that depressing fact could still take her by surprise.

She and Aimee had lived next door to each other and been pretty much inseparable from when they could walk. It was a friendship significant for its complete lack of drama. Even their arguments over the Rats had been good-natured because most of the time, they were completely in sync. They were going to conquer the world together. How, they didn't know. They just knew they'd be standing side by side when they did.

Except Aimee wasn't even twenty when she'd drowned in the Kickaha River down by the Butler University Common. All anyone knew was she'd died alone, some time between midnight and sunrise.

The police investigators ruled it a suicide.

Leah had refused to believe it. She'd never have used the word 'depressed' to describe her best friend. But then the journal Aimee's parents had given their daughter the year before she died surfaced.

Leah didn't recognize the Aimee who wrote those entries.

She recognized the handwriting and the people Aimee talked about. She'd even been at most of the events she'd described, but they were unrecognizable seen through the eyes of the Aimee writing in her journal. Like a poetry slam at Kathryn's Café they'd gone to with a bunch of friends. It had been a really fun night with lots of joking and laughing until this one poet just floored them with the intensity of his words and heartfelt delivery. At the time, they'd all been swooning with crushes on him.

In the journal, Aimee barely wrote about the slam. Instead she filled a couple of pages questioning what everybody was thinking about her, what this significant glance had meant, whether that innocuous comment had been a diss.

The journal held endless variations of the same. No matter how benign the situation, Aimee's perception of it was that everybody was judging her and finding her lacking. She kept asking over and over again: Why was she alive? What use was she?

The final entry in her journal transcribed a partial lyric from the Rats' song "Save Me":

> *If I coulda saved you, saved you, saved you;*
> *You just woulda played me, played me, played me.*

Losing her best friend was like losing her right arm, and reading the journal sank Leah deep into a depression of her own. It was as though the Aimee she'd grown up with had been a phantom of her imagination.

Ironically, it was the Diesel Rats that pulled Leah out. She started out listening to them to try and figure out why their music *couldn't* have saved Aimee, only to find that it was able save her.

So why not Aimee?

If Jackson Cole actually was alive, that was the one question she'd want to ask him, but she didn't think he'd have an answer either.

The question she'd asked herself most was: Why hadn't she seen what was going on? How good a friend could she have been to have missed Aimee's self-doubt and torment?

Leah's guilt still lingered all these years later. Would spewing this mess onto paper do anybody any good? It certainly wouldn't be the book that Alan was counting on.

She started writing all of this down—memories and questions both —and didn't look up until she heard the sound of an engine. Closing her notebook with her pen inside to keep her place, she watched a beat up old pickup truck pull into the motel's parking lot.

She had a moment to wonder if she was safe sitting out here by herself, without even the flimsy door of the motel room between her and the two men she could see in the pickup. But it was too late to bolt because the headlights picked her out, blinding her for a moment before the vehicle pulled in closer, then came to a stop.

The passenger's door opened and one of the men got out. He exchanged a few rapid-fire phrases in Spanish with the driver, then closed the door. The truck pulled away and the stranger gave Leah a curious glance. He was white, maybe in his late fifties, tall and in good shape, wearing jeans, cowboy boots, and a blue flannel shirt with a fringed leather vest overtop. Everything about him had seen a lot of wear, from his weathered face to his clothes. As he walked in her direction Leah knew a moment of fear. He seemed to sense her discomfort because he stopped a few yards away.

"Ma'am," he said and tipped a finger to his brow. "You're up late— or early, I suppose, depending."

Ma'am? Leah thought. She was at least twenty years younger than him. She had time to hope he was just being polite, and then he smiled, which made his whole face light up. The tension eased in her shoulders.

"I slept for a lot of the drive down from Las Vegas," she said, "so I thought I might as well do a little work since it's too dark to go for a walk."

"You're from Vegas?"

She shook her head. "From Newford. It's just a cheaper flight to Vegas, even with the car rental."

"I hear you. Me, I'm from right here at the Silver Spur Motel, room number ten. Name's Ernie."

"I'm Leah. And you're either up late or early yourself."

"Guilty as charged." He studied Leah for a moment, his gaze dropping to her notebook, before he added, "What kind of work do you do?"

"I'm a writer."

"Journalist?"

"Sort of. I've written a bit on social politics, but mostly I write about music. What about you? And please." She indicated the free chair. "Have a seat. I'd offer you a coffee, but…"

"Jerry's Roadhouse opens in a couple of hours," he said, waving a hand in what she assumed was the direction of the restaurant. "They've got good coffee, good food."

He sat down across from her, leaning back in his chair. "So you're here on a story?"

"I'm not sure. I'm looking for a guy who used to be in a band back in the sixties, but honestly, I doubt I'm going to find him."

"What's his name?"

Leah didn't know how to answer that. It was unlikely he'd know anything about Jackson Cole's whereabouts, and even less likely that he was plugged in to one of the Internet gossip sites, but she didn't want even a whisper of this story to get out. Because if Cole *was* alive, it would be the story of the century. Right up there with proving that Elvis wasn't dead.

Again he picked up on her discomfort. "Hey, don't worry. I know you reporters need to keep your scoops close to the vest. I was just making conversation."

"I'm not really a reporter," she said.

"You're a journalist—right. I've got a story for you. You hear much about migrants back in Newford?"

"You mean the illegals?"

"Yeah, nobody likes that term."

Leah nodded. "I'll keep that in mind. But to answer your question, I did a piece on Malo Malo last year when they came through town in support of Los Lobos. They were telling me how they get stopped and asked for papers all the time, even though they were all born and grew up here."

"That's become a pretty common story," he said. "But I was thinking more of the undocumented migrants. The ones who get across the border and try to make a new life for themselves stateside. The problem is, a lot of them don't understand just how brutal the desert can be. The only time they get on the news is when there's a bust, or they're found dead in the desert. Even then, it gets buried in the back of the paper and rarely makes the six o'clock."

He paused for a moment, then added, "And let me tell you, a whole lot of them die out there—from dehydration in the summer, or freezing in the winter. Not just men. Women and children, too."

"I didn't know that."

He put his hands behind his head and looked up at the stars. "Yeah, it's not really First World news, is it? They're trying to escape poverty and living under the threat of the cartels, coming here to work the shit jobs we don't want, but if you listen to some people, you'd think they were Satan's spawn, good for nothing except to be drug runners and whores. Except when you meet them and talk to them, you realize they're just desperate people looking for better lives for themselves and their families. And isn't that what America's all about? Everybody here's an immigrant—except for the Indians, and hell, they came from someplace else themselves, just a longer time ago."

His voice was quiet, matter-of-fact, but passion burned in his eyes.

He refocused his gaze on Leah. "Sorry," he said. "I just get going sometimes. I know whatever story brought you here must be important to you, but what's happening to these people is a story that needs telling too, especially by white voices since nobody's going to listen when it's told by someone with brown skin."

"No, that's okay," Leah told him. "It's..." Interesting, she was going to say, but that was almost patronizing. She settled on, "It's tragic. I've never really understood xenophobia."

He gave her a blank look.

"Fear of foreigners," she said. "Racism. I honestly don't understand it."

"You and me both." He stood up, pushing his chair back from the table. "I should hit the sack. It was nice talking with you, Leah. Sorry for bending your ear like that. I hope your story works out for you."

She smiled. "Me too."

As she watched him walk down to his room, she opened her notebook again and thought about the things he'd been telling her. Pen in hand, she began to write, asking the questions on paper, where perhaps they'd make a little more sense instead of having them bang around inside her head.

What made a rock star faking his own death—if that was the real story here—more important than these people Ernie said were dying in the desert? It wasn't, of course, but she knew which story would soar into the blogosphere, and which wouldn't.

And yes, if that big story was going to happen, she wanted a piece of it. But that wasn't the only reason she was pursuing it. It wasn't even to ask why the Rats' music hadn't been enough to keep Aimee alive. Not anymore. Now she was just as invested as any Diesel Rats fan. More so, perhaps.

She certainly knew more about them than most people. She'd researched and written so much about them—interviewed countless friends, acquaintances and many of the people who'd worked with the band. She listened to their music with more of a discerning ear because, beyond the records and bootlegs, she'd been privy to early demos, studio outtakes and otherwise unavailable concert recordings that—impossible as it might seem—still hadn't made it onto the Internet's pirate sites.

She probably knew the Rats better than she knew her own friends. And that was why she couldn't dismiss the idea of Jackson Cole finding a way to make the world believe he was dead so that he could start over. He'd been through so much toward the end. She thought he would have been stronger, but no matter how much research you did —how many stories you read, how much music you listened to—you could never actually get inside another person's head.

She closed the notebook, got up and stretched. The sky seemed a little lighter to the east, but she didn't have the energy to walk around the motel again to wait up and watch the sunrise.

She had a long day ahead of her and for once she'd do the sensible thing and try to get a couple of hours' rest before they drove out to the rez.

22

STEVE

My stomach does a little flip as we step away from Sammy's office. I'd like to say I'm getting used to this mode of travel, but so far, every time it happens I feel a little more freaked out. It hits me like a hammer in my gut that tells me nothing is necessarily as it appears and leaves me grasping for something—anything—to ground myself. But it's impossible to do when, in a heartbeat, I've stepped from an interior office to the top of a high red rock ridge with the mountains washing away in all directions like a vast ocean of stone.

I let go of Calico's hand and grab hold of the nearest boulder, waiting for the feeling to go away.

Calico chuckles. "You'll get used to it," she says.

"Says you."

"Because it's true. You've been doing this for years—you just didn't know it. Now it's just time for your brain to catch up with what the rest of you already knows."

"The rest of me is what's got me feeling unsteady on my feet," I tell her.

"No, that's just your brain sending out orders about the way it *thinks* you should be reacting. Stop thinking about it so much and you'll feel a lot better."

"Fine."

It's not even close to fine, but I learned a long time ago there's no point in arguing with her. I decide to change the subject and point at the bighorn head she's still carrying by one horn like it weighs nothing.

"So this has never happened before?" I ask.

"What? Cousins getting killed by hunters?"

I nod.

"Sure it has. And I know what you're going to ask. What happens to the hunter all depends on the kin of the victim. But most times, if we're in animal form when it happens, no one has a problem. You know, so long as the hunter approaches his kill with respect, uses all he can, and gives thanks for the bounty. We all have our part to play on the wheel of life."

"You'd be okay with somebody eating you?"

She shrugs. "If I'm stupid enough to get caught, sure. Everybody's got to eat."

"I'm not sure I'm comfortable with that idea."

"Nobody goes looking for it. But life isn't ours to keep. We only get to hold it for a little bit and then we've got to pass it on. It's like that for everybody. Even the *ma'inawo*. Even the thunders. And when you go, wouldn't you rather nourish somebody with the meat you can't take with you?"

"Well, when you put it like that," I say, then stick my finger in my throat.

She ignores my sarcasm. Instead she studies me for a moment. "Are you okay enough to move on?"

I push away from the boulder that's been grounding me and roll my shoulders. "Sure," I say. "Where to?"

"The aunts and uncles say a bunch of the tribe are sitting around a fire near the community center, telling stories, holding a vigil of sorts. I thought we'd bring Derek to them."

"The aunts and uncles?"

She points to the saguaro cacti forest on the slopes below where we're standing. I remember Morago calling them that one night around a campfire, telling me how the saguaro hold the spirits of the Kikimi who have lived a good life. He waited expectantly until I asked the question he was waiting for: What happens to those who live a bad life? They come back as people, he told me.

"I thought that was just a story," I say to Calico.

She smiles. "Everything's a story and more of them are true than maybe you think. They're all part of the wheel of the world."

She holds out her hand. "Shall we go?"

Doesn't matter how we travel, I tell myself. I can still be grounded.

Yeah, because that's worked so well for me so far.

But I take her hand anyway and off we go again.

23

THOMAS

Morago and Reuben were the only ones who didn't seem surprised when Calico stepped in out of nowhere carrying the head of a bighorn sheep in one hand, the other pulling Steve in her wake. Steve seemed a little unsteady on his feet, but he regained his balance quickly.

Around them, everybody fell silent. No one moved except to stare in their direction. Thomas glanced at Jerry, where he was holding up the wall of the community center. The deputy straightened up, hand going to his holster, but he just stood there staring like everybody else.

While their appearance surprised Thomas as much as anyone else, he recovered more quickly. All things considered, this had already been such a weird-ass day, what was one more improbable event to add to the list? He remembered Auntie telling him if you walked once with the *ma'inawo*, you had a foot in their world forever after.

The shaman stood up from his chair. "*Ohla*," he said.

"*Ohla*, Morago," Calico replied, but her attention was on William Strong Bow.

Dropping Steve's hand and taking the head of Derek Two Trees by both horns, she walked through the silent crowd to where William sat by the fire. She went down on one knee and held it out, offering it to him. The head appeared weightless in her hands, but when William took it, he grunted and the muscles stood out in his arms to keep the head aloft. That made Thomas realize that while the bighorn blood was strong in William, he wasn't a *ma'inawo*.

"*Ohla*, cousin," Calico said. Then she added in a formal voice, "I am so sorry for your loss. We have made what recompense we could, but any further retribution you would consider due, we have left to be bound by the wisdom of you and your kin."

William cleared his throat, then spoke in a shaky voice. "You have, um..." he said before he stopped and swallowed. "This is a great service you have done for my clan," he said. Tears streamed down his face.

Calico touched his knee. "You would do no less."

William managed a nod. Someone brought a blanket and William laid the bighorn upon it.

Calico rose and walked back over to Steve.

"We all give you thanks," Morago said to them both. He paused a beat, then added, "Should we be expecting a visit from Sammy and his boys?"

"Probably," Steve told him. "But Calico made sure he gained certain...insights, so he might just be coming for some advice."

Reuben stepped up to stand beside the shaman. "Advice on what?" he asked.

"How to tell the difference between animals and cousins," said Steve.

Reuben scoffed. "Are we're talking about the same Sammy Swift Grass we all know and would like to stake out on an ant hill?"

Steve nodded. "Or he could come riding in with guns blazing. It all depends on how seriously he took Calico's warning."

"What did she say to him?" Reuben asked.

"I'd be interested in hearing that too," Jerry said.

Thomas remembered a story about how the *ma'inawo* never broke their word. Jerry probably remembered that story as well, but even if Calico were to carry out her threats on Sammy, what did Jerry think the tribal police could do? It wasn't like you could lock up somebody who'd just step away into another world whenever they wanted.

"Relax," Steve told Jerry. "It's not like she threatened to disembowel him or anything." He shot Calico a glance and she grinned back.

Thomas wondered if he was the only one to notice how—just for a moment—her teeth all seemed sharp and pointed.

"And I seriously doubt," Steve went on, "that Sammy's got anything planned for tonight. He's going to be too busy dealing with a dissatisfied client to be thinking of coming down here."

The answer seemed to appease Jerry. If anyone else was unconvinced, they didn't bring it up.

Morago went and put a hand on William's shoulder. "Instead of worrying about Sammy," the shaman said, "we should take Derek up to Ancestors Canyon so he can start his next journey on the wheel." He looked around the rest of the group. "I'd like to have everything ready for a sunrise ceremony," he said.

The next few minutes were busy as the fire was covered with dirt and the men got their vehicles ready. Most of them drove off to collect other tribal members, leaving only a few behind. Reuben and a couple of his dog boys. William, Steve and Calico. Morago and the deputy. And Thomas.

"Ride with me," Reuben told the shaman, opening his passenger door.

Morago shook his head. "I'll ride in the back with William."

William bent over to lift Derek's head, but Calico stepped up, hoisted it easily and got into the back of the pickup. Morago and William joined her, and the dog boys sat beside Reuben on the bench seat in the front of the cab.

"I know what you're thinking," Morago told Steve, "but come as far as the mouth of the canyon with us."

Steve hesitated, then gave a nod. He joined the others, and then there was only Jerry, who wasn't coming, and Thomas, who figured he'd be walking home now, seeing how he'd been the one to drive here in Reuben's truck.

"You too," Morago said, offering his hand to Thomas.

Thomas let the shaman pull him into the bed of the pickup.

"Everybody set?" Reuben called from the cab.

Morago gave the roof of the cab a slap with his hand and then they were off. Grabbing the side panel, Thomas lowered himself down to sit on a wheel well. He retained his hold on the panel for balance as the truck bounced over a series of washboard bumps. Calico sat with William, the two of them with their knees up, backs to the cab, Derek's head on the blanket between them. Calico had a grip on one horn to keep the head from sliding. Across from where Thomas was sitting, Steve steadied himself on the other wheel well, while Morago sat on his haunches in front of him. The pickup lurched and bumped on the uneven road, but the unsteady ride didn't seem to affect the shaman's balance.

"I don't know why you wanted me to come," Steve said to Morago. "You're not going to talk me into taking part in any kind of ceremony."

Thomas leaned a little closer to hear over the sound of the motor and the wheels on the rough road.

"Because you don't walk the Red Road," Morago said.

Steve nodded. "Either you're born into a tribe or you're not—it's that simple. I may not know what the hell I am, but I know it's not a wannabe Kikimi."

"No one in the Painted Lands would ever think that of you."

"Still not going."

Morago nodded. "I know."

"Then why am I here?"

"We need to talk. Someone's come looking for that girl you found."

Thomas nodded to himself. It was just as he'd thought. Morago did know something about the kidnapped girl.

"Are you sure it's Sadie they're after?" Steve asked.

"How many other teenage white girls do we have running around the rez?"

Steve nodded. "Point taken. Who came looking?"

"Deputy Hernandez from the sheriff's department, with her father in tow."

Morago gave Steve a quick rundown on what had transpired in the parking lot. When Thomas glanced at Calico and William, they didn't appear to be listening.

"This kidnapping story is such bullshit," Steve said when Morago was done. "Her old man's the one that drove out here and threw her away."

"I know," Morago said. "And the deputy knows there's something not right about the father's story, but she's a minor, so he still has to investigate."

"Of course he does."

Steve looked back down the road. The moon had almost set. They were in the canyons now and there wasn't really anything to see except for vague outlines of rocks, cacti and scrub.

"You'll have to take the girl back to town," Morago finally said.

"And do what with her?"

Morago shrugged. "I don't know, but she can't come to the school. Take her to the bus station and give her some money."

"I'm not going to let her be thrown away a second time."

"We don't know that she was really thrown away," Morago said. "What if she's in on it?"

"In on what? Look, her father dumped her in the middle of nowhere. I saw it happen. He had no idea that I or anyone else would find her. And how would she get in touch with him if they were running a con? She doesn't even have a phone."

"When I stopped by Aggie's yesterday," Morago said, "the girl was on the computer. She could have been communicating with her father right then. Or she could have used Aggie's landline."

Steve shook his head. "I just don't see it—not unless Sadie's an Academy Award class actor."

"Well, you've got to do something. She's safe at Aggie's for now, but that's not going to last. Deputy Hernandez said her father knows how to work the system. He was already yelling at the deputy about involving the Indian Bureau, demanding they get FBI choppers up in the air above the rez."

Reuben's pickup slowed down. Thomas looked past the cab to see they'd reached the entrance to Ancestors Canyon. The pickup pulled over to the side of the road and Reuben killed the engine.

"I could bring Sadie to my place," Steve said. "Nobody'll find her there."

"Are you sure you want to take that chance?" Morago asked. "The two of you alone out there—what if she calls foul?"

"Calico will be with me."

The doors of the pickup opened and Reuben and the dog boys got out of the cab.

Instead of jumping to the ground right away, Thomas cleared his throat. "Is this all true?" he asked Morago and Steve. Thomas knew crappy things happened to people, even here on the rez. And he knew kids weren't immune to being victims. But it seemed especially wrong to him when people treated their own kids like that. Parents were supposed to protect their children. The whole extended family was supposed to be a buffer against the bad things that could happen.

The two men exchanged glances.

"Is what true?" Morago asked.

"What you're saying about this girl—that her father just threw her away."

"Yeah," Steve said. "One hundred percent. I was camping on a headland out near my place when I saw the car stop and the girl was pushed out. Then the car just drove away."

"So what her father was saying back at the community center was total bullshit."

Steve nodded. "From what I've heard, it's been a lot worse for Sadie than just getting dumped along the highway."

"If any of that's true," Morago murmured.

Steve shot him a look and the shaman shrugged, holding up his hands in defeat.

But Thomas didn't hear him. Instead he was picturing Santana and Naya in his head. He was remembering what had happened to Rebecca Spotted Pony's little girl, Giselle. Rebecca had met a new guy at the Indian Market in town and brought him home. A couple of days later she went out to party and left Giselle with the stranger. It wasn't the first such tragedy on the rez. It was just the latest.

"I hear about something like that," Thomas said, "and then I think about it happening to my sisters—it makes me feel a little crazy."

"I hear you," Steve said.

"So if you need help with anything, just let me know."

Steve studied him for a moment, then nodded and stood up. He offered Thomas a hand and pulled him to his feet.

"I hope it doesn't get to that," Steve said, "but I appreciate it."

"Appreciate what?"

They saw Reuben standing at the back of the truck, looking up at them.

"That when the time comes," Morago said, "Thomas is ready to stand up and do the right thing."

The shaman jumped lightly to the ground, followed by the others.

Reuben gave Thomas a light punch in the upper arm. "Hell, I could have told you that," he said.

Thomas ducked his head in embarrassment. He wanted to say, then why can I not wait to get away from the rez?

It was just like an elder to try to make it all about the tribe when the reality was, he just didn't like bullies. And he'd only come to the community center earlier because Auntie had asked him to. But nobody wanted to hear that—not while they were all pumped up on tribal pride—so instead of explaining, he shrugged and walked around the pickup to look out toward the canyon.

The last time Thomas had been here was when they laid his Aunt Lucy—Auntie's sister—to rest. A lot of the rez members were Catholics and they were buried in San Miguel Cemetery on the outskirts of Santo del Vado Viejo, but Ancestors Canyon was where the traditionalists were brought.

Thomas remembered there'd been spirits everywhere that day—not just vague representations of the animal clans he could sometimes see hovering on people's shoulders, but crowds of the kind he usually only spied in ones and twos from the corners of his eyes. Some of them were strange creatures, part human, part animal. Others were like ambulatory cacti with occasional human faces and limbs. Most of them remained incorporeal, but a few had taken human form to mingle with the mourners, comforting them with a touch on a shoulder or an arm.

Though he knew they meant him no harm, it had been a disconcerting experience at the time, and one he wasn't eager to repeat.

Looking up the canyon now, he could see the spirits beginning to gather in the growing light cast by the dawn pinking the peaks of the mountains beyond the canyon. He watched in fascination as many of them came down the almost sheer cliffs here at the mouth of the canyon, as sure-footed as desert bighorn.

Like Steve's friend Calico could, a good number of them manifested in curious hybrid forms. The mix of animal and human was mostly subtle. He saw a woman with long hare ears hanging like braids along either side of her face, standing with another two who had small antlers lifting from their brows. A man with a subtle sheen of scales on his skin seemed to simply glide down the red rock walls of the canyon, moving effortlessly like a lizard or snake. But others were unmistakably alien, such as the coyote head on another man's shoulders, pointed ears pushing up through the flat brim of his hat, or the tall woman with the head and torso that seemed proportionately far too small compared to her four long limbs. Or maybe that was just the poor light.

Thomas was mesmerized by her until the woman turned in his direction. As soon as their gazes met, he quickly looked away, hoping the shiver that had travelled up his spine hadn't shown on his face.

He let his attention wander after that, never lingering for long on one figure. The spirits murmured quietly to one another until suddenly they all fell still and turned as one to look farther down the canyon.

"Uh-oh," he heard Calico say from behind him.

Following their gaze, he saw what she and the other spirits had already sensed approaching.

The black dog with a broad head and broader shoulders came first, standing as tall at the shoulder as a small pony. But it was the woman walking behind the dog that grabbed and held his attention.

Like the dog, she was tall and her hair jet black, but there the resemblance ended. She was reed thin, almost insubstantial, with a nimbus of darkness following in her wake like a long enveloping cloak of black mist. Her features were slender and bird-like, her eyes set wide on either side of a nose as sharp as a beak. Hovering on her shoulders was the vague impression of a giant raven's skull.

She moved soundlessly on bare feet except for a strange clicking sound that arose with every step. It wasn't until she came closer that Thomas realized it came from the hundreds of small bones woven into her braids and hanging by threads from a dress that hung in rags and tatters from her shoulders to just above her ankles.

The cousins all moved out of her way as she passed by—not from fear, he saw, but from respect. Still, while they might not be afraid, something about her made Thomas shiver down to the very marrow of his bones and woke goose bumps on his arms.

"Who—" Thomas had to clear his throat. He turned to Calico, who now stood at his side. "Who is she?"

"It has to be Night Woman," Calico said in a voice as quiet as his own.

Thomas might have said, I thought she was only a story to frighten children, but after today, he knew better. In a night crowded with spirits and cousins, why shouldn't the spirit of death be abroad as well?

"What's she doing here?" Thomas asked.

Like everybody else, he couldn't take his gaze from the approaching woman and her giant dog.

"What do you think?" Calico replied. "She's come for Derek. And maybe for whoever killed him."

She never came for Auntie, Thomas thought. Seeing her now, he was just as glad. But still it made him wonder why that was. Before he could ask Calico what the difference was, the tall woman's gaze found his, caught and held him so that he couldn't move, couldn't speak, could hardly breathe. The night lay in her eyes, dark and unfathomable, and there was something older still that intensified the shiver in his bones. His testicles rose up toward his body and his throat went as dry as the desert around them.

And the longer she held his gaze, the more sure he was that they had met before. When or where, he had no idea. He wasn't even sure she'd looked the same. But he knew those dark eyes.

24

SADIE

S adie was gasping for air by the time she got back to her bedroom. She shut the door, dropped the blanket and leapt onto the bed, balling up in a tight fetal position to try to keep from shivering. It didn't help. The tremors ran up and down her limbs and her teeth chattered until she stuck the edge of her left hand in her mouth. Biting down on it brought her a small measure of control.

It took a few minutes before she could finally sit up. She leaned over and picked up the fallen blanket, then wrapped it around her shoulders and stared at the door, expecting the worst. Her fingers were still closed on the handle of her utility knife. She wasn't sure if she still wanted to cut herself or use it as protection against the monsters she'd seen outside.

She tried to convince herself they were just people in disguise, weirdos like Steve and his girlfriend with her fox ears and antlers, which couldn't be real either. They were probably some cult of freaks who had to dress up like animals to get it on.

Except…except…

When that bird-headed man had turned from the fire to look at her, his eyes, feathers and movement had all been too bird-like to be a mask. They could get away with fooling you in a movie, but CGI didn't work in real life.

Were the freaks going to come after her now that she'd seen them?

Her grip tightened on the knife.

There was no chair in the room or she would have jammed it under the doorknob—though did that actually work, or was it one more bullshit thing from the movies? And what about the window behind its curtains? What was to stop them from smashing it in?

She forced herself to get off the bed and tiptoe over to it. Hand trembling, she moved the curtains aside barely enough to peer outside. There was nothing to see, only the dark bulk of the mountains.

Her heart leapt into overdrive as an ominous clicking sound entered the hall outside her room.

Sadie'd always thought she was a little tougher than other kids. I mean, she'd dealt with Reggie's crap for all these years, hadn't she? Listening to some of the worst stories the foster kids told, she knew she'd never let anyone pull that shit on her, didn't matter who they were or where they sent her. Maybe cutting and dope wasn't the best way to deal, but it worked for her. She always found something that worked. There was always an angle, a way you could play people.

But monsters were different. The ones out there were real, and they weren't people. Her fear shattered her ability to think rationally.

The weird sound came closer and she imagined huge bird feet clawing at her door, a massive beak pecking out her eyes. Sadie stood ramrod stiff, staring at the wood panels. She thumbed the blade of her knife out from its handle, but when the door popped open the knife fell from her hand and she let out a scream.

And felt like a fool.

It was only Ruby—her nails clicking on the floor outside before she'd pushed the door open with her snout. Now the dog sat and looked at Sadie, head cocked as if to ask, what is *your* problem?

Sadie slid down until she was sitting on her heels. She picked up her knife, palming it from sight when Aggie appeared in the doorway. Her gaze went from Sadie on the floor with a blanket wrapped around her, to Ruby sitting in front of her.

"Is everything all right?" the old woman asked.

Sadie waved the hand that wasn't hiding the knife. "Yeah, yeah. No need to panic. I just had a bad dream."

Aggie's eyes narrowed.

"Seriously," Sadie said. "That's all it was. Freaked me out but then I woke up and it's all better now."

But she could see as the words left her mouth that it wasn't going to fly. The old woman knew there was more to it than some nightmare.

"What did you see?" Aggie asked.

"It was just a dream. Who remembers anything from a dream?"

Aggie sighed. "It's important."

"Why?"

"Because dreams can be messages and this house is a potent place for dreamers. You wouldn't be the first the spirits have contacted within these walls."

"Yeah, except I'm not an Indian."

Aggie's steady gaze remained fixed on her. "The soul has no colour."

"I wouldn't know," Sadie said. "I'm not sure I even believe in souls and that kind of stuff."

Ruby made a throaty sound, somewhere between a grunt and an almost inaudible woof.

Aggie nodded. "I agree," she said to the dog. "I don't believe her either."

Really? Sadie thought. Pretending that the dog could actually understand their conversation. Creepy much? But then she remembered the animal people around the campfire outside. She studied the dog, but all Ruby did was fix her with a mild gaze.

"Can she talk?" Sadie asked, looking up to Aggie.

"Everything can talk," the old woman replied. "The trick is, not everybody knows how to listen. Now, what did you see in your dream?"

"I..."

Never had a dream, she almost said. But that wasn't what Aggie wanted to hear. So Sadie told her about dreaming she woke up and went outside, seeing the people around the fire. How when they turned to look at her, they were all like the things in Aggie's paintings —not really people, but not completely animals, either.

"I freaked out and ran back to the house," she finished, "and that's when I woke up. Then I heard Ruby at the door and I thought my dream was coming true. That these monsters were really coming to get me and I hadn't been dreaming. When Ruby pushed the door open I pretty much lost it."

Under the blanket still wrapped around her, she clenched and tightened her fingers around the knife. She imagined drawing the sharp blade against her skin and how all the crap building up inside her would flow out like air from a balloon. Maybe one day so much would come out that the only thing left of her would be a heap of skin on the floor.

"Hmm," Aggie said. She studied Sadie for another long moment, then nodded and turned away from the door.

"Hmm?" Sadie repeated. "That's all you've got to say? What about dreams having meaning? What message are those monsters supposed to be?"

Aggie looked at her over her shoulder. "They aren't monsters," she said, "and you weren't dreaming." Then she stepped away down the hall.

Sadie scrambled to her feet and brushed past the dog.

"If they're not monsters," she shouted at Aggie's back, "then what would you call them?"

"Friends," Aggie replied without turning.

She paused at the doorway of her own bedroom to face Sadie.

"Don't make me regret having invited you into my home," she said.

Then she shut the door quietly, but with a finality that left no doubt that this conversation was done.

"Well, fuck," Sadie said.

She went back to her own room. Ruby lay on the floor, her gaze following Sadie as she walked from the door to the bed.

"What are you looking at?" Sadie asked.

She heard Aggie's words in her head—*everything can talk*—but the dog hadn't gotten the memo and didn't answer.

"Here," Sadie said. "Take a picture of this."

She pushed open the blade of the utility knife and drew it quickly across the flesh of her forearm. Not too deep. Just enough to let the new pain swallow some of the old.

She sucked in a breath of air through her teeth and slid down the side of the bed until she was sitting on the floor beside the dog, her arm propped up on her knees. She watched the blood well up, and for the first time today, she felt relaxed. In control.

The dog whined, but didn't look away.

25

STEVE

I don't know exactly what's going on here, but I can't be the only person that's completely weirded out by the woman and her dog. The dog's huge, sure, and maybe that's not so strange in and of itself, but the woman has a goddamned bird skull on her skinny-ass shoulders. I don't mean she's wearing it like a hat or some gruesome headdress—it seems to really *be* her head.

Impossible, yeah, I know, because where are you going to find yourself a raven almost as big as that giant dog?

The rest of the crowd in the canyon looks like they escaped from some carnie freak show, but the skull-headed woman is the one that's really giving me the creeps. It's the long distinctive beak where there should be a face, and the darkness inside her eye sockets. I can't see anything in there, but I still know there's something looking out at me. And if that's not enough, sometimes it seems as though she has the ghost of a raven sitting on her shoulder. When it's there, a second serious gaze is fixed on me. Then it changes its focus and regards Thomas with equal, if not more intensity.

Calico's in front of me, standing beside Thomas. She's still holding Derek's head by one of its horns. I overhear what she tells Thomas— that this is Night Woman. I've heard the stories. According to them,

Night Woman's the spirit of death. I've seen more than my fair share of crap today, but this makes no logical sense. Death doesn't go walking around except in spooky stories to scare kids. Death is a state, not a person.

The problem is, my gut tells me different. I haven't been this spooked in a long time, not since I fell off that cliff all those years ago and broke my leg. Those few airborne moments were pure terror, from when my foot slipped on some loose stones, to my plummet to the ground below.

I guess I was lucky it was Possum who found me, not this woman. He said the mesquite I hit on the way down saved my life because it broke my fall. I didn't know that at the time. I just remember lying there for what seemed like forever, a green stupid kid who thought he could tame the mountains and had just run smack into a big voice of dissent.

I was filled with dread, lying there all on my own, miles from anywhere, but it was nothing like the terror of the fall. I've never wanted to feel that again, but looking at this skull-headed woman, that same sense of foreboding fills the pit of my stomach.

I start when a hand clasps my shoulder, but it's only Reuben.

"What the hell is going on here?" I ask him.

He shrugs. "Damned if I know."

I look at Morago. As the shaman, he might be able to answer that question. He's been standing close enough to hear us, but now he just pushes by to join Calico and Thomas. William stays behind us by the truck, as though he's riveted to the ground. Either his fear or his sorrow is paralyzing him. Probably a bit of both.

I can hear vehicles in the distance, but they seem to belong to another world. My throat's dry. The air tastes of dust.

The big dog moves aside when it reaches Calico and Thomas, making room for his mistress. The air seems to shift around her shoulders and the raven skull transforms into a woman with long black hair and eyes like midnight. A vague memory of the skull hangs like an aura around her shoulders. The ghost bird that was on her shoulder isn't there anymore either, but I still feel the weight of its gaze watching from somewhere.

I don't like the way the woman is looking at Thomas. Then she turns her attention to Calico, and I like it even less.

"Is she really Night Woman?" I ask Reuben.

Reuben grimaces. "Oh yeah. Unless there's another raven woman running around looking that spooky."

I don't even know how to begin to get my head around that.

"So what's she doing here?" I ask. "Does she show up to give every cousin a big send-off?"

"I don't know that it's got a lot to do with our brother, except it makes a good excuse for her to be here."

"But—"

"*Ma'inawo* like her don't show up unless something big's going down—not that they'd ever let us in on it. But they've always got an agenda."

"What's hers?"

He shrugs. "No clue. But it's sure to screw up our lives.

"Hang on," he adds as the woman starts to speak.

"You have done well, little cousin," the raven woman tells Calico. "Our brother would have had a long journey to find his way home, had you not intervened. His ancestors would not have been present to welcome him. His kin would not have been able to celebrate his time on the wheel and send him home."

Okay, that doesn't sound so bad, I think, as Calico makes some innocuous response.

But then the woman seems to stand a little taller and says, "And you have dealt appropriately with the five-fingered being that killed him."

She says it pointedly, like a statement, not a question.

"No, señora," Calico says. I've never seen her so hesitant. "It was not my place to speak for the Bighorn Clan."

The woman lifts her gaze, looking around until she settles on William, who's still by Reuben's truck. Other vehicles are pulling in behind it now, the sound of their engines muttering in the early morning light, but the woman has no trouble making herself heard above them.

"And how has the Bighorn Clan dealt with the killer?" she asks him.

William gazes at his feet. "We...that is..."

The woman frowns as William's voice trails off. I'm not a hundred percent certain what's going on here, and I sure don't want to get involved, but I'm guessing that whatever hierarchy she represents, this is a cousin thing. From Calico's uncharacteristic politeness, to the way everybody is being cautiously respectful around the woman, this Night Woman is close to the top of the *ma'inawo* food chain.

But she's not *my* boss.

With that simple realization, the raw feeling in the pit of my stomach goes away and takes the unreasoning fear with it.

She's not my boss, and her superiority annoys me.

I'm an American. Her presence here is like the Queen of England showing up at my Airstream. I'd give her the respect you'd give anybody of her station, but it's not like the Queen of England's got any hold over me—not the way the skull-headed woman obviously has over the cousins here. So I can stand up to her where they can't.

"Not killing anybody in retaliation," I say. "That was my call."

Morago turns to look at me and shakes his head, plainly telling me to back off. But in for a dollar...

"I warned them what they could expect if it happened again," I add.

The woman cocks her head to look at me, the ghost bird back on her shoulder for a moment, mimicking the motion. Night Woman's eyes are as dark now as the eyeholes of her skull were when she first arrived.

"Did you now," she says.

Calico is shaking her head along with Morago, but I plunge on. "It was the right thing to do," I say. "The tensions between the traditionalists and the casino crowd are always running high. Something like this could have been a tipping point."

"Why should I care about that?"

"No reason you should. You don't have to live here like the rest of us do."

She doesn't respond right away. Instead, she studies me for a long moment. There's no sound except for the wind. It's as though everyone is holding their breath.

"And my dead cousin?" she asks finally, nodding at Derek's head. "Who speaks for him?"

"Well, no offence, ma'am, but you don't look like Bighorn Clan to me. His kin have already had their say."

She draws her head back in disbelief. "And left it to a five-fingered being to handle?"

I shrug. "Not entirely, but they wanted a message delivered, and then to have their brother brought here for proper burial."

The woman lays a hand on the head of her dog and it turns its enormous face to look at her.

"I think I like this human," she says. "What about you, Gordo?"

A loud rumble comes from the dog's massive chest. The woman gives me a thin smile that never quite reaches her eyes.

"Thank you for your help in this trying time," she says.

"Anything to help, ma'am."

Calico and Morago are shaking their heads again, but my words are already spoken.

The woman nods. "I will hold you to that," she says. I could swear the ghost raven on her shoulders flutters its wings and grins at me.

I see Morago roll his eyes. Calico gives a heavy sigh.

The woman turns to Morago before I can clarify what I meant.

More and more cars and pickups are pulling in along the side of the road. I see a lot of familiar faces, many of them in traditional garb.

"*Ohla*, Ramon Morago," the woman says.

"*Ohla*, señora," the shaman responds. "It's unfortunate that we meet under such sorrowful circumstances."

The woman shrugs. "There is no need for sorrow. Life and death are only different positions on the wheel."

"Of course," Morago says. "Which is why we are here to celebrate our friend's life. Will you join us?"

The woman steps aside and makes a motion with her arm to usher us into the canyon. Morago walks past the woman and her dog, followed by Calico. When the woman falls into step behind them,

Reuben, Thomas and the other recently arrived tribal members join them in groups of three and four.

I step back, out of the way.

I feel a tug on my sleeve. "I didn't expect to find you here."

I turn and smile at Aggie. "I'm not really here."

Her eyebrows go up.

"I mean, I'm not going into the canyon." I look past her. "Where's Sadie?"

"Still asleep, I imagine. She's a bit of a trial, that girl."

I nod. "Yeah, and it could get messy. Apparently her father showed up at the community center with a deputy from the sheriff's department, claiming that he'd seen her kidnapped by an Indian driving a white van."

"But—"

"Oh, it's complete crap. Morago says even Jerry Five Hawks didn't buy it. But there's still going to be an investigation. It's too serious an accusation for there not to be."

Aggie shakes her head. "Why would he abandon his daughter in the desert and then come to the rez with a story like that?"

"Beats me. But I'm going to go collect her before the police start knocking on doors. I don't want you messed up in this."

"And you'll do what with her?"

"Take her back to my place—at least for now. Unless the police can see into the otherworld, they'll never find her there."

Aggie puts a hand on my arm. "Don't do that. There's something off about this whole situation. Just wait until the ceremony is finished and we'll put our heads together with Morago and figure something out."

I hesitate. I hate the idea of Aggie getting in trouble because I decided to play Good Samaritan, but she's right. There is something off about all of this. We need to think it through and play it smart.

"Okay," I tell her. "I'll wait for the two of you at your fire pit."

Her eyes crinkle and she squeezes my arm. "What do you know? It turns out you can take advice."

I let her have her moment.

"I won't be more than a couple of hours," she says.

I nod. "Long enough to catch a snooze," I say.

"Hey, how'd you even find out about this ceremony?" I ask.

"I had a crow come knocking on my window a half hour ago."

Here's how far gone I am after the past couple of days: I don't even roll my eyes.

"You should get going," I tell her.

She starts to go, but turns around. "That girl," she says. "Sadie. She's pretty messed up and I don't know that she can be fixed."

"Still, we've to try, right?"

"I don't know that she *wants* to be fixed."

"That's harsh."

"Maybe. But what if it's true?"

She turns away again and this time I watch as she joins the last few stragglers making their way into the canyon.

The drums start up as I head off down the road, but I hardly hear them. I'm too caught up in thinking about what Aggie had to say—so much so that I don't realize a car has stopped beside me until Jerry Two Hawks calls to me through its open passenger window. It takes a moment for me to register the tribal police crest on the side of the door and whose voice I heard.

I lean in the window. "Hey, Jerry."

"*Ohla,*" he says.

"What brings you out here?"

"You."

That gives me pause.

"We were asking around on the casino side about the white van," he says. "You know, the one that the father says was used to grab the girl?"

"I heard about it."

"We've got another witness besides the father. Says you were driving the van, and it was Reuben who grabbed the girl."

"You know that's bullshit. I don't have a van, white or any other colour, and neither does Reuben. Check with the DMV."

"We already did, but it's not much of an argument. The van could have been stolen."

"Jesus, Jerry. You don't actually think that Reuben and I would—"

He cuts me off. "You think I'm an idiot? Of course I don't. But I still need to take statements from the two of you. It's talk to me or talk to the sheriff's department."

We both know it's not an either/or. Reuben and I will be talking to both whether I come with Jerry now or I don't. Probably the FBI and the Bureau of Indian Affairs as well. A white minor being kidnapped is big news, and they'll all want a piece of the pie. Everybody wants to be the hero and get the promotion.

Everybody except for me.

"Reuben's in the canyon," I say.

Jerry nods. "I'll talk to him after the ceremony. But maybe we could start with you?"

If I were Calico, I could just step away into the otherworld and good luck with catching me there. But I'm not and she's busy. And anyway, this'd all still be waiting for me when I got back.

I sigh and open the door, slide into the passenger seat.

"Who's this second witness?" I ask.

"Sammy Swift Grass," Jerry says as we pull away.

26

LEAH

Leah couldn't sleep, so an hour after she'd lain down she was back outside, sitting on a low stone wall behind the motel watching the sun rise. She found herself wishing she'd brought her phone out, but she didn't want to miss a moment by going back inside to get it. A camera never captured this sort of thing properly anyway, or at least not in her experience. So she stayed where she was, listening to the morning bird chorus as the sky slowly lightened in a blush over the Hierro Maderas Mountains. She could actually see the shadows of the mountains receding, the higher the sun rose.

When Marisa came around the side of the motel to join her, a half-dozen quail went bobbing into the underbrush, startled by the sound of her footsteps crunching in the dirt. A ground squirrel scolded her before it too scurried from sight. Marisa sat down on the wall beside her.

"You're up early," she said.

"I couldn't fall asleep," Leah told her without turning from the view. "I guess I got enough on the drive down."

Marisa nodded. She looked at the sunrise. Lifting her hand, she covered up a yawn.

"Pretty," she said.

Leah nodded. She could think of a hundred glorious descriptions for that sky, but "pretty" worked just fine. When the sun finally popped up above the mountains she felt like applauding.

"I need coffee," Marisa said.

"This guy told me there's a good diner just down the road."

"What guy?"

"I met him last night when I was sitting at the little table out in front of our room."

Marisa turned to look at her. "In the middle of the night, in the middle of nowhere, you meet a guy?"

"It's not like that. He was just coming back from work or whatever, and stopped to chat for a few minutes."

"Cute?"

Leah laughed. "More like grizzled. He looked like a real desert rat. But he was nice."

"Let me get this straight. Do you make a habit of chatting up strangers you meet in the middle of the night?"

"He had kind eyes."

Marisa shook her head. "I need coffee," she repeated.

JERRY'S ROADHOUSE was pretty much what Ernie had promised. It was a long building, part adobe and part wood frame, with a tiled roof and a dirt parking lot. Like the motel, it had seen better days. But the coffee was strong, with a bottomless cup, and the breakfast special was a generous helping of eggs any style, sausages, biscuits and gravy, with freshly squeezed orange juice and a couple of pancakes on the side.

The main difference from back home was that the waitress brought them each sides of salsa and green chilies. Her name tag read "Janis" and she seemed genuinely happy to see them, unlike the hipster servers and baristas back in Newford, who often seemed slightly put-upon when they actually had to take an order. Janis's face lit up when Leah told her that Ernie had recommended the place to them.

"So where did you meet Ernie?" she asked.

"We're staying at the Silver Spur," Leah told her, "and I was sitting outside our room last night when he came in from work or wherever."

Janis smiled. "Did he tell you he was working?"

"No, I just assumed it was work. He didn't look like a partying kind of guy."

"You can say that again. Ernie's one of the last of the old desert rats. He spends pretty much every night out in the mountains. I think he can see better than a coyote in the dark."

"So what does he do?" Marisa asked.

Janis shrugged and refilled their coffee mugs. "Who knows? Stares at the stars? Makes friends with the javelinas? I expect that mostly, he just wanders around."

"What about the migrants who get lost out there?" Leah asked. "He must run into some of them."

A wall suddenly went up behind Janis's eyes. "I wouldn't know anything about that," she said and started to move away from the table.

"It's just he was talking to me about them," Leah said. "I'm a writer —a journalist. He told me I should be telling their stories."

The waitress paused. "He said that?"

Leah nodded.

Janis looked around the restaurant before returning her attention to them. The warmth was back in her eyes. "That's something that doesn't get talked a lot about round here," she said. "It's like politics or religion. People have their own ideas about the issue and there's no shifting them. Get on the wrong side of that argument, you could find yourself finishing it from the inside of a jail cell."

Leah and Marisa exchanged surprised looks.

"For real?" Marisa said.

Somebody at the long counter called for a refill.

"Hold your horses, Fred," Janis called to the man. "Be right there." She turned back to their table. "Ask Ernie if you want to know more about it," she said in a quiet voice. "It's not my story to tell."

"Well, *that* wasn't weird," Marisa said as the waitress walked away.

Leah nodded. "Except we live in a whole different world, so we shouldn't judge."

Marisa studied her for a moment. "You've got a look in your eye."

"It's just...I've been thinking about it ever since I talked to Ernie last night. What am I doing chasing around after the ghost of Jackson Cole when there are real, important stories to tell? Maybe I should be writing something that has more meaning than trying to get inside the head of some spoiled rock star."

Marisa laughed.

"Okay," Leah said. "So I don't think Cole was ever exactly that, and if he is still alive and living around here, he's certainly not that now. But what are the chances he's actually alive? And if he is, would the world be a better place because I tracked him down and exposed his secret hideaway?"

"Probably not," Marisa said. "But really, I can't answer that and neither can you. It might mean a lot to his fans."

"But if he's alive, he walked away. Who are we to drag him back into the limelight?"

Marisa shrugged. "Don't get ahead of yourself. Let's see what this Abigail White Horse has to tell us. It might not be a decision we ever need to make."

Leah looked at the old Coke clock behind the lunch counter.

"It's pretty early to drop in on her," she said.

"Probably. But we can do a drive by, make sure we can actually find the place. If it looks like nobody's up, we'll just kick our heels for a while."

"I suppose it's a plan," Leah said.

She finished her coffee and they took their check to the cash.

"So what are you girls up to today?" Janis asked as she rang them in.

"We're driving up to the rez," Leah told her. "We're hoping to interview an artist named Abigail White Horse."

Janis nodded. "She's a nice lady. Her paintings give me the creeps, but her, I like."

"You know her?"

"Not really. But Ernie takes me to the powwow every summer and I've met her there. Too bad you girls didn't come a few months earlier. The Kikimi know how to throw a party. Even Ernie cuts loose a little."

"We'll try to make it back sometime," Marisa said. She paid the bill over Leah's protest and asked for a receipt. "It's a business expense," she told Leah.

"You have fun today," Janis said as she made change and printed out a receipt. "And make sure you bring water."

"We're only going to the rez. It doesn't look that far on the map."

"It's not. But like Ernie says, the first rule of going into the desert —doesn't matter for how long—is to bring plenty of water."

"We will," Leah said.

AFTER LEAVING JERRY'S ROADHOUSE, they backtracked a few blocks into town until they found a gas station where they could top up the gas tank and buy some bottled water. Leah entered Abigail White Horse's address into the GPS on her phone while she waited for Marisa to come back to the car with the water.

"Ready to navigate?" Marisa asked as she slipped into the driver's seat.

Leah nodded. "Left out of here, then take your first right on Jacinto. It'll eventually take us all the way to the rez."

"Sweet."

"Looks like it might get a bit tricky after that."

Marisa smiled. "Which is why I have you."

Once they got out of town, Leah drank in the austere landscape, appreciating every subtlety of faded colour. She loved how the shape of the land wasn't hidden by swaths of trees the way it was in the hills back home. Instead, she could see every nuance as the spartan panorama spread away from the highway, rolling into the distance like the dry waves of a dusty sea.

When she said as much, Marisa shot her a quick glance before returning her attention to the highway. "You're not serious, are you?" she said.

"What do *you* mean?" Leah asked.

"They call these 'badlands' for a reason. There's nothing but sand and cacti. I don't know how anybody can live out here."

"I think it's beautiful."

Marisa laughed. "And you also think there hasn't been any good music since the Diesel Rats packed it in."

"That's not true."

Marisa laughed again. "Kidding."

They passed a sign announcing that they were entering the Kikimi Painted Lands, quickly followed by a place called the Little Tree Trading Post. The dirt parking lot was empty, but it was still early in the morning, so it was probably closed. Leah hoped they'd get a chance to stop in on the way back. She checked her phone.

"We make a left in another mile or so," she said.

They missed the turn, but since they were the only car on the road, Marisa just backed up. The GPS led them through reddish hills dotted with mesquite, cacti and dried brush until they topped a rise to see a rutted lane that led down to a pair of adobe buildings, one obviously the main house, with a smaller structure up on the side of the hill behind it.

"That's it," Leah said. She peered through the windshield. "Although how are we supposed to figure out if anybody's up?"

Marisa pointed to a figure sitting on the porch at the front of the main house. "Somebody's up," she said.

She steered the rental down the lane, stopping where it opened into a yard between the two buildings. A half-dozen dogs came running and barking to meet them and Leah shrank back in the car seat. They looked like a mix of German Shepherd, coyote and pit bull, their fur the same dusty colours of the landscape—muted reds, yellows and tans—and all she could think of was the time a neighbour's two dogs had chased Aimee and her across a park when they were kids. She'd been nervous around dogs ever since.

The figure on the porch proved to be an old Native woman. She watched their approach, but made no move to rise and meet them.

Leah caught Marisa's arm as she started to open her door. "You're not going out there, are you?"

"Kind of hard to have a conversation with that woman if we stay in the car."

"But the dogs—"

"I'm not scared of dogs," Marisa told her as she opened her door.

The pack crowded around her as she got out, but she ignored them until she'd closed the door and was able to step away from the car. Then she stood still with her hands open on either side of her thighs to let the dogs take in her scent.

Leah looked up to where the woman had been sitting to find that she'd stood up and was coming to meet them. Swallowing her fear, Leah got out and braced herself as the dogs left off pushing their muzzles against Marisa's legs to take a turn at crowding around her instead.

"*Ohla,*" the woman said. "Are you lost?"

"I'm Marisa and this is Leah," Marisa replied, "and I guess that depends on whether you're Abigail White Horse."

"I am, though most people just call me Aggie." She glanced at Leah and added, "Just push them away if they're bothering you."

To Leah's surprise, the dogs were far more gentle than she'd expected. One in particular, a female with a red coat, looked up at her with big brown eyes, her tongue lolling from the corner of her mouth with what seemed to be pure goofy amusement.

"No, I'm fine," Leah said. She reached down to give the red dog a tentative pat and the animal leaned into her, pressing against her leg.

"I don't get many visitors," Aggie said, by which Leah assumed she meant she didn't often have a pair of white girls drive up to her house. "How can I help you?"

"We were interested in your art," Marisa said.

Aggie smiled. "You're welcome to have a look—especially considering that you drove all the way out here—but you should know in advance that none of it's for sale."

"We know that," Marisa said.

"I hope we haven't come by too early," Leah added.

"I'm usually up early, if not this early," Aggie told them. "But today I just got back from a memorial service for a friend of mine. We had a dawn ceremony for him back in the canyons."

"Oh, we're so sorry for your loss," Marisa said.

Leah nodded. "We can stop by some other time."

"Don't worry about it," Aggie said. "That's not how it works around here. Our brother's dead but that doesn't mean he's gone. He's just got himself a new place on the wheel. It's not as if we won't see him again."

Leah and Marisa exchanged glances.

Aggie smiled. "That only sounds woo-woo if you don't already live a spiritual life. Round here, the borders between this world and the otherworld aren't as solid as you might be familiar with. Come on. I'll show you my studio."

Leah blinked at the sudden switch in subject. She and Marisa exchanged another look, then hurried after Aggie, who had already set off up the hill to the smaller building. The dogs trailed along on either side of them.

"I mostly do portraiture," Aggie said when they joined her on the porch of the studio. She ushered them inside. "Right now I'm working on one of my friend Hector, but I think I'll stop and see if I can capture a good memory of Derek while the ceremony's still fresh in my mind. I haven't done a painting of one of the Bighorn Clan for a while, and I can already feel the sweep of those horns as they take shape under my brush."

The dogs sprawled on the porch while Leah and Marisa stopped just inside the doorway to look around. The smell of turps was pungent, and skylights let the sun splash light into every corner. Standing on a large easel was Aggie's current work in progress—a striking profile of a hawk's head on the shoulders of a man. The bird had a band of leather around his head. Strips of leather festooned with shells, beads and feathers trailed from the band down his back.

Leah looked from it to the other paintings. They were all similar to the one on the easel or those Alan had found in his Google search back at the Art's Court in Newford—curious combinations of humans mixed with animals, birds or reptiles.

"So...portraits?" Marisa said.

Aggie nodded. "I'm no good at making things up."

"I mean, are you saying these aren't...symbolic?"

"Heaven's no. I can only paint what I see."

"But..."

"I think I already mentioned that the borders between the worlds are awfully thin around here."

Marisa looked around, eyes wide, then walked over to an old battered sofa under the window. She moved some books to the floor and sat down where they'd been.

Leah drifted deeper into the studio, studying the paintings on the walls, others in stacks leaning against the walls. She had the same feeling looking at them as she'd gotten sitting outside the motel room last night and driving through the hills to get to Aggie's place. That everything was different, but familiar as well. That she was a stranger, but she had come home.

She could have stood there and soaked it all in for hours, except she suddenly realized that no one had spoken for some time. She turned to see Marisa still on the sofa looking a little shell-shocked, while Aggie leaned against a long table crammed with paint tubes and glass jars with the handles of paint brushes sticking up out of them.

Leah cleared her throat. "These are beautiful," she said. "Thank you so much for letting us see them."

"But that's not why you're here."

Leah shook her head. "No, but just getting to see your art would be more than enough reason for the whole trip."

"Hmm," Aggie said. She pushed away from the long table. "I think this calls for some tea."

She gestured for Leah to sit by Marisa, then fetched three clay handleless mugs from a stack on the table behind her. She put them and a thermos on the crate in front of where Leah and Marisa were sitting. Pulling a chair over for herself, she poured them each a mug from the thermos and sat down across from her two visitors.

"Usually," she said, "people I don't know come here for one of two reasons: they either think I have some special knowledge that will set them on a spiritual path, or they want to buy one of my paintings. More rarely, they hope to study under me or have come to invite me to speak at some conference or workshop. But what's interesting here is that I always know they're coming."

"I'm sorry," Leah said. "We should have called ahead."

"That's not what I mean. When I say I know they're coming, the local gossips tell me. Crows. Hawks. Sparrows. Sometimes it's one of the javelina boys, or perhaps one of Cody's younger cousins—Cody being the original Coyote."

Marisa looked at the old woman over the rim of her mug. "When you say these names, do you mean tribes or—"

"No," Aggie cut in. "I'm being quite literal."

"You can talk to birds," Leah said. "And wild boars and coyotes."

Aggie shook her head. "I talk to spirits. I'm one of the tribal elders, but where most of us consult with human members to help them deal with the world of the spirits, my time is spent with spirits helping them adjust to the world of the five-fingered beings."

"The, uh...?" Leah began.

Aggie held up a hand and wiggled her fingers. "It's what the *ma'i-nawo*—the spirits—call men and women because they only have the one, five-fingered shape."

"Ma'in..." Leah tried.

"*Ma'inawo*. It's what they call themselves, at least they do so here in the Painted Lands. It means 'cousin.'"

"So you help spirits who look like animals."

"No, they are animals, but they can wear human shapes as well. They've been here since the long ago, when Raven pulled the world out of that old pot of his and set the wheels of our lives in motion."

"This is...weird," Leah said. "You know it's weird, right?"

Aggie regarded her steadily with no change in her expression, so Leah turned to Marisa for backup, but Marisa only shrugged.

"This last day or so seems full of portents," Aggie went on. "There was a child whose parents threw her away. A friend of mine who finally learned to actually see the world in which he lives. Another friend shot by a hunter. The appearance of Night Woman at the dawn ceremony. And now you two showing up on my doorstep without the gossip of even one cousin preceding your arrival."

Leah didn't know what to say.

On the sofa beside her Marisa stirred. "Why are you telling us this?" she asked Aggie.

The old woman shrugged. "Sometimes when you speak riddles aloud they begin to make sense."

"But not today," Marisa said.

"Not today," Aggie agreed.

Leah looked from one woman to the other, then settled her gaze on Marisa. While her friend had seemed taken aback when they first came into the studio, she now appeared to be completely at ease. "You don't seem too freaked out by any of this," Leah said to her.

"I suppose I'm not," Marisa said.

Leah didn't consider that any real answer at all. But before she could ask Marisa to elaborate, Marisa turned to Aggie.

"Have you ever heard of numena?" she asked.

Aggie shook her head.

"Maybe you have another name for it," Marisa said. "It's when an artist paints a picture that speaks so clearly to..." She looked lost for a moment. "To its spirit in the otherworld, I guess. The painting speaks so clearly that the spirit crosses over and becomes real. No matter how outlandish the subject's appearance, they show up exactly as depicted in the painting."

She glanced at Leah, then returned her attention to Aggie before going on. "It's only special artists that can do it. Make this pathway, I mean."

"I've never heard of such a thing," Aggie said.

"So you didn't call the spirits to you through your paintings? And the reason you won't sell any isn't because their lives are tied to the physical safety of their paintings?"

"No, they're simply portraits of beings who already exist."

"Marisa—" Leah said. "You've seen this before?"

Marisa nodded. "You know Isabelle's daughter Izzy? And her girl-friend Kathy? Izzy's not Isabelle's daughter. She's Isabelle when she was twenty-something and her best friend was Kathryn Mully—the writer who killed herself. Both these girls are numena that Isabelle painted into existence. So's John Sweetwater and about half the people living on Wren Island."

"*What?*" Leah said. "You're saying they're all...all..."

"Numena. But now that they've crossed over, they're just people. Well, except for some of the faerie creatures she paints."

Leah bent over with her face in her hands. "I'm going crazy," she muttered.

"I'd like to meet your friend Isabelle," Aggie said. "And perhaps some of her friends, too."

"Isabelle doesn't travel much," Marisa said. "Maybe I can put the two of you together on Skype."

"I don't know how—"

Marisa didn't let her finish. "Don't worry. I can set you up. But the point of all of this is, I thought you were like Isabelle."

"You came here to have me bring someone across through a painting? But why? Couldn't your friend Isabelle do it for you?"

"No, no. I thought you'd already done it with someone. Leah, show her the picture."

Leah pulled out a printed copy of the image that had been emailed to her, and passed it over to Aggie.

"That's one of your paintings, isn't it?" she said.

Aggie nodded. "Where did you get this?"

"Somebody emailed it to me yesterday." She paused before adding, "It wasn't you?"

Aggie shook her head.

"Because the thing is," Marisa said, "the man in that painting looks just like a musician named Jackson Cole, who's been presumed dead. He disappeared after a plane crash around forty years ago. Or rather, the painting looks like Cole might if he'd been alive all these years."

"I don't know anyone named Jackson Cole."

"Used to play in the Diesel Rats?" Marisa tried. "They were huge back then."

"I don't really follow popular music—never have."

"But it is your painting?"

Aggie glanced at the picture again and nodded.

"Then, if you didn't send it to Leah, who did?"

Aggie lifted her gaze. She looked past them, out the window to her house.

"I think I have an idea," she said.

27

THOMAS

For the first time at a medicine ceremony, Thomas paid attention to what the singers around the drum were actually singing. He let his pulse be set by the heartbeat rhythm of the drumming, shifting his feet in time where he stood, echoing the steps of the dancers who moved in a shuffling line around the drummers.

These stories were different from those he'd heard in powwow songs. They celebrated specific aspects of Derek's life, but they also ran through the complete lineage of the Bighorn Clan, going further back than Thomas had ever imagined anyone could remember. As he listened to the songs, he found that he could hold every word and name in his own memory as well, the genealogy unwinding inside his mind like a golden rope that had no beginning and no end. Except there were always beginnings and endings, and the songs talked about them, too, of journeys already taken and others that lay ahead on the ghost roads of the otherworld where Derek would soon be travelling.

Sometimes Morago led the singing, other times it was one or another of the Aunts, the women elders of the tribe, holding smudge sticks that Thomas could smell even where he stood. His mother was there among them. The dog boys were part of the dance, as were the deer women dancers. Among the latter he could see his sisters. Santana looked around herself as she moved—she could see everything, just as Thomas could, while Naya simply danced. He even saw Auntie standing off on her own, holding his little brother William by the hand. She mouthed the words to the songs, though she didn't let any actual sound escape her lips.

Most of the tribe was participating the way he was: shuffling their feet in time to the drumbeat. *Ma'inawo* were everywhere, some no more than ghostly apparitions moving with the dancers, others standing in a loose circle around the tribe.

And then there was Night Woman and her enormous dog. Whenever he looked in their direction, the woman was watching Morago, but the dog would turn dark eyes on Thomas and hold his gaze until Thomas felt uncomfortable and had to look away. The dog's eyes carried knowledge of something Thomas was pretty sure he'd rather know nothing about. He couldn't tell if it was some private history, or a promise of something still to come. All he knew was that if he let that secret knowledge pass from the dog to him, he'd never be the same again.

But even the presence of the dog and its mistress couldn't make Thomas leave. His desire to be a part of this, triggered back in the community center parking lot, was still strong—so much so that he found himself wondering if someone had slipped a fetish into his pocket and put a spell on him to make him feel this way. He had to stop himself from checking his pockets.

He paid more attention as Morago and the Aunts invoked the blessings of the four directions. They stood in a circle, turning in each direction, the Aunts lifting their smudge sticks so that the pungent smoke rose up to meet the morning sun, while Morago took a pinch of tobacco from his medicine bag and tossed it into the air.

Thomas's gaze went to where Derek lay on a platform of old saguaro ribs tied together with leather rope. The platform was about six feet from the ground and the bighorn's head and body had been placed together as though they had never been severed. But unlike the head, which had been stored in the freezer at Sammy's hunting lodge, the body had been out in the sun all day and the smell of decay carried even to where Thomas was standing, not quite masked by the Aunts' smudge sticks.

Other platforms dotted the Ancestors Canyon, but only the bones of longer departed tribe members remained. Scavengers worked quickly. Vultures, ravens and the sacred crows of Yellowrock Canyon.

Thomas wasn't sure he cared for the idea—neither becoming feed for the canyon's carrion eaters, nor being buried in the ground, as were the Catholic members of the tribe. He thought he'd prefer a Viking funeral, his last remains disappearing into ash and smoke.

When the invocation ended, the drumming stopped and the whole tribe gave a farewell cry to Derek's spirit. For one moment, glittering in the light of the rising sun, Thomas thought he saw the vague shape of a warrior standing over Derek's body, then the image was gone and the tribe's cries faded into echoes down the canyon. The spirit people drifted away as though riding those echoes. Calico was the last of them to go. She gave a quick look around the canyon—searching for Steve, Thomas supposed—then vanished with the others.

Thomas backed up a little to make way as people began to leave the canyon, not quite sure why he wanted to stay. Auntie winked at him as she went by. His mother looked solemn as she walked with the Aunts, but she had a smile for him. When Santana and Naya approached, holding hands with William, who was in between them, Santana stopped long enough to give Thomas a hug.

"*Ohla*, big brother," she said. "It's good to see you here."

Thomas remembered driving out to Steve's, the two of them talking about how they wanted to get away. Right now Santana seemed a million miles away from that girl in the truck.

"I'll be home soon to take you guys into the city," he said.

"We'll have your breakfast ready," Naya said.

William let go of her hand long enough to give Thomas a fist bump, then the three of them went off. Reuben stepped up in their wake, one of the last to leave the canyon.

"Are you still coming to the sweat tonight?" he asked.

Thomas nodded. "Hey, can you tell me something?"

"Sure."

"Do you know how to see an enchantment?"

His boss's eyebrows went up. "You think somebody worked some medicine on you?"

"I don't know what to think. It's been a weird day and I don't really feel myself."

"It's not really the kind of thing I know that much about," Reuben said. "You should ask Morago or your mother."

"Except what if it was one of them?"

What if it was Reuben? he was also wondering, but he could see no guile in Reuben's face.

"They wouldn't, Thomas. Trust me on that."

"Yeah, I didn't really think so. But this…whatever this compulsion is…it's pulling me into the traditions."

Reuben gave him a rueful look. "And you don't like that."

"I don't understand it."

Reuben nodded. "I get that. Have you checked your pockets? Somebody might have slipped a little something into one of them."

"I thought of that, but why would anybody even bother?"

He put his hands in his pockets as he spoke, then felt the world go still as he pulled out a small black feather.

His gaze went to where Morago and Night Woman stood, her dog sprawled half asleep in the red dirt beside her. Now he knew where that sense of familiarity had come from. Her age and shape were different, but he'd bet anything the woman talking to Morago was the same one who had come to the trading post this morning.

"What is it?" Reuben asked.

Thomas opened his hand to show the feather, but his gaze remained fixed on Night Woman. "She was in the trading post this morning," he said. "She bought a Coke and asked for directions to the casino."

"Night Woman? Are you sure?"

Thomas nodded. "She looked different—younger. She didn't have the dog and she was driving a long black Caddy. But we had the counter between us, so how could she have gotten this into my pocket?"

He made a fist, closing the feather tightly against his palm.

"They say she's been here since the world began," Reuben said, a frown creasing his brow. "You get that many years under your belt, you can probably do a lot of things the rest of us can't."

Thomas was only half listening. He took a step toward where the shaman and Night Woman were standing, but Reuben grabbed his arm and pulled him back.

"You don't want to do that," he said.

"I need to find out if she did this to me. What she wants."

"Yeah, but don't do it with that chip on your shoulder. You need to be smart about this."

"So what would you do?"

Reuben shrugged. "Hear her out. Talk as little a possible. Try not to look like you want to drive your fist into something."

All good advice.

Thomas took a steadying breath. He eased the tightness of his fingers so the feather was only loosely enclosed. "Okay," he said. "I can do that."

Reuben laid a hand on his shoulder and squeezed. "Good man."

"But I'm getting rid of this," Thomas said, holding up the feather.

Reuben stopped him before he could throw it away.

"Hold on. If that thing's full of medicine, you don't want to leave it where anybody can stumble across it."

"Right," Thomas said.

He started to hand it over, but Reuben backed up a step, shaking his head.

"That's not warrior business," he said. "It's shaman business. We'll let Morago deal with it as soon as he's finished—"

He broke off as Jack Young Deer, one of his dog boys, came running up to them.

"Jerry wants to see you at the station," Jack said.

Reuben nodded. "I'm kind of in the middle of something."

"Sure," Jack said. "But he told me to tell you if you don't come in right now, it's out of his hands and you can expect a visit from the sheriff's office."

"He say what it's about?"

Jack shook his head. "But he's already brought in your buddy Steve."

"Crap. This is Sammy's doing. He wants that head back so that his big brave hunter can get it mounted."

Reuben turned to Thomas. "I need to deal with this or we'll have all kinds of authorities tromping around in here."

"I'm fine," Thomas told him. "Go."

Reuben nodded. "Since you're using my truck can you give Morago a ride back to the center?"

"No problem."

"And remember. When you're talking to Night Woman, don't look angry, and say as little as possible."

"Got it. Go see Jerry."

Reuben sighed. "Right. Let's go, nephew," he added to Jack.

Thomas watched them leave. When he turned around again, it was to find both Morago and Night Woman looking at him. His own gaze went down to the feather in his hand. He closed his fingers around it again and walked over to where they waited.

28

SADIE

The sound of a car coming down Aggie's lane woke Sadie. She was slouched under the window in the bedroom, still wrapped up in the blanket. The dog was gone, the door to her room closed. She was still trying to figure out what had awoken her when she heard a car door open. Clutching the blanket around herself, she got up, went into the kitchen and stood at the door where she could look out.

A blond white woman she didn't recognize stood outside a fancy car that was parked in the lane. She was letting the dogs smell her. Sadie was about to turn away when the passenger door opened. She recognized this second woman right away, though she'd only ever seen her picture on the masthead of her *Rats on the Run* blog.

Sadie watched as Aggie went to greet her visitors.

What the hell was Leah Hardin doing *here*?

She hurried back to the bedroom to get dressed. By the time she returned to the kitchen and looked out again, everybody was gone. Since all the dogs were sleeping on the little casita's porch or in the dirt near the bottom of the steps, Sadie figured Aggie must have taken the women into her studio. Fingering the fresh scab on her arm, she tried to figure out what to do.

Somehow Leah had tracked her down—or maybe, tracked Aggie down. Right now they were talking about Steve and her, and Aggie was blabbing everything, which meant there'd be no money coming her way.

And Aggie was going to be seriously pissed.

Sadie wanted to smash everything in sight. To put her foot through the paintings, one by one. Totally trash the place.

It wasn't fair. This had been her one chance to get free and now it was gone.

She wanted to scream. Tapping the knife in her pocket, she thought about dragging its blade across her arm and letting the anger and hurt out before she swelled like a balloon.

She could hardly breathe.

She dug out the knife and pushed the blade in and out, in and out of the handle.

The only thing stopping her from cutting was because that was what they wanted. They wanted to take everything away from her and let her bleed out on the floor.

Well, screw them.

She started for the front door, then returned to the kitchen and yanked open the cupboards until she found a canteen. Filling it with water, she went back to the door and eased it open.

She listened for the dogs as she quietly closed the door behind her. Keeping the house between her and any line of sight from the studio where the dogs were, she walked west. Downhill. Into the desert.

Cacti reared on all sides and she had to weave back and forth between saguaro and clumps of ocotillo and cholla. Did every freaking thing out here have to have a thorn?

She didn't realize she was crying until she got so congested it was hard to breathe except through her mouth. She wiped her nose on the sleeve of her hoodie and squatted on her haunches for a moment, sucking in big gulps of air.

She was so sick of this.

New plan.

Somehow, she had to get back to the city. She didn't care how she got there or how long it would take. It didn't matter if she had to walk the whole way. She'd wait until nightfall, then sneak into the house when Reggie was sleeping, bash him over the head, and take off with whatever she could lay her hands on that she might be able to sell. She'd take his credit cards and his car, too. Hell, maybe she'd throw him in the trunk and dump *him* in the desert while she was at it. See how he liked it.

She wasn't sure what she'd do with her mother. But knowing Tina, she'd be drunk, passed out, and sleep through everything, so Sadie wouldn't have to make a decision. As for the foster kids, at this point she couldn't decide if she'd be bringing Aylissa along with her or not. Maybe she'd let Aylissa make that call. But she couldn't bring the younger ones.

Shading her eyes with her hand, she looked west. There wasn't much to see except for hills and desert scrub. She wasn't exactly a whiz at geography, but she did know Santo VV was on a plain, and the rez was in the mountains, so after leaving Aggie's house, she worked her way down, following arroyos, dirt roads and little winding paths, always heading west.

It took her a good twenty minutes before she finally topped a rise and could see a blacktop below. She lifted her gaze and there was the smudge of the city in the distance.

Yes!

But before she could start down the hill a hand grabbed her shoulder.

She shrieked and tried to break free, but her unknown assailant's grip was too strong to escape. Then she was turned around and stood face-to-face with Steve's furry girlfriend Calico.

"What the fuck is your problem?" Sadie yelled. Again she tried to yank herself free but the woman's grip was too strong. "Seriously. Let me go."

"What's the connection between Sammy Swift Grass and your father?"

Sadie gave her a blank look.

"Just answer the question," Calico said.

"I don't even know who this Sammy guy is and what do you care?"

"Not the right answer."

She gave Sadie's shoulder a sharp tug, then took a step and the whole world seemed to go rubbery under Sadie's feet. Calico let her go and Sadie was so dizzy she staggered a few steps before falling to her knees in the dirt. She felt like she was going to hurl, but nothing would come up.

Calico stood watching her impassively until Sadie's world stopped spinning. Then the foxalope woman crouched down until their eyes were level.

"Let's try it one more time," she said. "Why are they framing Steve?"

"I have no idea what you're talking about. Framing him for what?"

"Kidnapping you."

"The only person going around kidnapping people is you."

Calico grimaced, showing a mouthful of teeth that were way too pointy and sharp. Sadie shivered but she didn't back down.

"I swear, until right now, I've never been kidnapped," she told Calico.

"That's not what your father says. He told the police he saw two Kikimi drag you into a van. Then Sammy steps up and says it was only one Kikimi—that Reuben Little Tree dragged you into the van and Steve was the driver."

"Yeah, well, I don't know any Reuben guy neither."

Calico studied her for a long moment, eyes narrowed. "If I leave you here," she said, "you'll never find your way back."

"Nice try," Sadie said, pointing to the rise where she'd been standing just before Calico grabbed her. "But I know the road's right over there."

"Is it?"

What kind of a weird-ass question was that?

"Why don't you go have a look?" Calico said.

Sadie waited a moment to see if Calico was serious, then stood up. She casually stuck her hands in her pockets, feeling better when her fingers closed around the handle of her knife.

Grab me again, freak, she thought as she walked back to the top of the hill, and I'll cut your stupid hand off.

But then she started to feel sick to her stomach again.

The road wasn't there. The smudge of the city wasn't on the horizon. There was just desert as far as she could see.

"You're not in your own world anymore," Calico said.

Sadie hadn't heard her come up behind her, and she jumped at the sound of Calico's voice.

"How…how's this even possible?" she managed.

Calico made a loose gesture toward the desert below. "So you can stay here for the rest of your life," she went on, "which, let's face it, wouldn't be that long for a city girl like you, or you can start being helpful."

Sadie shook her head. "I can't help you. I don't know these people you're talking about. I don't know how Reggie hooked up with them. I don't know anything."

"Maybe not. But you can come with me to the police station so they can see you haven't been kidnapped.

"Steve won't let me just take him away where they can't find him," Calico added. "He says this is a human problem, so we have to deal with it like humans do."

Sadie's fear of Calico and this strange world was swallowed by her bigger fear of the freak-storm that would come down on her if she went up against Reggie like this. It was one thing to sneak into his bedroom and smash his head in while he was sleeping, but face-to-face? When he was awake?

"And then what?" she said.

Calico gave her a puzzled look.

"What happens after I do that?" Sadie said.

"You can do whatever you want."

"Yeah, it doesn't work like that in my life. I don't know what Reggie's up to, but if I mess it up, I'm dead. He'll beat the crap out of me."

"And what makes you think *I* won't if you don't help Steve? He's only involved in this because he helped you."

"You think I chose my fucked up life? Think again, lady. Go ahead.

Do your worst. Beat me up. Leave me here. I don't care. But I'm not going anyplace where Reggie can get his hands on me."

"I can take you to the police station whether you want me to or not."

"I'm sure you could. But if you do, I'll just say you were in on it with Steve and the other guy you mentioned."

Calico glared at her. "Don't think I'm bluffing."

"I'm not bluffing either. I just don't care anymore. That's what happens when people like you push people too far."

"What do you mean, 'people like you'?"

"You, my old man—you're stronger than people like me. You can beat me up, so you get to tell me what to do."

"You think I'm…"

Calico's voice trailed off.

"Just like my old man?" Sadie said. "Yeah, you're acting just like him. You order me to do whatever you want or the hammer comes down. What I feel, what happens to me—you couldn't give a shit, could you?"

Calico regarded her for a long moment, then gave a slow nod of her head.

"You're right," she said. "I don't care about a self-centered little shit like you. But I care about Steve. So start walking."

She gave Sadie a little push to punctuate her demand.

Sadie pulled away. "Hey!"

"Walk."

"Why? Where are we going?"

"The tribal police station."

"I already told you, I'm not going to—"

Calico gave her another push. "Walk."

"What? You've got no magic spell that'll just whisk us there?"

"I do. But I want you to have the time to think about the consequences of making the wrong choice."

"I'm not changing my mind," Sadie said.

"We'll see."

Sadie tightened her grip on the handle of her knife. First chance she got, she'd cut Calico a new one with it.

"Yeah," Sadie said. "We'll see all right."

Calico met her bravado with a flat stare.

"Walk," she repeated.

Before Calico could give her another shove, Sadie turned and started down the hill where the road she'd seen no longer existed.

29

STEVE

I'm wondering if I did the right thing, having turned down
Calico's offer for help when she came by the tribal police station
earlier. She just popped in out of nowhere, sitting in the chair
beside me as soon as Jerry stepped out to answer a phone ringing in
the other room. She wanted me to go with her right then, but I told
her I couldn't and tried to explain.

I don't think she really understood.

This whole situation's got nothing to do with Sadie—not her old
man or the bogus kidnapping—and *everything* to do with Sammy
pulling this stupid scam because Calico and I reclaimed Derek's head.
At least that's the reason *I'm* here.

Whatever game Sadie's dad is playing is anybody's guess. The idea
that Reuben and I kidnapped her is pure bullshit and doesn't make a
lick of sense. Everybody knows it, but we still have to go through the
motions. It's deal with it here and now, or it gets right out of control
and Reuben and I find ourselves sitting in county, awaiting trial. If I
go on the run—or rather, disappear from the middle of the tribal
police station—it'll just postpone the inevitable and escalate my problems. Plus I can't very well abandon Reuben.

"But if things take a turn for the worse," I told her, "I'll welcome your help."

She frowned.

"Just let me try it my way first," I said.

Studying me for a long moment, she finally nodded. "Okay, but call my name if you change your mind. I'll be listening for you."

She disappeared just as Jerry hung up the phone in the other room.

When he comes back in he looks around. "I thought I heard somebody else in here," he says.

I shake my head. "Nope. It's just me and the spirits."

He gives me a considering look. "I always heard you weren't into that kind of thing," he says.

"You mean Kikimi traditions?"

He nods.

"Doesn't mean I don't have my own traditions."

Jerry gives another slow look around the room. "I hope those traditions don't include kidnapping teenage girls," he says.

"You don't seriously think I'd do that."

"No," Jerry says. "But I've been wrong before, and whatever else Reginald Higgins might be, he's on the money about one thing: nothing feels right about any of this."

Before I can frame a reply, the front door of the station opens and Reuben walks in, and I start to wonder for the first time what we're going to do if we can't make Jerry believe us.

"You KNOW this is a load of crap," Reuben says.

The two of us are sitting across the desk from Jerry. Outside, in the time we've been talking to Jerry, the sun's been up for a couple of hours, making long shadows and taking the chill out of the air. I try not to think of how I could be getting some sleep, or even out walking in the high country instead of dealing with this bullshit problem. I wouldn't be here at all if I hadn't felt compelled to play white knight for Sadie in the first place. But what was I going to do? Leave her there on the side of the road where her old man dumped her?

"Sammy's just jumped on this bandwagon," Reuben goes on, "because we gave him a hard time about one of his hunters. And his story doesn't even fit with what the father told you, so what the hell are we doing here?"

"I need to—"

"What happened to the father anyway?" I ask. "I thought you'd pulled him in."

"I did. I brought him here and then had a deputy from the sheriff's department drive him home."

"And then you hooked up with Sammy."

"I didn't 'hook up' with him. He went into the sheriff's department and they asked me to round you up."

"Of course they did," Reuben says. "So they've got you jumping through their hoops."

Jerry sighs. "I know the story he's telling doesn't add up. But Sammy's also a respected businessman and if he makes an accusation like this, and it involves a minor, we have to look into it."

"I'm a respected businessman too," Reuben says, "but I guess a casino trumps a trading post any day of the week."

"It's not like that and you know it."

"Maybe. But I'm in here answering your questions while he's not."

"He already gave his statement to the sheriff's department."

"So we do the same with you," Reuben says, "and we walk out of here?"

"I wish it was that simple."

"I've got twenty of my dog boys will tell you where I was Thursday night."

"I'm sure you do," Jerry says. "But to anybody off the rez, they're going to think your boys vouching for you might seem a little biased, and Steve's saying he was out alone in the desert all night. We're going to need more corroboration than just his word."

He looks from me back to Reuben. "You have to understand," he says. "Break a kidnapping case, deliver a solid arrest to the DA's Office, bring the victim in safe—that all looks good on a cop's record, doesn't matter if you're with the feds, the sheriff's department, or even the Bureau of Indian Affairs. Everybody's looking for a promotion."

"What about the tribal police?" Reuben asks. "They feel the same way?"

Jerry shrugs. "The chief does."

"What about you?"

Jerry gets a faraway look in his eyes. "You know what the happiest time in my life was? When I was herding sheep on my grandfather's land. That was after Dad took off to follow the rodeo circuit, and me and my little sister Annie and my mom moved in with her parents. I missed my dad, but God, did I love living out on that ranch. We never had much of anything, but we grew squash and corn and beans, and ran those sheep, and we made do. I didn't start school until I was ten, and I thought I was going to die when they took me out from under those painted skies."

"And your point is?" Reuben says.

I put a hand on Reuben's forearm. "Let him finish."

This is a side of Jerry I never knew, but I totally understand. Once you've lived out in those dusty hills, you never want to leave. If I lost what I have here, my heart would break and I don't think it would ever recover.

"Mom loved her parents," Jerry says. "Respected them, too, but she wanted more for Annie and me. We were always a traditional family, but she pushed me to become a cop and that's why I'm here today. I can't stand with either the traditionals or the casino crowd because, to do my job properly, I can't take sides."

"So?" Reuben says. "What's that mean for us?"

"It means I take the job seriously. It means that if the sheriff's department needs to talk to the pair of you, I'll make sure that happens. Just like I plan to interview Sammy myself. What's important to me is that we get to the bottom of what's going on here, not that somebody gets to score points. I don't care if it's you boys sniping at Sammy, or Sammy sniping at you. I don't care about anybody bucking for a promotion. That's not what this is about. It's about a teenage girl and what's happened to her."

Reuben slaps a palm on the desk. "And I'm telling you—we don't have anything to do with her."

That's not entirely true, at least it's not true for me. I get where Jerry's coming from. It's commendable that he puts his concerns for Sadie first. But I happen to know that none of it holds up. Not what her father says, not what Sammy claims he saw. Because I know Sadie's in no danger. She's way safer than she was with that piece of shit father.

"I can't go talking to the sheriff's department or the FBI," I say.

Jerry nods. "Look, I know something brought you to these hills and I've never asked what, or looked into it, because you've been a good member of the community. But I need you to step up now. You need to face up to whatever the hell you're running from and help me. There's a young girl's life at stake."

"I'm not living here because I broke any laws."

Jerry shrugs. "Granddad used to say this is an unforgiving land, but one where you can find forgiveness. Come with an open heart, live here long enough, and the sun and the desert will burn away anything you might have carried with you when you came."

"Some things can't be forgiven," I tell him.

Jerry gives me a sympathetic look. I buy his sincerity, but he's got it all wrong.

"What did you do, Steve?"

"I didn't do anything. It's what I let happen, and if I talk to your cop friends, it'll all come back on me."

"So you're an accessory."

"Not in the sense that you're thinking," I say. "It had nothing to do with the law."

"The girl—"

"I told you the truth. I was in the desert. Reuben and I didn't take her. If I were you, I'd be asking the hard questions of her old man."

I push my chair back and stand up.

"Sit down," Jerry says.

"No, I'm done here."

"Don't make me put you in a cell."

"You really think a cell can hold me?"

I can see him remembering how Calico and I just appeared out of nowhere back at the community center parking lot.

"Don't do this," he says. "I can help you."

His hand is edging toward his holster.

"Look," I tell him. "Let's cut the bullshit. You know the same as us that if we go to the other cops, we're already guilty. All they'll see is some desert rat, an Indian, and an easy solution to their problem. They're not going to listen to us, and you won't be able to do one damn thing to help us."

"I can't let you walk out of here," Jerry says. His hand drops to his gun handle, but before he can pull it out, Reuben is over on his side of the table pressing one hand on Jerry's shoulder so that he stops him from drawing his gun, and keeps him sitting at the table. Dog boys might not be *ma'inawo* but they're still faster and stronger than any normal person. I can see Jerry struggle but it's no use. He gets his free hand up where Reuben's holding his shoulder, but he might as well try to pick up his patrol car as pull off that grip.

"What the hell's gotten into you?" Jerry says. "That's resisting arrest. You say you've got nothing to hide, so why are you throwing everything away to go on the run?"

Reuben bends his head close to Jerry's.

"There are two worlds," Reuben says. "You know that, same as me. What you're trying to do here is make a man from one world obey the rules of another, and that's not going to happen. In my world, a man doesn't do what he knows is wrong just because somebody else tells him to. If you want to stick your nose up Sammy's shitty ass, that's your business, but you don't get to drag us up there with you."

Jerry tries to lunge out of the chair but he still can't move under Reuben's grip. "You sonovabitch!" he yells. "This has got nothing to do with Sammy."

"No?" Reuben says. "Then maybe we should all go have a conversation with him and see what he's got to say."

Reuben looks pointedly at me. "Steve," he says.

I sit there for a moment, then I get it. I come around the desk, grab Reuben's bicep, and he steps us all away into the otherworld. Jerry's chair doesn't come with us, and he falls down on his ass in the dirt. He recovers quickly and stands up, his hand going back to the butt of his gun, except it's not there anymore.

Reuben snagged it from its holster when we crossed over. Popping the ammo clip, he tosses the clip away into the brush. He checks the gun chamber for a round. Satisfied that it's empty, he hands it back to Jerry.

"Okay," Reuben says. "Let's go talk to Sammy."

Jerry looks around us and I understand his confusion. The tribal police station is gone. Everything he knows is gone. All he can see is miles and miles of desert scrub.

He stands up, stares at his useless gun for a moment, then holsters it and brushes the dust off his jeans. "Where the hell are we?" he asks. His tone is even, but it's plain that he's seriously pissed off, especially about losing his dignity.

"You shouldn't have to ask," Reuben says, "but this is my world." He spreads his hands. "We do things differently here. A man's measured on the weight of his word and what he does. So *this* is where we'll talk to Sammy."

"That's not going to change anything."

Reuben nods. "Then we're done. Let's get going, Steve."

"Wait!" Jerry says. "You can't just leave me here."

"Why not?" Reuben asks. He sounds genuinely interested. "You were going to turn us over to the sheriff's department and wash your hands of us. How's this any different?"

"I didn't go out and—" Jerry starts, then he breaks off.

"Kidnap some little white girl?" Reuben finishes for him.

Jerry drops his gaze and Reuben looks at me. "Whatever happened to innocent until proven guilty? Guess it's different when the Indian's got deep pockets. He can just make shit up and all his little toadies run around and make sure the chips fall the way he wants them to."

"You know it's not like that. It's just standard procedure to interview persons of interest in a situation like this."

"Will you listen to what you're saying? Why don't you use plain language instead of trying to cover up your bullshit with cop jargon?"

"I'm not—"

"And like I said, I didn't see Sammy in the tribal police station."

"I already told you. He was interviewed by the sheriff's department earlier."

"Yeah, and you took our story from us."

"They still want to talk to you."

Reuben nods. "Fine. We'll be here waiting for them."

Jerry wipes his brow with his palm then looks to me for help.

I keep my features bland.

"You backed the wrong Indian this time, Jerry," Reuben says, his eyes hard with anger. "And don't think I'll forget your playing at believing us. That grandfather of yours would be ashamed to see what kind of man you've become."

It's a low blow and I see it hit home.

"The world's not black and white," Jerry says. "Sometimes you have to make compromises for the greater good."

Reuben waves a hand. "There aren't any greys in my world—stick around here long enough and you'll figure that out."

"Take me back," Jerry tells him. "We can talk about principles when that girl is safe."

Reuben nods. "Yeah, *she's* the greater good. I'd expect as much from an apple like you."

Red on the outside, white on the inside.

Jerry's eyes flare with anger. He takes a swing that Reuben easily avoids. It puts Jerry off balance. Reuben gives him a little extra momentum, pushing him with the sole of his boot, and Jerry's on his ass in the sand again.

I'm feeling bad. This has gotten way out of hand. But if Jerry knew what I know, maybe he'd understand. I'm looking out for Sadie too. But I'm not going down just because Sammy's got a bone to pick with me. And I'm sure as hell not going to talk to any other lawmen.

Reuben points his finger at Jerry while he's still sitting in the sand. "Black and white," he says. "Right or wrong. In this place, there's no in between."

Jerry gets to his feet. I almost expect him to have another go at Reuben, but instead he keeps his distance. For the second time he brushes the sand and dirt from his pants. He still looks angry but there's a wariness in his eyes as well, like he just realized what a deep hole he's gone and dug for himself. I can see it plainly. He can't get out of here without our help. He's not even sure we're going to let him try to find a way on his own.

But he's a cop and he's tough—he has to be, to deal with some of the rougher elements on the rez—so he puts on a brave face. "Must be nice to be so sure of yourself," he says.

"I have to be," Reuben tells him. "I'm the tribe's war leader. I might make mistakes, but when I make a decision, I have to believe it's the right one. I have to believe it's the only one."

"Well, I don't have that luxury," Jerry says. "I have superiors that I answer to."

"And I answer to the Women's Council. But I have their trust. If I didn't, they'd replace me in a heartbeat."

This whole argument's gotten circular and I don't know how to stop it. Maybe it's something they just have to work out, but now's not the time or place.

I'm about to say as much, but then I see Reuben looking over my shoulder, his eyes narrowing as he tries to make something out. I turn to see Calico and Sadie in the distance, heat waves dancing between them and us.

"What the hell?" Reuben says.

I'm thinking the same thing.

"Who's that with your girlfriend?" Jerry asks as they get closer.

I don't bother responding. And then I don't know what the hell to say because Sadie gets this scared look on her face and points a finger right at me.

"That's him!" she cries. "That's the guy that raped me!"

30

LEAH

A ggie was silent as she led the way down the slope from the studio to her house. The dogs rose in a group as soon as they came outside, padding along on either side of them, their paws raising little puffs of dust in the dirt.

Leah stopped for a moment in the middle of the yard, captured by the view of the red dirt hills that danced off into the distance. Something swelled inside her at the sight. She could have stayed there all morning, but then Marisa called her name. She blinked and hurried to catch up with her friend, and the two women followed Aggie inside. The dogs dropped onto the flat stones outside the kitchen door, except for the red-furred one who trotted in behind them right on their heels.

"I'll get the girl," Aggie said.

She walked away down a short hall, leaving the two women time to admire the wealth of *ma'inawo* portraits that peopled her walls or were leaning five to ten deep against the baseboards. The art pulsed with life, the bright colours and startling images waking an array of stories in Leah's head that bounced, one against the other, until she wanted to write them all down in the same rapturous jumble they provoked inside her. Looking at Aggie's paintings, she could believe they *were* actual portraits. She could believe it was possible to call

beings to you from another world through the application of pigment
on canvas.

Leah glanced at Marisa. "How could you have never told me about
Isabelle?" she asked as she continued to make a slow circuit of
the room.

"It wasn't my story to tell," Marisa said.

"But you thought Aggie's art did the same thing as Isabelle's, didn't
you? I think our coming all the way out here on the basis of that little
bit of withheld information makes it my story too."

Marisa offered up a wry smile. "Whatever it was before, I suppose
that's true now."

"So tell me—"

She broke off when Aggie reappeared. The older woman was alone.

"She's gone," Aggie said.

"Gone where?" Marisa asked.

The old woman shrugged. "Who knows? She's a troubled child."

"But who is she?" Leah asked.

"Her name's Sadie, and I don't know much more about her other
than her father drove her out into the desert and dumped her. A friend
of mine found her and brought her to me."

Leah remembered the return address of the email that had brought
her here: sadinsan@gmail.com

Which could read as an abbreviated "Sadie in Santo del
Vado Viejo."

"*She* sent the email," she said to Aggie.

"Probably. That's what I wanted to ask her."

Aggie walked over to a stack of paintings that leaned against one of
the walls, lifted one out and brought it over to them. "She could have
used the camera on the laptop to take a picture of this to send to you."

Leah studied the painting the old woman handed to her. Looking
at the original, the subject looked even more like an older Jackson
Cole than the image file had. "Who sat for this?" she asked.

"A friend of mine named Steve."

"What's his last name?"

Aggie shrugged. "Never asked."

"So you aren't close?"

"I didn't say that. I said I didn't ask. What's important to me is who a person is, not who they once were. I accept the gifts of what I'm told and don't push for more."

Which sounded far more altruistic than most people.

Leah dug in her purse and came up with a copy of *Burning Heart: The Jackson Cole Story*, the first book she'd written about the band. Flipping through the pages, she found a good picture of Cole. "Do you think your friend Steve could have looked like this forty years ago?"

Aggie looked down at the picture and shrugged. "Who knows? Anyway, it's not important. This is now, not forty years ago." She handed the book back to Leah. "Now let's see if we can find the girl. What do you say, Ruby?"

The question was directed at the red dog who sat up, then trotted to the front door as if she understood exactly what her mistress was asking.

Leah and Marisa exchanged glances.

"So is Ruby," Leah asked. "Is she one of your...you know..."

"*Ma'inawo?*"

Leah nodded.

"They're not *my ma'inawo*," Aggie said, "and you'd have to ask Ruby that question."

The dog turned, her gaze meeting Leah's with a disarming intelligence in her deep brown eyes.

"Uh, maybe some other time," Leah said.

Aggie chuckled and opened the door. The dog held Leah's gaze for a moment longer before she followed the old woman outside. Once they were out of the house, the dog took the lead, taking them on a winding path through the cacti and brush.

The old woman was able to move at a surprising speed for her age, with Marisa close behind her. Leah lagged in the rear, trying to absorb everything around her while still keeping pace with her companions.

It was a losing battle. Her surroundings were everything she'd imagined they'd be while sitting outside her motel room last night, and she longed to go exploring at a much slower pace instead of hurrying after Aggie and the others. The tangled thickets of prickly pear and cholla were just as fascinating as the towering heights of the saguaro. And there was so much wildlife—more than she'd expected in a landscape such as this. The scurrying quail. A rabbit that was as startled as she was. Doves breaking into flight. An honest-to-god roadrunner, which looked nothing like the cartoons she remembered as a kid.

She paused by a jumble of stones when she saw a flash of brown movement and was delighted to catch a glimpse of a small lizard.

"Leah!" she heard Marisa call.

She hurried on, glad she was wearing sneakers as she picked up her pace on the uneven ground. Following the sound of Marisa's voice, she jogged up a hill to find the two women and the dog waiting for her at the top. From where they stood, they could see a two-lane blacktop following the contour of the land below.

"The trail stops here," Aggie said.

Leah peered down the hill again. "Do you think someone picked her up and gave her a ride?"

"No," Aggie said. "I mean it stops right here where we're standing. She walked this far, then went into the otherworld."

"The…otherworld," Leah repeated.

Aggie nodded.

"How's any of this even possible?"

Leah turned to Marisa, who shrugged.

"I know for a fact," Marisa said, "that Isabelle's numena came from somewhere else by way of her paintings. So I believe that other worlds do exist."

"Except this isn't a painting."

"No," Marisa agreed. "But why shouldn't there be more than one way to move between the worlds?"

"Oh boy."

"Do you still want to talk to Sadie?" Aggie asked.

Leah gave an uneasy nod.

"Then we have to cross over as well."

Leah thought about this unknown territory she was being asked to enter. What was it Dylan said? *You can always come back, but you can't come back all the way.*

The old stories said the same thing about fairyland: how, when you returned, you were no longer the same.

Except she wasn't starting that journey here, at this moment. She'd started it when she'd read Aimee's journal—that had been the first step she'd taken on this road.

And didn't *every* journey change you? Look at what she was already feeling after just coming to the desert and talking to that old man Ernie last night. The landscape, the plight of the people he'd described...

Change wasn't necessarily bad. It was just scary.

"Okay," she said.

Aggie offered a hand to each of them. "You might feel a moment of discomfort when we cross over, but it passes quickly."

Leah and Marisa exchanged glances. Marisa raised an eyebrow, Leah shrugged, and then they smiled at each other as they each took one of Aggie's hands and let the old lady take them into the other-world, red-furred Ruby leading the way.

Leah knew she was anthropomorphizing the dog, but she was sure she saw a glint of laughter in those dark eyes.

OVER YONDER

31

THOMAS

What Thomas wanted to tell Night Woman was: Who the hell do you think you are, casting some damn spell on me? But he remembered Reuben's warning. *Don't look angry and say as little as possible.* So when he got to where she and Morago were standing, all he did was hold the black feather out to her. "I think you left this behind at the trading post," he said.

Morago looked from her to him, clearly surprised at their familiarity with one another. Night Woman merely took the feather, a twinkle of amusement in her eyes. On her shoulders her raven aura manifested, then peered down with great interest and clicked its beak.

Thomas waited for some difference, once he no longer had the feather, but nothing changed. He felt exactly the same after it left his fingers as he had before. Apparently, whatever medicine she'd used to change him no longer required the feather be in his possession. Which probably meant the change was permanent.

He wasn't sure if he was disappointed or not.

"How do you two know each other?" the shaman asked, his voice casual.

Night Woman shrugged. "I stopped for a drink at the trading post."

"Did you find the casino?" Thomas asked.

Morago's eyes narrowed at the mention of the casino, and there was a long moment of silence. From somewhere in the distance Thomas heard the shrill *skree* of a hawk. He wished he were back on the highway with Santana, driving Reuben's sweet ride, just enjoying his sister's company. He wished Auntie had never sent him to the community center last night. He wished he were back at the trading post staring out the window at whatever new configuration the prickly pear made.

Basically, he just wished he was anywhere but here.

He sensed a deep underlying tension between Night Woman and Morago. You couldn't tell by looking at them, but the air was thick with hidden undercurrents despite their pretence of calm.

"What are you up to, Consuela?" the shaman asked.

"Consuela?" Thomas repeated. "Her name's Consuela?"

Morago nodded. "Consuela Mara, also known as the Morrigan, and at one time, she was Raven's bride."

Thomas didn't know who or what the Morrigan was, but he remembered the stories of Raven's bride—how they were wed in the long ago when the world was young, but now she presided on the opposite side of the wheel from where Raven stood. Raven had brought the world out of the darkness. She was a part of the darkness, curious to see what he had fashioned in that old black pot of his.

"I ask you again," Morago said, returning his attention to the raven woman. "What are you up to?"

"Nothing. I was thirsty. What business is it of yours, anyway?"

"I like to keep abreast of what's happening on the rez, especially when it involves spirits."

"Then you need better gossips and spies," she told him before turning to Thomas. "And no," she added. "I haven't had a chance to get to the casino yet."

But the shaman obviously wasn't ready to let her change the subject. "You saw her earlier today and didn't think to mention it?" he said, focusing his attention on Thomas now.

I didn't know I was supposed to answer to you, Thomas thought, but all he did was shrug and say, "I didn't know who she was. She didn't look like this. She looked like a supermodel."

Morago's brows went up.

"You know," Thomas said. "Hot." He felt a flush creep up his neck. It only got worse when Consuela gave him a smile like that of a contented cat. He could almost hear her purr and his neck got hotter. As she reached out a fingernail and ran it down his cheek, her raven aura fluffed its feathers, cocked its head at him and opened its beak. Thomas could swear it was laughing.

"Isn't that sweet," she said to him, but her gaze was on the shaman. "It's good to know not everyone is so frightened of me."

Thomas didn't think Morago was even remotely frightened. His eyes said he was pissed, but his voice was mild when he spoke.

"So why are you here, Consuela?" he asked.

This time, the raven woman answered him.

"Derek Two Trees wasn't the first to die at the hands of Sammy Swift Grass and his hunters," she said. "The kin of other victims have been speaking to the wind, asking for justice."

"Other victims?" Morago repeated. Whatever irritation he might have been feeling toward the raven woman seemed to wash away at this news.

Consuela nodded. The teasing look in her eyes was replaced with a hardness that sent a little shiver up Thomas's spine.

"Why am I only hearing about this now?" the shaman asked.

"They were *ma'inawo*, not Kikimi. The *ma'inawo* don't have a shaman to serve as their intermediary, so they offered their tobacco and prayers directly to Night Woman."

Morago gave her a long, dubious look.

"I know many of the stories about Night Woman," he finally said. "None of them say that she is such a powerful spirit as one of the thunders, accepting prayers."

She shrugged. "Cousins have their own stories. Those stories say Night Woman walks the hours between sunset and dawn to ensure that forgotten wrongs don't go without redress. She's a formidable force, by all accounts."

"So she's a vengeance spirit," Morago said.

"More a spirit of fairness. Even the *ma'inawo* may be in need of a champion at times."

Morago nodded. "And you're theirs."

Consuela shook her head. "No, not at all. But I can do my part to see that justice is served for the cousins whose prayers I've heard."

Thomas saw the doubt in Morago's eyes. "I see," the shaman said. "I appreciate your coming by to tell me about this."

"I'm not just being neighbourly," Consuela told him. "I'm here because I would like to have a member of the Kikimi as a witness to attest that whatever action I deem necessary is just. *Ma'inawo* clans are sticklers for propriety, and they wouldn't want my judgment to cause any trouble between your peoples. Will you be my witness?"

Morago hesitated and Thomas suddenly realized that the shaman wanted to be elsewhere. It probably had something to do with the white girl he and Steve were protecting.

"Why is this a difficult question?" Consuela asked.

"It's not difficult, but it's not simple, either," Morago began.

"I'll go with you," Thomas said, surprising himself as much as he did the shaman.

Reuben's warning came back to him again—*say as little as possible*—but it was too late to take the words back.

Consuela smiled. "Well, isn't this a nice surprise." She turned to Morago. "Does he have the authority to speak for the tribe in this?"

Morago studied Thomas for a long moment before he smiled as well. "Of course he does," he said.

Thomas looked from one to the other, trying to ignore the raven aura above Consuela's shoulders. The bird was grinning and waving its wings, as though beckoning him to join them.

What had he gotten himself into?

"If I may have a moment with Thomas?" Morago said to Consuela.

"Of course."

As the shaman took Thomas aside, Thomas realized it was really happening. He had just agreed to accompany a spirit out of myth to do…he wasn't sure exactly what. And not just any spirit. She was out for vengeance, so she was probably going to tear Sammy to pieces right before his eyes. Thomas wasn't particularly fond of Sammy, but he didn't hate him the way some of the people on this side of the rez did. And he really wasn't interested in watching him die.

"Thank you for this," Morago said. "It's not often I have to deal with crises on the rez and in the spiritworld at the same time."

Thomas barely heard what he was saying. "I don't know what I was thinking," he told the shaman. "I don't even know what to do. If she's just going to kill—"

Morago laid a hand on his shoulder. "You'll do just fine. It will be good for you. Observe, listen. Pay attention to what you see in both realms with your shaman's eyes and ears."

"But I don't have that kind of medicine."

Morago squeezed his shoulder. "How do you think you see the animal spirits of those walking around in the physical world?"

"I…"

"Exactly. I have only one caution: keep your own counsel. You are the tribe's ears and eyes, but *we* must make our decisions based on what you have witnessed. Make no promises and speak as little as possible."

Thomas wished he'd stuck to that before he'd opened his big mouth a moment ago. But he knew where the impulse had come from. He'd promised Steve and Morago he'd help them keep the girl safe. He just hadn't dreamed it would be with something like this.

"Ready?" Consuela called over to them. She looked impatient, while her ghost raven looked gleeful.

No, Thomas thought, he didn't want to join this pair. But he nodded.

"The cousins are just," Morago told him as he started to go. "Their word is their bond—like it is for us. No harm will come to Sammy if he is innocent."

Thomas wasn't convinced. "Except we know he isn't."

Morago shook his head. "So far as we know, Sammy isn't purposely targeting *ma'inawo*. All he has to do is convince Consuela of that."

"And if he can't?"

"Then he must face the consequences of his actions."

Thomas gave a glum nod.

And then he'd have to watch Sammy die.

32

STEVE

Sadie's good. She could almost have me convinced, except I know I never touched her, not even when she was expecting me to, the night we met. My gaze leaves her face to find Calico, and my foxalope girl gives me a look that says she never saw this coming. Truth is, neither did I. I have no idea what game Sadie's playing. Maybe Morago was right. Maybe this whole thing was cooked up by her and her father, though what they're supposed to get out of it is anybody's guess.

I want to tell Calico I understand why she brought Sadie here. That I know she meant well and I don't blame her, even though it made things a lot worse. But that'll have to wait until later. Right now I've got Reuben and Jerry to deal with.

"Steve—" Reuben says.

"Don't," I say without turning around.

"I have to ask, brother."

I sigh. "No. I never touched her."

I turn to look at him. He gives me a tight smile.

"That's all I had to hear," he says before adding, "Come on, Jerry, you know damn well we had nothing to do with this kid."

"You're not going to get away with it," Jerry says, ignoring him and staring at me.

I expected as much from him. He didn't believe me when I said I'd never kidnapped her, so why believe me now?

"Look at that poor kid," he adds.

"Yeah, poor kid," Calico says. "I think I'll kill her now." For a moment, the lower half of her face is a fox's muzzle. She bares her teeth and snarls, and both Jerry and Sadie flinch and go pale. She starts for Sadie, only stopping because I hold up a hand and call out her name. Sadie still cringes, her gaze darting between Calico and me.

I stare at Sadie until I'm holding her full attention. "You might try to bullshit about me," I say. "But if you drag anybody else into this little game of yours, all bets are off."

Trying to keep an eye on both Reuben and Calico, Jerry sidles around us until he's standing slightly in front of Sadie. "Nobody touches her," he says. "You'll have to go through me first."

I nod. "I'm hoping it won't come to that," I tell him, "but like I said, she's not getting away with this piece of crap story."

"He's the one who's lying," Sadie says, pointing at me.

I jab my finger in the air toward her. "Only one of us is a backstabbing liar."

"His real name is Jackson Cole," Sadie blurts out, raising her arm and pointing back at me.

Jerry turns and gives her a blank look.

She crosses both arms, looking both defiant and satisfied. "He used to be this hotshot rock star. You know—that old band the Diesel Rats? Wanna bet he gave it all up and ran away because he did something like this before? Celebrities all think they can get away with anything."

Jerry holds me with a considering look, probably not that different from the one I'm giving Sadie.

How'd she figure that out? She wasn't even born when the band fell apart.

But Jerry's focus is on the last part of what she said. "I don't care if he's the Pope," he says. "He's not getting away with any of this."

He eyes each of us in turn while keeping Sadie behind him. "Are you going to let us walk away?" he asks when he gets to Reuben.

"You see anybody stopping you?" Reuben asks.

"Walk away where?" Sadie asks.

"Back to the police station," Jerry says. "We'll be able to contact your dad and get you back with your family—that's if somebody here's going to help us return to our own world."

"Not our problem," Reuben says.

At the same time, Sadie's face blanches and she says, "I'm not going anywhere near my father."

Jerry turns to give her a puzzled look.

"Because...because..."

She didn't think this through. I can almost see the wheels spinning in her head as she tries to come up with some reason to stop from being reunited with her old man. Maybe they weren't playacting when she got tossed from her old man's car on Zahra Road the other night.

"Because," she finally says, "he's the one who sold me to Mr. Bigshot Jackson Cole in the first place."

"Your *father* did *what?*" Jerry says, unable to keep the disgust from his voice.

She looks at her feet, unable or unwilling to meet anybody's gaze, but she nods.

Jerry gives me a look like he wants to punch me in the face.

"You know," Calico says, "I'm beginning to understand why her father dumped her in the desert."

I nod. "Yeah, this just gets better and better."

"Just shut up, you sick freak," Jerry says.

I hold up my hands. "Hey, she's all yours." I look from Reuben to Calico. "Anyone volunteering to take them back?"

"No!" Sadie cries. "I'm not going back to him."

Jerry pats her shoulder. "Don't worry. I won't let your father or anybody else hurt you again. You'll be under police protection until we get all this straightened out."

"Yeah, good luck with that," I say.

Calico steps up. "I'll take them back."

I nod. "And then we need to get going."

"You won't get away with this," Jerry tells me, like repeating it is going to make it happen. "Don't think you won't pay for what you did."

"Somebody's going to pay," I agree.

The long day and night are catching up to me and I feel exhausted. All I want to do is get back to the trailer and shut the world away.

Possum was right. I should have turned away when I saw this girl dumped on the side of the road and never gotten myself involved. Except who am I kidding? I had to do what I could, no matter how it played out. I just hope to hell my good turn doesn't mess it up for anybody else.

"Do yourself a favour," I tell Jerry. "Don't let her take you down with her."

Reuben nods in agreement. "You're going to regret playing the big hero, Jerry."

"What the hell's that supposed to mean?"

"You'll find out," I say. "My advice? Try not to be alone with her because that's going to come back and bite you on the ass."

Calico steps forward, offering a hand to each of them. Jerry reaches out to take her hand with a resigned look in his eyes, but Sadie backs away. I realize she's going to take off and I give a mental shrug. I'm beyond caring about that kid anymore. Let her run. But then we hear a dog bark and Sadie freezes.

Aggie's red dog appears, running out of the heat haze that makes the desert scrub to the west look all wavy. Behind Ruby we see Aggie approaching with a pair of white women that I don't recognize, one blond, the other dark-haired.

The fair-haired woman is very pale, her palm on her belly, looking like she's about to throw up, but as they get closer she seems to recover. I twig to what she was feeling. It's a good thing it doesn't last long.

Sadie shrinks away from Ruby when the dog pads over to her.

"Get away," Jerry says to the dog. He's still in protector mode.

The dog sits on her haunches and looks at him with a cocked head. She gives a bark and Calico laughs. "Yeah," she says to the dog. "He is wound pretty tight."

Aggie and her companions reach us.

"Who's wound tight?" Aggie asks.

Ruby barks again.

"Oh, he's been like that ever since he went off to the police academy," Aggie says. "He's just never been able to get himself grounded again."

"Standing right here," Jerry says.

Aggie smiles. "So you are. *Ohla*, Jerry Five Hawks. How's your mother?"

"She's fine."

"And your sister? Is she still working at that gallery in Phoenix?"

"She's fine too. Aunt Aggie, what are you doing here?"

Aggie looks at Sadie. "Well, somebody used my computer to send an image of one of my paintings to Leah here." She nods to the dark-haired woman. "I wanted to find out if it was Sadie."

"How would she be using your computer?"

"She was staying with me."

"Hold on, now," Jerry says.

While they're talking, the blonde has been studying Sadie with interest, but the dark-haired woman doesn't even look at the girl. Instead, she seems weirdly transfixed on me.

"What do you mean, she was staying with you?" Jerry asks.

"I was not," Sadie says. "I don't even know any of these women."

"I'm Marisa," the blonde says cheerfully, lifting a hand.

Nobody pays her any attention.

Aggie's eyebrows go up. "Of course she does—well, she knows me at least, *and* my hospitality." She gives Sadie a pointed look then returns her attention to Jerry. "What are *you* doing here, Jerry?"

"Sadie was kidnapped by Steve and Reuben, and I'm trying to get her back. She also says that Steve raped her."

The dark-haired woman—I think Aggie called her Leah—draws her head back in a puzzled frown.

"That's ridiculous," Aggie says. "Steve found her out on Zahra Road after her father threw her out of his car. He brought her to me while we waited to see if Morago could find her a spot in the school."

"It's a serious accusation, so I still have to investigate," Jerry says.

"Of course you do," Aggie says.

She turns to Sadie, her face softening. "Child, I'm sorry it had to come to this. You must be so ungrounded, to repay the good turn that was done to you with these lies."

"I'm not lying. You're lying."

Aggie nods. "Have you shown him the bruises from when your father hit you, and the scars of your self-inflicted cuts?"

Sadie points to Jerry. "He's going to protect me—from all of you."

"That's good to hear. Perhaps he'll also be able to protect you from yourself."

"Can you take them back?" I ask Aggie.

"Of course."

"Then we'll be going," I say.

Except before we can leave, Leah steps up to me, her eyes still filled with wonder. "You're really *you*. Jackson Cole. I can't believe it."

I find a smile. "Now, I haven't heard that in a while. I used to get it all the time, forty years or so ago, back when I was a lot younger and Jackson was still alive. 'Course, having the same surname as my famous cousin didn't help. Personally, I never saw the resemblance like others did."

She turns to her friend Marisa. "It's really him."

"Nice to meet you, ma'am," I say, letting my drawl deepen. "Good luck, Jerry."

Then I'm walking away with Calico on one side, Reuben on the other.

"Are you just going to let them walk away?" I hear Sadie ask.

"Don't worry," Jerry says. "This isn't finished."

33

LEAH

There was no question in Leah's mind that it had really been Jackson Cole. Older, sure, but not nearly as much as one would expect. For one thing, there was no grey in his light brown hair. He was slightly grizzled and his skin leather-browned from the sun, but he was aging gracefully—still as handsome as ever, and very much alive. And it wasn't only his features that gave him away. She'd listened to hundreds of interviews and rehearsal tapes. That was definitely his voice.

And now—after all these years of having a head full of questions to ask him, after the impossibility of his still being alive right in front of her—he was simply walking away.

She gave Marisa a helpless look.

And what was this drama they'd walked into? None of Sadie's accusations jibed with her own mental picture of Cole, formed from listening to his music and interviewing people who'd known him. Aggie's version of what had happened was far more in line with what she supposed Cole was really like. But could she really trust those suppositions? Leah had never actually met the man. She'd never been inside his head. Everything she knew was secondhand from talking to those who'd known him, and poring over lyrics and interviews.

"We need to get back, Aunt Aggie." Jerry said. "Will you take us now?"

"Of course," the old woman said.

She offered her hands to them. Marisa and Leah joined hands, then Leah took Aggie's, but suddenly Sadie bolted. The red dog went charging after her, nipping at her heels and herding her back to where they waited.

"Get that thing away from me," Sadie pleaded. "You don't understand. Reggie's going to kill me."

"Nobody's killing anybody," Jerry said. "And we'll have a better chance of figuring things out once we get out of this place."

He grabbed Sadie's hand, then reached for Aggie's outstretched left palm.

"It won't be as bad this time," Aggie told Marisa.

Leah hadn't felt anything when they'd crossed over before, but the nausea had hit Marisa hard. This time, Leah stayed close to Marisa in case she needed support. Marisa's features were white as they arrived in the glaring light of the parking lot of the tribal police station, but she waved off Leah's hovering.

"I'm okay," she said. "Just a little queasy again."

"Aunt Aggie," Jerry said. "I have another favour to ask of you. Will you stay with us until someone from Children's Services can get here?"

Aggie nodded, then turned to the women. "Can you find your own way back to your car?"

"If we have to," Marisa said. "But if it's okay, we'll stick around. We might be able to help since we work with kids back home in Newford."

Leah was too distracted to respond. She was looking in the direction that Jackson Cole and his companions had walked, except instead of empty desert, she saw a road leading up to the rez and the ranches and farms that lay between the station and the foothills.

Jackson and the others were nowhere in sight. Not in this world.

The dog came up beside her and leaned against her leg. Absently, Leah stroked its red fur.

"Or perhaps I should say," Marisa went on, "I'll stay on. I think Leah's got somewhere else to be."

Leah lifted her head, brought back to the present moment. "What?" she said.

Marisa smiled. "I'm thinking you need to go after Jackson Cole—or whatever he calls himself here."

"It's too late for that now," Leah said, her shoulders slumped. "I'd never find him again."

"You don't know that."

"Oh, come on," Leah said. "It'd be bad enough if he'd just walked off into the desert, but now he's in some whole other world." She shook her head. "I can't believe it. He was standing right in front of me and I just let him walk away."

"It's frustrating," Marisa agreed. "That's why you should go after him."

Aggie nodded. "And contrary to what little miss here has been saying, you'll be perfectly safe. Steve keeps to himself, but he's got a big heart. You'd be hard pressed to find someone on the rez he hasn't helped—" she looked pointedly at the police officer, "—including your uncle, Jerry."

The cop flushed and looked away.

"But I wouldn't know where to begin." Leah said. "Crossing over and figuring out where he's gone."

"Ruby can take you and track him down."

Leah gave the dog a dubious look.

"We flew all the way here," Marisa said. "You wanted a story. This is a story."

Leah sighed. "Except I'm not sure I want to write it anymore," she said.

Marisa nodded. "Maybe you only feel that way now. The one thing I do know is that you need to have an actual conversation with him. If you don't deal with this while you can, it's going to nag at you forever."

"You're right, I know. It's just…" Leah looked over at Aggie. "Is he or isn't he Jackson Cole? And what did he mean about his famous cousin?"

Now that she thought on it, she recalled that Jackson did have a cousin who'd been part of the band's extensive entourage. She couldn't remember his name or what he'd looked like. When she tried to picture him, a beard and a ball cap were all that came to mind. She was pretty sure he'd been a roadie or a guitar tech, and she remembered trying to track him down for an interview because supposedly, he'd been the one who first taught Jackson how to play guitar. But she'd never been able to connect with him.

Could the man from Aggie's painting be Jackson's cousin?

"I only know Steve as Steve," Aggie said. "He's never talked to me about family. Who knows who he was before he came to the Painted Lands?"

"Aunt Aggie?" Jerry said. "I really need to get things rolling here."

The old woman nodded, but her attention remained fixed on Leah.

"Okay," Leah said. "I'll give it a shot." Her gaze went to the dog, then back to Aggie. "What do I do?" she added. "Hold her paw?"

Aggie laughed. "No. Just rest your hand on her shoulders and let her walk you back across. Her name's Ruby."

"And she knows where to go?"

"She will, once she crosses over." The older woman stepped closer and tapped Leah lightly on the forehead. "Don't think so much."

That was easy for her to say—this was all old hat for her. Even Marisa seemed nonplussed. Leah felt she was more in the cop's camp on this aspect of it. From his eyes she could tell he was quietly freaking out on the inside, the same as she was.

But all she said was, "Okay."

Marisa came over and gave her a hug. "Chance of a lifetime, kiddo," she whispered in her ear. "No matter what happens, have you got a story."

There was that.

Leah gave Marisa a quick smile then laid her hand on the red fur between Ruby's shoulders. "Here goes nothing," she said as she let the dog walk her back into the otherworld.

"Or here comes everything," she heard Marisa say as she left the police station behind and was back in the magical desert.

34

JERRY FIVE HAWKS

This was officially the worst day of Deputy Jerry Five Hawks' life, and he'd had more than his share of bad days. What really bugged him was he should be feeling good. He'd rescued the girl. Bottom line, her safety had come first. So that was a win. A big win. For himself as well as for the police department. Except right now, he wasn't sure she'd ever needed rescuing.

All he wanted to do was go home and put this day behind him. He'd been on duty for almost eighteen hours with no end in sight, and the sick feeling in the pit of his stomach hadn't come only from the nausea he'd experienced during the impossible passage between the worlds. He stuffed that in a corner of his mind to deal with later, because the reality of the otherworld was the tip of a whole other iceberg that he wasn't ready to face. Right now, he was trying to deal with the idea he was pretty sure he was on the wrong side of all of this, and there wasn't a damn thing he could do about it.

Thinking that, looking at the girl, made him feel a whole other side of bad. Here on the rez, he'd seen too many cases of abuse dismissed, and he didn't want to be guilty of not acting on her behalf. But considering the way the girl kept embellishing her story, how it didn't quite fit with Sammy's version, and what he knew of the men she was accusing, he wasn't sure that you could pin these atrocities on Reuben and Steve. Reuben was the tribe's War Leader, for Christ's sake, chosen by the Women's Council, and Steve... Well, Steve had been a fixture on the rez for as long as he could remember. Kept to himself a lot, but was always ready to lend a helping hand. Easygoing, mild-spoken.

It was hard to see either of them through the girl's eyes. But if they were guilty, how was he supposed to deal with criminals when they could just walk away into another world and there was nothing he could do to stop them?

In the end, he could only do what he always did in uncertain situations: follow protocol.

"Aunt Aggie?" he said. "We need to get things rolling here."

He waited until the old woman finished talking to the two white women, then tried to quell the uneasy roll in his stomach when the dark-haired one and Aggie's dog vanished back into the otherworld.

Don't try to figure it out, he told himself as he led Sadie into the station. Aggie and the blond woman—her name was Marisa, he remembered—followed behind. Ralph Long Ridge was on duty and looked up in surprise to see them coming through the door. His gaze went toward the room where Jerry had been taking statements from Reuben and Steve a few minutes ago, then back to Jerry coming in the front door.

"Where'd you come from?" Ralph asked. "I never even saw you leave."

"I went out the back. I need you to call Child Services and ask them to send somebody down here." He glanced to see where Sadie was, then added in a lower voice, "Tell them to send a nurse, too, and have her bring a rape kit."

"Why—"

Jerry didn't let him finish. "I also need you to put out an all points on Reuben Little Tree and Steve Cole, AKA..."

His voice trailed off. Did he really want to go there? To give credence to the idea of Jackson Cole being still alive, alias Steve Cole, was going to take this investigation into the crazy world of supermarket tabloids. Although what he'd already experienced this morning was worse than any Elvis sighting.

Ralph was waiting for him to finish, pen in hand.

"Just the two of them," Jerry said. "I need to call the chief."

Ralph nodded. "Roger that."

But first, Jerry had to get Sadie settled until the people from Child Services could get here. After that he'd call the chief.

He had Aggie lead the girl into the next room. Marisa came along, looking around herself with interest. He wanted to ask her what she knew about all of this, but reminded himself: follow protocol.

"I don't want to be in here," Sadie said. "Not with her." She pointed at Aggie.

"It's just for a few minutes," he told her. "You'll be perfectly safe."

"Am I under arrest?"

Jerry blinked. "What for?"

"So you can't keep me here? I can just leave?"

He shook his head. "I need you to stay here until somebody from Child Services shows up. They'll explain all your options."

He waited until she took a seat, her body stiff with reluctance. Aggie pulled a chair back from the table and set it so that she was facing the girl. Marisa was studying the topographical map on the wall.

The first thing Jerry did when he went into the main area and sat at his own desk was unlock the bottom drawer and replace the missing clip in his revolver. Then, bracing himself for the flack that was coming his way, he dialed the police chief's number.

35

SADIE

Sadie glared at the old lady. Everything had spun way out of control and Aggie's calm gaze just pissed her off more. Aggie was like everybody else, thinking she knew it all. The difference was, she wrapped her superiority up in this phony Indian spiritual crap. But Sadie didn't buy it. Just because the sicko monsters in her paintings were real didn't mean you'd be a better person just because you knew the story of your pizza before you ate it.

"Why are you doing this?" Aggie asked.

The truth was, Sadie had no idea. To get back at Calico, she supposed. When she saw the cop she'd just said the most hurtful thing that came to mind. From there, it went spiraling downward.

But it wasn't her fault. If people hadn't interfered, none of this would be happening. Leah Hardin was supposed to email her back and offer a bunch of money for the information Sadie had. They'd figure out a way to pay Sadie off, and she'd walk away rich—end of story.

But no. Instead they'd all screwed it up on her. Leah, by coming here. Aggie, for talking to that idiot Leah. Calico, for being so damned mean and pushy. Not to mention her stupid old man, for making her life a constant miserable hell in the first place.

It was so infuriating. She'd been *this* close to getting away from everything horrible in her life. *This* close to starting over again some-where else, where there'd be no one to boss her around or give her their stupid advice.

"We can still fix this," Aggie said.

It was like she'd read Sadie's mind and still thought anybody cared about her freaking stories and Indian wisdom.

News flash, old lady: I'm not an Indian. And I'm not one of your freak show animal people either. Your crap's not going to work for me.

Sadie wasn't stupid enough to buy into the promises either Aggie or Jackson Cole had made to her. Nothing was easy and nothing was free. With her old man, she knew the price she had to pay to survive, and she'd decided she couldn't pay it anymore. With these people, who knew what they'd want to carve out of her soul?

She stood up. "Yeah," she said, "I'm not going to be doing this anymore."

Aggie rose to her feet as well. The blond woman turned from the map she was studying to look at them.

"You need to back off," Sadie told the old woman.

"Don't do this," Aggie said. "The people here just want to help you."

"Thanks, but no thanks."

She was close enough to walk to the city now, and once she got there, she knew she could disappear. She'd figure out some new angle, some way to get out from under everybody's thumb and be her own person.

She started to push by Aggie but the old woman wouldn't move out of the way. Instead, she reached out and grabbed Sadie's biceps, trying to stop her from leaving.

Sadie didn't have a choice. The old woman wasn't giving her a choice.

So she reached into her front pocket, yanked out her utility knife, and with a practiced flick of her thumb the blade was out. She slashed hard at Aggie's stomach.

The sharp blade cut deep, and for a long moment the two of them stared at each other. Sadie watched the calm brown eyes flare with shock and pain. Aggie's grip tightened on Sadie's arms, then she let go to grab at her belly. Flowers of bright red blood blossomed on Aggie's top. When she pushed her hands against herself, it welled up between her fingers.

"Oh my god," Sadie heard the blond woman say as Aggie dropped to her knees, still clutching at her stomach.

Then Sadie was pushing past Aggie, out of the room racing for the front door. She saw Jerry and the cop at the desk stand up, but before they could come after her the younger woman started shouting.

"I need some help in here! Call for an ambulance!"

The cops hesitated, then the one at the front desk picked up his phone as Jerry dropped his. He tried to get around his desk to make a grab for Sadie, but he was too slow. She pushed a rolling chair in his way and he fell over it, crashing to the ground and leaving Sadie free to make her escape.

The blond woman was still yelling when Sadie pushed through the door, out into the parking lot.

She was closer to the city than she'd been at Aggie's house, but it would still be too long a hike, especially with the cops after her. Scrambling over to the first pickup with the Kikimi Tribal Police logo on the door, she peered in through the window. Score. The keys were inside. A moment later, she was too.

The truck started up with a cough of exhaust before the engine smoothed out. Sadie put it into drive and spun out of the parking lot, gravel and dust spitting out from behind the wheels. She gave a one-finger salute out the window as she drove away.

36

THOMAS

When Thomas joined Consuela, he saw a car parked at the mouth of the canyon that hadn't been there earlier. And not just any car. It was an early Ford sedan, glossy black in the morning light, customized with a long sloped back like the low riders the Mexican kids drove in the city, except its chassis rode high on big fat wheels.

"Oh, that Gordo," Consuela said, chuckling under her breath. "He does like his jokes."

Gordo was the name of her monstrous dog, Thomas remembered, then realized he hadn't seen the animal since they'd started talking to the raven woman. Maybe the creature could only be out at night and vanished with the coming of dawn. Maybe it had turned invisible. It was hard to know what to expect anymore.

"Do you want to drive?" Consuela asked as she started walking toward the car.

"What happened to your Caddy?"

Consuela shrugged. "I have many ways to travel. Today it seems I'm being chauffeured in some kind of hot rod—unless you'd rather I drove?"

Are you kidding? Thomas thought. He'd love to get behind the wheel of that car. He started to wish Santana were here until he remembered whose company he was in.

"No, I'm good," he said, trying to sound nonchalant. "Where are we going? To the casino?"

"Eventually. I thought we'd take a little detour first."

Thomas wasn't sure he liked the sound of that, but he opened the driver's door anyway. Before he got in he checked the backseat to make sure there was no vicious canine waiting to rip his throat out, then he turned for a last look in Morago's direction. Surely, the shaman would realize this was a mistake and call him back. But the tall man only nodded to him and smiled.

Why, Thomas wondered, was he the only one to think any of this was weird?

Consuela slipped into the passenger seat, looking younger than she had when she'd been standing outside the car. By the time she shut her door she was a twin for the woman who'd come by the trading post this morning, except she was wearing slim camouflage capris with a scoop-neck white T-shirt tucked into the waist. Thomas caught his gaze going to the scoop of the T-shirt and quickly looked away, but not before he saw her raven aura smirk. A flush crept up from under his collar.

He closed his own door and the car started up by itself, making him jump.

Don't freak out, he told himself. Morago believed he could do this, so it was time he thought the same.

He cleared his throat. "So...do you even need me behind the wheel?" he asked.

"Oh, don't worry," Consuela said. "Gordo's just playing a joke on you."

Okay. So she had a dog that could turn invisible, as well as a raven aura sitting on her shoulder. He checked the rearview, but the backseat was still empty. The absence of anything to see didn't fill him with confidence, but he did his best to hide his misgivings.

"Where to?"

"Take a right out of the canyon."

Thomas nodded. He knew the road ended in another couple of

miles at the base of a mesa that held the ruins of an old village of the pueblo people, so he supposed that was where they were going. He wondered if they were going to hike all the way up to the ruins. He'd find out soon enough. But in the meantime, he had other questions.

"Why did you leave that feather with me?" he asked.

"It was left to wake you up."

"I wasn't asleep."

"Are you sure? What about your connection to the tribe?"

"I have that without needing to be woken up."

"Then why are you so set on leaving?"

Thomas sighed. Were they gossiping about him in the otherworld too?

"How would you even know, and why would you care?" he asked.

"I'm a friend of your Aunt Lucy."

"You mean my Aunt Leila. Aunt Lucy's passed."

"No, I mean Lucy."

Thomas took his gaze from the road for a moment to give her a confused look.

"Has no one ever explained to you," Consuela said, "that there is no such thing as linear time? What people call the past, the present, the future—it's all happening at the same time."

"Of course it is," Thomas said and somehow managed to not roll his eyes.

"I'll grant you most people tend to live in one set of moments and ignore the rest. But that doesn't make the fact of it any less true."

"I don't believe in fate," Thomas told her. "I don't believe that our lives are already all laid out for us."

"I don't either."

"But—"

"Weren't you listening? It's all happening at the same time."

"Then why does it seem linear?"

"Because," she said, "that's how we choose to view it."

"This is crazy."

"If you think this is crazy, wait till you see what comes next."

He glanced over to find her smiling, then returned his attention to his driving because they were running out of road. He moved his foot from the gas pedal to the brake.

"No, don't slow down," Consuela said.

The only way to the top of the mesa was a narrow switchback path that led up through the cacti and scrub, barely wide enough for an ATV. The road ended in a small turnaround. If they didn't slow down, they were going to smash right into a tall wall of red rocks.

"Yeah, I don't think so," Thomas told her.

Her raven aura began to cackle madly.

He slammed on the brakes but instead the car sped up. He tried hauling on the wheel but it had a mind of its own and kept them straight on a collision course with the rock face.

His knuckles whitened on the steering wheel. "I'm not some frigging immortal *ma'inawo!*" Thomas yelled. "I can't survive this."

"Use your shaman's eyes," Consuela told him over the cacophony of the ghost raven's calls and his own shouting.

"I don't have any—"

But then it was too late. Thomas shut his eyes and crossed his forearms in front of his face, bracing for the impact while he cursed the woman, her crazy aura, and her haunted car.

The impact never came.

When Thomas dared to open his eyes it was to find they were cruising down a long dirt road that went off into the desert as far as he could see. He put his hands back on the steering wheel and tried the brakes again, and this time the car slowed, finally coming to a stop. He put it in neutral, then laid his head against the steering wheel. His heart drummed in his chest and he was covered in a fine sheen of sweat. When he was finally able to sit up again, his hands shook so badly he had to keep a hold on the steering wheel.

He glared at Consuela. "What the hell was that all about?"

"You have the sight," she said. "I thought you would see the road."

She wore an apologetic look, but once again her raven aura had its head tilted back in laughter.

Thomas bristled. "It's not funny. I thought we were roadkill."

She smiled. "But we're not."

"Yeah, no thanks to you."

"You mean, thanks to us, you travelled between the worlds unscathed."

Us? he thought. He checked the rearview but the backseat remained empty. So she either had somebody in the trunk or a ghost. Or maybe she was referring to her raven aura.

At least his pulse was finally starting to slow down. The sweat had evaporated in the desert heat. His hands didn't feel so shaky anymore. He took a steadying breath.

"That's right," he said. "Thanks to you."

Both she and the raven aura still wore amused smiles.

"I still don't know what you find so funny in all of this," he said.

"Funny?" She shook her head and her expression changed. "This is serious business. We go to determine the guilt or innocence of a man of your tribe. Reuben says he has faith in you, but I'm not so sure you speak with the will of the People when you're so disconnected from them."

"So you came and gave me a feather to wake me up because you saw this would be a problem in the future."

She started to speak, but Thomas cut her off, adding, "Why don't you just look ahead and see how it all turns out?"

"It doesn't work like that."

"No? Then how does it work?"

"First, we go see your Aunt Lucy."

Thomas looked away from her and pinched the bridge of his nose. "You're making my head hurt."

"I don't mean to."

"But why can't you just look ahead to see what happens?"

"Because I can't remember how to do that anymore," she said.

Thomas let out an exasperated sigh. "Is this some kind of *ma'inawo* Alzheimer's?" he said.

"No, it's—do you know anything about Norse mythology?"

Thomas shook his head. "Not really, unless you count the Thor comics and movies."

"One of their chief thunders was named Wodan, and he had two ravens: one named Memory and one named Thought."

That twigged a recollection in Thomas. "That actually sounds familiar," he said. "Except they called him Odin in the comics I read, and he was this big hairy dude with only one eye. But he did have these two ravens, one on each shoulder."

"Except they aren't two separate ravens," she said. "Or at least they weren't always. At one time, they were a single bird, but something— the passage of time, some accident of fate—split them, and their names each represent their own part of the original bird. One holds all of its memories, the other lives day to day with only that day's thoughts."

"How are storybook ravens relevant to you losing your…" But then he thought he understood, hard though it was to believe. "Are you trying to tell me that *you're* one of Wodan's ravens?"

"No. But this is something that can happen to old *ma'inawo* corbae—the crow and raven clans. We learn to not hold on to every- thing we've experienced. We compartmentalize our experiences and memories so that we're not trying to deal with our entire history all at once. But sometimes we lose track of those hidden parts of ourselves, and they wander off to have lives of their own."

Thomas's gaze went to her raven aura, now preening its feathers, giving him the odd smug glance.

"Yes," she said. "Si'tala is my memory. She stays with me, but we can't communicate with one another."

"I guess that sucks."

She shrugged. "It has its benefits. For a *ma'inawo* as old as I am, it makes the weight of all the years less of a burden since I can't remember them."

"How many years are we talking about?"

She gazed out the window. "That I do remember. I was born in the long ago, soon after the world was born. I wasn't there to see Raven stir his pot—like his crow girls, or Cody and Old Man Puma were—but not long after that I remember stepping from the shadow realms into the world he had made for us all."

She looked back at him, smiling at his doubtful expression. "You don't believe that Raven created the world?"

"I don't know. I suppose. It's what I was taught. But I've always wondered about the other religions. The Christian god is supposed to have created the world in seven days."

"*Their* world—not ours."

"I don't understand."

"Here in the dreamlands, all times and all possibilities exist at once, and some of them are reflected in the first world. Now, can we keep driving?"

"To meet my dead aunt."

She rolled her eyes and Thomas held up his right palm. "Okay, okay," he said. "One last question."

"And that is?"

"If you can't access your memories of the past and future, how did you know to leave the feather for me yesterday morning?"

"I didn't leave it."

"But you said I needed to wake up."

She nodded. "But I wasn't the one who took the initiative to do so. I usually try to stay out of people's personal business.

"Then who…?"

His gaze went again to Si'tala, the raven aura. The ghostly bird seemed far too pleased with herself.

"Never mind," he said.

He put the Ford in gear and pulled out onto the road. With the vehicle's fat tires, the ride was pretty smooth, all things considered. There was no traffic, obviously, but habit had him checking the rearview and he was surprised to see a big eighteen-wheeler in the distance.

"Looks like we've got company," he said.

Consuela turned to look out the back window.

"That's not right," she said.

He glanced her way. "What isn't?"

"They're not supposed to be around here today."

She faced the front again and leaned forward, peering at the road that lay before them. Out of the corner of his eye he saw the raven aura, Si'tala, her expression now deadly serious, keeping her full attention on the road behind them.

Thomas had no idea what Consuela expected to see ahead. There were mountains in the distance, but he knew from his own experience of living in the foothills of the Hierro Maderas that the mountains ahead were actually a lot farther away than they appeared. Between the mountains and the car was a stretch of desert scrub with the road cutting straight through it as though it had been drawn by a ruler.

"Who's back there?" Thomas asked. "And why are you so worried?"

"I'm not worried."

Thomas glanced at her again. "Well, you look worried," he said, "and so does she," he added, tilting his head toward them both.

His gaze went back to the rearview. The big truck was gaining on them. "And if it's something that makes the spirit of death nervous, then I figure I should be, too."

He gave the gas pedal more pressure and the Ford picked up speed.

"I'm not the spirit of death." Before he could question that, she added, "Gordo is. We just choose to travel together. And he's not *the* spirit of death, either. He's *a* spirit of death. Do you think Death has the kind of time to visit every dying person individually?"

"But—"

She cut him off. "Right now I need you to pay attention. When I say make a sharp right into the scrub, just do it. No arguments, no discussion. Got it?"

Thomas glanced at the speedometer and then the rearview. Even at ninety miles an hour, the tractor-trailer was rapidly gaining on them.

Great. Thomas thought. He was in the otherworld with the travelling companion of the spirit of death and he was about to die. Who was going to see his spirit off when no one in his family or his tribe even knew where he was?

"Turn—*now!*"

Thomas didn't hesitate. He let up on the gas and hauled on the wheel. As the Ford started to slide into a turn, he goosed the gas a couple of times until the car was travelling at a ninety-degree angle to the road they'd left, then he floored it again. The car shot forward and he saw that they were almost upon a steep dip made by a dry wash cutting through the scrub. The Ford was bouncing on the uneven terrain, taking out cacti, which he knew would be ruining its perfect glossy finish, but he didn't care. What he cared about was that wash.

There was no way they were going to jump it—even at this speed—
and they were too close to turn aside.

But then the wash was gone.

As was the desert.

Instead they were roaring up a narrow road of packed red dirt with
red rock cliffs rising hundreds of feet tall on either side of them. He'd
taken another momentary glance in the rearview right before they sped
into this new world, but it had been long enough to see the long, black
eighteen-wheeler follow them off the road.

If that thing caught up with them here, it would run them over
like they were a slow rabbit and flatten them.

"Stop at the top of the road," Consuela said.

Thomas nodded. "And then what?"

"Then we climb up one of those cliffs and hope Gordo can
stop them."

Thomas didn't bother to look around for the dog. The way things
were going today, it would just magically appear somehow.

He was *so* regretting having volunteered to replace Morago.

But it was too late for regrets. Right now he had to survive. Later
he could yell at the shaman.

When they got to the top of the incline he braked hard and threw
the Ford into park. Glancing back, he watched the black eighteen-
wheeler appear on the road behind them. He heard its gears down-
shifting as it started its own ascent. Not bothering to shut off the
engine, he popped his door, jumped out, and scrambled to where
Consuela was already waiting for him at the bottom of the cliff.

"Can you climb?" she asked.

Clearly, she'd never grown up on the rez. That was pretty much all
the kids did in the Painted Lands, scampering up and down the sides
of the canyons for hours at a time. It's not like they had Xboxes. Some
families on the traditional side didn't even have TVs.

He didn't bother answering. Instead he just started up, his zigzag-
ging path determined by where he could find a decent handhold. He
half expected her to turn into a raven and just fly up—it was that kind
of a day—but instead she clambered at his side, flashing him a grin
whenever he glanced her way. Her raven aura was nowhere to be seen.

Halfway up, they came to a good-sized ledge and paused to take stock of what was happening below.

Thomas blinked. That old customized black Ford was gone. An oversized Gordo sat in its place, awaiting the arrival of the tractor-trailer as it roared its way up the last part of its ascent.

37

LEAH

L eah almost felt like an old pro when Ruby led her back into the otherworld desert. She'd already done this and she hadn't even suffered the vertigo that Marisa had. But as they left the parking lot of the tribal police station and moved into the otherworld, the red fur under Leah's hand changed texture from fur to cloth, and the next thing she knew a young Native woman was rising from all fours to stand upright beside her.

The dog was gone.

No, Leah realized, her pulse quickening. The dog wasn't gone. She'd changed into this woman.

Except that couldn't be.

Images of Aggie White Horse's paintings flashed through her mind and she remembered the old woman's words.

They are animals, but they can wear human shapes as well.

Heart racing, Leah took a couple of quick steps back from where the woman stood.

"*Ohla,*" the woman said. "Don't be nervous. I'm just Ruby in another form."

Leah swallowed hard and tried to seem cool, like she saw this kind of thing every day. From the worried look in the woman's eyes, she doubted it was working.

She didn't know why she was so freaked out. The woman version of Ruby certainly didn't appear to be dangerous. She wore jeans, hiking boots and a red and black checked flannel shirt over a white T-shirt. Her long red hair—the same colour as the dog's—was pulled back in a loose braid. Peeking out from under the collar of her shirt was a neck tattoo of a bird in flight. Only the head, shoulders and one wing of the bird were visible, the wing rising up behind her ear.

For a moment, Leah fixated on that—how strange it was that a dog would have a tattoo of a bird on her neck.

She cleared her throat and straightened her shoulders. "I'm not nervous," she said. And she promptly sat down on a nearby rock because her legs felt like jelly, or maybe the ground felt like jelly. She wasn't sure which. She just knew she had to sit down before her legs gave out.

She lowered her head between her knees until she no longer felt faint. When she raised her head again the young woman was still there. Ruby sat on her haunches a few yards away. She studied Leah, head cocked to one side.

"I'm sorry," Ruby said. "Sometimes I forget how strange this might seem to someone who has never experienced it before."

"That's me. Feeling a little freaked out, to be honest."

"So I see. But is it really so different from stepping between worlds?"

"Um—yeah."

"How so?"

"It's just…" Leah didn't know quite how to explain, so instead she said, "I did an online quiz once and according to it, my spirit animal's a spider."

Ruby's eyebrows went up. "Are you worried that you're going to turn into one while you're over here?"

"What? No. I mean—that's not going to happen, right?"

"Not unless you have cousin blood, and I can sense that you don't."

"Right. Of course not. Sorry. I'm just nervous so I'm babbling."

Leah stopped herself from going on. She took a deep breath and let it out. Ruby said nothing. She gave Leah the impression that she could easily spend the rest of the day sitting there in the sun, soaking up the heat. Considering how fall was so much chillier back in Newford, the warmth felt wonderful, though Leah was a little thirsty. What she wouldn't give for one of the bottles of water that were in the rental back at Aggie White Horse's place.

"So," Leah said, "you can turn into a dog."

"Not exactly. I was born into the Red Dog Clan. What I can do is turn into a human. Reuben's boys turn into dogs."

"Reuben?"

"The guy who was with Steve. It's a tribal thing. There's something in their blood that allows those who join the Warrior Society to be able to change into dogs."

"But you're really a dog?"

"Is that such a bad thing?"

Leah shook her head. "No, it just seems strange—from my perspective, I mean. Which do you like better?"

"Definitely being a dog. We don't have your drama—like what was going on back there with Sadie and Steve and everybody. When we're not playing, we just lie around and take it easy, explore a little, sniff each others' butts."

Leah's eyes opened wider and Ruby laughed.

"Just seeing if you're paying attention," she said. "Are you feeling any better?"

"Actually, I am. You being a dog seems to make perfect sense now."

"Good, though I have to say that if we were both dogs, we would have gotten to this understanding a lot more quickly. Now I want to ask you something."

"Go ahead."

"Why is it so important to you that Steve is this person you say he was? Why can't you just accept who he is now? Maybe he was that person once, maybe he wasn't—but either way, why does it matter to you?"

Leah didn't say anything for a long moment.

"If you'd asked me that a week ago," she finally said, "I would've had an easy answer for you. Now it's gotten more complicated."

"Complicated how?"

"I'm not so sure anymore that it's anybody's business—you know, a famous person's private life. Especially when there's so much else going on in the world, bad stuff that affects ordinary people's lives."

"If that's the case, why do you still feel this need to confront Steve?"

"I don't want to confront him so much as ask him a question."

"And if you don't like the answer?"

Leah shrugged. "Then I have to live with it."

Ruby studied her for a long moment before she finally nodded. "Okay," she said. She stood up, the motion an effortless flow.

Leah wasn't sure she'd be able to manage to stay upright, but she got up from the rock anyway. She swayed for a moment until Ruby put a hand on her bicep, steadying her. "Will you be all right?" she asked.

Leah nodded. "But I could use a drink. You don't have a water bottle magically stashed away somewhere, do you?"

Ruby lifted her head, her nostrils working.

"Better," she said after a moment. "I smell a spring…" She turned slowly, then pointed to some distant rocks. "That way. Can you make it that far, or do you want me to get you some?"

"And carry it in what? Your mouth?"

"I hadn't thought of that."

"I can make it as far as those rocks," Leah said. "Maybe you can tell me what the deal is with that kid Sadie while we're walking."

Ruby's brow furrowed. "I don't know what to tell you," she said as they started across the desert scrub toward the spring. "I usually don't have any trouble reading you five-fingered beings, but she's complicated."

"Five-fingered beings?" Leah asked, falling in step beside her.

Ruby lifted a hand and wiggled her fingers. "You're born with five fingers on your hands."

Leah smiled. "And you're born with paws."

Ruby nodded.

"Why are you having trouble reading Sadie?" Leah asked.

"We dog clans tend to be impetuous," Ruby told her. "We jump in because something feels right rather than thinking it through. We form these immediate bonds with people and because of our nature, we remain loyal to them long past the time that anyone else would have cut themselves loose. But we can't. We're too trusting and loyal, and we keep expecting the best from those we befriend."

"None of which sounds like a bad thing."

"Tell that to the dog chained up in somebody's yard, or the one that gets cuffed every time the five-fingers around her are in a bad mood."

Leah frowned. She'd never had a pet dog or cat. Not even a fish. But she wasn't so naive as to think that pets were never mistreated.

"Okay," she said. "That sucks. But what does any of that have to do with Sadie?"

"I always seem to be drawn to damaged humans—the ones that need help. When Sadie arrived at Aggie's place I could smell the bruises and cuts on her. She was scared of me—she was scared of the whole pack—but I thought maybe I could help her."

"But you couldn't."

"Not when half her hurts were self-inflicted. She cuts herself."

Leah nodded. Kids like that showed up from time to time at the Arts Court back in Newford. Kids that did more harm to themselves than to anyone around them, and all you could do was try to be there for them. Maybe gently suggest counseling in a way that made it seem like it was their idea. But mostly, you had to show them you'd stay the course, no matter how messed up they were. Or got. It wasn't easy. Mostly, it was heartbreaking.

"What did you do?" she asked.

"Nothing," Ruby said. "I didn't know what to do."

"It's hard to know what to do in a situation like that."

Then Leah thought of what Ruby had said about being drawn to damaged humans. She remembered that when Ruby was a dog, she lived with Aggie.

"So is Aggie—"

"Damaged?" Ruby replied before she could finish her question.

"It's just, when you said—"

Ruby laughed. "Aggie's the most well-adjusted person I know, *ma'inawo* or human. I live there because those dogs are my pack. The Red Dog Clan have always lived on White Horse land."

They were at the rocks now and Leah scrambled up, following the route Ruby took. Water trickled from a seep higher up, forming a clear pool in the rocks below, the bright sunlight glinting on its surface.

"Where does the water go?" Leah asked.

Ruby shrugged. "Back into the ground?"

She cupped her hands and drank. Leah followed suit and was startled at how cold the water was. She drank again before joining Ruby where she sat on a slab of red rock up above the seep.

For a time, Leah simply got lost in the view. From this vantage, the desert scrub seemed to go on forever, flat and unending, but having just walked through a part of it to get to the spring, she knew how the deceptive the look of the terrain was from this height. Down there, the land was broken up with hidden washes and any number of dips and swells.

Finally she turned to her companion to find Ruby with a faraway look in her eyes, her brow creased.

"What's the matter?" Leah asked.

Ruby gave her a quick smile. "Oh nothing. I was just thinking about Sadie."

"How she might be hurting herself?"

Ruby shook her head. "Partly. But after her performance back there, I'm more worried about her hurting somebody else."

"We should go back."

"No. I told Aggie I'd bring you to Steve and keep you safe."

"Steve can wait."

Ruby gave her a sharp look.

"Really," Leah said. "You can find him any time, right? So let's go back and make sure everything's okay."

"You're sure? You flew all this way…"

In truth, Leah wasn't sure. But nothing had turned out the way she'd expected it would and she felt she needed time to process it. She certainly hadn't expected to find Jackson Cole actually alive, and meeting him had not gone well. If he *was* Jackson Cole. Maybe he really was Jackson's cousin. Who knew?

And then the conversation she'd had with the old desert rat last night at the motel was still echoing in her head, making her question not just what she was doing here, but what she was doing with her life.

She had too many questions and not nearly enough answers.

Somebody else's problems were a perfect distraction. Not that she wished problems on anybody, but since they were there, she might as well let them take her outside of her own head.

"I'm sure," she told Ruby.

The young woman's grin made her whole face light up. She jumped to her feet and reached for Leah's hand.

"I know a shortcut back," she said.

38

THOMAS

The boom/hiss of the tractor-trailer's air brakes rose in the air, echoing back and forth in the canyon.

Thomas stared down the rock face at Gordo, teeth bared, crouching on the ground where the Ford had been. He remembered what Consuela had said about her and the dog being travelling companions. When the Caddy had pulled into the trading post parking lot, the dog hadn't been there. It was the same when the Ford had sat at the mouth of the canyon waiting for them. Both of the vehicles were black. Like the dog. And now the dog was huge, and the Ford was nowhere to be seen.

"Are you serious?" Thomas said. "Gordo shapeshifts into a car? What is he—a Transformer?"

"A what?"

"You know, the little toy cars that you can twist around and turn into robots?"

"Don't be ridiculous," Consuela said.

But he was longer listening to her. With the truck stopped, the doors of the cab opened and a trio of enormous men stepped out onto the road, one from the driver's side, two from the passenger's. They were tall and bulky with muscle. One was a black man with a shaved head. The other two had a Native cast to their skin and features, but Thomas didn't recognize the tribe.

"Who are they?" he asked.

"It's a salvage crew."

"Salvaging what, exactly?"

"Anything alive that's travelling down the roads of the dead. It's usually old vehicles—something that's been invested with so much love that when they're finally set aside, their spirits keep driving, except now they're heading down the highways and byways of the spirit realms. If they happen to stray onto one of the roads of the dead, they become fair claim to the salvagers."

"Vehicles invested with love."

Consuela nodded. "Cars. Pickup trucks. Bicycles from one's childhood. Even old wagons and carts. Anything that somebody drove and loved enough to give it a life after it's been scrapped in the first world."

"So why have they been chasing *us*? Gordo wasn't some scrapped vehicle in another life, was he?"

Her raven aura appeared on her shoulder, eyes wide, and shook its head, but it was Consuela who answered. "They're after you."

"That's nuts. I don't have some inner car totem."

"No, but you're alive and you were on the roads of the dead. That makes you fair game."

"So were you. Unless you're…" He let his voice trail off.

"Alive, dead," Consuela said. "That kind of thing doesn't apply to beings like Gordo and me."

Thomas turned his attention back down to the road. The salvage crew was approaching Gordo with wariness. Then one of them looked up and saw Thomas. He pointed and said something to his companions, then they all looked up and started moving toward them. When the first one reached for a handhold, Gordo growled, a big, chest-deep rumble that Thomas swore was making the rock ledge they were perched on shake. He could see the huge dog bunching its muscles, ready to pursue the salvagers. But before he could spring at them, the tractor-trailer's horn blasted and the big vehicle lurched forward, cutting him off.

"Tell me somebody's driving that thing," Thomas said.

He turned to Consuela. Again, her aura was no longer present.

"It doesn't matter," she said. "It's enough to keep Gordo busy and they'll be after us."

Sure enough, the salvage crew were already climbing up toward the ledge. Gordo was behind the truck, no longer in sight.

Crap, Thomas thought.

But he didn't pause to argue. He scrambled up the cliff after Consuela, the threat of the salvagers enough to make him take chances with precarious holds he never would have normally trusted.

He didn't look down as he climbed—he'd learned that lesson the hard way as a kid, when he'd almost broken his leg from a fall. Instead, he concentrated on the lip of the cliff above. He took the same route Consuela did, which made the climb a little easier, though no less dangerous.

As they neared the top of the cliff he noticed something funny about the sky. There appeared to be lines running across it, parallel to each other. It wasn't until they'd scrambled up the last few feet that he realized what he was seeing. That wasn't a sky above them—not a real one. It was a sky painted on boards. The sheer impossibility made him giddy with the absurdity of it all.

He pulled himself up onto the cliff top. "Well, thank God for that," he said, collapsing on his back.

"What are you *doing*?" Consuela said. "They'll be up here soon and there aren't any boulders we can roll down on them."

Si'tala suddenly manifested on her shoulders, urgently pumping her body up and down as though doing knee bends.

Thomas grinned and waved a hand at them, then pointed upward. "See that?" he said.

"I'm not blind," Consuela answered. "Give me a hand. Those boards look old. With any luck we can push enough of them aside to get out of here."

Thomas shook his head. "That just tells me that all of this is a dream. This whole day has been weird from start to finish, but come on. A sky painted on a bunch of boards that stretch as far as we can see? Let the salvagers come. I'm going to wake up at some point and all of this will have been meaningless anyway."

Consuela dropped to his side. She grabbed him by the shirt and pulled his face right up to hers. In his peripheral vision, Thomas saw Si'tala's raven eyes peering at him with equal urgency.

"We can't save you from them!" Consuela yelled. "These are the dreamlands and you're not here like you usually are, your spirit travelling while your body lies asleep in its bed. *You* are here, and if those salvagers catch you they'll suck the life out of you the same way they do anything else that strays onto their roads. That's what sustains them."

"This is insane."

She let him go and he fell back to the rocks. She stared down at him, the bizarre slats of the painted sky behind her. Si'tala studied him as well, her expression dark and unreadable.

"Stay and die," Consuela said, "or accept what you can't believe and live another day. You have a choice, but the window is closing with each moment you wait."

Thomas thought of his sisters and brother. Of his mother and Auntie. If he were gone, who would take care of them?

The charity of the tribe, he supposed. But his family was *his* responsibility. Taking care of them was his job.

He'd been accepting the impossible all day. Why stop now?

"Okay," he said.

Consuela stepped close and lashed out with one foot. Thomas dodged the blow but it wasn't aimed at him. He heard someone grunt, the sound of hands scrabbling for purchase. A distant thud.

"That buys us a moment," Consuela said.

"Did you kill him?"

"No such luck. He landed on the ledge." She cupped her hands. "Let me give you a boost. See if you can reach those boards."

Those boards.

This was insane.

But he got to his feet, put a foot in the saddle of her hands. She lifted him up, over her head, her arms straight. She was stronger than he expected and held him steady as he used the heel of his hand to hammer against the nearest board.

It burst upward in a cloud of dust and dirt that came back down in a shower with bits of old, rotted wood. He was blinded by the bright light of another sky beyond the boards.

How was that even possible?

Don't think, he told himself.

He grabbed hold of another board on one side of the rectangular hole he'd just made and hammered it with the palm of his free hand. More debris showered him. The light grew brighter.

"Hurry up!" Consuela called.

He leaned a little to the side, bracing himself by his grip on the one board. Consuela continued to hold him steady as the heel of his hand drove up into yet another board. A fourth, a fifth. By then there was enough room that he could pull himself through by turning to one side. He got a grip on the board with his free hand and hauled himself up.

Without bothering to look where he was, he lay flat out and reached down a hand.

"Move back," Consuela told him.

He did as she said and a huge raven rose up out of the hole he'd made. He looked back down to see the top of the cliff, the men climbing, the truck on the road far below, trying to run over Gordo's enormous body. Tires spun, sending up clouds of red dust, but the truck couldn't budge the dog.

Vertigo hit him and he would have tumbled back down through the hole if Consuela hadn't grabbed him by his belt and pulled him back.

"We need to get moving," she said.

Thomas stood up and looked around. They stood in the ruin of an old barn in the middle of some desert. Half of one wall remained of the structure. The rest had tumbled down uncountable years ago. No other structures were in sight except for a stone fireplace that stood in the midst of another mess of dried and broken wood. There was no break in the desert. The scrub spread out as far as he could see to every horizon.

"What about Gordo?" he asked.

"He'll get to us when he can. He wouldn't miss a visit with your Aunt Lucy."

My dead Aunt Lucy, Thomas thought.

But all he did was brush the dust and debris from his clothes, shake out his hair, and nod. She wanted stoic? He could play stoic.

"Then we'd better head out," he said.

Consuela started to walk, picking what appeared to Thomas to be a random direction.

"What about the salvage crew?" he asked, falling in step with her.

She shrugged. "Now that we've made it to here, we can lose them. But I'd stay off the roads of the dead for the next little while."

"Wasn't my idea in the first place."

"Don't think I won't hear about it from your aunt."

All things happen at the same time, Thomas thought. So had she known beforehand that they would escape? And if so, why hadn't she known that they'd run into trouble in the first place?

On her shoulders, Si'tala looked at him as though she could read his mind. She rattled her beak. It made no sound, but Thomas heard a vague clatter inside his head.

39

JERRY

Jerry shoved away the chair that had tripped him, and got to his feet. He hesitated, torn between going after the girl and finding out what was happening with Aggie.

"I need a first aid kit and some duct tape—quick!" Marisa yelled out. That settled it.

"On it!" Jerry called back. He grabbed a white case with a red cross on it from the shelf beside his desk, then tried to think of where they kept duct tape.

"Here," Ralph called as he tossed the roll to Jerry. "Ambulance is on the way."

"Get an APB out on that kid," he told Ralph as he ran toward the holding room.

Ralph nodded, then pulled his gun and went out the door after Sadie.

Jerry knew he wasn't going to catch her. He'd already heard one of the pickups start up and go tearing out of the parking lot.

What a clusterfuck of a day.

But there was no time to worry about Sadie, or the chief, who was still on the line, or the suspects that were supposed to be in his lockup but had escaped into some otherworld desert.

He ran into the holding room and dropped down beside Aggie. There was too much blood. How could there be so much blood already?

Why wasn't that ambulance here yet?

Aggie's eyes were closed, but she was still breathing. Trouble was, she was bleeding out. Marisa had both hands pressed against Aggie's stomach. The old woman's blood oozed through her fingers.

"When you're ready," she said, "we'll get her blouse up and try taping some bandages to her stomach."

Jerry nodded. And then pray it was enough until the ambulance got here.

He opened a couple of large gauze pads from the first aid kit and sandwiched them together. "Ready," he said.

Marisa pulled up Aggie's top and Jerry pressed the pads against the bloody wound. "We should be cleaning this," he said.

"Yeah, we should," Marisa agreed as she picked up the roll of duct tape. "But let's stop the bleeding and let the hospital worry about infection."

She pulled free a long strip of the grey tape and cut it with her teeth. Jerry adjusted the position of his hands so that she had room to tape the pads in place. Two more strips of tape, and the gauze pads were completely covered and tightly held in place.

"Can I get another pad?" Marisa asked. She used this one to gently sop around the edges of the tape to make sure no blood was seeping from under them.

"Where the hell's that ambulance?" Jerry muttered.

Marisa checked Aggie's pulse. Satisfied that the old woman was still with them, Marisa cradled her head on her lap and murmured soothingly to her.

Jerry stood up, wiping his hands with tissues, then going to the door to look out toward the main office. Nobody was manning the front desk, so he supposed Ralph was still out chasing that damned girl. Then he remembered he'd left the chief hanging on the other end of the phone.

He started back to his desk, but before he could reach it, the front door opened. Marisa's friend Leah and a young Indian woman he didn't know came through. The stranger lifted her head like an animal sniffing the air. Then she made a beeline for the room where Aggie lay.

"Not so fast," Jerry told her.

He grabbed for her, but she brushed off his hand and he swore he could hear a low growl as she went by.

"Hang on there," he said, turning after her.

His hand went to the butt of his gun. "I said—" he started. But the siren of the approaching ambulance pulling into the parking lot outside was enough to distract him.

"What's going on?" Leah asked when he looked her way.

"Honestly?" he said. "The worst day ever."

He went to the door to usher the paramedics in, studiously ignoring the faint shouting he could hear coming from his phone as he went by his desk. He led the medics back to where Aggie lay, Leah trailing behind them.

"Who did this to her?" the young woman was asking Marisa.

The blonde was still cradling Aggie's head on her lap. She gave Jerry a helpless look. He wasn't surprised at her being intimidated. The stranger loomed over her, radiating danger.

"You need to back off," he told the woman, hand still on his gun.

The paramedics stopped because he was blocking the doorway.

"I'll back off when someone answers my question."

"Please," Marisa said. "Let the paramedics through."

Jerry moved to one side as the paramedics entered.

"Get out of the way and let them help her," he said to the woman. The stranger blinked, then gave a brusque nod. She retreated a couple of steps away so the medics could get to work.

"Who are you?" Jerry asked.

"A friend of Abigail's."

"Yeah? If you're such a good friend, how come I haven't seen you around before?"

"Abigail doesn't only have friends in this world," the woman said.

Jerry so didn't want to get back into that crap.

"Her name's Ruby," Leah said from behind him.

The paramedics were easing Aggie onto a stretcher. Marisa stood up, looking from Leah to the stranger.

"Well, Ruby—" Jerry started, but whatever he'd been about to say dried up inside him when he started remembering.

Ruby.

Aggie had a dog named Ruby whose fur was the same colour as this woman's hair.

The dog Ruby had gone into the otherworld with Leah, and now Leah was back, and there wasn't any dog around.

He hated where this was going.

"The girl did this," Marisa said. "Sadie."

Ruby nodded. "That's all I needed to know."

She stopped by the stretcher and tenderly touched Aggie's cheek with the back of her hand. Then she lifted her head, a grim look in her eyes. "Her life is in your hands," she told the paramedics. "I hold you responsible for what happens to her."

A moment later she was stalking back into the front office.

"Hey, wait!" Jerry called.

She moved so fast that she was out the door within seconds.

Marisa pushed past him and followed the stretcher. "I'm going with Aggie," she said. "Does she have any family we can call?"

Jerry shook his head. "But I'll get word out to the rez."

Leah came over and grabbed Marisa's arm. "Are you okay?" she asked.

"Except for watching that girl—oh, you mean all this blood on me."

"Well, yeah."

"It's not mine."

"You should change."

"There's no time," Marisa said, turning to catch up to the medics.

"Then I'm coming with you," Leah told her. "We can swap clothes at the hospital and I'll go back to the motel to get something clean."

Marisa nodded, distracted.

At first the paramedics weren't going to let them in, but Jerry came out and told them it was okay, saying the first thing that came to mind.

"They're Aggie's granddaughters," he said.

He watched the ambulance pull away, standing out in the parking lot until it had disappeared down the road, then finally returned to his desk. He wanted to put his head down and not have to deal with any more crap. Instead, he picked up the phone and began to explain the situation to the chief.

40

ABIGAIL WHITE HORSE

Aggie had been here before—in dreams, in spirit, if never in the flesh. That being the case, she could only assume things were not going well for her back at the tribal police station after Sadie had knifed her.

She vaguely remembered the surprise she'd felt. The flash of pain. The sudden weakness. Drifting away while someone repeated her name over and over, asking her not to leave them.

"It's not like I have a choice," she wanted to say as the dark cloud washed over her, but the words never left her mouth. They died somewhere between her thinking them and her tongue, then curled up and went to sleep in a corner of her mouth.

And she found herself here.

Pragmatic as Aggie was, she didn't waste any more time in shock at Sadie's attack. It was what it was, and if this was how the wheel turned for her today, who was she to protest? In truth, it was almost worth it to be here so unexpectedly because she loved this place as she did nowhere else.

She stood on a ledge, high in the mountains—which mountains, she couldn't say, but they bore some resemblance to the Maderas she knew so well. Below her, the wild benighted terrain spread out in a cluster of jagged peaks, rolling off into the distance like so many waves of a vast and stormy sea of stone. It was usually night when she came here, but she had never had trouble seeing in the darkness. Sometimes when she came in the daytime she saw eagles riding the winds. They would fly close to where she stood and dip their wings in salute before gliding on. Other times, she would simply stand and listen to the song of the winds. She would remember a time when she was young and in love, and stood in a place like this with more than a memory at her side.

She knew from previous visits that if she followed the ledge it would switch back and take her up to the top of the peak—a large flat platform with a jumble of rocks strewn about like a child's discarded toys. She went there now, walking easily along the ledge, unconcerned with the drop below. The switchback took her up a gentle incline and then she stood with only the night sky above her and what felt like the whole of the world spread out below.

For a long time she simply drank in the beauty. She realized she wouldn't really mind if she never returned to her body.

"Now that's some view."

Turning from the panorama, she found Old Man Puma lounging on a nearby rock.

Although he lived up in the mountains behind her house, Aggie didn't see him often and even then, it was usually in his mountain lion shape. Today he was in another familiar guise, that of an old man with hair the colour of his *ma'inawo* fur, dressed in a white cotton shirt and jeans. His feet were bare.

The *ma'inawo* loved to tell stories about him. Lately, they were all amused with the rumours that he was training a small group of young *ma'inawo* who were driving him to distraction. It was even said that one of them wasn't a cousin, but a five-fingered being. Aggie wasn't sure how much stock to put in the stories since *ma'inawo* were just as likely to make things up if they didn't have any actual gossip to relate, and she didn't know him well enough to ask.

"*Ohla*, Diego," she said. "I'd offer you some tobacco but I didn't know I'd be seeing you."

"That's okay. I never smoke up here. We're already so close to the thunders we don't need to try to get their attention."

"Just as well," Aggie said. "They wouldn't have any interest in an old woman like me anyway."

"You'd be surprised what interests the thunders." His yellow-green eyes looked past her to the view before he added, "Our mountains were like these once. Untouched, unpeopled. No jet trails in the air. No hikers or hunters."

His full name among the *ma'inawo* was Diego Madera, and it was said that the mountains were named after him. She, too, remembered what it was like to see the incursion of civilization into the foothills of what had once been all wild land.

"Sometimes people make poor neighbours," she said.

"The Kikimi have been good neighbours for a very long time now."

"Even with the casino and the hunters Sammy brings into the mountains?"

Diego gave her a curious look. "Those ones aren't really Kikimi anymore," he said. "Not when they've turned their backs on their traditions."

Aggie had never thought of it like that before.

They fell silent for a time. Aggie didn't know what was on her companion's mind, but she wasn't thinking of anything. She let her eyes drink in some more of the mountains, let her ears listen to the music the winds made. But eventually she came back to wondering why she was here.

"Am I dead or am I dreaming?" she said.

She didn't realize she'd spoken aloud until Diego answered, "Maybe a little bit of both."

She turned to him again. "The one, I can understand, but how can you be a little bit dead?"

He shrugged. "It depends on how close you are to dying, I suppose. What happened anyway?"

He was looking at her midriff. When she looked down herself she saw all the blood on her blouse. Lifting the fabric revealed pads of gauze held in place with duct tape.

"Huh," she said. "I never noticed that until now."

Then she told him about Steve bringing Sadie to her place and everything that had followed.

Diego frowned. "She cooked with you? She ate the food you made together? She drank your tea?"

"She's troubled."

"That's no excuse."

"I know." She sighed. "I suppose kindness might have killed me. Still, there are worse ways to go. And what did Crazy Horse say?"

"*Hóka héy,*" Diego said. "It is a good day to die. But it's also a good day to live."

Aggie smiled. "True. I still have stories to hear. Portraits to paint." She looked down at her bloody blouse again. "If I don't make it back to my body will you tell the other *ma'inawo* not to take it out on the girl?"

"If you don't make it back to your body, there's nothing I can do to stop them. Still, I'll pass along your message if the winds haven't already done it for you."

"Is that what they do?" Aggie asked. "Because I hear their song, but not the words."

"The winds don't have words the way you and I do," Diego told her. "But most cousins know their language." He laughed. "And it's certainly easier than deciphering the language of the mountains. The stones can take a half a day just to say '*ohla.*'"

"It's a wonderful world," Aggie said. "I'm going to miss it."

"Go back, then. See if you can't wear your skin for a few more years."

"I get a choice?"

"There are always choices. Maybe you'll return to your body to find it's failed. But maybe you'll fit right back under its broken skin. If you survive, come see me. I know the story of a good healing medicine."

Aggie touched her stomach. Her blouse was wet and her fingers came away red.

"I can't feel that," she said. "There's no pain. Is that a good or a bad sign?"

"It's a sign that you're not making your choice. Close your eyes. Decide to live or let go."

Aggie nodded and did as he said. As soon as she closed her eyes she felt as though she was floating in the starred sky that had unwound above them. She could no longer feel the rock underfoot. She couldn't hear or feel the wind. She wasn't sure if she was deciding to live, or letting go.

And then she was no longer aware of anything at all.

THOMAS

As they walked through the desert scrub, Thomas kept turning around to look at the ruins of the old barn behind them until finally a dip in the land hid the structure from sight.

"Don't worry," Consuela said. "They won't follow us here."

"You said that before. What makes you so sure?"

"Because now we walk the roads of the living," Consuela told him.

Roads? Thomas thought. He couldn't even spy a deer trail.

"But you'll need to be careful," she went on, "the next time you're on one of the roads of the dead."

Her ghostly raven twin nodded at him from her perch on Consuela's shoulder.

"If I ever get home, I don't plan on walking anywhere except in the world where I was born."

Consuela nodded. "Good plan. Unfortunately, you don't always get to choose where the wheel takes you."

"That's true. I might get hijacked again by some crazy immortal lady who can turn into a bird."

Consuela frowned at him, but the ghostly Si'tala threw back her head and cackled.

"This did not go as I intended," Consuela admitted.

Thomas figured that was about as much of an apology as he was going to get.

"So let's go find Sammy and get this over with," he told her.

"We will. But we're so close now. Don't you want to see your aunt?"

His dead aunt.

Not particularly.

But Consuela was pointing to a plume of smoke ahead. "It's not far now," she said.

Thomas remembered what Morago had advised him before he'd gone off with Consuela.

Make no promises and speak as little as possible.

That hadn't gone well so far. He was probably lucky she hadn't already turned him into a toad or a lizard. Maybe that was still to come.

"Sure," he said, to mollify her if nothing else. "We've come this far, we might as well talk to my dead ancestors."

"Just one."

He nodded.

"And in this place," Consuela added, "she isn't dead."

Thomas sighed. "So let's go see her," he said.

His head was starting to hurt again. He'd seen Aunt Lucy dead, laid out in their cabin before the funeral. He'd seen her brought to Ancestors Canyon, her body a slender twig shape under a sheet.

But in this place, apparently, she was alive.

This place.

He tried not to think of how the ground underfoot was only a few inches of dirt over wooden boards that provided the sky for a whole other world than this. Not that he trusted this world, either. He kept stealing surreptitious glances at the cacti and stunted trees they passed, expecting them to be made of painted cardboard or wooden cutouts. And was that a real sky above them or the underside of yet another world?

Out of the corner of his eye he could see Si'tala studying him as they walked along. For a change, there was a sympathetic expression in her dark eyes, as though she knew what was going through his head. Then, as they walked down into a dry wash, she lifted from Consuela's shoulders and flew on ahead.

Thomas stopped dead in his tracks and watched her go. He'd never seen anything like that before. Animal spirit auras—so far as he'd seen —did not leave their hosts. They were auras, manifestations of their host's animal blood, not separate entities capable of individual expression. Consuela's aura had been different from the start, but he hadn't realized how different.

Consuela looked back at him from the top of the dry wash's far bank. "What is it?" she asked. "You're not having second thoughts, are you?"

Thomas could only point to the sky behind her. "Si'tala," he finally said. "The raven. She flew from your shoulders."

Consuela nodded. "Yes, she does that from time to time. Are you coming? I can smell your aunt's beans and flatbread from here."

Before he could ask how that was possible—that an aura could extract herself from her host—Consuela disappeared from view. He guessed there was no point in asking about the invisibility acts Si'tala could pull, either.

He sighed and scrambled up the embankment, pushing through a gap between two palo verde trees and sidestepping the thorny arms of a cholla to catch up to her. Then it was too late to even try to pursue the subject because they'd reached…no, not his aunt's house. His aunt was dead. *Someone's* house.

It was a ranch-style structure, longer than it was wide, with adobe walls and a roof of saguaro ribs. It had a dirt yard in front with a small corral to one side, a pair of outbuildings on the other that were little more than shacks. It seemed verdant here compared to the arid landscape around them. Thomas noted what must be a spring-fed pond just past the shacks. Green reeds and grasses grew up along its shore, spreading off into a small meadow just beyond. A tall river oak and a few large mesquite trees were also clearly benefitting from the water.

In the shade of one of the mesquites was an adobe oven—the source of the smoke that Consuela had pointed out earlier. Standing in front of it, cooking, was a woman with long braided hair, dressed in a plain cotton skirt and embroidered blouse. Thomas felt a shock of recognition when she lifted her head and smiled at their approach.

She looked just like his mother had when she'd been a young woman, who in turn had borne a strong resemblance to her two aunts, Lucy and Leila. Si'tala was perched on the chimney of the oven, obviously unfazed by the heat. Lying in the deeper shade close to the trunk of the mesquite was a large black dog, happily gnawing the meat off a soup bone. Thomas felt a small shiver go up his spine. The dog resembled Gordo, but Gordo was back there in the salvagers' world.

"*Ohla*," the woman called to them. "You took your time. Gordo told me you'd be here a half hour ago."

Okay, Thomas thought. So not only could death spirit Gordo change size—or Transformer-like, turn himself into a vehicle—but he could also transport himself to another world at will.

Still, that latest bit of information seemed trivial compared to this woman's strong resemblance to his family.

She laid down the utensil in her hand and stepped away from the adobe oven, opening her arms wide. "Thomas!" she said. "Come give your old Aunt Lucy a hug."

She didn't look old and she didn't look at all like his Aunt Lucy—or at least not the one the family had accompanied to the Ancestors Canyon after she'd died. That Aunt Lucy had been withered and all dried up, like a sad little figure of cacti ribs and braided dead grass, woven into human shape. She hadn't seemed human. She'd no longer looked like any of the Corn Eyes women except for her surviving sister, Leila.

This woman was vibrant and young, full of life.

"How is this even possible?" he asked.

From the oven's chimney, Si'tala cocked her head as if to say, after all that's happened today, you have to ask?

"How is it not possible?" Aunt Lucy said, as enigmatic as the Aunties ever were.

And as he let her embrace him, he knew that however impossible it might seem, it was his Aunt Lucy.

His arms went around her and he held her tight.

"What are you doing here?" she asked. She pulled back but held his face in her hands for a moment longer, as though she was memorizing every element of his features.

"I have no idea," Thomas said, then nodded toward Consuela. "You'll have to ask her. She brought me here."

Aunt Lucy looked at the raven woman.

"He's drifting away from the People," Consuela said. "I thought you could talk some sense into him."

Aunt Lucy looked back and forth between them, then settled her gaze back on Consuela. "We each have to define our own connection to the tribe," she said. "You should know that."

"But all he wants to do is go away."

"Then that's his definition, and who are we to argue?"

"But—"

Aunt Lucy shrugged. "Some of us are content to never see the next canyon while some of us have the wind in our hearts. So it will take him a little longer to connect. Sooner or later, everybody comes back."

"I'm standing right here," Thomas said as they talked about him.

Si'tala's shoulders shook with silent laughter.

"I know," Aunt Lucy said. "And just look at what a fine young man you've turned out to be. Your mother must be so proud of you."

"Everybody comes back," Consuela repeated. "But they don't necessarily come back better. Look at Sammy Swift Grass. Turning his back on the People. Opening that casino. Hunting cousins in the mountains. Now isn't the time to leave the Painted Lands to find oneself."

"I'm not some hero who can stop Sammy," Thomas said before Aunt Lucy could respond. "Nobody's going to listen to me. And why do you even care? You're *ma'inawo*, not Kikimi."

"Except what happens on the Painted Lands affects my people too," said Consuela. "Do you think there is so much free range left that the cousins can live wherever they choose? We've had our lands stolen too—without even the dubious benefit of a treaty for the five-fingered beings to break. The Maderas were a last refuge for many of us, but now we're being hunted there, as well."

"You should be talking to Morago, not me."

"I did. But when I came to him, he gave me you. Remember?"

Thomas nodded, unable to hide his regret. "And I'm only here to watch you kill Sammy," he said. "All your problems will be solved then."

Consuela glared at him and Thomas took a step back. "I have yet to speak to Sammy," she said. "Do you think I would kill him out of hand without allowing him to explain himself?"

"I have no idea how you expect this to play out. But I'm pretty sure Sammy will be dead when the dust settles. Don't pretend you haven't already decided that."

"I have made no such decision. And even if his life does need to be taken as a blood-debt to the *ma'inawo* that were slain, it won't change anything. Someone else will only step up to take his place."

Consuela glanced at Aunt Lucy. "They need to remember the ways of the People. How the Kikimi respect their neighbours and the land that hosts them."

Looking directly at Thomas, she added, "But how can this happen when someone such as you, gifted with a shaman's vision, wants nothing more than to leave?"

"Why do you even need a shaman's vision?" Thomas asked. "All time happens at once," he said. "Isn't that what you told me? Past, present and future. So you already know how this turns out, right? And if it's already happened, what makes you think any of us can change it?"

Consuela pointed to her raven ghost sister. "She knows, not I."

Thomas remembered what Consuela had told him when they were first driving through the otherworld—how it was Si'tala who had left the feather to wake his connection to the traditions. What had the raven aura seen in the future to make her do that?

"The future isn't permanent," Aunt Lucy said. "The decisions we make today affect both the past and the future."

"You know that doesn't make any sense," Thomas said.

"Not now," Aunt Lucy said. "Not to you." She took his arm and steered him toward an old wooden table on the far side of the oven. "I've prepared a meal for you. Come sit with me and tell me what it is you hope to find, away from the Painted Lands."

42

STEVE

"So who do we go after first?" Calico asks after we've put some distance between us and the others. "Sammy or the girl's father?"

"I don't see how we have to do anything," I say. "Things'll play out and people will know we're innocent."

"I'm thinking Sammy," Calico goes on, as though I haven't said anything.

"I'm with you," Reuben says.

I stop dead and wait for them to look back at me. "Seriously?" I say. "Anything happens to either of them, it'll come back on us. Maybe it'll even lend some weight to the kid's crazy accusations."

"So?" Calico says.

Reuben nods, agreeing with her.

"What's the problem?" Calico asks. "Justice is done and you can stay safely in the otherworld. What do you need that we can't send somebody over to get for you?"

"My life. My place. The people that I know."

Calico smiles. "Says the lone wolf who spends most of his life alone in the desert."

"But it's because I choose to, not because I have to. And what about you, Reuben? Are you willing to give up everything to live here in the wilds? The trading post? Your dog boys? Being the tribe's War Leader?"

Reuben frowns. "From what I could tell, that was Sammy's story, not hers."

"You think the kid won't jump in on it, if it serves her? Are the Aunts going to keep you on if you can't show your face in the rez? What about the heat all of this is going to bring down on the entire tribe? The reputation of stealing and raping white kids?"

"He's right," Reuben tells Calico.

"Maybe about the kid and her crazy father," she says. "But Sammy needs to learn there are boundaries he can't cross, no matter how much money he's got to throw around."

I shake my head.

"I'm not saying *we* kill him," she says. "We just need to show him some major consequences. A couple of months trying to make it on his own in the otherworld might do the trick."

"And when *he* disappears—maybe for good?" I ask. "Who're they going to blame?"

I look to Reuben for support, but his usually cheerful features have settled into a stern mask. "If we let Sammy get away with what happened to Derek, not to mention his lies about us," he says, "it'll just happen again. And it *will* happen."

"Is that your hate-on talking, or something you honestly believe?"

"Does it matter? It's still true. You know it is."

And I do. But I still can't help but feel there's got to be a better way of dealing with this. I've gone all these years off the grid, minding my own business and staying under anybody's radar. How the hell could it all have gone off the rails so fast?

One good turn is how. Not minding my own business, like Possum always told me to. But it wasn't like I could leave the kid out there on her own in the middle of the night.

"Who was that woman that thought she knew you?" Calico asks.

"Beats me."

"Hell, even I've heard of the Diesel Rats," Reuben says, "and no offense, Steve, but you're no Jackson Cole."

Except there's something in his eyes that tells me he knows different.

I sigh, but play along with him. "Tell me something I don't already know."

Reuben grins. "'Course, I've never seen you cleaned up."

"And you probably never will," Calico says.

This is good, I think. Let them rib me, we'll all relax.

But then Calico's smile goes away. "So do we just grab Sammy," she says, "or his big white hunter as well?"

"Sammy," Reuben says before I can answer. "The hunter wouldn't be here without him, and if we deal with Sammy, there won't be any more of them."

"Okay," she says. "So it's settled. Anybody want something to eat before we take him on?"

"I could do with a burrito and some water," Reuben says.

I start to speak but Calico holds her hand up. "Don't worry," she says. "I know what you'll want." She takes a step and disappears, and then it's just Reuben and me out here in the desert scrub.

"How the hell does she *do* that?" I say.

"It's a *ma'inawo* thing," Reuben says. "Some of them can move great distances when they switch between the worlds, so long as they're going to a place they've been before. Otherwise, you have to be careful, especially moving from the world we know to these changing lands. If you're on the top floor of a skyscraper and you step over, you'll find yourself plunging twenty stories through the otherworld air until you hit the ground. Not pretty."

I study him for a moment, then look away, letting the expanse of desert and hills do its calming magic for me.

"What?" Reuben says.

I look back at him.

"Don't blame the messenger," he says. "I didn't tell you to move to the Painted Lands and hook up with a *ma'inawo* girl. I'm just trying to educate you."

I sigh. "I think I liked my life better two days ago, when everything was simpler. And I should have just let somebody else find that girl."

"Like you'd ever turn your back on anyone who needs a hand."

"I'm not some fucking saint," I tell him.

He grins. "That we can both agree on. But come on, Steve. You know what the Aunties say. You can pretend you don't have troubles, but that doesn't make them go away."

I've never actually heard any of the Aunts say that, but I nod because it's true.

"So how come *you* can't do it?" I finally ask.

"Do what? Pick where we want to cross over?"

I nod.

"We're not *ma'inawo*," Reuben says. "The dog boys are a tribal thing. Our shapeshifting and theirs—it's two completely different things."

"I don't get it."

"It's not something to get. It's just how it is."

"Okay," I say, "so tell me this. There are girls running with your pack—why are you called dog boys?"

"We've got women, too," Reuben says, "but we're all called dog boys. I don't know why. And before you get all PC on me, I know it's sexist, but nobody seems to want to change it. It's like everybody talks about deer women, how they'll try to woo you away into the changing lands, but the stags are just as horny."

He smiles. "No pun intended."

"Is that what happened to me? I got wooed away into the otherworld?"

"What do you think?"

"I don't think it was anything like that."

"Me neither. Calico might have some antelope in her, but she's no deer woman. She's got too much trickster in her."

The subject of our conversation steps back from her errand just at that moment. She's carrying a couple of paper bags, one of which has a grease stain on the bottom.

"You know, it's not polite to talk about a lady behind her back," she says.

"But we were only saying good things," Reuben tells her, "so does that still count?"

She tosses the bag with the greasy bottom to him. He catches it easily, opens it up and hands around burritos. Calico's bag has water bottles, which she shares in turn. We sit down right where we are and dig in.

"I asked around about Sammy," she says, mumbling through a mouthful of burrito.

"What did you do to him?" I ask.

"Oh please. Give me some credit. I wouldn't cut either of you out."

"I thought we agreed we were going to lay low for a while."

She shakes her head. "You agreed to that. We didn't."

"What she said," Reuben says before he takes another bite.

I sigh. "I think I liked you better before," I tell her.

She frowns. "What's that supposed to mean?"

I can see she's miffed, but I can't seem to stop myself. "Back before," I say. "You were more fun. Not so…bloodthirsty."

She stops eating. "I could say the same about you."

"I'm not bloodthirsty."

"No, but you're not much fun anymore, either."

"Hey, Bickersons," Reuben says. "Do I really need to be in the middle of this?"

I almost snap at him, but I realize he's right. And so's she. I've let this take away everything I love about these mountains. And my friends. I look from one to the other, my burrito uneaten in my hand.

"You're both right," I tell them.

"I usually am," Calico says with a smile. I'm glad that she's trying to ease the tension too.

"What am I right about at the moment?" she continues, teasing me.

"I'm letting this get under my skin," I say. "And we do need to deal with Sammy. But can we leave it at that? Sammy's a problem here on the rez. But I don't want to take anything out on Sadie. After the cops clear us, we never have to see her and her old man again."

Reuben lays a hand on my forearm and gives me a squeeze. "This isn't exactly the rez," he says, "but I'm glad you're on board."

"And we leave the freak show that's the Higgins family out of it?"

"I don't even know who you're talking about," Reuben says with a smile.

I turn to Calico, but she's not even listening. All her attention is on a pair of crows riding the winds above us, their caws blowing away in fading tatters. She's gone paler than I've ever seen her before.

I call her name and she turns to me.

"Aggie's in the hospital," she says. "Sadie knifed her in the police station."

"*What?*"

But I heard exactly what she said, and my whole body's gone cold.

"They say she's asked that nobody go after Sadie," Calico adds.

"They?" I ask.

Reuben just points to the crows who are now flying off. "The *ma'i-nawo* aren't like us," he says. "They understand all the languages we've forgotten and the ones that were spoken before we ever showed up."

"Did they say how Aggie is?" I ask Calico.

"She's in intensive care. Those two women we saw earlier are with her."

I set my burrito on the ground beside the water I haven't tasted yet and stand up. "Okay, that's it," I say. "I told Sadie she can crap all over me, but she can't go after my friends."

Calico's standing now too. "Aggie said no. We have to respect her wishes."

"But if she doesn't make it," Reuben says, "all bets are off."

"Do the police have her in custody?" I ask.

"No."

"It's my fault Aggie got hurt. I should've never brought that kid to her."

"You had no way of knowing."

"But how could she be that good an actress? Christ, maybe she's hell on her family, too. Maybe that's why her father dumped her."

"No, I saw him at the community center," Reuben says. "He was just as much a piece of work. The crows say anything about us teaching him a little respect?"

"He's not worth it," Calico says. "In the long run, hurting him will just blow back on you ten times as hard."

Reuben sighs. "I suppose."

He understands, but he doesn't like it. I know exactly how he's feeling. I so need to hit something right now.

"Now I'm really in the mood to see Sammy," I tell them.

Calico smiles without any humour. "That, we can do."

"All we need to do is track him down," Reuben says.

Calico shakes her head. "We don't need to. Like I said. I asked around while I was getting our food. A hawk uncle told me that he's back up in the mountains at the hunting lodge."

"Perfect," Reuben says, then he asks Calico, "You have any short-cuts in this part of the dreamtime to take us there?"

She responds by offering each of us a hand.

43

SADIE

What she really wanted to do was point the pickup in whatever direction would take her the farthest away from the city, pedal to the metal, *hasta la vista*, assholes. But she knew as she pulled out of the parking lot of the tribal police station that could never happen. The cops would grab her before she got ten miles out. Driving in the direction she was headed, they'd have her even sooner. A teenage girl driving a stolen police vehicle toward Santo VV? She'd be a cinch to find, especially since there was only the one road from the tribal police station to the city. Before very long she'd probably have the combined might of the tribal police, sheriff's department and state cops on her ass. Maybe the FBI, too. But unlike the thousands of square miles of desert and mountains that spread north and east and south, she could lose herself in the city and survive.

She just needed to get there.

The first thing she had to do was abandon the truck as soon as possible, though not before she ate up as many miles as she could. The less time she had to spend on foot, the better. She'd had enough of tramping around in the bush scrub to last her for-freaking-ever. But she also didn't want to leave the truck abandoned on the side of the road. She might as well spray paint "Here's your starting point" on it if she did that.

She was still trying to figure out the best thing to do when a "Do Not Enter When Flooded" sign popped up on the side of the road, indicating a dip coming up ahead. She slowed down as she drove down the sharp incline. When she got to where the dry wash crossed the road, she turned the truck to the right and drove up the wash. Luck was on her side—there'd been no other cars to see her turn off.

The course was narrow. Branches and cacti scratched at the sides of the truck as she wound her way along the dry sandy bed. But in moments the road had disappeared behind her. The only way she'd be spotted now was from the air.

She headed north for a while, trying to decide when and where to dump the truck. It had been at least ten minutes since she'd made her escape. Would they have called in the choppers yet?

She started eyeing the palo verde trees, looking for a place where they grew thick enough to form a canopy above the wash. Then she thought of better place to abandon the truck. A funnier one, too.

For a long time the scariest dudes in Santo VV had been the 66 Bandas. The gang had ruled everything north of the San Pedro River. There were other gangs, but they kept to their own little neighbourhoods. Nobody was as ruthless as the 66ers. They could get away with pretty much anything since they had the backing of the Garza Cartel. Gangbangers were scary enough, but nobody was stupid enough to get on the wrong side of Mexican drug lords.

Except somebody had, a year or so ago. Another gang took the 66ers down, the Cartel hadn't retaliated, and things had been quiet for a long while now. But Sadie knew from the gossip at school that the 66ers were regrouping and were using their old clubhouse again—a property that backed right on to this dry wash.

She grinned. Just let the cops go looking for witnesses around the 66ers' compound. Nobody in that neighbourhood would be stupid enough to talk about anything. And if that wasn't enough, the Latino kids at school said a witch lived in the house right beside the 66ers.

Two days ago, Sadie would have laughed off the idea of a witch.

Now she wasn't so sure. But it didn't really matter. People just had to think she was real. Between her and the gangbangers, that part of the barrio would be the safest place for somebody wanting to disappear.

Which was exactly what she planned to do.

It took her another few minutes to reach the 66ers' compound. The clubhouse was a one-story adobe ranch with a red tile roof, various kinds of cacti clustered up against the walls. Between the wash and the house, the yard was strewn with various kinds of cars and motorcycles, a lot of them wrecks. A few raggedy mesquites and dying river oaks lined the edge of the property.

Because she was still in the trough of the dry wash, which was lower than the terrain it cut through, all that might be seen from the clubhouse was the top of the pickup with its band of police lights. She killed the engine, put it in neutral and let the pickup roll to a stop. Pulling the keys out of the ignition, she got out of the cab and lobbed them into the scrub on the far side of the wash away from the house before she continued north on foot.

"Hey!" somebody yelled from the direction of compound.

Sadie looked over her shoulder to see some big Latino guy trotting from around the house and heading in her direction. Behind him were a pair of others. She quickened her pace, breaking into a run when she heard a gunshot. The bullet pinged off a tree and went whining off into the scrub.

Crap. This wasn't going the way she'd expected.

It was her own stupid fault. She hadn't thought this through. Sure, it would piss off the police to have to collect their pickup at the back of a gangbangers' clubhouse. But of course it would also piss off the gangbangers. She hadn't thought about the engine noise soon enough.

A second shot made her duck, but the bullet came nowhere near her.

She dared another quick glance behind her and saw that one of the gangbangers—tall and skinny with freakishly long legs—was gaining on her.

Time for plan B.

She scrambled up the bank of the wash and ran across a dirt yard, right up to the front door of the witch's house. Looking back again, she saw that the gangbangers had stopped at the edge of the property. Interesting. They weren't even shooting at her anymore. Maybe she could just cut across the witch's yard and lose herself in the barrio. But then one of the men made a waving motion with his arm and two of them set off at a trot, circumventing the witch's yard as they made their way to the front of her property.

Which left her with only one course of action.

As she returned her attention to the witch's door she remembered the strange beings she'd seen in behind Aggie's place, the animal people gathered around a fire. If they were real, if the gangbangers were too scared to chase her onto the witch's property, then maybe there was more to the witch than just stories.

Double crap.

Before she lost her nerve, she lifted her hand and rapped sharply on the witch's door. For a long moment there was no response, but just as she was getting ready to knock again the door swung open and an old dark-skinned woman stood there, regarding her with curiosity. She didn't seem particularly scary. Her long hair was in a single braid that hung down the front of a plain white cotton blouse. She wore a dark skirt underneath and looked like some Mexican kid's grandmother. But there was something in her eyes that made Sadie put her hand in the pocket of her hoodie and close her fingers around her utility knife.

"Is there something you want, girl?" the old woman asked in a gravelly voice after the two of them had stood there for a while regarding each other.

Sadie cleared her throat. "Sanctuary," she said. "I want sanctuary."

"This isn't a church," the old woman said.

Sadie rolled her eyes. "You think I don't know that?"

The old woman cocked her head a little and studied her with eyes so dark they seemed to swallow all light. "Sanctuary from what?" she finally asked.

"Cops, mostly. Right now, gangbangers."

The old woman nodded. "I see. And what have you done to earn their combined ire?"

It took Sadie a moment to figure out what she'd said.

"With the cops, it's complicated, but part of it is that I stole one of their pickups. The gangbangers are mad at me because I abandoned the cops' truck in the dry wash at the back of their property."

"That would do it. And what do the cousins want with you?"

"The who?"

The old woman nodded at something over Sadie's shoulder. When Sadie turned, she saw a young Indian woman standing equidistant between the two groups of gangbangers. She wore jeans and a red and black flannel shirt over a white tee. Her red hair was in a braid. There didn't seem to be anything special about her, but even with the distance between them, Sadie could see that the woman had a serious hate on for her.

What the hell? What had she ever done to that bitch?

"I have no idea who that is," she said. "Is she your cousin? Or the cousin of one of the gangbangers?"

"'Cousin' is what the animal people call themselves."

"Animal people," Sadie repeated slowly.

She remembered the paintings in Aggie's home. The fire last night and all the half human, half animal beings gathered around it.

Aggie's friends.

And she'd cut Aggie open with her knife back at the cop shop.

Sadie glanced at the woman again. "She looks human to me," she said. "I thought they were, like, a mash-up of animals and people."

"They can look as human as you or me."

Of course they could, the freaks.

"I might have pissed one or two of them off," she admitted. "Is that a problem?"

"I don't do business with either the police or my neighbours next door. But many of the cousins are customers of mine, so I can't help you."

"You're just going to let them kill me?"

"Is that their intent?"

"How would I know? I didn't even know they existed until last night, and now all of a sudden they're all up in my face."

Sadie massaged her temples with her hands. When she took them away, she tried again. "Please. Isn't there anything you can do?"

"That depends. This isn't a charity. What do you have to offer for my services?"

"I don't have any money." Sadie thought about what witches usually wanted in stories or movies. "I suppose you want my firstborn kid or something. Or maybe my soul."

"Is that what you're offering?"

Sadie wasn't sure she believed in souls and afterlives and crap like that. But if this old witch was willing to barter for hers, then she sure as hell wasn't giving it up.

"Does it have to be *my* soul?" she asked.

For the first time the old woman actually looked interested. "No," she said. "But it has to be given up willingly."

"Well yeah," Sadie told her, though she'd known no such thing.

"And if the promised soul isn't forthcoming, then yours will be forfeit."

Sadie had to think on that for a moment to figure out exactly what the old woman was saying. Really, what was with her? She couldn't talk like a normal person?

"That won't be a problem," she said. She'd figure it out later. Truth was, right now she'd say any damn thing just to get out of the mess she was in.

The old woman stood aside and ushered her in.

"What's your name?" Sadie asked as she went by.

"Around here, people call me Abuela," the woman said from behind her.

Sadie didn't speak Spanish, but she understood enough to know that only meant grandmother.

"My name's Sadie."

"I know."

Sadie turned around, startled that the old woman would know her name. But then she realized that it was easy to say you knew something after you'd already been told as much.

Abuela smiled. There was something in her eyes that said she knew exactly what was running through Sadie's mind.

"So, Sadie Higgins," Abuela added. "Who do you know that will offer up their soul in return for your safety?"

Okay, Sadie thought. How the hell did she know my whole name?

Abuela smiled. When she closed the door behind her, Sadie realized she might be in more trouble inside the witch's house than she'd been outside of it.

44

THOMAS

Aunt Lucy was every bit as good a cook as his mother and Aunt Leila. With the simplest of ingredients, it seemed that the three of them could each make meals that would be the envy of any of the great chefs of the world. Thomas's mouth began to water as soon she set a plate in front of him: flatbread heaped with a chili of tepary beans, roasted corn, squash and peppers, all of it topped with shredded lettuce, sour cream and a chunky salsa of diced tomato, chipotle, cholla buds and green chilies.

"Where do you get all this stuff?" he asked.

Aunt Lucy pointed to the other side of the pond, past the river oak and the mesquite trees.

"I've got a garden over there," she said, then smiled. "I share it somewhat reluctantly with the local rabbits and deer. The rest I get from town."

Thomas nodded. Everything seemed so normal. Sitting round the table eating a homemade meal. The sun shining. The desert spread out around them, mountains in the distance. It felt familiar and strange all at the same time. It felt like home except the meal had been made by his dead aunt, and his companion was supposedly the ex-wife of the raven who'd created the world, the three of them being watched by the ghost of a raven and a dog that was a spirit of death.

And he wasn't sure he even wanted to know what a town would be like in this world.

That reminded him of how he and Consuela had gotten here in the first place.

"Do you know what's under the ground of your yard?" he said. "A whole other world, separated from us by a bunch of boards and a few inches of dirt."

Aunt Lucy just looked at him.

"It's true," he started to tell her, as Consuela and her raven twin began to laugh. "What?" he asked. "You saw it, the same as me."

"I did and I didn't," she told him. "Those boards you pulled away were just a passageway between the world we left and this one. The only reason there was a sky painted on boards is because that's what your shaman sight saw."

"I'm telling you, I don't have some shaman sight."

Aunt Lucy reached across the table and put her hand on his. "But you do," she said in a gentle voice.

Thomas looked at her, his surprise plain.

"All the men in the Corn Eyes Clan do," she continued. "Some of the women, too."

"What does that even mean?"

She settled her gaze on his. "You know exactly what it means. You see deeper into the world than most people do."

Thomas couldn't argue with that.

"Except I don't want to be a shaman," he said.

"Who says you have to? You could run with Reuben's dog boys."

"I don't have *ma'inawo* blood."

"Neither do they," Aunt Lucy told him. "Their dog aspects grow from Kikimi traditions. You could wear the same four-legged skin as any of them."

Thomas shook his head. "That doesn't appeal to me any more than being a shaman, which it looks like I'll end up as, whether I want to or not."

"And who says you have to be either?"

"I—I don't know. I just assumed it would be expected of me, what with Morago looking for an apprentice."

"That's right," Aunt Lucy said. "He comes back, doesn't he? I mean, he came back—it all depends on your when."

"*Morago* went away?" Thomas asked, unable to hide his surprise. He couldn't imagine the shaman being away from the rez. "Where would he even go?"

"Everybody leaves at some point," Aunt Lucy said. "Look at me— here I am. Some of us just don't go as far as Morago does." She smiled and added, "Did."

"But *where* did he go?"

"You'll have to ask him."

Thomas nodded, then went back to eating because it was easier than trying to understand just how weird his life had become.

Gordo had been following the conversation too, or at least that was how it seemed to Thomas. But now the big black dog dropped his head on his paws once more, the now-meatless bone lying forgotten on the dirt beside him.

Thomas sopped up his plate with his last piece of flatbread. He was about to put it in his mouth when he noticed Gordo watching his every move. It was so much like the begging gaze of any of the rez dogs that he forgot what Gordo was and tossed it over. Gordo's mouth opened wider than should have been possible and the flatbread disappeared into its depths like a pebble dropped into a canyon.

Si'tala made a small guttural sound of approval from her perch.

"I don't know why you feel the need to go anywhere," Consuela said.

Thomas tore his gaze from the dog to give her his attention.

Aunt Lucy shook her head, amusement plain in her eyes. "Says the woman who has been on one road or another for as long as I've heard stories of her."

"I just feel there has to be something more out there," Thomas said, responding to Consuela.

That made Aunt Lucy laugh. "Of course there is more—how could there not be? You need only travel a few canyons from your home to find more."

"It's hard to think of travelling anywhere when you have no money and a family to support. Being poor gets old really fast."

"How are you poor?" Consuela wanted to know. "And in whose eyes? You have your family and friends and your tribe. You have the Painted Lands to host your journey in the world."

"All of which is well and fine," Aunt Lucy said before Thomas could respond. "But it doesn't help when you feel all the possibilities of your life slipping away and there's nothing you can do to stop it from happening."

Thomas shot a grateful look at Aunt Lucy. "That's exactly what it feels like," he said.

Consuela made a noise in the back of her throat and looked away. Though he didn't agree with her, Thomas was a little envious of how certain she was of, well, pretty much everything. She didn't seem to have any doubts, whereas he would second-guess or even third-guess the simplest decision. Which maybe wasn't such a bad thing, considering how when he'd acted on impulse—like stepping in to give Morago a hand—he'd ended up in this situation.

"You're seeing something different now," Consuela said. "How do you like it so far?"

"Other than almost being in a couple of car wrecks and having a gang of mutant salvagers out for my blood?"

"What salvagers?" Aunt Lucy asked.

Thomas jerked a thumb in Consuela's direction. "Ask her. I'm still not sure I completely understand."

Aunt Lucy's features darkened as Consuela explained.

"What were you thinking?" she demanded when the raven woman was done.

"That the boy needs to accept his responsibilities to his people—the sooner the better."

"And now his soul is forfeit if he should ever stray onto one of those damned ghost roads."

Consuela glared back at her. "It was nothing I planned."

"And when he dies?" Aunt Lucy continued, her voice getting louder. "Where will he go? Where will his soul be *safe*?"

From where Gordo was lying splayed out in the dirt soaking up the sun, the big black dog lifted his head, dark gaze swinging between the two women.

Aunt Lucy shook her head. "You corbae are as bad as Cody ever was."

Consuela ignored the slight. "Si'tala would never have woken his connection to his people's traditions if she didn't see that it would be needed in the future," she said.

Thomas was having trouble concentrating on what they were saying. He was still trying to get past his soul being forfeit. What the hell did that even mean?

It was really time he disengaged from all of this craziness.

"Time out," he said.

Both women turned to him.

"I can't figure out half of what you're saying," he told them. "Maybe it'd be better if we just go do what we set out to do. The sooner that gets over with, the sooner I can get back to my actual life."

"But she—" his aunt began.

Thomas raised a hand, palm out. "Don't want to hear it."

"Your 'actual life'?" Consuela said. "What makes you think this isn't—"

Thomas waved his hand back and forth. "Don't want to hear that, either. Let's just go find Sammy and be done with all of this."

Gordo stood up as though he understood every word. And he probably did, Thomas thought. Si'tala straightened in her perch. She gave her back feathers a ruffle, her gaze fixed on Thomas.

He stood up from the table and inclined his head to his aunt. "I appreciate the meal, Auntie," he told her. "And it was weird, but really good to see you. But now we need to go."

"I understand," Aunt Lucy said, rising as well. She came around the table and gave him another hug, adding, "Don't let anyone do your thinking for you."

"I won't."

She smiled. "No. I see that you already trust in yourself. That can be a hard road at times, especially when everyone around you claims to know a better route you should take. But in the course of your life, that trust will serve you well."

Thomas stepped from her arms and focused on Consuela, who was standing now as well.

"You know I had no intention for things to get so complicated," she said.

"I don't know any such thing," Thomas told her, "but it doesn't really matter, does it? Can we just get going?"

"Of course." Consuela looked to his aunt. "Thank you for your hospitality, Lucy."

Aunt Lucy just nodded stiffly, still visibly upset with the raven woman.

"Come, then," Consuela said to Thomas. She began to walk back into the desert.

Si'tala left her perch and floated to Consuela's shoulder. Thomas gave Aunt Lucy a smile and a shrug. Gordo brushed his head against Aunt Lucy, then stopped beside Thomas, tongue lolling. As Thomas began to follow the raven woman, the dog fell in step beside him.

"So, no magic portals?" Thomas said, when he caught up to Consuela. "Gordo here doesn't turn into a jeep or something?"

"We'll be there soon enough," she said.

Her voice sounded tight and she didn't look at him. She was obviously still ticked off as well.

Like any of this was his fault, Thomas thought. But for once he was going to follow Morago's advice and keep his mouth shut.

45

LEAH

Marisa looked a lot better. Instead of letting Leah go back to their motel room for a change of clothes, Marisa had gone down to the hospital gift shop where she bought herself a T-shirt. She cleaned up in the public restroom, drying herself with paper towels. Wadding her bloodstained shirt into a ball, she discarded it in the garbage bin before coming back upstairs to intensive care where Leah was sitting in the waiting room. Leah looked up and shook her head at the unspoken question. There was still no news.

Marisa settled beside Leah on the sofa. Her jeans still had splatters of dried blood on them, but she no longer had the look of a victim from some slasher movie.

The sofa wasn't particularly comfortable, but it seemed a better option than the single-seat chairs in the room. Its back cushions were too hard and the seat sagged in weird places, but neither of them paid any mind to personal discomfort. They just kept looking up at the door, expecting someone to arrive with an update on Aggie's condition. But time dragged on and no one came.

Marisa had told the nurse in charge they were Aggie's granddaughters, which had garnered them a dubious look. But one of the paramedics told the nurse that Deputy Two Trees had spoken up for them, so they were allowed to stay. What really sealed the deal was when Marisa gave them her credit card to put on file in case Aggie or her relatives couldn't afford to pay the hospital bill.

The waiting was hard. Leah barely knew Aggie White Horse, but she still felt an inexplicable connection to the old woman, and was horrified at what had happened to her.

"How screwed up is that kid's life," Marisa said after a few minutes had passed, "for her to do something like this?"

Leah nodded. "It's nothing we can imagine. But we've seen the results of the damage before. Remember Brian Parker?"

"Oh God, that was a nightmare. The whole Arts Court almost got shut down because of his accusations."

"But a part of what he was saying was true."

"The neighbour…" Marisa began.

"Exactly. So what part, if any, of Sadie's story is true? Something must have happened to her. Somebody damaged that kid before she started lashing out."

"That doesn't give her a pass on hurting Aggie, or on what she's been claiming, because she obviously can't be trusted."

Leah sighed. "No, but if someone doesn't figure this out, she's just going to get worse."

They broke off, lifting their heads at the sound of someone approaching the waiting room. The stranger who appeared in the doorway was tall and lanky, with a dark complexion and startling amber eyes. Leah wasn't sure if he was Latino or Native American. He wore jeans, cowboy boots and a black T-shirt with a fringed buckskin jacket overtop and a straw cowboy hat. His long russet hair trailed down his chest in a pair of braids.

Leah felt a pang of disappointment as their hope for news died. "You're not the doctor," she said.

"And you're not Abigail's granddaughters unless she's done a very good job of hiding you over the years."

Though his features were stern, he didn't seem to be too upset about their deception.

Leah tried to figure out who he was. He was too young to be a husband. Maybe he was Aggie's son? The weird thing was, she felt like she'd seen him before, but in some other context.

"They wouldn't let us stay unless we were family," Marisa said. "We didn't want her to be alone in case she woke up and no one had come from the rez yet."

The man nodded and came all the way into the room.

"That was kind of you," he said. "*Ohla.* My name's Ramon Morago and I'm not family either."

Marisa introduced Leah and herself, then added, "But they're letting you stay? Please don't make us leave before we know if Aggie's going to be all right."

"No one will make any of us leave," he assured them.

He looked from one to the other, and Leah couldn't help shake the feeling that he was looking past their faces, right under their skin and straight to their hearts.

"You were there when the girl attacked Aggie?" he added.

Marisa nodded. "But I don't know if it was actually a planned attack," she said. "Sadie was trying to leave and Aggie stood up to stop her, and then I'm not sure exactly what happened because the next thing I knew, Aggie was collapsing and there was blood everywhere. And Sadie took off."

"Jerry said your quick thinking probably saved Aggie's life."

Marisa shrugged. "I hope so. I just did what anybody would do."

"Or what we wish they would do," Morago said. He shook his head. "I warned Steve that girl would be trouble."

"Steve?" Leah asked. "You mean Jackson Cole? We met him on the way to the police station."

Morago studied her for a moment, then he smiled. "Is that who he told you he was?"

"I... What do you mean?"

"It's just... Where do I begin?"

He pulled a chair over in front of them and turned it so that he could rest his forearms across its back. "You know Jackson Cole's dead, right?" he said in a quiet voice. "Died in a plane crash, a long time ago."

"Yes, but—"

"Oh, I know. There are always rumours. But the thing is, you're not too far off with Steve. He's a Cole, but not the famous one. He's Jacko's cousin."

Jacko? Leah thought. Who was this guy? Only Jackson's band and crew referred to him as Jacko. But all she said was, "His cousin? The Steve Cole that Jackson played with as a kid?"

Morago nodded. "They grew up together back in Texas, had that little band and everything."

"Jackson always said that it was Steve who got him into music—taught him to play the guitar."

"He sure did. And Steve's maybe the better guitar player of the two, but he didn't have Jacko's vision, or his gift for words and melody and arrangements. Play something for Steve and he can play it right back to you, but he can't bring the magic out of nothing. Not the way Jacko could."

"You talk like you knew him," Leah said.

"That's how I met Steve—we were both part of the Diesel Rats' road crew. I packed it in and came back to the rez before all the heavy crap went down—you know, Sully ODing, Marty taking off, Toni banging Conway. It just turned into a bad scene, as we used to say."

Leah stared at him, sorting through images in her head: memories of old photographs, concert and home movie footage, newspaper and magazine clippings. Her main focus was almost always on the band, Jackson in particular, and she hadn't really paid as much attention to the hangers-on and crew.

"You were really part of the Diesel Rats' road crew?"

Morago nodded.

"And now? Are you still involved with music?"

Morago laughed. "Not the way you'd think. I came back home to the rez and now I'm the tribal shaman."

After everything she'd already experienced today, Leah didn't find it hard to accept that the man in front of her was a shaman who could probably work real magic, which made her wonder why he didn't use that magic to help Aggie.

"Can't you just heal Aggie?" Marisa asked, obviously thinking the same thing.

"I could try. The trouble is, she's not home."

Leah and Marisa exchanged puzzled looks.

"What does that mean?" Leah asked.

"Her spirit's gone off wandering somewhere. I need her to be in her skin to work any kind of medicine on her." At their continued blank looks, he added, "My medicine speaks to the spirit. It teaches the spirit how to heal itself. But her spirit is no longer in her body, so I can't sing to it."

"But she's still alive," Marisa said. "How can she not have a spirit or soul anymore?"

"Oh, she still has a spirit. That's what makes us who we are. It's just, you know how when you sleep, your spirit travels to other worlds?"

The two women shook their heads.

"Trust me," Morago said. "It does. We all visit the dreamlands when our bodies are sleeping, but we don't all remember those journeys we take."

"So she's...dreaming?" Marisa asked.

"In a manner of speaking. We need to wait for her spirit to return to her body before I can sing my medicine song. Until then, we must trust to the medicine of the five-fingered beings to keep her alive. We can only wait and pray for her safety."

It was a lot to take in. Marisa and Leah exchanged glances.

"I feel like I'm still in the otherworld," Leah said.

Marisa nodded. "And waiting's hard."

"It is," Morago agreed. "Especially in a situation such as this, when we have no control."

They fell silent, and once again time began to drag.

After a while Leah asked, "Did you really work with the Diesel Rats back in the day?" She spoke as much to distract herself as out of curiosity.

Morago took out his wallet and pulled a worn picture from one of its slots.

"That's Steve and I at the beginning of the last tour," he said as he passed it over to Leah.

Marisa leaned closer to have a look for herself as Leah studied the photo. It was black and white, marred by a crease and dog-eared edges. But it was easy to make out the features of the two men, one Native American and one white. Morago and—it looked so much like Jackson Cole sitting there beside him. Shorter hair than Jackson had ever worn, a little more buff in a sleeveless tee and jean cutoffs, but if no one had told her beforehand, she would have thought it was Jackson.

Leah felt a sense of *déjà vu.* "Is this part of a larger picture?" she asked.

The two men appeared to be in a crowd of some sort, but only hints of the other people remained. The edge of a shoulder. The side of a knee.

When Morago nodded she got out her phone and went online. After a few moments of searching she found the photo she was looking for. It was a famous shot—the last time the whole band had been alive and before the acrimony set in. As Morago had said, it was taken at the beginning of the final tour, the band and full road crew posing on the bleachers of a stadium in California. She expanded the view to find Jackson Cole, then moved the focus of the screen around, examining the faces until she reached the portion with Morago and Steve that the shaman had in his cropped version.

How had she never noticed the close resemblance between Jackson and his cousin? She'd known Steve existed—he was a big part of Jackson's early history, the two of them growing up in Texas a few blocks from each other, playing music together in high school. But there weren't a lot of pictures of him, and those that she could recall never seemed to show all of his features. He was always turning away, bent over a guitar or some gear. One of those guys who shunned any focus on himself as a center of attention. And really, didn't everybody fall by the wayside when it came to the bright, larger-than-life star that Jackson Cole had been?

"When I was leaving," Morago said, "I told Steve that if he ever got sick of the rock 'n' roll life to come look me up. I have to admit I never expected him to actually take me up on it. But some forty years ago, who does Possum bring by, but Steve Cole with a broken leg. Fell off the side of some canyon and snapped it right in two. He's stuck around ever since."

"I wish I hadn't started off on the wrong foot with him," Leah said, "because I'd really like to talk to him about Jackson and the band. You, too."

Morago laughed. "I can't tell you much. Roadies didn't hang around with the headliners. We just did our jobs. But I can tell you that even before I left, I could see the writing on the wall. I don't mean the exact details of what went down in those last days, but you could feel the train wreck waiting to happen. And we all knew there was going to be some serious fallout when Jacko found out about Toni and Ben's little something-something on the side."

Leah hung on to his every word. She might have tried telling herself she was going to move into a different kind of journalism, but after all her years studying the band, finding a whole new source of information such as this was like stumbling upon a gold mine.

"There has to be something you can tell me," she said.

Morago regarded her for a moment, then he smiled.

"I don't know if this ever made it into the stories about the band," he said, "but you know the old urban legend about how Elvis traded places with an Elvis impersonator, and he's still alive because it was the impersonator who died in that Graceland bathroom?"

Both Leah and Marisa nodded, eyes wide.

"Well, I know for a fact that Jacko was trying to talk Steve into swapping places with him toward the end. Not forever. Just long enough for him to get his head together again."

Leah couldn't help herself. "And did they?"

Morago shook his head. "Jacko got on that plane first."

Leah wanted to ask him more, but just then the doctor came into the room. He had such a serious set to his features that everything Morago had been telling her faded away.

46

JERRY

There was no way around it. The chief was pissed and Jerry didn't blame him. Everything that could have gone wrong with this situation had, leaving Jerry feeling like an idiot. He might as well be standing with his pants around his ankles for all the competence he'd shown. The worst of it was Aggie being knifed right in the station by the "victim" of a bogus kidnapping, who then stole one of their own trucks from the parking lot out front to make her escape.

"Are you telling me this kid hot-wired one of our pickups?" the chief had demanded.

Jerry'd had to admit that the keys had been in the ignition.

"Who leaves their goddamn keys in the goddamn ignition?" the chief had yelled.

We all do, Jerry'd thought, the chief included, but he hadn't said that. He knew what had made his boss so angry. It wasn't just the sloppy mistakes, but how they couldn't be hidden from the sheriff's department, the FBI and Indian Affairs. They made the whole force look bad. And the chief would have to take the heat for it.

Jerry knew he should have listened to his gut. He never should've tried to hold Steve and Reuben. He should have put the girl's lying ass in a cell as soon as he got her to the station, locked the door and thrown away the key. But that was easy to say after the fact. At the time, Sadie Higgins had seemed to need his protection. She'd been so damned convincing that he'd swallowed every bit of her bullshit.

All he could do now was try to salvage what he could as quickly as possible, even if that meant driving every damn road in the county.

His radio crackled and Ralph's voice came on.

"We've got tire tracks running off into a wash just a few miles west of the station, on Calle Esmeralda. Bob says his people are pretty sure she never made it to Santo VV, or at least the truck hasn't been spotted anywhere in the city, so she must've gone off-road here."

"You're there now?" Jerry asked.

"Standing right here looking at the tracks—same tread as on all our trucks. You want me to wait for you?"

"No, go ahead. I'm ten minutes away on Redondo. But be careful, Ralph. This kid's as wily as a coyote."

"Copy that."

Jerry flicked on his lights and siren, pulled a U-turn, and headed back in the direction of the city.

47

RUBY

R uby stared at Sadie and the witch from the edge of the witch's property and wished she could sever the incongruous bond she'd formed with the girl. For what Sadie had done to Aggie, she deserved to have her throat ripped out, but instead the bond made Ruby want to do everything she could to protect her, regardless of how the girl had betrayed them all.

She sighed. The loyalty of the dog clans was so messed up sometimes.

And she was a fool for always wanting to take the broken ones under her protection.

Ruby whined in frustration, a barely audible sound that came from the back of her throat.

She didn't know what to do. Sadie had added to the problem by pissing off the 66 Bandas when she'd dumped that tribal police pickup right on the edge of their property.

She was fully aware of the two groups of bandas also watching Sadie and the witch, just as they were aware of her. Earlier, one of the men had made an off-colour remark when she'd stepped out of the desert into the dry wash, but she'd turned and snarled at him, baring a mouthful of dog canines that had the gangbanger stumble back in surprise. He'd quickly recovered his bravado, but when he took a step toward her she'd pointed a finger at him and growled, "Don't."

Surprisingly, he'd lowered his gaze. Now the men kept their distance. They were wary of her, muttering comments to each other, but none of them had summoned up the courage yet to make a move in her direction.

That would come—it was only a question of when.

She was also aware of the dozen or more crows that had landed in the boughs of the mesquite trees overhanging the wash. Most of them gathered in the tree above her, but a couple flew over to the witch's house just as Sadie and the witch were going inside. A few moments after the women disappeared, one of the crows drifted down from his perch on lazy wings, transforming into a dark-skinned man just before his feet touched the ground beside her.

"Word is," he said, "the girl isn't to be harmed."

Ruby didn't bother to look at him. "Go away, Manny."

When he didn't respond she turned to see him studying the closest group of gangbangers. There were two up by the road on the other side of the witch's property, but the ones in the wash had multiplied to a half-dozen. A couple of them carried baseball bats, but one of them, with a tattoo of a Maltese cross on his shaved head, had a rifle in his hand. It was pointed at the ground at the moment, but just as she'd arrived she'd heard him firing it at Sadie.

The look in his eye was wary. He'd seen her canines, heard her snarl. Seen Manny drop from the tree, turning into a five-fingered being. But his caution was slipping and he didn't seem as intimidated anymore, which wasn't good because that meant it was a short step now to his taking action.

"I don't think you're making friends," Manny said. "Whatever happened to you? You used to be such a friendly pup."

"Piss off," she told him, but she smiled as she said it.

Manny was one of the crow boys who roosted in Yellowrock Canyon. Tall and dark-complexioned, with hair as luxurious and black as the feathers of their crow shapes, they were an unruly lot, but she'd always liked them. There were usually a few of them around Aggie's place, ready to play or laze in the sun and swap tall tales with the pack.

"What are you doing here anyway?" he asked. He nodded with his chin to the low adobe building. "Do you know who lives in that house?"

Ruby nodded. "The witch they call Abuela."

"The *formidable* witch they call Abuela. She's supposed to be an *hechicera*—the kind of witch that controls spirits."

Ruby shrugged. "I'm not here to cause trouble with her or the bandas. I just want the girl."

Manny studied her for a long moment, then cocked his head. "To keep her safe," he said. It was a statement, not a question, and he didn't bother to hide his surprise. "After everything she's done."

"I made a mistake, okay? She smelled of bruises and blood. I didn't know she was cutting herself or would hurt anyone else. I thought she needed protecting."

Manny nodded. He didn't say what she'd left unsaid: that she had not done a good job of it so far. But that was the problem with anyone who didn't live under your own skin. You couldn't predict who they really were, what they would do. All you had to work with was hope, which eroded a little more every time somebody let you down.

"And now?" Manny asked.

"She still needs something, but I don't know what it is, or if I can give it to her." She paused, then added, "Or if I'd even want to."

One of the crows that had been perched on the witch's house drifted back in their direction. He became a man as gracefully as Manny had, landing on two feet without so much as raising a puff of dust.

"Hey, Ruby," he said. "*Ohla.*"

"Hey, Xande."

"What's happening over there?" Manny asked, tipping his head in the direction of the house.

"The kid just promised Abuela a soul in return for protection."

"Protection from *what?*"

Xande shrugged. "Gangbangers. Cops. Us."

Manny scoffed. "Seriously? *Us?*"

"Hey, *you* may be a little baby crow, but I can kick ass."

Manny punched Xande's shoulder and they both laughed.

"Whose soul?" Ruby asked, fearing for Aggie, lying in the hospital.

"Either she didn't say, or I didn't hear," Xande told her. "But I do know that the soul has to be willingly given. And if the kid can't come up with payment, her own soul is forfeit."

Ruby rubbed her face. Could this girl be any more clueless?

"I have to put a stop to this," she said.

"And how do you expect to do that? They've already made their bargain."

"I'll think of something."

As she stepped into the witch's yard she felt the sudden interest of the gangbangers. A couple of them stepped toward her and she paused.

"You want us to take care of them?" Manny asked.

Ruby shook her head. "That'll only exacerbate the situation."

"Listen to you with your big words."

"Seriously. Let's try to leave them out of it."

Manny nodded. "No problem."

But he made a slight motion with his hands and the crows in the tree above them rose from their perches and landed again in branches above both groups of gangbangers. The men that had been moving stopped and eyed the birds warily.

"Wait," Manny told Ruby as she started to move again. "You know this is a bad idea."

She ignored him and strode across the yard. Manny and Xande exchanged glances, then shifted to their crow shapes and flew ahead. They were perched above the witch's door by the time Ruby reached it.

Ruby flung the door open and stepped inside, followed by the pair of crows who flew a circuit of the room before settling on the backs of chairs on opposite sides of the room.

Sadie shrank away from Ruby and hid behind the old woman.

Abuela gave each of the intruders a long look before her gaze finally settled on Ruby. "Normally," the witch said, "visitors have the courtesy to knock before entering." She smiled, but there was a warning in her eyes. "This is the home of a witch. You take your life in your hands with such behaviour."

"I don't see a witch," Ruby told her. "I just see an old woman who steals the medicine of the thunders and pretends it's her own. Pretends this land is her own."

"I do no such thing. My people have been here since—"

"You stole this land from the tribes, who stole it from the *ma'i-nawo* before you or the other Europeans ever arrived. All you five-fingered beings are liars and thieves."

Anger flashed in the old woman's eyes. "You dare question my integrity?"

"When it begins with the lie of how this land is yours?"

The witch scowled. "If you wanted to claim ownership, you should have done a better job of holding on to it."

Ruby laughed. "No one owns the land. You might as well say you own the sky. It makes about as much sense." Then she let her humour fall away. "The girl is under my protection."

"Is she now? Then why did she come to me to ask for the same?"

"Because she's a stupid child who doesn't think and takes no responsibility for her actions."

"Don't let her near me," Sadie said. "I don't know who she is, but she's a crazy woman."

"You know me," Ruby said. "My name is Ruby."

Sadie's features went white. "Oh crap. She's going to kill me. You need to get rid of her—right now."

"I told you I would protect you against those who mean you ill," the witch said, "and I will do so. But our bargain doesn't include protecting you against those who mean you well."

"This is such bullshit," Sadie said.

"However," the witch went on, "should she attempt to harm you, I will deal with her, and when I'm done she won't be troubling you—or anybody else—again."

Ruby held the witch's gaze. "I doubt you'll find me as easy to deal with as the five-fingered beings you're used to dazzling with your stolen medicine."

"You'd be surprised," Abuela told her.

Manny changed shape, sliding down from his perch until he was lounging in the chair, one leg thrown carelessly over its arm.

"You might want to reconsider that kind of threat, señora," he told the witch. "If you kill her, you'll start a clan war between yourself and every canid from the mountains to the ocean."

The old woman turned to look at him. "You think I'm afraid of *dogs*?"

"Did I say 'dogs'?"

Abuela frowned. "Speak plainly."

"I did. You'll become the number one target of all the canid clans. Every wolf, coyote, dog, fox... Well, you get the picture. And then there are the big guns. If justice serves, you might get the attention of Cody, and you know how Coyote likes to mess with you five-fingered beings."

The witch waved a hand, feigning indifference. "I'll worry about that when the time comes."

Manny nodded. "If Aggie dies, that time's coming sooner than you might like."

"Aggie?" the witch repeated. Her gaze went from Manny to Ruby, and they could see her make the connection. "Do you mean Abigail White Horse? What have you done to her? I thought dogs and crows were her friends."

"We are. We didn't knife her and put her in the hospital."

"I have no quarrel with her," the witch said.

"No, but you're protecting the one who is responsible."

The witch fixed her dark gaze on Sadie.

"Hey, it was an accident. She's just some old lady—why would I want to hurt her?"

"Why, indeed?"

"I said it was an accident."

Abuela's attention returned to Manny. "What's done is done," she said. "The bargain has been made, and no matter what the dog thinks, I do not break my word."

Ruby growled low in her chest, but didn't speak.

"And speaking of the bargain," the witch said to Sadie, "it's time you upheld your side of it. You owe me a soul."

Sadie nodded. "Sure, but I have to go get it."

"All things considered," the witch said, "I would prefer you have your volunteer come to meet us here. You can use my phone."

"That's not really going to work."

The witch's brow went up.

"Chill," Sadie told her. "I'm not planning to rip you off."

"Then what is the problem?"

Sadie sighed. "Look, the soul I'm getting for you belongs to my old man. He just doesn't know it yet."

"You did hear me when I said it must be willingly given?"

"Sure I did. I have a plan."

The witch remained silent, waiting.

Sadie gave another heavy sigh. "Okay, okay. You want the deets? I mean to pay the old fuck back for how he treats me. I'm going to the house tonight while he's asleep, and taking a baseball bat to him. Once I get going, he'll do whatever it takes to make me stop—including giving up his soul. It's not like he cares about it anyway."

Ruby felt her heart sink. The child was on a downward spiral and she wasn't sure there was any chance that she could be saved. But Ruby knew what she had to do.

"You can have my soul," she told the witch.

A broad smile spread across the old woman's features. "Can I now?"

"Ruby!" Manny said, jumping up from the chair. "What the hell are you doing? Look at that kid. You think she's worth it?"

Ruby shook her head. "But she's under my protection, so I can't let her do this."

Manny glared daggers at the witch. "This is messed up."

"Free will," the witch said.

"Wait a sec'," Sadie said. "Isn't this supposed to be *my* decision?"

"Oh, let's see," Manny said, his voice heavy with sarcasm. "Haven't you already done enough?"

"Hey, smart mouth—" Sadie began, but Ruby cut her off.

"Get her out of here," she told Manny. "Take her wherever she wants to go."

Sadie shook her head. "No. I'm not going anywhere. This is between me and Abuela, so you just butt out. If she's taking anybody's soul, she's taking mine."

Ruby smiled. Maybe there was hope for the child yet. But all she said was, "Manny?"

Manny stepped up and took Sadie by the arm. When he started to move her toward the door she tried to yank herself free, but he held on tight.

"Ouch! Some protection here?" Sadie demanded of the witch.

"There's nothing I can do," Abuela told her. "He means you no harm."

As Sadie continued to struggle, Xande shifted to human form and joined Manny. Between the two of them they half dragged, half marched her out the door.

Ruby waited until it closed behind them. She could still hear Sadie yelling, but she put the girl from her mind and turned to the witch.

"So how does this work?" she asked.

RAVEN WINGS

48

STEVE

I'm not just getting used to Calico's way of travelling, I'm starting to enjoy it. And I especially enjoy the look on people's faces when you just step out of nowhere into their space, the way we do in Sammy's office at the hunting lodge. He's behind his desk, with Dave Running Dog sitting on a couch by the window. They both stand up, eyes wide, mouths agape. Man, I love it.

Dave takes a run at us but Calico gives him a casual backhand that sends him crashing into the wall. Sammy winces, the surprise in his features turning to fear. We stand there for a few moments, not saying anything until I see his courage coming back.

"We decided to forgo the white van for this kidnapping," I tell him before he can speak. "That's what always trips criminals up, pulling the same crap over and over again."

"Now look—"

I wag a finger at him, cutting him off. "Uh-uh. I'll *tell* you when you can talk."

We decided before we got here that I'd handle this part of it. Calico's too pissed off for any kind of finesse, and Reuben's just going to push all the traditionalist-versus-Casino-crowd buttons.

"You're lucky I'm here," I tell him. "Calico says we should kill you, and I have to admit I can see the appeal of that because then we'll be done with you once and for all. There's a lot to be said for never having to see your sorry ass again.

"Reuben wants to dump you in the mountains," I continue. "Oh, not the Maderas. The ones in the otherworld. I'm leaning a bit more that way because I'm not really a bloodthirsty kind of guy. Mind you, there's no guarantee you won't die of exposure."

I give him a smile. "You figure it out yet? I'm the deciding vote."

His gaze shifts between us.

By the wall where he fell, Dave pushes himself up to a sitting position, which earns him growls from both my companions. He puts his hands up, palms out. "I don't want any trouble," he says.

"Then why are you toadying around this piece of work?" Reuben asks, nodding in Sammy's direction.

"Come on, man. It's just a job. I had nothing to do with ratting you out to the cops."

"See, that's part of the problem," I say. "Ratting us out presupposes that we're guilty of something."

"I didn't mean it that way."

"I know, Dave. But unfortunately, now you're a witness."

"Don't kill me, man. I won't say anything to anybody."

"He probably won't," Reuben says. "Who's going to listen to him? He's going to start talking about people appearing out of thin air and grabbing his boss?"

Calico's been staring hard at Sammy through all of this. The little bit of bravado he was showing a few moments ago has vanished, sucked away like rain on the thirsty desert dirt.

"Let's deal with the boss first," I say. "Okay Sammy. You're up. What've you got to say for yourself?"

His eyes can't stay in one place. We're spread out enough that he can't focus on one of us without the other two disappearing into his peripheral vision.

"I—" He clears his throat. "What do you want me to say? You told me not to kill any of those spirit animal people and I didn't."

"No, instead you told the cops that we kidnapped some girl."

"That was a mistake—I see that now. I'll tell them I was wrong."

"But you weren't."

He looks puzzled. "I wasn't?"

"You weren't 'wrong.' You were outright lying to them."

I don't know where it comes from, but he finds a little backbone. "What did you expect?" he says. "You disrespected me."

"So you thought fair payback was for us to be thrown in jail and have our reputations dragged into the gutter."

"I just wanted to mess you up. They probably weren't going to charge you on my say-so."

"So that makes it okay?"

"I'll fix this, okay? I'll talk to whoever you want."

I shake my head. "Maybe you should shut up again because the more you talk, the more I'm leaning toward Calico's way of dealing with you."

"You don't kill people over something like this!" he yells.

I shrug. "Ever disrespected a gangbanger? You know what their reaction would be?"

"Come on. We can work something out. You want money? I can throw in a couple of grand on top of clearing things up with the cops."

I turn to Calico. "You need to get him out of here before I take a swing at him myself."

She nods. One moment she's standing beside me, the next she's over the desk and has Sammy in a neck lock.

"What are you waiting for?" Reuben asks.

"Shh," she says. "I'm just calculating elevations so that I don't drop him off the side of a mountain on the other side."

"Wait…no," Sammy wheezes. It's hard to talk when someone's cutting off most of your air. He pulls at her arm, but he might as well be trying to break a python's grip.

Calico simply ignores him. "Got it," she says. "I'll be right back for you."

Then the two of them vanish.

"Jesus Christ," Dave says. "Are you really going to kill him?"

I look over to where he's slouched against the wall. At least this time he didn't piss his pants.

"Haven't decided yet," I tell him.

A moment later, Calico's back.

Reuben points a finger at Dave. "Keep your mouth shut. Remember this: no matter where you go, we can find you."

Calico adds a little punctuation mark by showing him a mouthful of sharp fox teeth.

"I swear, I swear!" Dave tells us.

Calico growls and turns away, but I see the twinkle in her eye. She'd as much bite him as I'd kidnap Sadie Higgins, but he doesn't know that. She offers Reuben and me her hands.

"Ready, cowboys?" she asks.

Reuben smiles. "I think I feel insulted."

"What? A Kikimi can't ride the range and be a cowboy?"

"Jesus, don't you two start," I say.

Calico laughs and steps us away. The exhilarating rush of the passage between the worlds comes to an abrupt halt when we reach our destination and see we're not the only people with an interest in Sammy Swift Grass. Calico dumped him on a small plateau high up in the tallest mountains I've ever climbed. As far as the eye can see, the peaks run off in all directions. The air is thin and at least ten degrees cooler than it is in the desert. The sky's an impossible blue, specked with condors in the distance, turning slow circles on updrafts.

But none of that is what grabs our undivided attention. It's not the view, or the sky, or even Sammy standing in front of us, his pants scuffed from an obvious fall. It's what's on the other side of him: a jet black helicopter, engine still, its rotors slowly turning until they come to a standstill.

Sammy doesn't even notice our arrival. Like us, his entire focus is riveted on that big metal machine. With its sleek lines, the tinted windows and black metal, it's like some computer gamer's wet dream. It doesn't look real. It looks CGI.

"What the hell?" Reuben says.

I glance at Calico and she's just as surprised as we are. "That wasn't here when I dropped Sammy off," she says.

"Well, it's sure here now," Reuben says. "The damn thing looks like a black ops chopper or something out of a sci-fi movie."

I give a slow nod of agreement. "Except I thought our world didn't intrude here."

"Normally it doesn't," Calico says. "But the elders say anything is possible, somewhere in the otherworld."

The cockpit door cracks open and we all tense up.

Reuben turns to Calico. "If they've got guns or lasers or some kind of crap like that, you get us the hell out of here."

Calico nods. "Pronto."

But it turns into a whole other kind of crazy when the last person in the world I'd expect to see drops down to the ground from the helicopter: Thomas Corn Eyes. Following him is Night Woman, that strange raven woman I saw at Ancestors Canyon when the tribe was laying Derek Two Trees to rest. She doesn't have the ghostly giant raven's skull superimposed above her shoulders anymore, but there's that regular-sized raven perched on one of them again, and it's just as ghostly—more the idea of a bird than the bird itself.

"What's *she* doing here?" I ask Calico, pitching my voice soft.

"I have no idea."

"Thomas, you crazy Indian," Reuben yells. "Where did you get that machine?"

"That's no machine," Thomas says. "It's Gordo, Consuela's big black dog." He looks at the raven woman and adds, "I'm pretty sure he's some kind of Transformer."

Night Woman rolls her eyes.

Consuela? A dog that's a Transformer? I'm thinking Reuben's right about the crazy. Thomas has been smoking some serious weed or gotten into somebody's peyote stash. But then—

I'm standing right there watching it happen and I still don't believe what I'm seeing. The helicopter seems to quietly implode on itself, growing smaller and smaller until that black dog from Ancestors Canyon is standing there. Still big, but no longer the size of a small pony. More like a mastiff.

The helicopter's gone like it never existed.

"Seriously?" I hear myself saying. I want to sit down on the ground before my legs give way. It's all I can do to stand upright. "What the hell is this?" I ask Calico and Reuben, but they're looking as stunned as I'm feeling.

Sammy's already sitting on the ground, staring with bug eyes as Thomas and his companions approach.

The black dog lies down a few yards from Sammy and fixes his gaze on the casino owner. Night Woman stops beside her dog, but Thomas comes right over to us and gives Reuben a hug.

"What are you doing here?" Reuben asks.

"Morago sent me. I'm supposed to be the eyes and ears of the tribe while Consuela here kills Sammy."

We all look at her. She looks calm, but her ghost raven has its head cocked, staring at me intently.

"I'm *not* here to kill him," Night Woman says.

Thomas shrugs. "She says. But she's here to judge him on behalf of the *ma'inawo*, and you tell me: How else is it going to go?"

"Do you know what he's talking about?" I ask Calico.

She looks tired, which isn't like her. "I don't know anything anymore," she says.

Reuben's shaking his head. "I don't get it," he says to Thomas. "Yesterday I had to work just to get you to agree to come to a sweat, and now—"

"Her bird put a spell on me so that I'll embrace tribal ways."

Reuben looks confused. "What bird?" he asks.

"The one on her shoulder," I say.

"I don't see a bird," Calico says.

"It's kind of ghostly, like it's hardly there," I say. I'm not sure how to explain it any better than that, so I focus on Thomas, instead.

"How's embracing tribal ways working for you?" I ask.

He shrugs. "I'm here, aren't I?"

"Maybe she could get the bird to put a spell on Sammy," I say.

Speaking of whom, Sammy finally twigs that things are not going his way. He starts to stand, but Reuben puts a hand out and pushes him back down. He doesn't even look at Sammy while he's doing it. Instead, his gaze is fixed on Consuela. "What's the Spirit of Death got to do in our business?" Reuben asks.

"She's not the Spirit of Death," Thomas says before the woman can answer. "Gordo—the dog—is. She's only his travelling companion. And apparently there isn't *a* spirit of death—there's a bunch of them, because how can death be in all the places it has to be at the same time?"

"Santa Claus seems to do pretty well," I say.

That gets me an elbow in the side and a quick grin from Calico.

"So why are you here?" Reuben asks Consuela while I study the dog, trying to figure out how it can change into a helicopter. The physics make no sense at all.

The woman holds her head high. "I am here as Night Woman, for the *ma'inawo*," she says. "Sammy Swift Grass must answer for the deaths he has caused."

"I haven't killed *anybody!*" Sammy says, his voice pitched way too high.

Reuben gives him a light cuff on the back of his head. "Shut up."

"Wait," Calico says, her brow furrowing. "What do you mean, 'as'? You're not Night Woman?"

Consuela shakes her head. "I took the idea of her from *ma'inawo* stories to make sure that justice would be done."

Calico looks pissed. "So you're just like the rest of us cousins, only older."

The raven woman holds her gaze. "How is this relevant?"

"It tells me you don't belong here. This is between the local cousins and the Kikimi tribe. *You* have no say in any of it."

"I'm here to help."

"Like you 'helped' me?" Thomas asks.

The woman turns to him. "That was Si'tala's doing, not mine."

I want to ask who Si'tala is, but Thomas is already talking.

"Si'tala didn't sic a bunch of salvagers on me," he says.

"You did *what?*" Calico demands of Consuela at the same time that Reuben says, "Those things are real?"

"Oh yeah," Thomas says. "And when I die, they get to eat up my spirit in the ghost lands."

"I don't know or care who this 'Si'tala' is, but *you* need to leave," Calico tells the raven woman.

"Careful," Consuela says. "I'm not some besotted five-fingered being that will jump to do your bidding."

That dig, I assume, is directed at me, but I don't really care what some woman I don't know thinks, even if she does have a dog that can change into a helicopter.

I step in front of Calico and the raven woman's attention fixes on me—both her and the bird on her shoulder.

I hear Calico make a little growl of annoyance behind me, but I decide to keep it simple.

"Like Calico said," I tell Consuela. "We can handle this. Without your help."

The woman draws her shoulders back, eyes flashing. Her ghost raven seems more fixated on me than angry. The dog lumbers to its feet and seems half again larger than it was when it lay down. Its gaze is fixed on me as well, eyes so dark they seem to swallow all the light around us.

I don't know why we don't just give Sammy to her. It's not like we weren't considering the idea of throwing him off the top of this mountain ourselves. But there's something else going on here now that's about more than Sammy. What I do know is that Calico's ticked off, Reuben's unhappy, and I'm not letting this woman run roughshod over either of them without a fight.

Suddenly the ghostly raven leaves her shoulder and flies across the distance between us. Even though it's semi-transparent, I can see every edge of its glossy feathers, the gleam of its bill, the light in its eyes. I'm transfixed until I realize it's going to collide right into me. By that time, it's too late.

I start to duck, but the bird's trajectory and speed drive it right into my chest.

I don't mean it bangs up against me. It shoots itself right inside of me.

For a long moment I stand there, too stunned to react. An icy coldness bursts in my chest, rapidly spreading throughout my body. An odd metallic taste fills my mouth. I realize that what I'm tasting is blood. I've bitten my tongue.

I try to lift a hand to my mouth, but my arm won't move.

Then something explodes behind my eyes and I can feel myself falling, toppling like some old tree struck by lightning. My friends are shouting, but they sound a million miles away.

Then there's nothing more.

49

LEAH

L eah braced herself for the worst as the doctor cleared his throat. Marisa couldn't wait.

"What's wrong?" she asked, jumping to her feet. "Has something happened to Aggie?"

The doctor shook his head. "No, it's just that there's a man at the nurses' station who insists on seeing her. He's a really big guy and he's making the nurses nervous. They want to call security, but I thought I'd better ask if you know him. Maybe you can calm him down."

"What's his name?" Morago asked.

"He says it's Diego Madera."

The name meant nothing to Leah, but Morago immediately stood up.

"I'll talk to him," he told the doctor.

"Do you know him?" Leah asked as she followed him down the hall.

Marisa walked ahead of them with the doctor.

Morago nodded. "He lives up in the mountains. On the rez, they call him Old Man Puma."

"Why?" Leah asked.

"Because he's an old mountain lion spirit who was here when the deserts were still an ocean. They say the mountains are named after him."

"You mean, after his family?"

Morago shook his head. "No. After him."

"But that's—" Impossible, Leah had been about to say. But with all she'd experienced so far today, she wasn't sure the word held a real meaning anymore.

They came around a corner and there he was. She had to admit to a little disappointment. Not that Diego Madera wasn't an imposing figure. She'd just expected him to be bigger than life, somehow—decked out like a vaquero of old in fancy boots and jacket, with a big gaucho hat decorated with silver and turquoise, like Pancho Villa might have worn.

But the man waiting at the nursing station was dressed casually—cowboy boots, jeans, a plain white cotton shirt. His hair was a tawny gold, his skin tone a light brown. He was tall, shoulders broad, hips lean. His eyes, she saw, when he turned at their approach, were a penetrating green-yellow.

"Morago," he said when they reached him, "tell these people I need to see Aggie."

"*Ohla*, Diego. Aggie's not with us right now."

"I know that. I just saw her in the spirit realms. I told her she had to make a choice: live or let go. She let go."

The doctor, nurses and Marisa all looked as confused as Leah was feeling. But Morago only frowned.

"Why would you say that to her?" he asked.

"I thought I was helping." He looked past Morago to where Leah and Marisa were standing. "Who are you?"

"These are Aggie's granddaughters."

Diego studied them for a long moment, then nodded. "I have to see Aggie," he said, "but the five-fingered beings are objecting."

Leah didn't think anybody could stop this big man from doing whatever he wanted. But then she realized he was simply being polite. The look in his eyes told her it was only for the time being.

"To do what?" Morago asked.

Diego's attention turned to the shaman, his surprise plain. "To call her back—what else? But I need the connection her body can give me, so that she actually hears me."

Morago nodded. "Let him see her," he told the doctor.

"I'm afraid that's not—"

"This isn't about science medicine," Morago said, cutting him off. "It's time for spirit medicine.

"Go on," he added to Diego, nodding toward the door. "Try not to break the windows."

"What do you mean?" Marisa asked. "What's he going to do?"

"Just as he said, he's going to call her spirit back. But he has a loud voice."

The doctor started to move forward as Diego opened the door to Aggie's room, but Morago stepped in front of him.

"My patient—" the doctor started.

Morago cut him off. "She's my patient now. She's under the care of the spiritual leader of the Kikimi people."

"You mean that man?" the doctor asked, pointing at Diego through the observation window. Diego had closed the door to the room and was approaching Aggie's bed.

"I'm speaking of myself," Morago told him.

The doctor backed away. "Call security," he told the nurses.

Leah watched Diego at Aggie's bedside on the other side of the window. The vibrant woman she and Marisa had met this morning seemed diminished, her form overwhelmed by the invasive life support system that was keeping her alive. Leah was inclined to agree with the doctor. If she was in such bad shape that she needed all of this to survive, they shouldn't be messing with it.

Movement by the window caught her eye. She lifted her gaze to see that a line of crows had settled along the outer window ledge, black feathers gleaming, dark eyes on Aggie, as though they understood exactly what was happening. Diego pulled a chair over to the bed and sat down.

"You told me when I arrived," Morago was saying, "that you had no medical explanation for her coma. That her wound, while serious, shouldn't have caused this reaction."

"Your point being?" the doctor said.

"That this is a spiritual matter and needs to be dealt with by those with expertise in that kind of medicine."

"This is a hospital," the doctor said. "Not some shaman's tent out on the rez."

"I'm going to ignore that offensive remark for Aggie's sake," Morago said. Before he could go on, a door banged open at the far end of the corridor and two large security guards trotted in their direction.

Leah glanced up, distracted by the noise. She saw the pair of security guards, saw as well a half-dozen other men enter the corridor behind them. Black-haired and dark-skinned. Tall and broad-shouldered. Leah wondered if they were from the rez.

They didn't seem to be moving quickly, yet they were rapidly gaining on the guards, and in moments, had flanked them, two men to each guard. Behind the counter of the nurses' station, the male nurse reached for the phone. Before he could pick it up, one of the men leaned over and put his hand over the nurse's. The nurse tried to break his grip, but Leah could see that the dark-haired man was simply too strong.

From beside her, Marisa suddenly grabbed Leah's shoulder.

"Oh my god," she said in a strained voice.

Leah turned back to Aggie's room to see that Diego's face was *changing.* Broadening. Becoming something other than human. In moments, his head became that of a mountain lion. She watched in captivated fascination as he leaned forward, his mouth opening wider than should have been possible. She remembered what Morago had said a few moments ago.

He has a loud voice.

She braced herself for the roar that was going to come, except as Diego continued to lean forward, his head began to disappear followed by the tops of his shoulders. She sensed the doctor stumbling back— an understandable reaction, she thought, given that her own legs had turned to jelly.

Again Morago's words returned to her.

He's going to call her spirit back.

That was where his head had gone. He was half in the otherworld, calling to Aggie.

"You see," she heard Morago say behind her, "not everything's the way they taught you in medical school."

"I—I—"

"Don't worry, doc. Nobody's planning to hurt your patient. We all have her best welfare in mind."

Leah pressed her face a little closer to the observation window. She had no idea where Diego's head was—what world it was in—but most of him was still visible.

Leah noticed a slight movement in Aggie's hand. Her fingers were beginning to twitch.

Marina's grip tightened on Leah's shoulder. "Did you see that?" she murmured.

Leah nodded. Her gaze rose a little to see that all the crows perched on the window ledge—and there had to be seven or eight of them, depending on the moment—were staring intently into the room. Behind them, more crows swooped in and out of sight, riding the wind. They seemed to be taking turns on the ledge.

"Our brothers are just as concerned as we are," an unfamiliar voice said from behind them.

They turned to find one of the black-haired men there. Leah blinked, looking back at the crows outside, and then to the stranger. She felt a small chill go up her spine. The man was even more handsome up this close. Though perhaps striking was a better description. His dark features were chiseled. Nose a little long, cheekbones prominent. Like the men in the hall, his complexion was considerably darker than Morago's. And where did anyone get hair that thick and black and glossy?

He held out his hand to Marisa. "I'm Gonzalo, and I want to thank you for looking after our friend the way you did." His gaze travelled from Marisa to Leah. He smiled, but the humour didn't reach his eyes. They were too shadowed with worry.

Marisa shook his hand. "When you say brothers..." she began, then let her voice trail off.

Leah knew just what she was going to ask, because the same question had immediately risen in her mind.

Gonzalo nodded. "We're all Yellowrock Canyon Corbae—winged, or five-fingered."

Leah wanted to be cool about it all, but it was hard when there was a man in Aggie's room whose head and shoulders had disappeared.

"Will he be able to call her back?" Marisa asked Gonzalo.

The crow man shrugged. "I don't know." He paused, studied them both for a moment, then added, "How do you know Aggie?"

"We don't, really," Marisa said. "But we were with her when she was hurt and she…she's the sort of person who inspires loyalty, even if you've just met her."

Gonzalo smiled. "I like you."

Leah caught movement in her peripheral vision. "Something's happening," she said.

By the bed, Diego's head and shoulders were still thrust into the otherworld, but on the bed itself, Aggie's body had risen until it was floating a few inches from the mattress. Leah flashed on too many late-night demonic possession movies. Things always started to get bad when people began floating.

She watched in morbid fascination as Aggie continued to rise. Then the body began to rotate, horizontally. "The IVs!" she cried.

And not just the IVs. There was Aggie's oxygen and who knew how many sensors monitoring her vital functions.

Pushing past Morago she yanked open the door and ran into the room.

"Wait!" he yelled.

She didn't. There wasn't time.

She darted across the room. Climbing up on the bed, she put her arms around Aggie's legs and held on. She was able to stop the body's spinning motion, but it continued to rise despite her best efforts to pull it back down to the bed.

"Get away!" she heard Morago cry.

She turned to see him halfway between the door and the bed, but then her vision distorted. Morago's body seemed to elongate, legs and head and shoulders growing long and thin, while his torso widened to impossible proportions. It was like looking in a funhouse mirror. He reached a weird, rubbery arm toward her that wobbled as though it had no bones, and was flapping in the wind, then her vision went black, her ears popped, and she was falling.

Falling.

Falling.

Aware, but unable to access any of her senses.

She wished she could pass out.

All she could do was fall.

50

SADIE

Sadie struggled in the grip of the two crow men, but they forced her outside without any apparent effort on their part. They let her go once they were in the witch's yard and she made an immediate scramble back toward the door. The one Ruby had called Manny grabbed her bicep before she'd taken more than a couple of steps, and she was brought up short. She punched him with her free hand. Her knife was in the wrong pocket for her to reach, or she'd have cut him just like she had the old woman.

"Fuck you, pervert!" she yelled as she tried to pull free.

Manny half smiled in response, but there was no humour in his eyes.

"We'll take you anywhere you want," he said, "except back in there."

"But Ruby—"

"Paid the price for the bargain you made. That can't be undone."

"It was supposed to be Reggie, not her."

He let go of her arm and she immediately reached in her pocket for her knife.

"Looking for this?" Manny asked, holding up the box cutter.

She lunged for it. "Give that back!"

Manny eluded her with an easy sidestep and she lost her balance, falling to her knees.

"Yeah, I don't think so," he said.

Neither of the crow men helped her to her feet. She started cursing them as she got up, but once she was standing, the words dried up. She stared past the crow men to where the gangbangers were now having a confrontation with two members of the tribal police.

"Oh crap," Sadie said, ducking her head and turning away.

"Don't worry," Manny said. "They can't see you. You made a bargain with the witch to keep yourself safe, remember?"

Sadie dared a glance in the direction of the cops. She recognized Jerry, the one who'd brought her back to the station, as well as the fat man who'd been behind the desk. Jerry's attention left the gangbangers to look toward them for a moment before he returned to the gangbangers.

Sadie couldn't believe it. How cool was this?

"He really didn't see us," she said.

"He didn't see you," Manny corrected her. "He saw us, but we're not on his radar. Now where do you want to go?"

"So…what?" she said, ignoring his question. "I'm invisible to anybody who wants to hurt me?"

"Pretty much."

Sadie nodded. "Okay. Then I want to go home."

"What's the address?" Manny asked.

She told him.

"I'll walk her, Xande," he said to his companion. "You and the boys can follow by air."

Xande nodded. He gave Sadie a scowl, then turned and walked toward the dry wash. Sadie watched until he was under the mesquite on the far side before turning back to Manny.

"What's his problem?" she asked.

"You."

Sadie frowned. "None of you like me very much, do you?"

"Is there any reason that we should?"

"Like I care. But if you've got such a hate on, how come you can see me?"

"We promised Aggie we wouldn't kill you and we promised Ruby we'd take you to wherever you want to go. We don't break our word. So whatever spell the witch used doesn't affect us. We don't like you, but we won't harm you."

"Huh."

"Now let's get going."

He turned from the wash and headed back across the witch's yard toward the street. Sadie fell in step with him.

"Can I have my knife back?" she asked.

"No."

"Why not?"

"Because you'll attack me. And since I can't kill you, I'll have to cripple you, and that means I'll have to carry you all the way."

"Jesus, sympathetic much?"

He didn't respond.

When they reached the street, Sadie turned for a last look at the witch's house and tried not to imagine what was happening to Ruby.

"I wouldn't try to cut you," she said.

"You already did try, but I had your knife."

"You grabbed me first."

"I'll grab you again if you don't start walking."

Sadie's retort died as she heard a weird sound. She turned around again to see what had to be a couple of hundred crows rise up from the mesquite trees along the wash. It was their wings, she realized, as they flew by overhead. The sound of all those wings.

She shivered and quickly started walking at Manny's side down the street. She tried not to think of the fact that he was one of them—a man that could change into a crow. Or maybe it was the other way around. It didn't matter. Either way, it was just too creepy.

Most of the flock disappeared from sight, but at least twenty or thirty kept pace as Manny led her out of the barrio and onto Mission Street. Some of the birds made lazy circles in the sky above them. Others flew from power line to rooftop to cactus to tree, going only short distances so that they were always in sight.

51

THOMAS

Thomas stared in shock as Steve began to collapse, but Reuben and Calico moved quickly, calling his name and bracing him on either side until they could ease him to the ground. Once they had Steve lying prone on the rock, Calico stood up and glared at Consuela, murder in her eyes.

The big black dog growled a deep threatening sound. Calico quickly bared her teeth, then ignored the dog and turned back to the raven woman. Looking at the three, Thomas realized that Gordo was directing his displeasure at Consuela, not Calico. The dog kept staring at Consuela's shoulder, as if searching for Si'tala.

Reuben straightened up as well. "You may be from some old corbae clan," he said to Consuela, "but that means nothing out here. You'd better fix whatever the hell you've done to Steve, or all the mojo you've got stored up inside you won't be enough to stop us from taking you apart. Even that oversized dog of yours is pissed at you right now."

"She sent her ghost raven into him," Thomas said. "It flew right into Steve's chest before he went down."

"I had nothing to do with it," Consuela said. "Si'tala has a mind of her own."

Reuben looked confused. "I didn't see any raven."

"Steve flinched like he'd been hit," Calico said, "but I was behind him. I couldn't see what was happening."

"It was her bird attacking him—she calls it Si'tala," Thomas told them. "Her ghost raven. It's like…her shadow or something."

"She has a mind of her own," Consuela repeated.

Thomas nodded. "She likes to blame it for anything she doesn't want to take responsibility for herself."

The raven woman shot him a sour look.

"I don't care what the bird is," Calico said, "and I don't care what or who's to blame. Get it out of him—*now*."

"I can't," Consuela said. "I wouldn't know where to begin."

Thomas had witnessed Si'tala's autonomy, such as it was, so he might have felt some sympathy for Consuela if he hadn't had such a crap day because of her.

Calico nodded. "Then maybe I'll start tearing pieces off of you until you start to remember."

The raven woman stood taller. "You could try," she began.

Gordo suddenly seemed to double in size. He rose and walked stiff-legged toward Consuela until he was directly in front of her, lips curled up, showing teeth. Consuela seemed surprised, but she held up her hands in a placating manner.

Thomas exchanged a puzzled glance with Calico and Reuben. Why was the woman's dog taking their side?

"It wasn't my doing," Consuela said to the dog, then she looked up and sighed. "Fine," she continued. "This is all I know: there are dream-lands within the dreamlands." She paused and met each of their gazes. Calico nodded for her to continue. "I think my sister has taken your friend into his own inner world. Into his mind."

"But *why?*" Thomas asked.

"You'll have to ask her. But to reach them, you'll need a shaman or dreamwalker."

For a moment, no one spoke, then they all turned to Thomas.

"Don't look at me," Thomas said. "I'm no shaman."

"Perhaps not yet," Consuela said. "But you have a shaman's sight. You might be able to see into your friend's mind and call them both back to us."

"I wouldn't even know how to start."

"Well, I'm no expert," Reuben said, "but Morago would probably lay his hands on Steve's temples and…" His voice trailed off and he shrugged. "Yeah, I don't know either."

"Medicine is a matter of will," Consuela said. "It's a conversation between you and the spirits. Anything else—the laying on of hands, burning tobacco or smudge sticks—is merely a focus."

"So what do I do?" Thomas asked.

She shrugged. "What the shamans did in the long ago, before they had their rituals and songs. You make it up. You decide what you want to do, and you will it to happen."

Thomas gave a helpless look to the others, but neither Reuben nor Calico had anything to offer.

Gordo had lain down again, almost the size of a normal large dog at the moment.

Sammy sat off to the side, a glazed look in his eyes.

"I guess she's right," Reuben finally said. "Shamans didn't always know how to work their medicine. At some point, they had to learn how to do it, just as Jimmy Cholla had to teach the first dog soldiers how to find their animal shapes. Somebody had to figure it out."

"But that somebody's not me," Thomas said.

Reuben shook his head. "You don't know that. You can't know it until you try."

"I…" Thomas's voice trailed off. He looked away to where the otherworld mountains marched to the horizon under skies so blue they didn't seem real. But after the past couple of days, nothing seemed quite real anymore. He turned to Consuela.

"That feather I gave back to you," he said. "Do you still have it?"

52

STEVE

"You're awake."

I blink my eyes open to find myself lying on some big flat rock with Consuela Mara sitting cross-legged beside me. Her hair falls down to frame her face as she leans over me, peering into my face with interest.

I can't see much beyond her features and the huge expanse of blue sky behind her. The air's thin and the wind blows endlessly, which makes me think we're still high up in the otherworld mountains. But I also get the sense that only the two of us are here.

"Where am I?" I ask.

The question appears to amuse her.

"I have no idea," she says. "Somewhere in your mind, I assume."

"Somewhere in my…" I shake my head and try to think. The last thing I remember is that damned raven woman sending her ghost bird to attack me.

Except that's not quite right.

The bird didn't attack me. It went *inside* me.

"You're not Consuela," I say. I don't know how I know it, but as soon as the words slip out, I'm sure that I'm right. There's something different—softer—in her eyes, but she looks enough like Consuela to be her twin.

I push myself to a sitting position and she scoots back a few feet without getting up.

"That's true," she says. "I'm Si'tala."

"Are you related to Consuela?"

"In a manner of speaking. You could think of me as her shadow sister. Her memory, given what substance it can glean from the medicine of the wind and mountains."

Like that makes any sense.

"So what are we doing here?" I ask instead.

She smiles. "I wanted to talk to you."

"I can think of easier ways to get my attention."

She nods. "But I can only speak to you in a situation such as this."

"Where you fly inside my head."

She nods again, then gets a sympathetic look. "What is this place?" she asks. "It seems so desolate."

"Depends on your definition. If we're really inside me, this looks an awful lot like the place I imagine when I'm meditating. I find it restful."

She turns her head in a slow half circle, taking in the starkness surrounding us. I don't have to look. I know what's here. A flat island of a plateau on a mountaintop in the middle of nowhere. No matter what direction you face, there isn't one damn thing to see except for the endless sky. No other mountains, no other land at all.

Si'tala finally turns from the view to face me again. She moves closer until there's maybe a yard between us. Four feet, tops. She looks far more innocent than her sister. Her gaze searches mine.

Slowly, her face lights up in a radiant smile. "You have nothing to regret," she says after a moment.

"Excuse me?"

"We've already had this conversation," she says, "but since you don't remember, I'm happy to have it again."

"You know," I tell her. "I get that weird-and-mysterious plays big with you *ma'inawo*, but if you're hoping for any kind of meaningful conversation, you're going to have to cut the bullshit. In other words, either say something that makes sense or shut up."

I give her a hard stare, but her smile never falters. It's the real thing. Whatever's happening here amuses her to no end, which pisses me off just a little more. The worst thing is, I don't get the sense she's laughing at me. She's laughing with me, only I don't get the joke.

"Let me start again," she says. "You see that the world is a much different place than you once assumed it was, correct?"

I don't know how she knows that, any more than I understand how a ghost raven can turn into a woman—who's sitting with me inside my head—in a place I only imagined.

For the moment, I decide to play along. "How do you know what I see or don't see?" I ask.

"Patience. Just answer me—is this true or not?"

I give her a reluctant nod.

"Given this new worldview," she says, "do you allow that you might be unfamiliar with some aspects of it?"

I wish she'd just get to the point, but I give her another nod.

"You asked who I was earlier, and I told you I'm Consuela's shadow sister, but you don't know what that means, do you?"

"You said something about being her memory."

She claps her hands together like a pleased kindergarten teacher and sits back a little. "When you live long enough, memory can be a burden. Consuela walked the first days, not long after her husband drew the world out of that big fat pot of his. She has more memories than she knows what to do with."

"Ohhkay," I say slowly, but I'm pretty clueless as to what she just said.

Her eyes twinkle, which tells me she knows how I'm feeling.

"Every cousin handles the weight of all these memories differently," she says. "Some live only in the moment—they literally can't see the past or future anymore. Some are more judicious—they might allow themselves a hundred or so years to hold in their minds. Some go mad."

"What about Consuela? Where does she fit in—the latter category?"

She shakes her head. "Some cousins put their memories into a shadow-self and let it fend for itself, unless they want access to one thing or another that the shadow knows, but they have forgotten."

"And you're her shadow."

She nods. "But she hasn't accessed the memories I hold for a very long time, and I'm becoming my own person. As the years go by, I'm less and less bound to her. One day soon, I'll find someone to make a body for me from wind and mud, and I won't be a ghost bird anymore —or a woman who can only talk to someone by entering their mind."

"I guess I can see how that would suck."

She tilts her head and looks at me thoughtfully, as though trying to decide whether to share an intimate secret. "You may have noticed," she finally says, "that Consuela is unhappy. For whatever reason, she has kept more bad memories inside herself than good, letting me hold the happier ones. That's been good for me, but by her very nature, she's been acquiring more and more bad ones as time goes on. If she gives them to me, I'm likely to become more like her."

I take a breath. May as well go the whole dang hog, as my grand-mother Sadie used to say. Do I believe everything she's telling me? After the last couple days, I either have to keep my mind wide open or just shoot myself in the head.

"So why do you want to talk to me?" I ask.

"I had a premonition," she says, "when I saw you this morning in Ancestors Canyon. So I had a look at your story—where you came from, where you're going."

"You can do that? You have access to—what? Everything?"

"Hardly. But when I meet someone, I can follow the patterns of their life. Past, present, future."

"What? You can travel through time?"

She shakes her head. "What most people don't realize is that all time happens at the same time."

"So you're saying you already know everything we're talking about right now? You know what's going to happen because, for you, it's all happening at the same time."

She nods. "Unless you change something in the past."

"Wait a minute. How do you change the past when you're living in the present?"

"Not the you in the present—the you in the past. It's happening at the same time. When you change something back then, everything else changes."

I scrunch up my shoulders, wishing I could pull my head in like a turtle. "You're making my brain hurt," I tell her.

She gives me a sympathetic smile, but doesn't say anything.

Si'tala is trying to be gentle, but I'm dog-tired and cranky. "So when do I die?" I say, unable to keep the edge out of my voice.

Her eyes widen. "Do you really want the answer to that?"

"No. I was just being a smart-ass. Look, you'll have to cut me some slack. These past couple of days haven't been the best I've ever had. It's all put me on edge, and that makes me mouthy."

I think harder about what's she's saying, and it hits me. If a person can go back in time…

"So when you…access…the past," I say. "You could fix a mistake?"

She nods. "If you can figure out how. But I should warn you, it rarely works out for the better. Some say that it merely creates another world, so that now there are two of you. One carries on in this world; the other has an entirely different life from that point on in some other world."

"You don't know how?" I ask. It comes out pretty harsh, but what I leave unsaid is, because you seem to know everything, lady.

As I'm staring at her waiting for an answer, she slowly crosses her eyes and gets a crooked smile on her face. She looks so ridiculous, I can't help but laugh.

"What are you—five?" I ask.

Her features return to normal and she giggles. "You just looked like you needed a smile," she says.

Okay, she and that twin of hers are day and night.

"You still haven't said why you wanted to talk to me," I try instead.

Her smile turns into an expression of longing. "That body I was telling you about?" she says. "The one I need in order to break from Consuela?"

I nod, remembering.

"I want you to make it for me." I see a flicker of hope dance in her eyes.

"Me? I'm a musician, lady, not a sculptor."

She nods encouragingly. "But the creative medicine is strong in you. I was going to ask the boy—Thomas. It's why I gave him the feather charm. I wanted to wake the shaman inside him. His medicine is strong and will grow stronger every year, especially once he starts training. But it will take time for him to grow into his potential, and I find myself unwilling to wait."

"If you need strong medicine," I say, "you should talk to Morago."

"Perhaps that's true. But he will require a favour in return."

"And you think Thomas or I won't?"

"I've no idea. I do know that whatever favour either of you might ask of me, it will be something easy to give. But Morago... Morago will ask me for something like bringing the tribe together again. To shut down the casino and everything that has grown up around it."

"And that's a bad thing because?"

"There is a purpose to everything," she tells me. "Sammy Swift Grass might seem like a divisive force at the moment, but there will come a time in the near future when it's he who will bring the tribe together once more. He and Thomas."

"You really think he's going to change out of the goodness of his heart?"

"What makes you think he doesn't have the best interests of the tribe in mind?" she asks, instead of replying.

"Because he's all about making money? Because he doesn't respect the traditions of his own people?"

"Much of the money he makes goes to the tribe—just as a portion of your earnings from royalties and publishing rights does."

"I don't know what you're talking about," I lie.

She shrugs. "Both he and the traditionalists will come to terms. They each have something to teach the other. And this will become important when water rights become an issue."

"Say what?"

"The city expands more and more every year. The same neighbour-hoods that have sprung up everywhere else in the city have already begun their march toward the mountains. Before long, all the new houses and schools and golf courses and businesses will require water, and where do you think they will get it?"

I shake my head. "I've never thought about it."

"When storms come, the water flows down from the mountains of the National Park and through the canyons. But the water itself is on Kikimi lands, between the two halves of the rez. The city will try to negotiate for the rights, perhaps build a reservoir. But it will have to be on Kikimi lands. What will happen if the tribe refuses? Or the city decides the asking price is too steep?"

I don't have to even think about that. It's an old story in the desert, and an older story when it comes to Native land claims.

"Trouble," I say.

She nods. "And it will require a man like Sammy to negotiate with them because he understands both worlds. Just as it will require the Warrior Society to stand guard and protect what belongs to the tribe. They will have to learn to work together. Why do you think the Women's Council let Sammy go ahead with his plans? Because they could see ahead to when they would need his expertise and the money that his enterprises raise."

I look at her in a new light. "You're awfully worldly for a ghost bird," I tell her with a wink.

This time, she doesn't laugh. She just keeps staring at me in earnest. I know she has only one thing on her mind.

"So you want me to sculpt a body for you," I say.

She nods.

"I'm crap as an artist," I tell her. "The most I can draw is stick figures. I'd hate to see what kind of sculpture I'd do. Believe me, you wouldn't want to be the butt-ugly thing that I'd put together."

She shakes her head. "It's the intent that's important," she says. "Not what it might look like."

I try to consider this from every angle, but my perspective is severely limited.

"And no harm will come to anyone if I do this?" I ask.

"Not directly. That is, it will not be by my intention. Consuela will not be pleased, but she can ask the thunders for help creating another shadow-self, if she even wants one. This would be a new beginning for her, as well. She might even decide to live in the present, and hold on to more of the beauty in life, rather than focus on her sombre thoughts."

Her eyes twinkle. "Or a hundred years from now I might trip someone," she says with a chuckle. "Only you can decide if it would be all your fault because you gave me a body."

I laugh and nod. Are parents responsible for what their grownup kids might do? Yes, because they brought them into the world. No, because you can't control another being. Nor should you try. Which makes me decide that it's time Si'tala had her independence.

"Okay," I tell her. "I'll do it."

The look of gratitude shining in her eyes is worth every stupid thing I've gone through today.

"Should I start now?" I ask. I look around, but all I see is rock.

"You need to return to your body first," she says. "And you have unfinished business to take care of before you can fulfill our bargain."

Before I can ask her what she means by that, she adds, "What do you want in return?"

I wave a hand. "You can owe me."

She smiles. "I knew you would say that."

"Because for you, the future's happening at the same time as right now."

She shakes her head. "No, because of the man you are. I don't even need to ask for your own promise that no one will be hurt by whatever favour you might ask."

"What did you mean by 'unfinished business'?" I ask.

She stands and points past the edge of the plateau, down to something that's out of my sight. This is my meditation place, so I know there can't be anything there, but I stand up anyway and see something floating out in the air. It's a body, I realize—a woman's body turning in a slow circle.

53

SADIE

It was a long walk with Manny down Mission Street to the neighbourhood where Sadie's family lived. Sadie's hands were jammed in the pockets of her hoodie, the right one reaching longingly for the utility knife that Manny had taken from her. Manny's long black hair swung loosely with his gait. He didn't speak to her. The crows continued to follow.

She missed her knife. The closer they came to the Higgins house, the more she felt the need to cut something. Herself. Manny. Some random stranger. She didn't care which right now.

Her crappy neighbourhood only made her mood worse. The yards were all dust and dead weeds and half-assed cacti, most of it browned and unhealthy. A few yards sported ragged palms, and most had at least one dead car, usually up on blocks. The pavement was cracked and rutted, the houses in poor repair. No wonder she was such a mess, growing up in this Loserville.

And here she was, back again, and the only way she'd be getting out this time was by going to jail or scoring some cash and running as far as she could. That dream of a big payday selling out Jackson Cole felt like it was centuries old, gone and turned to dust like the dirt underfoot. Now she'd settle for enough money to get a one-way bus ticket out of town. Maybe then she could start over again. It all depended on what kind of cash Reggie had lying around the house. And how many broken bones it would take before she got her hands on it.

But first, she had to get the drop on him.

"This is close enough," Sadie said when they were a block away from the house.

Manny nodded and stopped. "Here's something you need to remember," he said before she could head off on her own.

"Yeah, what's that?"

"Aggie dies and all bets are off."

Sadie took a step back from him. "You can't hurt me. You promised you wouldn't. And the witch made a bargain."

"That you paid for with the soul of someone who only wanted to protect you."

Sadie did feel bad about that. "I never meant—"

Manny cut her off. "Doesn't matter what you meant. What matters is what happens. And I didn't make you any kind of a promise. My clan made a promise to Aggie, and that ends with her death. So you'd better pray she doesn't die."

"I don't want her to die. I just want people to leave me alone."

"Guess you should have thought of that before you started pissing on anybody who came near you."

"The witch's magic will protect me."

She remembered how the cops hadn't even seen her when they were in the witch's yard.

"Maybe," Manny said. "Maybe not. But I think blood magic is stronger than anything a witch can conjure."

"What do you mean by 'blood magic'?"

"The magic that a blood debt can call up. Don't count on your witch's spells to save you if Abigail dies."

Then he changed right in front of her eyes. Man to crow, the transformation so fast that she never actually saw it happen. One moment Manny was standing there glaring at her, the next a big crow went winging up into the sky. Something clattered on the pavement where he'd been standing. She looked down, then bent and picked up her utility knife. She smiled and blew the dirt from it, slid the blade out then back in again. She did that a couple of times before she put it her pocket.

Her gaze went to the crows. They were still everywhere. In the trees, on the rooflines. She couldn't tell which was Manny. They all seemed to be watching her. Stupid asshole birds. She gave them the finger and walked on, toward the house. When she got one yard full of dirt and scrub away, she walked down the neighbour's lane to where their own little junkyard started with the rusted remains of a few cars and a pickup truck. A tall, ratty palm rose up at the back of the property, throwing what shade it could on the junked vehicles. Three crows up in the browning fronds watched her approach, like it was any of their business. Sadie ignored the birds and found a seat on the running board of the truck. From here, she could watch the house by peering around the front fender, but couldn't be easily seen by anybody in the house.

It was going to be a long wait until it would get dark, longer still before her parents would finally fall asleep. She took out the utility knife and played with the blade again, sliding it in and out, in and out. She should have stopped for water on the way here. She'd thought of it, but she didn't have any money, and it wasn't like stick-up-his-butt Manny would have spotted her any.

So. Here she was. Thirsty and bored, with way too much time to think and nothing to do except play with the utility knife.

She felt a little bad for what she'd said about Steve, and for cutting Aggie. But the old woman shouldn't have tried to stop her from leaving, and Steve needed to realize she didn't need anyone to plan out her life for her. Just because you were old didn't mean you knew anything, especially not if your idea of a good time was living in the frigging desert with a bunch of rocks and cacti. But basically, he'd been a good guy. He hadn't shared his dope with her, but he hadn't tried to fuck her, either. Most guys wouldn't have passed up the chance for a quickie.

She hadn't really meant to dump on him in front of the cops and his friends the way she had. That was all his stupid furry girlfriend's fault. She frowned, remembering how Calico had tried to bully her. She'd happily drop a big rock on Calico's head.

She peered around the fender. Still no movement in the house. Was Reggie home or wasn't he? For all she knew, he and Tina had gotten wasted and were sprawled out on their bed, completely oblivious to anything going on around them. It wouldn't be the first time that happened, especially on a Saturday. It wasn't like they had jobs or anything, but any excuse to get shitfaced would do.

She was still pissed at what had gone down back at the witch's house. Reggie's soul was supposed to be her payment to the witch, not Ruby's. It was a no-brainer. Reggie deserved the worst that could happen, but if he had a soul he wasn't using it, so it wouldn't even be missed. But Ruby…

Why the hell would Ruby even do that? It made no sense. But not much that people did made sense to her. Working at crap jobs. Living in this part of town. Or how about being a loser like Reggie, working twice as hard with his scams to make the same kind of money he could get from a real job?

She thumbed the utility blade out of its handle and in again. Leaning her head against the rusty door of the truck she looked back up into the palm tree. Now there were only two crows up there among the half dead fronds. The missing one made her feel uneasy, but when she looked around for it, too many others were perched in the area to figure out where it had gone.

A sound from the direction of her parents' house made her look around the fender again. The back door opened and Aylissa appeared, holding the door ajar while she shooed the two younger foster kids out. Riley and Gabriela looked nervous and scared, which had been pretty much their general demeanor from the first day Reggie and Tina had brought them home.

They were the children of some crack whore who was either dead or in prison—Sadie couldn't remember which. They'd only stopped being nervous around Sadie when they realized that she was getting the same rough indifference from Reggie and Tina as they were—worse, in fact.

The pair stepped out holding hands, looking younger than Sadie recalled, which was weird because she'd only been gone a day or so. Gabriela was the eldest of the two—six, to Riley's five. Other than that, Sadie only knew that their father had been Latino, their mother, white.

Aylissa was close to Sadie's own age, fair-skinned, where the little kids were a light brown, but her hair was a dark glossy black, where theirs was brown, and she usually wore it tied back in a loose chignon. Sadie watched her shut the door carefully, then lead the kids out into the backyard. The small leather satchel that was never out of her reach hung from her shoulder.

Sadie stood up to study the house, staying as much out of sight as she could behind the pickup. She couldn't sense any movement, but Tina and Reggie were pretty much the laziest people she'd ever met, so that didn't mean anything. She watched Aylissa take the kids across the yard, angling for where the packed dirt of the neighbour's lane at the back met that of the yard. They were probably headed for the playground, which was what Tina called the empty lot down the block where the neighbourhood kids hung out.

Sadie considered the house for another moment before starting off after them. She froze as a cop car pulled up in front of the house. A sheriff's department car, not one from the rez police, like that was going to make a difference. By this point they'd all be after her and here she was, out in the open. All they had to do was look in front of their noses.

If she bolted now, it would look suspicious and they'd be all over her. If she didn't, she'd lose precious time for getting away.

Crap, crap, crap!

While she was trying to decide what to do, one of the car doors opened and a big Latino cop got out. He did an automatic check of his surroundings, his gaze travelling past her as though she wasn't standing right here in front of his big stupid face.

She almost laughed out loud.

He couldn't see her. *Of course* he couldn't see her. The witch's spell was still working. He meant her harm, so she was invisible to him.

She turned away, ignoring the prickle of anticipation telling her that any minute, whatever was hiding her would fall away and he'd be after her. Keeping her hoodie up over her head, hands in her pockets, she slouched off after Aylissa and the kids and caught up with them at the empty lot.

Only some of the crows—a half-dozen or so—followed. Sadie ignored them.

The three kids were alone, facing away from Sadie's approach. Aylissa sat on a stack of three old tires watching Riley and Gabriela toss pebbles at a tin can that had been wedged into a sorry-looking prickly pear.

"Got any water in that bag of yours?" Sadie asked.

Aylissa started, but when she turned a big grin spread across her face.

"You're okay!" she said.

She didn't jump up and hug Sadie. They didn't do stuff like that, although right at this moment, Sadie could have used a hug. She settled for seeing three familiar faces, none of which belonged to someone who wanted to smack her in the head or throw her in jail.

"So are you rich now?" Aylissa asked. She pulled a plastic water bottle out of her satchel and tossed it over.

"That kind of fell through."

Sadie had a long drink before she put the cap on the bottle and tossed it back. Aylissa caught it easily.

"Life sucks that way," she said.

"No shit." Sadie smiled at Gabriela and Riley. "You guys okay?"

They both nodded, eyes wide.

"Did Reggie really drive you into the desert and throw you away?" Riley wanted to know.

Sadie wasn't surprised that Aylissa had told them. They had a pact: no bullshit between them.

"Yeah," she said, "but it didn't work out the way he expected. Is Reggie at home?"

"He's still at the cop shop," Aylissa said. "I heard Tina talking to him and they're pretty pissed off about him trying to scam them."

Sadie didn't let her face give away what she was thinking. Reggie wasn't even home. That figured. She didn't even get to slice him up a little and rip him off before she disappeared.

"The cops were pulling up to house when I went by," she said.

Aylissa gave her a surprised look. "They're taking Tina in as well?"

Sadie shook her head. "Doubt it. I'm pretty sure they're looking for me. I think I'm in a lot of trouble."

Aylissa frowned. "Why would you be in trouble? Reggie's the one who dumped you in the desert and then made up all these lies about you being kidnapped."

"It's what I did after," Sadie said. She glanced up a nearby saguaro where a solitary crow sat, watching. "The cops are looking for me and probably other people are too."

"We won't tell on you," Gabriela said, her face solemn. "We'll pretend like we didn't see you."

Riley and Aylissa nodded in solidarity.

"I'd tell you more," Sadie said, "but the less you know, the less they can try to pull you down with me."

"Like that's ever stopped the cops before," Aylissa said.

Sadie shrugged.

"So what are you going to do?" Aylissa asked. "Where can you go?"

"I don't know. Do you have any money?"

Aylissa dug into the pocket of her shorts and pulled out a wad of bills. She offered them to Sadie, who reached out and took the bills, riffling through them.

"There's got to be over a hundred dollars here," she said. "Where did you get it?"

"Reggie's wallet—not all at once. A few bucks here, a few bucks there."

"Sweet."

Sadie counted out twenty dollars and tried to hand the rest back to Aylissa, who put up her hands and shook her head.

"No. Take it," Sadie said, holding it out. "I appreciate having some money, but you guys might need some too, depending on what happens with Reggie and Tina. Social Services might finally figure out their scam and then you'll need a stake."

"This stuff you did," Aylissa said as she took the cash and repocketed it. "You're a minor. Can't you just say you're sorry you messed up?

They've gotta cut you some slack if you tell them about Reggie ditching you out in the middle of nowhere."

The world doesn't work like that, Sadie wanted to say, but she didn't have the heart, especially around the little ones.

"That's a good idea," she said instead. "I'll give it a shot."

Her gaze drifted to the saguaro where the crow had been perching. There were four of them on it now, one on the very top, the others scattered on the big cactus's arms.

Right. Apologize. Like Manny and his creepy buddies would even listen or care.

"I should go," she said.

"Let us know, once you find a place to stay," Aylissa said. "I've got another email addy Reggie hasn't cracked. Same name, but it's with Yahoo."

Sadie nodded.

She doubted it would happen. The next time Aylissa or the kids would hear about her, she'd be on the news. Going to jail. Or her body being found after she'd been ripped apart by birds.

Everything felt tight and awkward inside her, like her skin was shrinking, or her body was bloating. She needed to let something out —whatever it was when the blade of her knife pierced her skin and the blood came welling up. She needed to let it out now.

"Be careful," she said. "Don't let Reggie…" Turn you into something like me, she thought, but she didn't finish. She knew their stories, what they'd been through, what they'd lost, their struggles coming through the system. They were stronger than her, even little Riley and Gabriela. They wouldn't put up with Reggie's shit for as long as she had. Hell, Aylissa had pulled a kitchen knife on some perv in her last placement.

When it came to the four of them, Sadie knew that she was the weak one.

"Here," Aylissa said, handing her a fresh bottle of water.

"Thanks."

For a moment, Sadie thought they were going to hug. She didn't know if she wanted it or if it would make her explode.

"See ya round," she said before anyone could step closer.

She walked away. The familiar sound of wings came to her ears as the crows lifted from the big saguaro to follow, but she ignored them. She gripped the utility knife in her pocket. They could go screw themselves. Everybody could go screw themselves.

But she needed to do something before she frayed away into little Sadie pieces and was blown away by the wind.

Maybe that wouldn't be such a bad thing.

At least she wouldn't be able to feel anything anymore.

54

MARISA GRANT

M arisa was following Leah into Aggie's room when Leah simply vanished. Here, then gone faster than a blink.

Marisa stopped dead. She felt like a hole suddenly opened in her chest and a piece of her stomach dropped to the floor. Her senses were overloading on the chemical smells, the stark walls, the array of monitoring equipment. All of it battered away at her, circling around the sudden emptiness inside her.

"No!" she cried and lunged forward.

A hand landed on her shoulder, stopping her. "Don't," Gonzalo said. "This is the business of medicine men now."

She turned her head toward him. "But—"

"They can do something," the crow man told her. "We can only make it worse."

She let him pull her toward the window, still inside the room, but out of the way. Two more of the dark-haired crow men filled the door, effectively blocking any entrance. By the bed, Morago circled around Aggie's floating body until he reached Diego's side. When he touched the other man's arm, Diego's head and shoulders reappeared from the otherworld.

He looked from Morago to Aggie.

"Did you find any sign of her?" Morago asked.

Diego shook his head. He reached out to touch Aggie, but Morago pushed his hand away. "Leah did that and she disappeared," he said.

"Disappeared?"

The shaman nodded. "As soon as she touched her."

Aggie's floating body turned enough to pull various tubes and monitors out. A klaxon of alarms began beeping in discordance with one another.

"I need to get in there," Marisa heard the doctor say.

The tall crow men continued to block his entrance. "There's nothing you can do," one of them told the doctor. His tone was similar to how Gonzalo had spoken to her.

Morago and Diego were studying Aggie's body, ignoring the cacophony of sound. "It makes no sense," Diego said. "If her spirit is gone, her body should be done. But it still functions, even without the five-fingered beings' medicine."

"And you didn't see Leah on the other side, a moment before I called you back?"

"I was drawn to the last place I saw Aggie. Neither she nor the woman were there, but others were. Consuela and her dog. Calico, Reuben Little Tree, that boy who works for him, and Steve Cole. And that hollow man from the other side of the rez."

"Sammy Swift Grass?"

Diego nodded. "Steve appeared to be unconscious, with his head on Calico's lap and Thomas kneeling beside them, waving a little black feather in Steve's face."

"That makes no sense."

"Unless he was trying to use his medicine to revive Steve." Diego frowned. "I could sense Aggie nearby, as strongly as I can sense you standing in front of me, but I couldn't see her."

"Perhaps she's in a deeper echo of that mountain," Morago said. "The dreamlands get twisty, the farther in you go."

"I suppose," Diego said, "though I'm not entirely convinced that's the case here. She seemed so *present*."

Listening to them, Marisa felt as though she'd stepped into some surreal foreign film where, although the actors were speaking English, she still felt she needed subtitles. Simple though the conversation was, every word felt obscure and out of place, especially with the distracting sound of the beeping. She didn't know most of the people they were talking about, and it seemed to her that nobody was focusing on the actual problem at hand.

"What about Leah?" she asked. "Can't you follow where she's gone?" Her gaze went from Diego to the shaman. "And if your magic's so much better than what the hospital can do, why aren't you reviving Aggie?"

Whose body continued to turn in a slow circle three feet above the bed.

"She's right," Diego told Morago. "Enough talking. I'll follow Leah and you do what you can for Aggie."

Morago caught Diego's arm again as the mountain lion man stood up and reached for Aggie. "You don't know where she's gone. What if neither of you can make your way back?"

Diego pulled free of Morago's grip. "This is my fault for giving Aggie bad advice in the first place," he said. "So it's up to me to fix it."

He reached out again and this time Morago didn't stop him. Marisa held her breath, but when Diego did make contact with Aggie's body nothing happened. His grip stopped her circling motion and that was all.

Marisa's heart sank. "Now what do we do?" she asked.

Diego let go and Aggie slowly began to turn again.

"Now we wait," he said. "Whatever comes next is in the hands of the thunders."

"The who?" Marisa asked.

"The great spirits."

Marisa sighed and looked away to the window. Crows were still perched in a line along the outer sill, with more wheeling in the sky beyond. She let her back take a slow slide down the wall until she was sitting on the floor. This trip had turned into a complete disaster. Alan should never have talked Leah into coming out here. And what was she supposed to tell him and their friends back home? Yeah, Leah just vanished—no, I mean literally—and I haven't seen her since.

She shook her head. They couldn't just wait around for some

spirits to sit up and take notice. With all of Morago and Diego's magic, and the ability to step between worlds, there had to be *something* they could do.

"And if nothing happens?" she asked.

For a long moment she didn't think anyone was going to answer. Then Diego looked at her.

"Something always happens," he said.

55

STEVE

It's so weird. The woman's just lying there face up, like she's laid out in an invisible floating coffin, arms folded across her chest. Then her features come into view and I almost jump off the edge to get to her.

Si'tala grabs my arm. "You can't fly," she says.

"But that's my friend Aggie."

"I know."

"You said we're in my mind," I tell her. "Well, in my mind I can fly."

"We're not just in your mind," she says. "We're in a part of the otherworld that echoes your mind. The laws of physics still apply here."

I point out toward Aggie. "Oh yeah? Then how come *she's* floating?"

And that doesn't even start to address the question of what the hell Aggie's doing here, when she's supposed to be in the hospital. I look closer and see that under her folded hands, Aggie's blouse is red with blood. This is making my head start to hurt again.

"Well?" I ask.

When I tear my gaze away from Aggie to see why Si'tala isn't answering me, I find the raven woman staring up into the sky. It takes me a moment to figure out what she's looking at, but finally, I see that there's a speck up there. I assume it's a bird until I realize that it's another body dropping rapidly toward us.

My first thought is, where the hell is it falling from? My second is, if it hits this mountaintop, it's going to make a horrible mess. It sure as hell won't survive—if whoever the hell it is isn't already dead.

If we're in my mind, shouldn't I be able to do something? Will it to stop and float gently down to where Si'tala and I are standing? Maybe float out there beside Aggie?

But I can't do a damned thing.

I remember what Si'tala told me.

We're not just in your mind. We're in a part of the otherworld that echoes your mind. The laws of physics still apply here.

I might as well try to catch the moon between my fingers for all the help I can be.

I put my hands on Si'tala's shoulders. "Do something," I tell her.

She regards me calmly. "Do what?"

"I don't know. You're the *ma'inawo*. Make some magic."

She studies me for a long moment that seems even longer because all I can think of is that poor bugger dropping out of the sky.

"Fine," she finally says.

I stumble back from her as a pair of enormous wings explode from her back. Loose feathers cloud the air all around us. Then she throws herself off the mountaintop. A slow turn brings her below Aggie's floating body before she darts up, heading on a trajectory that will take her directly into the path of the other body that's plummeting down.

With everything I've experienced these past couple of days, this is still an amazing sight. My chest goes tight with emotions that I can't begin to articulate.

This is what angels look like, I realize, as I watch her rise higher and higher on those sunlit wings.

56

THOMAS

"Have you always been wound so tight?" the raven woman asked Calico.

"Shut up," Thomas said before Calico could respond.

Gordo rumbled a low growl, but when Thomas glanced at the dog, he saw its displeasure was once again directed at Consuela and no one else. The dog was panting lightly.

"Fine," Consuela said, frowning at the dog. "I was just making conversation."

Thomas hadn't spent much time in her company, but he already knew that was anything but the case. Consuela was what Jerry Two Hawks referred to as a shit-disturber when he was calling out the ringleaders of the kids getting into trouble around the rez.

"Please be quiet," Thomas said to her. "I'm trying to concentrate here."

Bringing *her* stupid shadow sister out of Steve.

Which was a ridiculous thing to even be thinking of, especially when he had no clue what he was doing. Use his will. Yeah, if that were so effective, he could just will himself right off the rez, not to some godforsaken mountaintop in the middle of the otherworld.

"Fine," Consuela said again.

She stalked off to where Sammy sat near the edge of the plateau, staring off into the endless sky with a dull expression on his features.

Calico touched Thomas's arm. "Ignore them. You can do this."

He looked from her earnest features to Reuben, who nodded in agreement.

"Medicine's medicine," he said. "If Morago thinks you've got it in you, then you need to believe that and find a way to pull it out."

"It will be easier to do here," Calico said. "Everything is magnified in the dreamlands. This is where your ancestors first found their connections to their medicine."

Easier? That depended on your definition of the word. Because nothing was easy when you didn't have a clue about what you were doing.

Thomas turned his focus back to Steve, trying to muster the same optimism Reuben and Calico seemed to have. He studied Steve's face, looking for something in the slack features that would let him see Steve the way he saw people with *ma'inawo* blood walking around the rez—how the ghosts of their animal aspects settled on their shoulders, or rose up from behind their heads. Not that he thought Steve had an animal aspect—the man wasn't even Kikimi—but maybe if he looked hard enough, he'd find some way into understanding the riddle of how the damn bird had entered him, and where they were now.

He held the crow feather up in front of Steve's face and moved it slowly back and forth. There was something familiar about the motion, and it took him a moment to realize it reminded him of the swaying steps of his sisters when they danced. That called up the memory of the first time he'd seen Santana coaching Naya in the arroyo behind their house. Santana had seemed so self-assured. Later that same day, he'd asked her where she'd learned the steps because he couldn't remember her ever taking lessons from anyone.

"I didn't need to take lessons," she told him. "The steps were already in here." She laid a hand on her chest. "Auntie told me all I had to do was reach inside myself because all Corn Eyes women know how to dance. Naya saw what I meant right away."

Maybe it would work for him, too. If he was born with shaman's eyes, then maybe all he had to do was reach inside himself and…what?

See with those shaman's eyes, he supposed. Consuela was certainly convinced he could. As was his dead Aunt Lucy, who wasn't dead in the otherworld.

The trouble was, he didn't know what he was looking for.

Studying Steve's face, trying to access something he didn't quite understand, the only thing that felt real was the slow back and forth motion of the crow's feather.

Odd, he thought, that Si'tala had put a crow feather in his pocket with the medicine to wake him up instead of one of Consuela's raven feathers. But maybe she did it because the lives of the crows of Yellowrock Canyon were so entwined in the lives of the Corn Eyes and White Horse families.

There were always crows around the house, lanky dark-haired men with their avian aspects floating on their shoulders. You'd see them on the cliffs and up in the arroyos, stopping by the porch to pass a few words, lending a hand with the heavier chores. Or the black-winged birds themselves, visiting with Auntie, perching on cacti and the roofs of the outbuildings, filling the air with their raucous songs.

When Thomas thought of crows, he thought of stories. There was an endless tangle of stories about them in the Painted Lands, but Thomas's favourites were the ones narrated by Old Man Crow, who lived half in the canyons and half in the spiritworld. The kids at the community center loved them too. Telling stories was one of the main things Thomas did with the kids. He got most of his from Auntie, though he'd also learned a few from Reuben and Petey Jojoba.

"Some tribes," Auntie told him once, "only tell stories in the winter."

"Why do we tell them all year round?" he'd asked.

She'd rapped his head with a knuckle. "Because the skulls of Kikimi children are so thick they need the repetition to actually learn something from them."

And his skull *was* thick. Everyone said that these stories were learning stories. That however implausible or arcane they might seem at first, if you understood the stories, you had the tools to live a good life. He remembered a favourite: "The Girl with a Heart of Stone."

OLD MAN CROW found a girl named Anna Long Ears weeping by a dry wash in the moonlight because she'd been born with a stone for a heart and had been told she would never be able to love.

Old Man Crow took Anna to see various ma'inawo and spirit guides, whose imparted wisdom fell upon her deaf ears. Finally, just as the dawn was breaking from behind the eastern mountains, Old Man Crow reached into her chest.

"See," he said. "Your heart's not a stone. It's an egg."

Anna stared wide-eyed at the object that rested in Old Man Crow's palm. She reached out a hand to touch it, but before her fingers could make contact, Old Man Crow took his hand away and put it back in her chest.

Her gaze was haunted when she lifted it to meet his.

"An egg's no better than a stone," she told him. "It still won't let me love."

Old Man Crow laughed. "No," he said. "At least not until you let it hatch."

"How am I supposed to—"

He didn't let her finish. "Look inside yourself. What do you see?"

"I…I…"

Then her eyes went wide again as the egg in her chest cracked and a cactus wren pushed its way out, small but full-grown. It fluttered its wings before it wormed its way up her throat and burst from between her lips to fly around and around her head, filling the air with its cheerful song until it finally winged away.

Old Man Crow plucked a small brown feather from her lips and held it out to her.

"Everything we need," he said, "to walk large and fulfill our potential can be found within ourselves. The trick is, no one ever looks for it there."

Anna took the feather from him. She was still dazed from her experience, but her smile grew wide, then wider. Inside her chest where the bird had hatched, her heart beat a strong pulse like a hoof-beat on the desert floor.

"Make a medicine bag and keep that feather in it," Old Man Crow told her. *"Whenever you begin to forget, you can take it out and be reminded of who you are."*

THOMAS STILLED the motion of the crow feather he held between his thumb and forefinger and gave it a closer look.

Was this why Si'tala had secreted the crow feather in his pocket? To remind him of this story as well as to awaken his feelings for the tribe and their lands?

"Do you know the thing about time?" he asked his companions without looking away from the feather. "How it's all supposed to happen at once—past, present and future?"

"Sure," Calico said, "though I don't know who can actually hold it all in their head at once."

"I'm not sure that I believe it," Reuben said. "It doesn't make any logical sense."

Since when did anything? Thomas thought, but Reuben's words made him look up. His gaze went to Calico. "So is it true or not?"

"Does it matter?" she asked.

"I don't suppose it does," he said.

He looked back at the feather, then closed his eyes. Maybe he had a rock in his chest instead of a heart, just like Anna Long Ears thought she did—something that disconnected him from his heritage. Maybe he didn't. But he could still use the story as a guide to visualize what he'd been told about looking inside himself. Except if he was going to imagine anything, he wasn't going to imagine a rock, but an egg. And inside that egg was the bird that was his shaman sight. All he had to do was let it crack open and fly out.

He pictured the egg. Pale blue, with darker speckles of various shades of brown. The bird inside was tapping away at it with its beak, a slow heartbeat rhythm that reminded him of Auntie's steady breathing when her gaze was caught on something beyond the horizon that only she could see. It was the shuffle-stomp of his sisters' dancing, following the slow and steady sound that the drummers beat from their instruments.

The egg finally cracked and he could see the bird within as it pushed its head out of the hole it had made. No cactus wren, like Anna Long Ears' had been, but a tiny perfect crow, cousin to its Yellowrock Canyon kin. He visualized it wiggling its way up his throat. He was doing such a good job visualizing it that he imagined he could actually feel its movement inside him.

Suddenly it was impossible to breathe. His airway was blocked. As he lifted his free hand to his throat, he heard a voice inside his head and could almost picture the tall, brown-skinned man speaking to him. *Everything we need to walk large and fulfill our potential can be found within ourselves. The trick is, no one ever looks for it there.*

It was the voice of Old Man Crow, rough and croaking, the way Auntie made it sound when she was telling one of her stories about him.

Thomas knew without a doubt that the bird he felt was his shaman's eyes crawling up his throat.

No way.

He started to massage his throat to loosen the blockage, but suddenly his mouth was full of feathers. He coughed and the little black crow flew out from between his lips.

"What the hell?" he heard Reuben say.

No kidding, Thomas thought, except he couldn't answer.

His eyes were closed, but he could see right through the lids.

He could see...he could see so far...so deep...

The endless sky grabbed his gaze and sent it spiraling off into ever more intense blues. He felt as though he could see right around the world. Right out of the world.

He was connected to everything. He was a part of the sky above and around him. He was just as big, just as blue. The wind was his voice and it sang a thousand thousand songs. He had roots that grew from his veins, from his nerves, from his bones. Roots that went deep into the rock below, slithering and sliding through tiny crevices, reaching for the heart of the world.

The immensity of the experience threatened to envelop him,

making it almost impossible to remember who *he* was, as a separate entity from everything else.

If this was how Morago saw the world, he had no idea how the man could function.

But suddenly, like the unexpected gift of a spectacular sunset, he could see exactly how Morago could be connected to everything and still go about his business.

That gift of understanding was enough to bring him back into himself.

With an effort, he turned his shaman's gaze to Steve's face and saw a whole other world inside the man's head. Implausible though it was, in there was a mountaintop like this one, with another Steve standing on it. That Steve had his head tilted back, all his attention focused on a woman who looked like just Consuela, except with big black wings and she was carrying off a white woman.

No, not Consuela. That had to be Si'tala in a mostly human form, doing Consuela's bidding. Remembering the runaround he'd been taken on today, he felt for whoever her newest victim was.

This stopped now.

He reached out with the force of his will and pulled the raven woman back. He ducked aside as the ghost raven came tumbling out of Steve, eyes blazing, beak open and screeching, though he still couldn't hear a sound she made. She caught her balance and rose high in the air. Thomas stood up, putting himself between Steve, Calico and Reuben and the bird as it came flying back.

He could feel the winds gather protectively around him. The sky was a pattern of medicine power, awaiting his word. He was rooted deep into the mountain under his feet, immovable.

"These three are under my protection!" he called, holding the crow's feather up. "You have no power over any of us!" The words appeared to have no effect and Thomas braced himself for some kind of ghostly impact, but Si'tala turned at the last moment of her plunging descent and flew off.

Thomas tracked her until she disappeared from sight, then tracked her further through his connection to the sky and winds.

"How's Steve?" he asked, keeping his gaze fixed on where Si'tala had disappeared.

"There's no change," Calico replied.

Reuben was looking at Thomas. "Who were you talking to?" he wanted to know.

Thomas finally turned and fixed his shaman's gaze on Steve.

There was nothing to see. He could no longer look inside the man, and his deep connection to the earth and sky washed away.

"No," he murmured. He wasn't done. Though he'd pulled Si'tala out of Steve, he hadn't brought Steve back.

But the medicine was gone. He was just Thomas Corn Eyes again, a young man holding this small crow feather between his fingers, standing on a desolate mountaintop with a sense of deep loss rising up inside him.

He started when Reuben put a hand on his shoulder. "Thomas? What just happened?"

"You didn't see the ghost raven?"

Reuben shook his head.

"I managed to pull it out of Steve," Thomas told him, "but the medicine's gone and I don't know how to bring him back."

Calico gently moved Steve's head from her lap to the ground and stood up. "Then I guess we do this my way," she said and started to walk across the plateau to where Consuela stood over Sammy.

57

SADIE

Crows followed Sadie through the neighbourhood all the way to Mission Street, but by the time she got to the busy intersection, she could only spot a pair of them. If one of the two was Manny, she couldn't tell. She didn't particularly care, either. Of more concern was the police car approaching from the middle of the next block.

Crap.

She was shaky now, her grip on the knife handle so tight that it was leaving an imprint on her palm. She needed to let the pain out, but she couldn't do it in public. Some do-gooder would try to "help" her because people could never mind their own goddamn business. But she was enough on edge that any cop looking at her would assume she was a junkie.

She turned her back to the street, hood still up, and feigned great interest in the window of the used bookstore on the corner. The cruiser went by at a crawl, but she could tell from watching its reflection in the window that the cop was like the ones back at the 66 Bandas' clubhouse. He cruised right by without even a glance in her direction. She was still invisible to anybody who wanted to hurt her. But just in case, she waited until the cruiser had gone a few blocks before she crossed to the other side of the street.

She slipped into a little grocery store down the block and managed to snag a bottle of water from a box at the rear of the store without getting caught. She thought maybe the young guy behind the counter saw her do it, but then felt sorry for her and let her get away with it. Loser. But she was grateful to finally have some more water. She'd finished the bottle that Aylissa had given her ages ago.

As soon as she was outside, she twisted the top off and glugged half the bottle. The water wasn't particularly cold, but even so, it tasted better than anything she could remember, and it helped ease her anxiety a little.

She still had a ways to go, and by the time she reached the Ghost Mall—what everybody called this abandoned shopping center on the far east side—she was really dragging her feet. It was all boarded up and covered with gang signs and graffiti. The parking lot was a dumping ground for junked cars and trucks, old fridges and stoves, and every kind of trash, all of it vying with the weeds, cacti and scrub that had grown up through the pavement.

The bandas had shut the place down, back in the day. There'd been so much vandalism and violence both inside the mall and out in the parking lot that the owners had finally closed up and moved farther north. A chain-link fence had been erected, but that hadn't stopped people from getting in. Sadie squeezed through a hole that had been cut in it. Farther along, she could see where somebody had driven a vehicle right through, following one of its original access roads.

Gangs had partied and squatted in the mall itself—mostly the Southside Posse, but also the Kings and some of Los Primos Locos from the west side. It was also a place where they'd once come to settle their differences, gladiator-style. But then something happened—ghosts had chased them off, older kids liked to tell the younger ones in the schoolyard—and superstitions were so strong that now everyone avoided the place. Dummies.

Still, Sadie watched for a long moment, a tickle of fear in her stomach—but what better place to hide? This was the last place the cops or anybody else would come. When she was satisfied no one was around, she crossed the parking lot, weaving a path around the buckled pavement and junk. Nobody was going to find her here.

The pair of crows that had been following her flew overhead to land on the roof of the shopping center.

Except for them.

She gave the birds the finger before going in through the front door, glass crunching underfoot as she stepped over its metal frame. It didn't smell nearly as bad as she'd thought it would, probably because the heat of the summer had burned away any hint of damp. Something scurried away, running deeper into the mall. A packrat, most likely. Nothing for her to worry about unless it could change into one of Aggie White Horse's animal people.

She walked down one of the corridors, feeling so tight and swollen by now that she surely must look like a balloon girl. It didn't matter that her reflection in the marble walls between stores showed the skinny kid she actually was. She knew what the pain and anxiety building up inside was doing to her.

It took her a while before she finally found an old clothing store that wasn't too trashed. Any merchandise had long since vanished, but the clothing racks remained, scattered haphazardly about like skeletal reminders of their original purpose. Dim light came in from a filthy skylight above the front of the store, its glass so encrusted with dust and dirt, it made the sky beyond look brown.

The inside of Sadie's skin was itchy now, as though hundreds of tiny mites were moving through her flesh. She made her way around the store's cash counter and slid down to the floor. Pulling the utility knife from her pocket, she thumbed the blade out and pressed its sharp edge against her forearm. She closed her eyes for a moment, allowing anticipation to build before she made the first cut.

She opened her eyes to watch the blood well up and drip down her arm, taking with it all the ugliness that had built up inside her since the last time she'd been able to ease the pressure. It oozed slowly, escaping the cut like a sigh. The world around her dissolved away and she was alone in the safe place where she was in control, nobody else.

"What the hell are you doing?"

She lifted her gaze. Manny stood at the end of the counter, looking down at her like she was a piece of dirt. She'd never even heard his approach.

"Fuck off," she told him, her voice tired.

He pushed his long hair back and shuddered. "Kid, why would you do that to yourself?"

Even in the dim light she saw the concern in his eyes, but she was too zoned out to muster the energy to be pissed off.

"Seriously," Manny said. "Have a little more respect for your body."

"If we're going for serious, you seriously need to fuck off."

He didn't answer. His gaze was locked on her bloody arm. Or maybe it was all the scarring that held his attention. Sadie couldn't really tell. She didn't much care, either, but her anxiety levels were lower now, so it didn't wind her up.

"Please," she said, thinking maybe politeness would work. "You should just go."

He shook his head. "I can't leave you like this."

Sadie stared at him until he finally lifted his gaze from her arm to meet her eyes.

"Look," she said. "I'm broken. Do you understand what that means? I'm not a good person. I'm never going to be a good person. People are always trying to fix someone like me. Ruby, Steve, Aggie. Now you. But we can't be fixed."

"But Aggie—"

"Means well. You all mean well. But I have to tell you, I kind of wish Aggie would just fucking die because then you and your crow men could kill me and everybody's problems are solved."

"You don't mean that."

Sadie could feel a new wave of anxiety building up inside her. Could feel herself swelling, her skin getting tight, even though she'd just made a cut and let it all out. This had never happened before. There was always a decent respite.

"You need to go," she said.

"So you can keep cutting yourself?"

"Why do you even fucking care?" She waited a beat, then added, "I think I liked you better when you didn't give a shit."

She held his gaze until he finally turned away. Closing her eyes, she listened to him leave. When he reached the hall the sound of footsteps changed to a sudden flap of wings. She took the utility knife and made a second cut across the one she'd made earlier. The relief was immediate. She took a rag from her pocket, found a clean spot in amongst the dried blood on it, and used it to soak up the blood.

Leaning her head against the wall, she looked up, half-expecting to see a crow watching her through the dirty skylight.

There was nothing there.

She closed her eyes. Thumbing the knife blade in and out, she let the emptiness that grew inside wash through her, numbing any need to think or feel.

For the first time in what seemed like forever, she felt at peace.

58

STEVE

One moment, they're in the air—Si'tala with her angel raven wings carrying the woman that I now recognize from back when Sadie was putting the hate on me. Lana or Leila or something. The next, Si'tala vanishes and the woman's dropping toward the ground. Luckily, it's only a dozen feet or so before she hits. I brace myself to catch her, but who am I kidding? Gravity's not on my side and I'm not as strong as one of the *ma'inawo*.

She hits me hard and all I manage to do is break her fall and get the wind knocked out of me. I lie there trying to catch my breath for a long moment, the woman sprawled across me. I'd move her off, but I can't muster the energy. She's the first to stir. She slowly pushes herself away, then sits beside me, a stunned look in her eyes. I still don't feel like I can do much more than lie here on the ground. Finally I manage to suck in a tortured breath. And another.

The sound draws her glazed eyes.

"You...okay?" I manage.

I watch her eyes clear until her gaze focuses on me. "I just had the weirdest dream..." she starts. Her voice trails off as she takes in where she is. The mountaintop, the endless sky. Me, sprawled on the ground by her knees.

"I'm not dreaming, am I?" she says.

I move my head back and forth.

She gets a puzzled look. "But I'm not freaking out. So I must be dreaming. Especially with you in it."

I get my hands under me and work myself into a sitting position. The world does a slow whirl before it settles again.

"You're not dreaming," I tell her.

"I have to be."

I don't bothering repeating myself. Instead, I wait for her to accept what she already knows.

"God, this is so weird," she says finally.

"No argument there."

She gives another look around us. "Where are we?"

"Inside my head—at least that's what Si'tala told me. Or we're in some part of the otherworld that I access through being inside my head. It's kind of confusing."

"And Si'tala is?"

"The winged woman who just saved your ass."

She gives a slow nod. "Right. Winged woman. We're inside your head. Nothing weird about any of this."

"How'd you end up falling from the sky?" I ask.

"Oh, the usual way," she says. "There was a woman floating above her hospital bed. When she started turning, I tried to stop her from pulling out her breathing tubes and IV, but as soon as I touched her, I showed up here." She pauses to look upward. "Or rather there."

Her gaze comes back to mine. "None of this freaks you out? I feel like I should be a total wreck, but I'm stupid calm."

"I fell down the rabbit hole a couple of days ago," I tell her. "After a while you get to the point where nothing really surprises you anymore."

She lifts a quizzical eyebrow.

"Well, before I found myself here," I say, "I met a dog that can turn itself into a full-sized helicopter."

"That's imposs—" She cuts herself off. I can completely sympathize.

"The woman in the hospital bed," I say. "Was that your friend? The blonde you were with when I met you earlier?"

"You mean Marisa? No. It was your friend. Aggie."

I nod. Of course it was. I point toward where Aggie's floating just out of sight below the lip of the plateau. "Go have a look," I tell her.

She stands up, then goes pale and sits right back down. "I don't understand," she says, hands on her temples.

"Welcome to the club."

We fall silent then. I have this urge to lie back down on the ground and close my eyes. Maybe I'll fall asleep and when I wake up I'll be back in my trailer.

"I owe you an apology," the woman says.

"For what? Falling on me?"

She smiles. "No, for giving you such a hard time back when we first met. I know you're not Jackson Cole."

"What changed your mind?"

"Marisa and I met another friend of yours—Ramon Morago. He told us all about you and your cousin Jackson. I don't know why I never twigged to it before, but God, the two of you could have been identical twins."

I nod. "People always took us for brothers."

"But you didn't really care for the limelight, did you?"

That's not really true. I loved it at first. But after a while, the public perception of Jackson Cole just swallowed me to the point where I no longer knew who I was anymore. The substances didn't help either. But that's not something I can tell her.

I settle for, "Once you see what crazy fame does, you just want to get as far away from it as possible. It's way easier being the guy on the crew with the baseball cap pulled down to hide any resemblance."

"I get it." She laughs. "You know, two days ago I'd have had a million questions for you about those days."

"But now?"

She gets a faraway look in her eyes. I wait until she comes back to me.

"I don't know how to explain it," she says. "I guess I finally realized that there are a lot more important things to write about than the little pieces of some rock star's life, especially one who's been dead for so long."

She suddenly looks horrified and covers her mouth. "No offense," she says. "I'm sure you must miss him—"

I raise my hand. "It's okay," I say, interrupting her. "I came to terms with it a long time ago," I say. "Maybe it's good that you're going to put your energy into writing about more important things."

She smiles. "For years I would have argued that, but I had a bit of an epiphany the morning I arrived. It was just a conversation with this old desert rat at the motel where we're staying, and I bet he has no idea how much the things he was saying made an impact on me."

"What made you such a Diesel Rats fan?" I can't help but ask.

"That's the funny thing. For the longest time I wasn't, but my best friend Aimee lived and breathed their music. It wasn't until she died that I really started listening to it myself."

"To keep close to her."

She shakes her head. "No. Aimee killed herself. I started to listen to the music to try and figure out why it couldn't save her. Then I just kind of fell in love with it myself."

She's looking off into the skyscape as she speaks.

I don't know what to say. Back in the Diesel Rats' heyday, I had a lot of fans tell me that. Hell, playing the music that saved them was what saved me back then. Until it couldn't anymore. Until all the crap in my life got to be so heavy that a simple song just couldn't keep that weight off of me.

I never thought of killing myself. But I did need to escape so badly that I traded places with my cousin. He was going to be the rock star and I was going to quietly vanish into the woodwork.

It would have turned out okay. Steve had stood on the outside while all the crap went on in my life. He'd watched it all play out, the good and the bad. I don't have a doubt in my mind that he would've made a better Jackson Cole than me.

But then that damn plane had to go down.

"People talk about art saving them," I finally say.

She looks at me.

I go on. "You know, reading this book, hearing that song, at just the moment when you need it most. And sometimes it's not just taking it in. Sometimes it's *making* art that saves a person. But it's not always enough. Sometimes nothing can save them, not even the loving support of family, or friends, or complete strangers who reach out to help. Maybe the hardest thing is discovering too late how good some people are at hiding how bad they feel."

"That was Aimee," she says. "I had no clue—nobody did. Not until we read her journals after...after she..." Her voice trails off and she sighs. "There are a lot of nights I've lain awake wishing I'd never read that damn journal."

"It's got to suck," I tell her. "I guess all we can hope is that the folks who didn't make it finally found the peace they were looking for."

"Do you really believe that?"

"Honestly, I have no clue. What I do know is, we can't beat ourselves up for things that happened that we couldn't control."

The words coming out of my mouth are ones I've heard before. From friends, when everything about the band was imploding. Later, from Possum and Morago. But as I say them now, it's like I'm hearing them for the first time.

I didn't make Steve take that flight. I didn't even ask him to change places with me. We just got talking one night, me bitching about how everything had turned to shit, Steve being sympathetic, then finally joking, "Hey, we should just change places for a while. I'll be the rock star, you'll be the roadie, and let's see how we like it. Bet you my Les Paul that you'll get over it pretty fast."

I don't remember exactly when it stopped being a joke. But there was no pressure on either side, once we'd decided. We both thought it'd be a laugh, and I really needed the break from the whole lifestyle.

He even called me just before his flight. "Hey, loser," he said, and I could hear the grin in his voice. "I've a girl and a bottle of sipping whiskey waiting for me on my plane. How's your evening shaping up?"

It was the last conversation we ever had.

But what happened to the plane wasn't my fault. Just like I didn't turn Sully into a hopeless junkie, or push Toni to start fucking Ben, or cause the accident that took Martin. And I sure didn't have any control over what Grandma did, killing her husband that way.

It was all just one thing on top of another, lying heavy on the endless expectations everybody had for me. The fans. The records execs.

Write another hit.

Play a killer show.

Channel all the shit in your life into something that makes money for everybody.

You're an artist—you're supposed to be tortured.

I'm not to blame.

How come I'm finally coming to terms with it now? Sitting here, in this impossible place, talking to some woman I barely know.

"You just went somewhere," the woman says.

I pull myself out of my thoughts to focus on her face. "Yeah, I guess I did. I was just listening to what I was saying to you and it's like someone hit a switch in my brain where it all actually made sense. I mean, saying you can't dwell on regrets always makes sense, intellectually. It's the believing in it that's so hard."

She smiles knowingly. "Can you teach me that trick?" she asks.

"'Fraid not."

She gives a slow nod. "I didn't think so."

"All I know is, it's taken forty years for it to sink in for me, so maybe patience is part of the process."

"I don't know that I want to live with it for forty years," she says.

"I hear you. Say, I don't know that I ever caught your name."

"It's Leah—Eleanor Leah Hardin, actually, but I never felt like an Eleanor."

"Leah suits you. You don't look like an Eleanor."

"What does an Eleanor look like?"

"Not like you? Morago's the man for names. He could tell you."

"Morago," she repeats. Then she stands up and walks back to the edge, where Aggie's still doing her slow spin, floating out there—hell, it could be miles above the ground. Who knows, in this place.

"There's got to be something we can do for her," she says when I join her. "You don't have a rope or something, do you?"

I shake my head. "When Si'tala grew those big raven wings I planned to ask her to get Aggie after she'd rescued you."

"That all feels like a dream now, there and then gone. What happened to her anyway?"

"No idea. I just hope we're not stuck here, because I don't know a way back."

"Out of your own head," she says.

I give a slow nod. "I'm still not really up on how that works."

"Maybe you just have to wake up."

"Except I wasn't sleeping," I tell her.

Leah looks at Aggie again. "Back when we first met, it seemed like you two were pretty good friends."

"You know the person in high school that everybody wanted to be friends with?"

She nods. "Though that wasn't me."

"Wasn't me either," I say. "But Aggie's like that. She's got time for everybody, and when you're with her, you've got her complete attention. I'd be hard put to find a better person."

"I got that. The moment Marisa and I showed up at her place, she welcomed us. We both felt an immediate connection to her."

Her voice trails off and I don't have anything to add. We sit down again, but this time near the edge of the plateau where we can keep an eye on Aggie.

"You know," Leah says after a while, "I didn't get here by dreaming or having some raven spirit bring me. All I did was grab Aggie's arm while she was floating above her hospital bed."

I get a feeling of dread as I realize where she's going with this. "Don't even think about it," I tell her.

"She's not that far out," Leah goes on as if I never spoke. "I bet if I took a running jump, I could reach her."

"Best case scenario, you reach her and manage to hang on. But then what? You can't bring her back and you'll both be stuck out there. Worst case scenario, you fall, and to tell you the truth, I don't know that there's a bottom."

"No, best case scenario is I reach her and she transports me back to the hospital."

I shake my head.

"Don't worry," she says. "I'll tell them where you are. Morago will know how to get you back, won't he?"

"It's not that," I say. "If you jump, all you're going to do is kill yourself or fall forever, which amounts to the same thing. Imagine falling for so long that you die of hunger and thirst."

"Come on. It makes sense for me to try this, or at least as much sense as anything else does. Ever since I got to the rez it's been one impossible thing after another. Why should this be any different?"

"Because if you're wrong, you die."

"And if I'm not wrong?"

I'll give Leah this: she's stubborn. But that doesn't always equate with wise.

"Are you ready to bet your life on that?" I ask her.

She's quiet for a moment, then finally sighs. "No, I guess not."

She turns away from where Aggie's floating to look across the mesa. "What's on the other side?" she asks.

She stands up before I can answer and walks to the opposite side. I give Aggie a last look, then follow after her.

"It's the same," she says when I reach where she's standing near the edge. "Minus Aggie," she adds. "I thought maybe there'd be a path down or something." Her shoulders slump in disappointment.

She's right. There's just another expanse of endless sky as far as the eye can see. It's obvious that there's nothing.

She turns to me. "So what is this place?" she asks. Holding up a hand before I can speak, she adds, "I know, it's in your head. But why *this* place? What's so special about it?"

"I guess everybody's got demons," I say. "This is where I come to beat mine. It's what I imagine when I'm meditating—that I'm on this huge mountaintop floating in the sky where nothing can touch me and I can't hurt anybody."

"You feel you've hurt people?"

I remember she thinks I'm my cousin, so I say, "I've certainly let them down."

Hurt swells in her eyes and she looks away. "Yeah," she says after a moment. "I know all about letting people down."

Neither of us talk for a while then. I lower myself to the ground, feeling stiff and sore from the impact of trying to catch her earlier. It's funny. If I'm just in my head, why are physical ailments bothering me?

Leah sits nearby, too close to the edge of the rock for my liking, and dangles her legs. "So why's Aggie here?" she asks. "If this is some private meditation place that only exists in your head, how would she get here? How would she even know about it?"

"She described it to me."

Leah lifts an eyebrow.

"It was a long time ago," I tell her. "Not long after I first moved to the area. She's the one who suggested I visualize a safe place where I could get away from my endless circular thoughts—just enough to get a breathing space. When I couldn't think of one, she described this mountaintop to me. She said it was the spot she always came to when she needed to feel grounded. Hers was in some actual mountains, but I didn't need a whole mountain range. I just needed the space you see here, away from everything, with only the sky around me."

"Bet you wish you'd used your own backyard now."

I think of the little canyon that runs off the tunnel behind my trailer.

"That would have been a good idea." I say.

"So how did she get to this place of hers?"

"She took some trail that switchbacked up to the top."

Leah leans over and looks between her knees.

"You mean like that one?" she asks.

When I get up to join her, she stands as well.

"I don't see anything," I tell her.

"Look harder," she says.

But when I do she takes off, racing for the other side. She's younger than me, wearing running shoes. By the time I realize what she's doing, she's already gone half the distance.

"Leah, don't!" I call out.

I start to run after her but there's no way I can catch up. She gets to the far edge and launches herself off, arms reaching out.

"Fuck, fuck, fuck!" I yell.

I know I'm too late. She's long gone. But I push myself harder, shoes slapping against the stone, and then—

59

THOMAS

T he last thing Thomas wanted was to watch a pair of *ma'inawo* have a go at each other. But Calico was pissed and Consuela didn't seem like the kind of woman who backed down from much of anything.

As Calico stomped over to where the raven woman stood, he shot a glance in Gordo's direction, but the big black dog didn't seem concerned. He lay with his head on his paws, gaze fixed on Sammy who crouched a few feet away from him.

Reuben called her name but Calico flipped him off without turning.

"We've got to stop them," he told Thomas.

Good luck with that, Thomas thought.

He was about to say as much when Steve suddenly started shouting, "Fuck, fuck, fuck!"

He sat up in an abrupt motion, eyes wide open. The movement was so forceful that both Thomas and Reuben took a step back.

Calico stopped in her tracks.

Steve got to his feet, swaying unsteadily. He probably would have fallen if Reuben hadn't stepped forward and caught his arm. Steve took a moment to steady himself, then pulled free and staggered to the edge of the plateau like a drunk about to step right off. He stopped where the stone met the sky and stared down, still swaying slightly.

"Steve!" Calico cried. She ran and grabbed him by the waist. He put his arm around her, but his gaze stayed on whatever he was seeing below.

"Was Aggie there?" he asked, pointing downward. "Just floating and turning in slow circles?"

"No." Calico stared at him, her features worried as though she thought he might have sustained some brain damage from whatever had happened to him. And if she wasn't thinking it, Thomas certainly was.

"So maybe Leah's all right," Steve said.

"What are you talking about?" Calico asked. "What *happened* to you?"

Steve pointed to Consuela. "Her ghost sister worked some mojo on me so that we ended up inside my head."

"You're not making any sense. First you were talking about Aggie, then Leah, and now you're talking about a ghost."

Thomas nodded in agreement. "But after what I've been through today," he said, "it's hard to make sense of anything. But Si'tala," he pointed at Consuela, "did fly into him."

Calico looked at Thomas, then glared at Consuela before returning her attention to Steve. "Okay," she said. "So why would she do that?"

"She was being kind, warning me about things to come," Steve said.

"Like a fortune-teller?" Reuben asked.

Steve shook his head. "No, it's this thing where she experiences everything—past, present and future—all at the same time. It's supposed to be a *ma'inawo* thing."

"Our elders talk about that as well," Reuben said.

"Except nobody actually lives that way," Calico said. "Or if they do, the stories say it drives them insane."

Now everyone turned to Consuela.

"Why are you all looking at me?" she asked. "I did the smart thing. I put all those thousands of years of memory into a shadow of myself. If anyone's crazy, it's Si'tala."

"And where is she now?" Thomas asked.

The dark woman bristled. "I don't know. She has a mind of her own." Consuela was feigning indifference, but Thomas could tell that she was perturbed by the ghost raven's absence.

"On our way here," Thomas went on, "you talked about this time business as though you live the same way as she does."

"As I told you, my lines of communication with Si'tala have always focused on what I pass along to her. I live in the present, while she holds the memories. I'll admit that she's acted strangely these past few days. Perhaps some madness has crept in."

"What was she warning you about?" Reuben asked Steve.

"She said we're going to need Sammy in the days to come."

"The betrayer?" Consuela said. "What use could anybody possibly have for him?"

Thomas glanced over to see that Gordo was still lying in front of Sammy, panting lightly, fixed on the discussion as though he understood every word.

Sammy was hugging himself, unable to stop shaking. It was funny. Thomas had never thought of the casino boss as a loser. A lot of other things, sure, but word had it that ever since Sammy had come back from university he seemed to have an answer for everything. He always came out on top.

Except for today.

"The city's expanding," Steve said.

"We don't need Si'tala to tell us that," Reuben said. "Anybody with half a brain can see it happening."

Steve nodded. "But she pointed out that they're going to run out of water and come after the tribe's water rights—by force if the Women's Council doesn't give in to them."

"They can't do that," Thomas said. "We're protected by treaties and laws."

A wry smile came over Reuben's face as he squeezed Thomas's shoulder. "That's never stopped them before," he said. "The only bones they ever throw us are the ones nobody else wants. It's always been like that."

Thomas's brow creased. "So how's Sammy supposed to help?" he asked.

"Si'tala says he'll be able to deal with whatever they throw at the rez in a way that the Aunts and the dog boys won't be able to."

"So it's a Kikimi problem," Consuela said.

"I suppose you could put it like that," Steve told her. "But it's a serious one. If the tribe loses the water rights—"

"Who cares about water rights?" Consuela cut in. "What about the cousins Sammy's trophy hunters have killed?"

Steve blinked.

"Where's the justice for *them*?" Consuela hissed. "And if you let him live, what's to stop him from bringing in even more hunters, which means more cousins will die."

"Hold your horses," Steve said. "We'll have to get Morago to teach him how to tell the difference, so that nothing like that can happen again."

Consuela shook her head. "That's not good enough. I came here to throw him off the mountain."

Thomas frowned at her. "I thought you said you were going to listen to what he had to say."

"I changed my mind."

"But your sister just told Steve—"

"I don't care what Si'tala said. She's not here, though she should be," she glanced around, as though willing the ghost raven to manifest, then scowled. "Anyway, the decision is mine."

Steve stepped away from Calico and stood directly in front of the raven woman. "How come your sister's so much smarter than you are?" he asked, frowning at her. "Don't you get it? Water rights are going to be a huge problem. Most of the runoff from the mountains passes through the Painted Lands. If the city needs it badly enough and they can't buy the rights, they'll find a way to take the rez away from the tribe."

Consuela glared back at him. "*You* don't seem to get it," she said. "The life of a cousin should never be worth a fistful of money. Sammy doesn't get to walk away from what he's done."

Thomas glanced over at Sammy, who looked like he was about to shit his pants.

Steve took a deep breath. "Look," he said, keeping his voice even. "I know where you're coming from. Sammy's a smug asshole and I like him about as much as I do the one-percenters he does business with. But he didn't *know* he was killing cousins. If the tribe's going to need his expertise when the shit hits the fan, they need to keep him around. Look at him. He's been scared to his senses. He can be taught to tell the difference so that nobody has to get hurt again."

Consuela shook her head. "It's not worth the risk or the effort. He still has his life, while theirs are gone. The debt he owes remains unpaid."

Steve shook his head then turned back to Calico. "Can *you* help me talk some sense into her?" he asked.

Calico looked at him. "She does have a point about the risk to us ma'inawo," she said. "Or are you just expecting me to blindly agree with you?"

"What's that supposed to mean?"

"I don't want me, or any of my friends, to end up with our heads mounted on a plaque in someone's den because of that asshole." She jerked a thumb in Sammy's direction.

Steve looked aghast. "Neither do I, but listen: Si'tala would never have told me—"

"No, *you* listen. Some ghost woman that you've befriended—who most of us can't even see—reads the future for you, and you don't even stop to wonder if what she's told you is true?"

Steve looked confused. "I thought cousins couldn't lie."

"We don't. But some will bend the truth if it serves them. Lies of omission, that kind of thing."

Steve tilted his head in Consuela's direction. "Like when she claimed to be Night Woman?"

Calico nodded. "Right. She just let us assume that was the case. And knowing how manipulative she can be, what credence does that give to what her ghost sister—who apparently might be crazy —tells you?"

Steve studied her for a moment before saying, "First of all, her sister is nothing like her. And second, I never agreed to killing Sammy."

Calico looked at him, defiance in her eyes. "So you're choosing to side with her and not even considering how I, or the other *ma'inawo*, might feel."

Steve groaned in frustration. "No. It's not like that. You *know* Sammy had no idea that Derek or any of the others were *ma'inawo*. How are people supposed to learn from their mistakes if you kill them before they even have a chance to try to do better?"

She lifted a hand and touched his cheek, then stepped away into some other part of the otherworld.

Steve stood staring at the empty place where she'd been standing. "What the fuck?" he said. He turned to Reuben and Thomas for help. Thomas was as baffled as Steve and couldn't offer any sort of explanation.

"She thinks you're putting the tribe ahead of her, and looks like she might be a little jealous, too." Reuben said.

Steve shook his head, his confusion plain. "Why would she think that? Even if Si'tala hadn't come to me with her story, I still wasn't going to be a part of killing Sammy."

"Then you should leave now," Consuela said. "All of you."

Steve's eyes narrowed. "No way, lady. Whatever beef you have with Sammy, you're going to have to go through me to get at him."

She gave him a feral smile. "That shouldn't be a problem."

"You might want to take that up with Gordo," Thomas said.

Consuela studied her companion. The big black dog had risen to his feet and seemed at least twice the size he'd been the last time Thomas had glanced in his direction. Gordo stood facing Consuela, Sammy behind him, and growled a warning.

"Fine," the raven woman spat. "Protect the murderer."

The dog gave a loose shake, nose to tail tip. When he was done he was even larger, his dark gaze still fixed on Consuela. The raven woman stared back at Gordo for a long moment, then, just like Calico, she stepped away. Here one moment, gone the next. Thomas didn't think he'd ever get used to it.

"Well, crap," Steve said. "There goes our ride home."

"You shouldn't have pissed Calico off the way you did," Reuben said.

"I didn't do anything wrong."

Reuben shook his head. "And so long as you keep believing that, she's going to stay pissed off at you."

"So we're stuck here for the duration." Steve looked from Reuben to Thomas. "Unless either of you guys...?"

"Worldwalking's not in my wheelhouse," Reuben said at the same time as Thomas shook his head. "I can do some simple crossovers but if I tried to do that here, we'd just end up stranded somewhere high up in the Maderas. That's if we didn't appear in the middle of the air between peaks and go splat, way down below."

Steve sighed and walked over to where Sammy was still sitting on the ground. He reached out a hand, sighing again when Sammy flinched.

"Nice," Steve said. "You did hear that I was the one saying you shouldn't be killed, right?"

Sammy nodded. After a moment he took Steve's hand and let himself be pulled to his feet.

"So do you understand what's happening here?" Steve asked.

"Yeah, I get it. No more hunting."

"No more hunting *ma'inawo*."

"Right," Sammy said. "That's what I meant." His gaze darted left and right. When it came to Gordo, he flinched and stared at the ground. The figure he cut was a far cry from the big chief Thomas usually saw strutting around the rez like he was better than everybody else, when he even bothered to come over to the traditionalists' side.

It was strange to see him like this. His designer jeans were coated with dust. His fancy shirt was dirty as well and had a rip in the sleeve. But the biggest difference was his red face, how he kept looking like he was about to cry. Maybe Sammy had an auntie who'd told him the traditional stories before he went off to the white man's university, and he was remembering them now. In a lot of those stories the bad guy didn't get off lightly.

Thomas listened as Steve continued to grill Sammy. "And you're going to learn the difference by…" Steve waited for Sammy to finish his sentence.

"Talking to Morago," Sammy finally mumbled in response.

"That's what I wanted to hear," Steve said. "But just so we're clear, you fuck up, and I'll take you down so hard you'll wish I'd never saved your ass today."

"Okay. I get it already. Can we just go now?"

"I wish it was that easy," Steve told him. He turned away and walked over to where the rocks dropped off, then stared out to where the mountains marched into the far distance. The way his shoulders were slumped, Thomas figured he was probably thinking more about Calico than he was about getting back to their own world.

"Hey, man!" Sammy called after him, his face pale. He obviously thought Steve was reconsidering saving him. "I said I'd do what you told me," he said in a pleading voice.

"Shut up," Reuben told him.

"But—"

"If we knew how to get back, we'd be doing it."

Steve never turned around.

While the conversation was going on, Thomas had been surveying the mountaintop. There had to be a way to get off. Earlier, he'd seen the sign of an old campfire—a smudge of coals enclosed by a circle of stones, too old to even hold much of a smell. If some of the people who came here weren't *ma'inawo*, maybe there was some kind of a trail they could find that would take them down. He was about to go looking when Steve turned around. "What about the dog?" he asked Thomas.

Gordo lifted his head, dark gaze settling on Steve's face.

"He's not actually a dog" Thomas replied.

"I know. That's the whole point. He's some kind of serious shapechanger, right? Can't he change into something that can take us off this mountain? Wasn't he a helicopter at some point, or was I hallucinating that?"

"He can change into all kinds of things," Thomas said, "but he's a spirit of death, so I don't think we want to owe him a favour."

"Let's worry about what he wants after we've asked if he'll help us."

"I know how this story ends," Thomas told Steve, "and it never ends well. *You* ask him."

"But you're the shaman," Reuben said.

"I'm not a shaman."

"You pulled the evil spirit out of Steve's head."

Steve looked puzzled. "What evil spirit?"

"Si'tala," Reuben said.

Steve shook his head. "She's not evil. She's just…different. Nice, actually."

"Careful, cowboy," Reuben said. "You better reign in those dreamy thoughts of yours."

Steve's mouth dropped open. "Are you kidding me?" he said. "Man, you couldn't be more wrong."

Reuben laughed and clapped him on the shoulder. "I know. I'm just not sure that your girlfriend does."

"Will *somebody* just talk to the dog? Get it to send us back?" Sammy pleaded.

"Shut up," Steve and Reuben told him at the same time.

Reuben turned back to Thomas. "Come on, kid. You can do this."

Thomas could see that Gordo had been following the whole of their conversation. The big dog also seemed a lot smaller than he'd been earlier—less the size of a horse, more like a large mastiff. More like, well, an ordinary dog. But there was nothing ordinary about the intelligence in his eyes as he watched Thomas walk up to him.

Thomas's first inclination was to put out his hand and say something like, "There's a good boy," the way he'd do with the rez dogs. He stopped himself and stuck his hands in his pockets before he did something stupid. This was not a dog. It was a *ma'inawo*. No, it was something *more* than a cousin. It was a piece of death.

He felt something in his right front pocket when he put his hand in and pulled out the black feather he'd used to work the medicine that had pulled Si'tala out of Steve's head. How could something so small have so much power?

He was so absorbed by the feather that he didn't notice the dog until it had closed the distance between them. Its tongue whipped out and snatched the feather from his grip. The big mouth closed and the feather was gone. Swallowed.

Gordo backed away and began to change.

It was hard to watch. At first, the black dog simply got bigger and bigger. But then it was like staring into the sun for a moment, and when you looked away, lights danced in your eyes and you couldn't see anything properly.

Gordo's shapeshifting was like that—impossible to actually see it happen, but when it was done, the jet-black helicopter was back and the dog was gone.

No, not gone. The dog had become the helicopter again, like some frigging Transformer.

A door opened on the side of the sleek machine and hung ajar.

"What did you give him?" Reuben asked.

Thomas didn't take his gaze away from what Gordo had become. "A feather. The one that Consuela—or Si'tala—slipped into my pocket back at the trading post when I first saw them."

"The one you were waving in front of Steve's face?"

Thomas nodded.

"Why would she give you a feather?"

"To wake up my spirituality, apparently. She said it fast-tracked my connection to my tribal responsibilities."

"So it was a charm."

"I guess. And she didn't hand it to me. She snuck it into my pocket."

Reuben shook his head. "That's not right. It's like slipping dope into somebody's drink and letting them think they're just losing their mind."

"I wouldn't know," Thomas began. He broke off at the sound of a scuffle behind them. Turning, he saw Steve trying to drag Sammy toward the helicopter.

"Are you out of your goddamn mind?" Sammy said. "There's no way I'm getting inside that thing."

"You want off this mountain," Steve told him, jerking his chin toward the machine, "there's your ticket out."

"Fuck that. I'm not riding in that dog's stomach."

"It's not a dog anymore."

"The hell it isn't."

Reuben left Thomas's side and went to help Steve. In the end, it took all three of them to drag the struggling Sammy to the door and hoist him inside.

The door shut on its own as soon as they were all in.

"You know how to pilot this?" Reuben asked Thomas.

Thomas shook his head. "But we don't need to. Gordo pilots himself."

"Okay, that's just a little creepy," Steve said.

Sammy lunged for the door. "Let me out of here! The fucking thing is eating us alive!"

Steve and Thomas grabbed him, one on either side.

"Tell you what," Reuben said. "As soon as we're airborne, I'll be happy to shove you out the door."

"Fuck you!"

His face went even paler as the helicopter rose from the rocks.

60

MARISA

They were a silent group. Morago stood on one side of Aggie's bed, head bowed in prayer or thought, Marisa couldn't tell which. Diego stood across from him on the other, gazing toward the window where the crows remained in a silent line on its outer ledge, but Marisa didn't think he even saw them. Manny, one of the crow men, sat in a chair near the foot of the bed. He had turned the chair around and crossed his arms on the back, supporting his chin as he watched Aggie.

Marisa sat with her back against the wall, looking toward the windows, her legs splayed out in front of her. She felt utterly defeated and the silence of her companions hadn't given her the slightest bit of confidence that she'd feel better any time soon.

After a while she took out her phone and found she had a couple of texts from Alan. She started to respond to the latest, but then erased what she'd written and dialed his number instead.

"Hey," he said when he picked up on his end. "I was hoping to hear from you."

Hearing his voice, she immediately felt better. "Hey, yourself," she said.

"So what happened with Jackson Cole?"

"You know that thing with Isabelle that we never talk to anyone about?"

She could almost feel him straighten up from wherever he'd been slouching. "Are you saying he's a numena?" Alan asked.

Diego shot her a curious look as though he could hear exactly what Alan was saying.

"No, turns out he's Jackson's cousin Steve," she said.

"So if a painting didn't bring Jackson Cole across—" Alan began.

"It's not about Jackson. It's about the place that Isabelle's numena come from. I've been on that other side. And Leah's lost somewhere over there."

"Whoa, whoa. Back up. You're been *where*?"

"Into the otherworld. Or maybe it's an otherworld, I don't know. It was surprisingly like ours, except there was no indication that people have ever been there. No roads, or houses, or anything. At least where I was."

"And you're okay?"

"Seems so. But did you hear me? Leah's gone."

She told him about their day, ending with the bizarre moment by Aggie's bed when Leah simply vanished. She looked past Diego as she spoke. Aggie's body still floated above the sheets, turning in a slow circle like a leaf caught in the lazy eddy of a current.

She described what she was seeing to Alan.

"I should never have talked Leah, or you, into going," he said.

"You had no idea any of this would happen. And to tell you the truth, I haven't seen her this engaged in ages. Maybe writing a book about Jackson wasn't what she really needed to nudge her out of her habits and routines back home. Maybe all she needed to do was experience something different. She's actually been talking about doing some serious investigative journalism here, and didn't seem at all disappointed when Steve turned out to be Jackson's cousin."

"But now she's vanished."

Marisa sighed. "Yeah, and doesn't that suck? What are we going to do?"

"I'm catching the first flight out there."

Marisa knew she should be saying something like, "You don't have to do that," or "There's nothing any of us can do." But the truth was, she felt as though she'd failed Leah and really needed Alan here to help her get through whatever had to be done next. She supposed the first thing would be to report Leah's disappearance to the police, except how did you even report a missing person who'd vanished into the otherworld?

"Marisa?" Alan said.

"I'd like that," she told him. They talked for another minute or so, then he signed off to check on flights.

Marisa started to put her phone away and paused. Opening her camera app, she switched from photo to video to record Aggie floating above the hospital bed in her slow, steady turning motion. She remembered how it had been with Isabelle's numena, how the reality of them kept slipping away from her memory like trying to hold on to mist. They had no proof. It was only by talking it through with Alan that either of them was able to keep what had happened from fading away.

Well, now she had proof. Not that she planned to show the video to anybody. There was no point in that. People would only think it was some special effects trick. But it would remind her.

She caught Diego smiling at her. "You're as bad as these children I have staying with me," he said. "They don't believe they're experiencing anything unless they can see it through their phones."

Marisa thought of any concert she'd gone to in the last few years and the sea of phones upraised in the crowd. "It's not like that," she said.

Before she could go on, Aggie's body suddenly dropped onto the bed. The bedsprings squeaked as the old woman landed, and Manny jumped to his feet so quickly that he knocked his chair over. Marisa was still registering Aggie's sudden return to the normal laws of gravity when Leah appeared directly in the air above Diego. Marisa assumed some sixth sense warned him because he stepped back with his arms outstretched before she struck him. He caught her as effortlessly as though it were all part of an act that they'd performed a hundred times, and gently stood her up beside the bed. He kept an arm around her shoulders until she regained her equilibrium.

Aggie sat up in the bed and looked around herself, her gaze finally settling on Leah. "Now, aren't you an interesting young woman," she said. Leah blinked back at her in confusion.

Marisa didn't blame Leah for her bewilderment. It was an odd first statement to come out of the old woman's mouth after she'd been comatose for hours.

Marisa jumped up and joined Leah by the bedside. When Diego stepped back, she gave her friend a hug. "Are you okay?" she asked, pulling back, but leaving her hands on her friend's shoulders. "I was so worried."

Leah nodded. Her gaze remained fixed on Aggie, but Aggie's attention was on Diego. "What were you thinking?" he asked her. "How could you just give up like that?"

"I wasn't giving up," Aggie said. "I was…I'm not sure what I was. Tired, mostly, I suppose. I'm human. All these extra years don't lie as easily on my shoulders as they do on a *ma'inawo* such as yourself."

"What extra years?" Marisa found herself asking.

Aggie didn't respond.

"When humans spend a lot of time in the ghost lands," Manny said, "they tend to live longer than the rest of you do."

"And I've spent more time there than most," Aggie added. "It seems like a miracle at first, but in the end, all you do is dream of sleep while the ashes of your body ride the winds to meet your ancestors.

"And no," she added, turning to Morago as though she could see his frown with other senses than her eyes. "I don't have a death wish. But when the child cut me, and Diego said I had a choice…" She shrugged.

"I never meant *that*," Diego said.

"Then you should be more careful when you waggle your tongue."

Manny grinned. "Now that's the Aggie White Horse who spits in the face of fate."

Aggie shook her head, but there was a smile in her eye. "What have I told you about catching more flies with honey?"

"Don't remember, don't care. I'm just glad to have you back."

Morago nodded. "*Ohla.*"

"I thought that meant 'hello,'" Leah said.

"It means many things," Diego told her. "In this context it means 'thank you.'"

"How long was I gone?" Aggie asked.

"Half a day," Morago said.

"And the child?"

"She's squatting at the Ghost Mall," Manny said.

"But she's unharmed."

Manny nodded. "Mostly. Though I can't say the same for anybody around her. That girl's poison."

"No," Aggie said. "She's been poisoned."

"And you can fix her?"

Aggie sighed. "Oh no. The only person who can fix her has always been herself."

She reached out and took Leah's hand. "Though I was content where I was, I thank you for risking your life to bring me back."

Risking her life? Marisa thought. She squeezed Leah's shoulder.

"It was no big deal," Leah said.

"It was a very large deal," Aggie told her. "I know that, and so do you."

"How did you get inside Steve's mind?" Leah asked.

Marisa gave her a surprised look as if to say, *say what?*

"Is that where I was? Interesting."

Marisa noticed the look that Morago and Diego exchanged. Aggie did too.

"How is that—" Morago began, but Aggie cut him off. "I'm tired," she said. "Let an old woman rest." She made a shooing motion with her hand. "You can debate where and why I was somewhere else."

Diego nodded. "I'll take you back to your motel," he told Marisa and Leah.

"Our rental's still at Aggie's house," Marisa said.

"I'll get someone to bring it by tomorrow," Morago told her.

He gave Aggie a stern look which she pretended not to see as Diego ushered Marisa and Leah out of the hospital room.

Manny picked up his chair from where it had fallen and sat down.

"You too," Aggie told him.

He smiled. "Make me."

61

SADIE

Sadie awoke with a start, unable to see anything in the pitch blackness. She didn't know what had woken her, or where she was, but then the horror show of the past day all came back to her.

She listened carefully for a minute or two, but heard no sound. Her body was stiff and sore because she'd slept away the afternoon and a good part of the night on the hard marble floor of this abandoned clothing store in the Ghost Mall. Now it was dark, and maybe she'd stayed safe, but nothing had changed. Her life was still shit. Twenty bucks wasn't going to last long and she had no place to go anyway, unless she went back home where Reggie would beat the living crap out of her.

She pictured his smug, creepy face—how he'd get that slow grin of his as he stood up from his recliner and took a step in her direction.

That wasn't going to happen. Not anymore. She was done being his private punching bag.

But the downside was, all she could exchange for living with Reggie and Tina was being homeless and on the run, and if today was anything to go by, she didn't think she could cut it.

While Sadie liked to pretend she had street smarts, she knew

Aylissa could run circles around her when it came to being tough. Even Riley and Gabriela were better equipped. Their bodies weren't like hers, a scarred road map of all the ugliness she couldn't keep bottled up inside.

She didn't know how they did it, how they were able to compartmentalize the crap they confronted in their lives when she couldn't. But Reggie wasn't as bad with them because Child Services checked in from time to time, and foster children represented money. Not so with Sadie, his natural born daughter—she was all cost and no benefit. Unwanted from the get-go, as he'd often reminded her. So at the end of the day, the other kids just weren't the mess that Sadie was.

But bad as her days usually were, this past one had really sucked. And the worst thing was she felt like she'd been channeling Reggie in the past couple of days, like all those years of living with him had turned her into some sketchy bitch version of the douchebag he was.

She bit at her lip until she drew blood. The metallic taste in her mouth helped keep the rising anxiety at bay.

If her life were one of those Hallmark special movies that Tina liked to watch, this was the point where she'd be trying to make amends to those she'd hurt, and get their forgiveness just in time for a happy fade-out to the next set of commercials. But she'd learned a long time ago that life was nothing like a Hallmark movie—at least her life sure as hell never was.

And as for forgiveness, she wasn't going to get it any time soon. Not after the things she'd done to all these people who'd genuinely been trying to help her. She'd pretty much tried to ruin Steve's life. She'd stabbed Aggie. But maybe the worst was what she'd done to Ruby.

What she needed was a way out—a permanent way out—but she didn't have the *cojones* for that, either. If she did—if she could just draw the blade of her utility knife across her own throat—she'd solve a lot of people's problems. And since she'd been so stupid making that deal with the witch, she couldn't even piss somebody off enough to kill her because the witch's spell made her invisible to anybody who meant her harm.

If it was going to get done, she'd have to do it herself.

She sucked at her lip and reached into her pocket, fingers closing around the handle of the knife.

Maybe if she had some dope she could find the nerve.

Then she heard something stir out in the hallway and her usual sense of self-preservation kicked in. The idea of killing herself vanished as though it had never crept up the back alleys of her mind to whisper in her ear.

"Who's out there?" she yelled.

The sound, whatever it was, stopped.

She scrabbled around on the floor, feeling for the mess of hangers she'd seen when there'd still been some light. It took a moment to find them in the dark. Grabbing a handful, she flung them in the general direction of the store's opening where they made a loud clatter out in the hall. She heard some kind of animal scurrying away. A packrat, maybe. But what if one of those creepy animal people had come to give her some payback? A hybrid scorpion man would make that same scratchy sound.

That scared her enough to get her to her feet. Her eyes had adjusted enough that there was the vaguest bit of illumination from the grimy skylight, but not much. She found her way to the main corridor of the mall mostly by inching her way forward, hands in front of her to avoid walking into display cabinets or clothing racks. She knew she was near the front of the store when glass crunched underfoot. The 'bangers must have had a field day smashing all the windows in this place. She just wished they hadn't pissed everywhere because out here in the hall it smelled like a urinal.

She stood quietly, listening. The only sound was her own ragged breathing.

Screw this, she thought. On top of everything else she didn't need to be in this freakshow of a place.

She eased her way in the direction of the main entrance, sliding her feet along the marble floor so that she was pushing glass away rather than stepping on it. Every so often she'd stop to listen. Nothing. But finally, the solid wall of darkness around her gave way to a diffuse light ahead.

It seemed bright when she finally made it to the entrance and outside. Darker than she'd ever experienced except for that night out in the desert with Steve, but nothing like the near absolute blackness inside the mall.

She stood by the entrance, looking around at the shadowed hulks of abandoned cars and other crap. It seemed like she had the place to herself, but she studied the parking lot for a long time before deciding it was safe to move away from the mall. She didn't get more than a half-dozen steps before she heard the sound of wings flapping, loud in the night air.

She'd forgotten about her own personal freak crow-stalker.

"Manny?"

She heard the sound of wings again, circling. They disappeared somewhere behind her and she heard the approach of footsteps crunching on broken glass. She turned in the direction she thought they were coming from.

"Come on, Manny," she said. "Stop screwing around."

"Manny's not here," a voice responded from the darkness.

It had the same timbre as Manny's—raspy and rough—but it definitely wasn't him. Sadie'd already heard enough of his annoying comments that she'd have known if it was him.

"My name's Gonzalo."

"Who the hell are you? Where's Manny?"

"He can't be here, so he asked me to look in on you."

Yeah, creepy much? She couldn't make out his features very well in the dim light, but he was tall and dark-skinned like Manny, and from what she remembered of the rest of his crew, they all kind of looked the same.

"What for? Where's Manny?" she repeated.

Gonzalo hesitated, then said, "He's at the hospital with Señora White Horse. She was concerned for your well-being, so Manny sent me to check on you."

It took Sadie a moment to figure out who that was. "So she's okay?" she asked.

"She's recovering, no thanks to you."

"Hey, if she hadn't—" Sadie broke off what she'd been about to say.

She took a breath and forced herself to at least sound calm. "I need to talk to her."

Gonzalo laughed without any humour.

"Seriously. I'm not going to hurt her."

"Because we won't give you the opportunity."

Sadie took the utility knife out of the pocket.

"Relax," she said when she sensed the crow man stiffen.

She drew back her arm and threw the knife off into the darkness. It hit something metal with a sharp *ping*, then clattered on the ground.

"See?" she said. "Now I can't hurt anybody."

Gonzalo stood silent for a long moment.

"Manny still says no," he finally said.

Sadie gave him a puzzled look, then realized he must have a Bluetooth earpiece.

"Give me your phone—let me talk to him."

"I don't have a phone."

"Then how can you...never mind. I get it. You're all magic people. You can change into birds and now it turns out you're telepathic. But that crap doesn't make you the boss of me. You tell Manny I'll find out what hospital she's in and I'm going to talk to her whether he likes it or not."

"I'll stop you."

Sadie smiled. She wasn't sure if he had superhero night vision on top of everything else, and she didn't really care.

"You know what?" she said. "You probably can't. I've still got that witch's spell working for me. I'll bet as soon as you try anything with me I'm just going to disappear and you won't even know where I am."

"Wait."

"No thanks. See you later, loser." She started to walk away.

"No, wait," Gonzalo called after her.

She paused, but she didn't turn around.

"He wants to know why you want to see Señora White Horse."

Sadie made him wait a couple of moments before she finally came back. "Tell him I want to apologize."

Gonzalo just stood there, but a moment later he said, "Manny says that's not going to change anything."

"You think I don't know that? But it's important to do it anyway."

Again there was the lag while Gonzalo mentally filled Manny in.

"For you or for her?" he asked.

"For both of us."

Pause.

"Okay," Gonzalo told her. "Manny says you can come by. But if you try anything…"

Sadie kicked the dirt. "What the hell am I going to try?"

Gonzalo gave a slow nod. "Come along then."

He set off, easily picking a way through the junk. Sadie trailed behind at a slower pace. When they got to the chain-link fence, Gonzalo hopped easily onto the top. He balanced there for a moment before jumping down on the other side. He didn't make a sound. Sadie thought she was going to have to climb it herself until she realized that he'd led her to a spot where someone had cut a hole in the chain-link.

Gonzalo looked back before continuing down the street. Sadie squeezed through the hole and hurried after him.

62

STEVE

The past few days have given me a whole new understanding of just how weird-ass the world can be, but this takes it to a whole other level. Because it's not just a helicopter with the damn thing flying itself. It's a dog that's turned itself into a helicopter. We're inside a dang dog. I remember my dad's old expression, *that dog won't hunt*, that he'd use when he was telling you something wouldn't work. This sure is a whole other dog story, and I'm as happy as anyone on board when we finally come up over a rise and there's Sammy's hunting lodge nestled in the pines.

I never even noticed the transition between the otherworld and here. But I don't care. All that matters is we're off that mountaintop.

The chopper takes us over the pines before coming down on a helipad on the far side of the lodge. Reuben pops the door open and we all pile out. I'm the last one. As soon as my feet touch the tarmac, the helicopter shrinks and is gone. Just like that, the big black dog is back sitting on his haunches staring at us. Or maybe not us. Maybe I'm being paranoid, but I can't shake the feeling that most of his attention is on me, expectant.

I break eye contact and look around. A path leads off under the trees, back toward the lodge, no doubt. At the edge of the helipad are a pair of ATVs. One's the usual two-seater. The other looks like a golf cart on steroids: big, fat monster tires, a roof overhead, probably seats six. After that, there's just the mountain dropping away, its forested slopes marching off into the deeper darkness below.

"Well, it's been real," Sammy says. He starts for the path, but Reuben grabs him by the collar of his shirt like a pup by its scruff and brings him to a stop.

"We're not done," Reuben says.

Sammy grunts and shakes himself loose. "We worked out what I need to do. Now you're not okay with it anymore? Make up your mind, Little Tree."

"It's provisional, depending on what the Aunts have to say."

Sammy rolls his eyes. I can feel Reuben's hackles rising and put a hand on his arm.

Reuben takes in a breath, lets it out. "But while I've got your attention," he finally tells Sammy, "the other thing you need to do is to treat the animals you hunt with respect."

"What's that supposed to mean?" Sammy asks.

"It means that when one of your trophy hunters bags a bighorn, you give sincere thanks to its spirit for the gift of its life. And you don't leave the carcass rotting on the rocks."

"Oh, come on. What do you expect me to do with it?"

"Lot of folks on my side of the rez would be grateful for the meat and hide. You can have one of your boys drop it off at the trading post and I'll see it goes to whoever needs it the most."

"You mean you'll sell it to them."

Reuben frowns. "See, that's the white man in you talking—no offense, Steve."

I wave it off.

Sammy's jaw is out. "People come out with crap like that when they've got nothing and need to bow and scrape to make ends meet," he says. "But I remember what it was like to be dirt poor, and I'm never going to live like that again."

"I'm never poor in spirit," Reuben says.

"Sure, that's what everybody who's got nothing wants to believe. Like the white man's Bible, where it says the meek are going to inherit the earth. But I've got news for you, Little Tree. That's never going to happen. The meek don't come out ahead. Not ever. Money's the game changer, even for a traditionalist like you. Once they get a taste of it, nobody turns their back on it."

"I wouldn't be so sure about that," I tell him.

Sammy laughs. "Says the desert rat who's got less than the poorest blood on the rez."

I look at him and then back at Gordo.

Sammy holds up his hands. "Hey, don't get me wrong." He nods in Gordo's direction. "I'll play the game your way because you've got the big gun pointed at my head. But don't kid yourself. Your ideals don't change the way things really work."

"You can say that after everything you've seen today?"

Sammy shrugs. "So the *ma'inawo* are real. I know they've got me over a barrel and I need to adjust my game to their demands. But off the rez? Outside of these mountains? How many of *them* do you see as CEOs or politicians? None. Want to know why? Because they're not the movers and shakers of the world. If they were, they'd be running it instead of humans."

I think about how Sammy was, back in the otherworld—so scared I was surprised he didn't crap his pants. But here, with that big hunting lodge on the other side of these pines—just one accomplishment out of the many he's managed to pull off—he's regained all of his old arrogance.

Reuben smiles as though Sammy's just said something particularly stupid. I've seen that look before when someone around him has messed things up.

"I guess you've got it all figured out," he drawls.

Sammy nods. "Damn straight I do." He points a finger at Thomas. "I know it's too late for Little Tree, kid, but if you ever want to make something out of your life, come see me. I can show you how there's more to living than eating dust and scrabbling to make ends meet."

"I'll keep that in mind," Thomas says.

Sammy shakes his head. "Yeah, sure you will."

He faces Reuben again. "Tell Morago I'll be by to see him." Then he turns away and heads down the path toward the lodge.

"Phone Jerry while you're at it," Reuben calls after him. "Clear up that bullshit story you tried to sell him about Steve and me."

Sammy doesn't stop, but he lifts a hand, thumb up, and keeps going.

Reuben turns to me. "I wish we'd just tossed him off the mountain."

"Me too, but you know why we didn't do that."

"Doesn't mean I have to like it."

He looks from Gordo to Thomas. "What do you think?" he asks Thomas. "Do we still owe the *ma'inawo* anything?"

Thomas looks at the dog. "How would I know?"

"I owe Si'tala," I say.

Reuben's attention jolts back in my direction. "What? I guess nobody warned you not to make bargains with *ma'inawo*."

"I guess not."

He sighs. "What did you promise her?"

"I told her I'd make her a body," I say.

"Out of what?"

I shrug. "She said it doesn't matter. Doesn't matter what it looks like, either. Apparently it's just my intent while making it that's important."

"What do you get in return?"

"A marker that I can call in when I need to."

Reuben sighs. "You should have talked to me or Morago before you agreed to anything."

"That wasn't really an option, considering where I was."

"Maybe so. But when you see how batshit crazy Consuela's turned out to be, do we really want another one of her walking around sticking her nose in everybody's business?"

I start to say something, but he waves it off. "It's too late now," he says. He rolls his shoulders. "Time we were heading back to our part of the rez anyway. But talk to Morago about this when you can, and maybe Calico, too, if you ever see her again."

"What's that supposed to mean?"

I get that look again. "Doesn't matter if she's *ma'inawo* or human," he says, "I know a pissed off woman when I see one, and that fox girl of yours has a serious mad on."

"Come on. She knows what I meant. And if she doesn't, she'll be back and we'll talk it out."

He shakes his head and looks at Thomas. "Is it just me or did you feel it, too?"

Thomas give him a puzzled look. "Feel what?"

"How the collective intelligence here just dropped another few IQ points," Reuben says.

"Real funny," I tell him.

His gaze is back on me. "I'm not joking, Steve." He gives his shoulders another roll, stretches the muscles in his neck. "Let's head out. It's a long way home."

He walks toward the path that Sammy took.

"Can't you just step us into the otherworld?" I ask.

"Sure. If you want to be in the otherworld version of this same mountain. Like I told you, I don't have the same gift of getting around as Calico does."

"Great."

After the past few hours, the last thing I feel like is a hike through the mountains. But Reuben stops at the big ATV.

"What?" he says. "You didn't think we were going to walk, did you? Sammy owes us the use of this machine."

He gets behind the wheel. When Thomas and I take our own seats, Reuben looks back at the dog.

"What do you say, big fellow?" he calls over to Gordo. "You want a ride?"

The dog stands up, takes a step in our direction, and disappears.

Reuben laughs. "Yeah, you couldn't just give us a lift?"

He starts the engine. It sounds loud and the head beams seem too bright as he steers us onto the rough trail that'll take us down the mountain.

63

LEAH

There was an old, rusty pickup truck out front in the patient drop-off zone. A white teenage boy dressed in a bright Hawaiian shirt, baggy shorts and sneakers leaned on one of its fenders. His hair was blond and messy, and even in the dim light from the lamppost overhead, his eyes were a startling blue against his tan. He looked like a surfer, Leah thought.

The boy straightened up as Diego led them in his direction.

"Dude!" the boy said. He grinned. "You never said there were going to be ladies."

"I didn't say there wouldn't be, either," Diego told him. "Now behave."

The boy nodded. Still grinning, he ushered Leah and Marisa to the passenger's side and opened the door for them. Leah eyed the bench seat, built to fit three.

"Don't worry," the boy said. "The boss man prefers riding in the back."

Leah glanced at Diego, who nodded and hopped into the bed of the truck. He gathered up what looked like a pile of horse blankets and made a seat for himself, his back leaning against the cab.

Marisa slid into the middle, then Leah got in. The boy went

around to the driver's side. Once he was behind the wheel he waited for them to buckle up, then called out the window to Diego.

"Where to, Boss?"

"The Silver Spur Motel," Marisa replied before Diego could speak.

The boy waited for a nod from Diego before he put the truck in gear and pulled away from the curb.

Leah hadn't known where the hospital was, and felt completely lost as they navigated through backstreets that all presented what seemed to be the same series of adobe buildings, dirt yards and cacti.

Neither she nor Marisa had a lot to say on the drive, but the boy behind the wheel kept up a constant stream of chatter. At any other time Leah would have been amused—the kid was smart and funny—but right now it just exhausted her, so she tuned him out, leaving Marisa to hold up their side of the conversation. Fortunately, Marisa seemed happily engaged enough.

Finally, the neon of their motel's sign came into view, and Leah began to feel grounded. When they pulled into the dirt parking lot and the boy brought the car to a halt, Leah popped her door and got out as quickly as she could.

"Thanks for the ride," she said, not really looking at either the boy or Diego.

"No probs, dude," the boy said. Diego lifted a lazy hand.

Marisa slid over and hopped onto the ground. For a moment, she looked as though she might lean back into the truck for a final word, but Leah stepped forward and closed the door.

"Drive safely!" she said, giving the pair a small wave. They heard the boy laughing as the pickup pulled away.

"You must be tired," Marisa said as they watched the taillights disappear. "You were so quiet on the ride back."

"I am beyond tired," Leah said, turning back to their motel room. She plopped down on one of the two cast iron chairs on either side of the table outside their door. "But it's mostly from all of this…I don't even know what to call it. Magic?"

Marisa sat across from her. "Magic," she repeated.

"You know. Otherworlds and animal people, floating people and falling, and just…everything. The world doesn't make sense anymore.

Take that kid in the truck. He looks like a kid, but what kind of an animal person do you think he is, really?"

"He's not necessarily any kind," Marisa said.

Leah gave her a tired smile. "Right. With Mr. Mountain Lion Head for a boss." She sighed. "I don't know what to think about *anything* anymore."

Marisa regarded her for a long moment, then looked off into the darkness.

"None of this fazes you, does it?" Leah said.

"It does and it doesn't. It's just… Look, if you want things to feel normal again, they will, if you let them."

"What's that supposed to mean?"

"I don't know why, but the way our brains are wired, we seem to forget any inexplicable things that happen to us, as though our minds prefer to file them away as impossible. Most people take comfort in not having to deal with this stuff. But if you do want to remember, you have to work at it or else you'll find some more plausible explanation for what you experienced, and it all fades away. Much sooner than you'd expect."

"I can't imagine forgetting anything about today. Ever."

"And yet you will, if you let it. Jilly told Alan and me about it after the whole business with Isabelle's numena, and we didn't believe her any more than you believe me right now. But we could feel it start to slip away within just a few days, so we made a pact to talk about it with each other and Jilly on a regular basis. I think it's pretty much hardwired in us now."

Leah put her face in her hands. "Oh God. Jilly. When I think of all the times I've teased her for her stories about faeries and ghosts and— what were those odd fey girls that she claimed lived in junked cars? Gummy-somethings?"

"Gemmin."

Leah let her hands fall away. "So that's all real? The things Jilly paints, the stories Christy tells?"

Marisa smiled. "Jilly, yes. But with Christy you might want to take them with a grain of salt. He's been known to make things up."

"God, I can't believe I'm stuck in a Christy Riddell story."

Marisa laughed. "It's not that bad."

"But now I get it," Leah said. "Why they're telling their stories, why Jilly does those paintings. That's their way of not forgetting—of getting the story out so that it becomes a part of the world we know, instead of this weird secret other place that only exists on the fringes."

"Yeah," Marisa said, an element of doubt in her voice. "Except I'm not really sure that telling their stories is such a good idea."

"Why not?"

"Well, some of these beings—these *people*—are my friends. If they don't want the publicity, what gives me the right to turn a spotlight on them? Shouldn't it be *their* choice when, or even if, they reveal themselves?"

Leah thought about that for a moment before she gave a slow nod. "That's kind of how I felt when I realized what I was planning to do if we *had* found Jackson Cole down here."

Marisa nodded. "But how comfortable are you about editing out the supernatural aspects of your experience? It's going to mess up your book."

"I don't even know that I want to write a Diesel Rats book anymore."

Marisa raised her eyebrows, but before Leah could explain, headlights turning into the motel's parking lot caught their attention. Leah thought about the old desert rat she'd met last night, but this didn't appear to be him. The vehicle was a sedan, not a pickup. But when the car parked in their room's parking spot, it was Ernie who stepped out.

"Hey, that's our rental," Marisa said, puzzled.

Ernie looked at them from across the top of the car and tipped a finger against his brow. "Ladies. I didn't think you'd still be out and about."

"Hey, Ernie," Leah said. She introduced him to Marisa, then added, "What are you doing with our car?"

Ernie walked around the front of the car to join them. "Alejandro —the guy you saw dropping me off last night? He got a call from Morago asking us to pick it up from Aggie's place and drive it here."

He shook his head. "Damn shame, what happened. Aggie's good people. I'm glad it looks like she's going to be okay."

Marisa nodded. "We really like her," she said.

Ernie laid the car keys on the table then dragged another chair over and sank down in it.

"Everybody does," he said. "Except for that psycho kid that attacked her, I guess."

"I'm sure it's not that simple," Marisa said.

"It never is."

They all fell silent for a moment.

"So, Ernie," Leah said. "Thanks for the tip about Jerry's Roadhouse. It was just what we wanted yesterday morning, and we enjoyed talking to your friend Janis."

"Yeah, she's something, all right." There was a real warmth in his eyes when he spoke. He gave a little shake of his head. "So how'd things go with that musician you were looking for?"

"It was a dead end."

"I guess that comes with the territory in your business."

Leah nodded. "But I was wondering if I could talk to you some more about what's happening out in the desert."

His gaze flicked to Marisa before returning to her.

"I haven't been able to stop thinking about the things you were telling me," Leah added.

He nodded. "I'm kind of beat."

"Oh, I didn't mean right now. I thought maybe sometime tomorrow, maybe early afternoon?"

"Sure."

"Ahhh…Leah," Marisa said. "We've got a late afternoon flight and we still have to drive back to Vegas."

"I know. I'm not coming."

"But—"

"Don't worry. Alan will still get his book—or at least a book. I see a long connecting thread from when I first got into the Rats, to being here right now."

"I'm not worried about a book," Marisa said. "I'm worried about you. This is a big decision."

"Yes, Mom."

Marisa frowned. "No, seriously, Leah."

Ernie stood. "Maybe I'll just let you folks work things out."

Leah nodded. "But what's a good time to get together?"

Ernie looked uncomfortable. "Pretty much any time after one," he finally said.

Leah grinned. "Great."

"See you then," Ernie said, picking up the chair putting it back in front of the room next door.

Marisa waited until he'd reached the door of his own room before she turned back to Leah. "When did you decide all of this?" she asked.

"Pretty much in the last five minutes. But I've been thinking about it since the first morning we got here. Sorry to spring it on you like this."

Leah waited for Marisa to tell her she was crazy—because it did feel a little crazy to her—but all Marisa asked was, "Where will you stay?"

"I don't know. Maybe I'll just keep the room. I've got a little money put away. I could probably stretch it for a couple of months—longer, if I can find some work."

Marisa gave a little shiver and hugged herself. "This is crazy."

And there it was.

"I know," Leah said. "But it feels right. My life's been this narrow little world of blogging and working at the Arts Court, and that's about it. Being here has opened my mind to all sorts of different things I could be doing. Like, maybe making a difference instead of focusing on the minutiae of a band that folded decades ago."

"But it—it's been your life's work. You've invested so much of yourself in the band."

"I know. Except when you think about it, I didn't learn anything. What did Jackson Cole say in song after song? Be your own person. Follow your dreams. Make a difference. I've done none of that."

"And writing about the migrants will change that?"

Leah shrugged. "I don't know. What I do know is that I always had just one question if I ever met Cole: Why didn't the band's music save Aimee?—and that's the one question that no one but Aimee could have answered.

"That casual conversation I had with Ernie on our first night was a literal epiphany for me. I haven't been able to stop thinking about it, and everything I've experienced since we got here seems to be leading me back to how I can help others. Make that difference. Not ruin Steve's life for the sake of a big story that's nobody else's business except his."

Marisa opened her mouth, then shook her head. "Why don't you sleep on it?" she said. "See if you feel the same way in the morning."

"I'm not going to change my mind."

"Still, sleep on it," Marisa said, then her eyes went wide. "Crap. I forgot that Alan's looking to get a flight out. I have to see if I can get him to cancel."

She got up and pulled out her phone as she spoke. "Remember," she said as she dialed.

"Yes, Mom. I'll sleep on it."

Marisa stuck out her tongue as she went into their room, leaving Leah to the desert night so rich with stars.

64

SADIE

Sadie's bravado had been fading during the whole long walk from the Ghost Mall to the hospital. Neither she nor Gonzalo had said another word to each other and that was fine with her. She wasn't in the mood to talk with anyone.

By the time the automatic doors opened for them at the front entrance, she felt empty and sad. She had no idea what she hoped to accomplish by seeing the old lady, and she couldn't imagine that Aggie would be particularly happy to see her. She dreaded seeing Manny, too —the quick disapproval in his eyes every time she opened her mouth or did anything.

She didn't even know why she cared. But it was too late to back out now, so she stuck her hands deep into the pockets of her hoodie and followed as Gonzalo strode into the elevator.

There'd been crows lining the hospital's roofline and perched on the mesquite and cacti out front, a couple of the crow men inside the hospital's entrance. There were two more in the corridor when they exited the elevator. They had all given her the same flat, hard stare as she went by. Sadie was pretty sure that, if not for the witch's protection, she'd be lying in a shallow grave right now somewhere out in the desert.

Which would probably be the best end to this whole crappy business.

Yeah, she'd pushed Gonzalo hard to come here, except once she saw the old woman, then what? She could say she was sorry, but after that, there'd be nothing for her. She hadn't just burned bridges, she'd blown them all into so many tiny pieces it was like they'd never existed.

If only she could just learn to think things through first. Ever since Reggie had dumped her out in the desert, she'd been out of control, like the rabid dog that the cops had shot on her street last summer.

Even right now, while she wasn't exactly foaming at the mouth, she was trying to figure some way out of this mess and wishing she hadn't thrown away her utility knife. She'd like to plunge it right into Gonzalo's arrogant back.

Stop with the crazy talk, she told herself.

If she had her knife, what she would really do was ease the growing pressure that was making her skin feel tight and her head all loco.

She took a deep breath. God, her throat was dry.

As they passed a restroom, she said, "I need to use the can," and ducked inside before Gonzalo could react. She ran the tap, drinking with cupped hands, then splashing more on her face. Lifting her head she saw some sketchy pyscho girl looking back at her from the mirror.

She bit hard on her lip and the scab broke open. The salty iron taste of blood filled her mouth and she felt herself calm a little.

Now the psycho girl in the mirror looked more like some pathetic street kid with a bloody lip.

She spit into the sink and watched the gob of spit and blood inch toward the drain until she turned on the faucet and washed it away.

She grabbed some paper towels. Wetting them, she gave her face and neck a good scrub to clean up the worst of the dirt and sweat. She used her fingers to comb her hair. Her clothes were grubby and smelled rank, like that hellhole mall, but there was nothing she could do about that. She put her mouth to the faucet and took another drink. Straightening up, she went back out into hall to find Gonzalo leaning against the wall, arms folded across his chest.

"You ready now?" he asked.

Sadie nodded.

They walked by a nurse's station to a doorway where another crow man was standing guard. Gonzalo ushered her into the room, but stayed outside.

Sadie ran her tongue over her cut lip and swallowed. The taste of blood was vague enough that it could almost have been a memory, but it helped.

Manny was sitting in a chair near the head of the hospital bed. He stood up when she came in. Aggie lay with her eyes closed. Her skin had a weird pallor, but that might have been from the fluorescent light coming through the large observation window. "There's not going to be trouble, right?" he said.

"What? No!" She peered more closely at Aggie. "Maybe I should come back when she's awake."

Aggie's eyes opened and Sadie took a quick step back. "Who says I'm sleeping?" the old woman asked.

Sadie moved warily to the foot of the bed. "How are you doing?" she asked, shifting from one foot to the other.

"I've been better."

"Yeah, about that. I'm, you know, sorry. That you got hurt. Um." She cleared her throat and tried again. "That I hurt you."

Aggie studied her for a long moment without speaking. Her gaze was so dark and serious that Sadie wanted to drop her own, but she couldn't seem to look away.

"I know that what happened at the police station wasn't entirely your fault," Aggie finally said. "You panicked and I was in the wrong place."

Sadie gave a slow nod.

"But that doesn't excuse how you treated Steve, the hurtful lies you told."

"I—I know."

"Perhaps your father's given you no reason to trust men, but you only have to consider Steve's kindness toward you to know that they're not cut from the same cloth."

Sadie nodded again. "It was wrong."

Aggie sat up a little with a grimace, waving Manny away as he moved closer to help her. Her gaze never left Sadie's. "I wonder," she said. "Do you really believe that, or is it only what you think I want to hear?"

It took Sadie a moment to realize that Aggie was asking her the question, not talking to herself. "Probably a little of both," she replied, surprising herself with her honesty.

"Huh." Aggie turned to Manny. "What do you think about that?"

The crow man's gaze remained harsh. "I think she also went and traded Ruby's soul for a witch's favours."

Oh, God. Ruby. That might be the worst of what she'd done.

"That wasn't supposed to happen," Sadie said, all her defensiveness back. "I had it under control, but then she had to go and offer herself."

"What *was* supposed to happen?" Manny asked.

Sadie turned to him, her jaw set. "I was going to beat Reggie over the head with a baseball bat until he agreed to do it."

"Who's Reggie?" he asked.

She shrugged. "My old man."

The unfriendliness in the crow man's eyes was still there, but now it didn't seem completely directed at her.

The old woman just looked sad. "There's something wrong with you," Aggie said.

Sadie clenched and unclenched her fists. "You think I don't know that? I hate myself and I'm angry all the time. I'm about as fucked up as you can get."

"It can be fixed," Aggie said.

For a moment, hope blossomed in Sadie. "You'd do that? Help me?"

Aggie nodded. "I would. I hope I get the chance to try. But you know what you have to do first."

Sadie's shoulders slumped. "What's that?" she asked, feeling the energy drain from her body.

"There's the world of the spirit and the world of the body," Aggie told her. "I can help you in the world of the spirit, but first you must set things right in the world of the body. If you don't fix this first, the spirits can't help you."

"Spirits," Sadie replied. She nodded with her chin at Manny. "You mean, like him?"

Aggie smiled. "Yes and no. Manny's from Yellowrock Canyon—a ma'inawo. People think of the ma'inawo as spirits, but when you consider the thunders—the big mysteries—they're more like little ones."

"So they're…little mysteries?" Sadie tried.

She didn't have a clue what that actually meant, and Aggie's "Exactly!" didn't help.

"So I've got to make things right with the cops," Sadie said, her voice dull.

Aggie nodded.

"You know they're going to put me away in some jail. They won't call it a jail, but that's still what it'll be."

Aggie nodded again. "Think of it as a time-out. And don't be shy of the counselors. I'm sure you have an excellent bullshit detector. If you trust any of them, don't be shy about accepting their help."

"And then what?"

"Then you come back and see me, and I'll teach you how to walk large. I'll teach you how to bring yourself back into balance with the spiritual world."

"Is that hard?"

Aggie shrugged. "Everything's hard, if it means anything."

But why did it have to be this hard? Why did she have to feel so bad all the time? Why did she have to always break whatever came into her orbit?

Not everything, she realized. She'd never hurt Aylissa or any of the other foster kids that had come through the house.

She remembered back in the Ghost Mall, thinking there was nothing left for her. But maybe she'd been wrong. Like Aggie said, it'd be hard. Facing the cops. Facing Reggie. Taking her medicine.

But hard made sense. With everything she'd done, she deserved hard.

She met Aggie's steady gaze. Here was the woman she'd put in the hospital with her knife, the woman who was still offering to help. Yeah, she was a space cadet, and yeah, all her mumbo jumbo about food having feelings was weird. All those crazy stories had come out while they were making what had pretty much been the best meal she'd ever eaten. But right now, Aggie seemed like a light in the darkness.

Sadie had tried it the other way. Reggie's way. The asshole way.

Maybe it was time she tried the space cadet way. How had Aggie put it? *Bring yourself back into balance with the spiritual world.* Sadie wasn't entirely sure what that meant, but she knew she'd never been in balance in her life, and it sounded a hell of a lot better than any of her other options.

She thought about her knife, how it provided a sense of release and helped her cope with being powerless. The knife was gone, but she still needed something—some kind of hope to take with her while going through the pile of crap she'd face as soon as she walked into the police station.

Now she wished she'd been paying better attention when they were making dinner at Aggie's house.

She felt like a little kid when she asked, "Will you tell me a story before I go? Something to help when the cops put me away?"

Aggie nodded. "Come sit here beside me."

Sadie edged her way around the bed to the chair where Manny had been sitting. He stepped back and leaned against the windowsill, arms folded across his chest. Not exactly friendly, but not as hard-eyed as he'd been earlier.

"The People of Turtle Island don't have all the same medicines and mysteries," Aggie said, when Sadie was sitting. "But from tribe to tribe, there are some stories and beliefs we hold in common. I'll tell you one of the oldest stories I know. I've heard many versions over the years, but this is how it's told around the campfires of the Kikimi."

LONG AGO, *Tía Sweet Smoke, an Aunt of the desert people, took her granddaughter Pela down from the mountains to trade with the river people. They left the Painted Lands early in the morning, but between trading and gossip, by the time they were returning home, the shadows*

had grown long before them, the sun was ready to find her bed in the mountains, and they were still hours from home.

Pela grew nervous as the darkness fell around them, but Tía Sweet Smoke wasn't worried. Why should she be? She knew the trail well, the moon would rise soon to light their way, and who would dare trouble an Aunt of the People? Everyone knew that while the men of their tribe had a magic that let them fight in the shape of dogs, the Aunts were magic. Medicine ran in their veins the way blood runs in ours.

But Pela was just a girl and the medicine hadn't yet come to her. She wasn't as fearless as her grandmother. When they heard something moving in the scrub nearby, she thought: demons, where her grand-mother thought: some animal, perhaps a ma'inawo.

They were both wrong, though Pela was partly right. When the moon rose, what they saw on the trail ahead of them didn't look like a demon—it looked like a young boy of the People—but Tía Sweet Smoke immediately knew it had the heart of a monster because she knew what it was.

A skinwalker.

In the dream of the world, skinwalkers are spewed forth from the darkest corners. Black witches abduct young girls from the tribe and impregnate them. The infants from these unions are nurtured with black magic and fed on the flesh of their own mothers. In time, they are taught how to take the shapes of other beings by wearing their skins. Doing this, they can even assume the likenesses of the dead.

One such creature was fearsome enough. It would be hard, but not impossible, for an Aunt to destroy it. But Tía Sweet Smoke could hear more of them in the scrub on either side of the trail—perhaps as many as half a dozen.

She put her mouth to her granddaughter's ear. "When I say run," she told the girl, "run as fast as you can and don't look back. Run as fast as you can, and then a little faster still. If—when—you make it back to the village, tell my sisters what you have seen. They will know what to do."

"But—"

"No argument. If you wish to live to see the morning, you'll do as I say."

Tía Sweet Smoke straightened up and walked briskly toward the skinwalker, her granddaughter trotting behind to keep up. The semblance of a boy grinned at their approach until Tía Sweet Smoke took a few quick steps.

"Run!" she cried as she grabbed the boy.

Pela darted past them and took off as fast she could run.

The skin the boy wore slipped a little under Tía Sweet Smoke's grip, pulling tight until the seam broke at the back of his head and she was staring into the face of a nightmare. A skinwalker's true shape has no skin, only a translucent sheath to hold the muscles and organs in place. Undaunted, Tía Sweet Smoke laid the palm of her hand in the center of the creature's face and spoke the beginning of a blessing ceremony.

Her medicine flowed forth, and where she held the skinwalker, his skin began to smoke, then burn. He cried out, writhing in her grip, but she held fast. She had extra strength, not from concern for her own safety, but for that of her granddaughter. She knew that some of the others might have gone chasing after Pela, but as soon as they heard their pack mate's screams, they would converge on her.

Tía Sweet Smoke was an old Aunt, and more than a match for one skinwalker. But not two, or three, or the five that attacked her as medicine cleaned the evil from the first of them. He burst into flame before the others could pull her away.

She fought, but there were too many. All she could do in the end was make certain that she held silent, so that no cries she might make would draw Pela back.

But Pela was already far away. Fear lent her feet wings. The moon rose and the path was easy to see, easy to follow. She arrived breathless at the village, calling her alarm. The dog boys came first, some in their human shapes, most of them in a dog pack. The Aunts arrived almost as quickly.

Pela told her story, tugging at the sleeve of this Aunt or another when she was done. "Come," she said. "We have to go help her."

But the Aunts shook their heads. "Our sister Sweet Smoke will survive or not by her own strength and will," Tía Marita told her. "If any of us were to go to her aid, it would leave the village undefended, for we are only strong when all are here."

Pela tried to pull away to run back to help her grandmother, but the Aunts wouldn't let her go. They waited with her near the mouth of the canyon, which was the entrance to the village in those days.

The dog boys patrolled the cliff top borders. Juan Carlos Morago, the tribal shaman, joined the Aunts. He leaned on a wooden spear that he carried as though it were a staff. Feathers and shells dangled from leather strips tied to its top, upon which a sharp flinthead stone glowed bluish-green with its own light.

The moon rose and set. And they waited.

The stars wheeled in a slow dance across the sky. And still they waited.

Finally, just before the dawn, a figure came up the trail. Pela gave a cry of joy, recognizing her grandmother before anyone else did. Tía Sweet Smoke was bloodied and bruised. She walked with her head bowed in weariness and a limp so severe she was almost dragging her leg.

But she was alive.

Juan Carlos walked out to meet her, banging the end of his spear in the dirt with each step that he took, raising little plumes of dust in his wake.

"Oh honourable sister," he said when he stood before her. "We can see that you fought long and hard."

Tía Sweet Smoke raised her head and nodded her appreciation for his words.

Juan Carlos banged his spear on the ground again.

"Hey ya, hey ya," he said.

Then he suddenly thrust the glowing flinthead straight into her chest.

Pela gave an anguished scream and it was all the Aunts could do to hold her back.

But it was not her grandmother who fell to the ground. It was some awful creature, wearing her skin. A skinwalker. It writhed and tried to pull itself up the haft of the spear, but Juan Carlos kept the creature pinned down until it began to smoke and finally burst into flame. Moments later, there was only the sharp end of the spear left in the ground with a circle of ash in the dirt around it.

Pela was never the same again after that night. She turned her back on the Aunts, and trained instead with the warriors, intent on learning dog magic from Marco Little Tree, the chief of the dog boys. But that magic he wouldn't teach her because, while she could outrun and outfight even boys older than her, she was always angry. She had focus, but no stamina because everything she did was fueled by anger, and that anger burned too bright and hot inside her. She was fierce, but she could never stay the course for any of the exercises they practiced.

Finally, Marco took her aside. He made her sit with him on the red rocks that jutted out high above the canyon. For a long time, neither of them spoke. They watched the Yellowrock Canyon crows ride the winds above the canyon, chasing each other in a rough and tumble game of catch-me-if-you-can.

"You understand," Marco said finally, "that it wasn't your grandmother that Juan Carlos killed."

Pela didn't look at him. "It doesn't matter. I still hate him. But I hate the skinwalkers more. I'm going to kill every last one of them."

"We defend. We don't take the fight to the enemy."

"You don't know what it feels like, this awful hole I have to carry around in my chest. How everything I see reminds me of her. It hurts so much. All I want to do is break everything around me."

"You're not the first to lose a loved one," Marco told her, "and sadly, you won't be the last. At some point in our lives, we're all forced to take up that burden, and there's nothing any of us can do to make that feeling go away. They say time heals, but I've found that all it does is blur the rawness."

"Then what's the point? Why love anything?"

"Love doesn't have a point," Marco told her. "It just happens."

Pela shook her head. "I don't want it to—not ever again. It hurts too much."

"Would you rather never have known your grandmother?"

Pela didn't answer. She kept her gaze on the distant mountains.

"Pela?"

Finally, she shook her head.

"The anger and hate you feel does you more harm than anyone else," Marco told her.

"But how do I stop feeling this way?"

"I don't know. What I do know is that each of us has two spirits constantly warring inside us. Think of them as hummingbirds fighting over flowers—and in this case, we're the nectar. One is made strong by our anger and greed and ego, the other by our love and kindness and compassion. In the end, we become whichever of the two spirits we allow to be the strongest."

Pela thought about that, then asked, "How do we know which one will win?"

Marco smiled. "That's the simple beauty of it. The one that wins is always the one that you feed."

"That's a terrible story," Sadie said. "I mean, it was a good story, but jeez, the crap Pela had to go through. And her poor grandmother."

Aggie nodded. "Remember what I told you when you stayed with me at my house? How the stories the People tell help us to understand the world we live in, and our neighbours?"

Sadie nodded.

"This is a story for the landscape that lies inside us," Aggie said.

"Yeah, I got that," Sadie told her, then she sighed. "You make it sound so easy. Feed the good spirit, starve the bad one."

"It's simple. That doesn't mean it's easy. At times in our lives, it becomes the hardest struggle we will ever face."

Sadie nodded.

Aggie took her hand. "I meant what I said. Come back when you are in balance with the physical world, and I will help you as best I can."

When she let go, Sadie stood up. She looked from Manny back to the old woman in her hospital bed. The hospital bed that she had put her in.

"Why would you want to help me," she asked, "after all I...after everything?"

Aggie smiled. "Maybe I'm just feeding the good spirit inside me."

Sadie nodded. She felt weird and flushed, but for some reason she wasn't itching to be alone somewhere with her utility knife.

"Okay, then," she said. "I hope you start, you know, feeling better and everything."

"Thank you. *Ohla*, Sadie."

Sadie nodded again. There wasn't anything left to say. She sidled past Manny.

"Sadie," Manny said as she reached the door.

She turned to look at him.

"You might think about tattoos instead of cutting. You still wear them like a scar on your skin, but they can tell different kinds of stories than the ones you've been putting on yourself so far. Better ones."

"Like you give a shit," was out of her mouth before she could stop herself.

"Actually, most people do."

"Not the ones I know."

"You need to meet some new people," Aggie said from the bed. "And remember which spirit to feed when you're with them."

"I guess I could give it a try," she said.

Then she was out the door and walking down the hall under the watchful gazes of the crow men guarding Aggie's room and the elevator.

65

THOMAS

The Corn Eyes' house was dark when Reuben let Thomas and Steve off at the end of the driveway. They thanked Reuben, then watched as he backed the ATV around to return the way they'd come.

It wasn't until the sound of the engine faded that Steve faced Thomas and extended his hand. "Drop by and say goodbye before you leave the rez," Steve said as they shook.

"What makes you think I'm going anywhere?"

Thomas could barely make out Steve's smile in the dark.

"What makes you think you're not?" Steve said. "Remember what I told you before. We can see that your family's taken care of while you go do a walkabout." He clapped Thomas on the shoulder and started up the road to where he could catch the ridge trail back to his trailer.

Thomas stood a moment longer before he trudged across the packed dirt of the driveway toward the porch. He was halfway there when he heard the rustle of a bird's wings. Peering closer, he saw one of Auntie's visitor crows opening and closing its wings as it strutted back and forth along the railing. Thomas smiled. The bird's antics made him think of a circus ringmaster.

Then he realized that someone was sitting in Auntie's chair.

He had almost reached the steps before he saw it was Auntie, still up, with Santana beside her in another chair. Santana stood up and met him with a big hug when he got to the top of stairs.

"What's this for?" Thomas said into her hair.

Santana pulled back to look him in the face. "I was so worried. Auntie said you were dead."

"I did not," Auntie said. "I told you he was in the land of the dead. It's not the same thing at all."

"God. You didn't tell Mom that, did you?"

Santana shook her head. "Auntie had me brew up a tea for her with special herbs that made her fall asleep."

"Really?"

"We kind of had to. She was so mad that Auntie had gotten you to go off with Morago and the others, we had to do something."

Thomas could just imagine the state their mother would've been in. "I'm surprised it worked," he said.

Santana shrugged and returned to her seat.

"And Naya and Will?" Thomas asked as he pulled over another chair for himself. "They're okay?"

She nodded. "They're sleeping." Before he could ask, she added, "Without the help of any tea. I was sleeping too until I woke up for no reason and came out to find Auntie talking to her crows."

One of which was still on the railing, though there were probably others in the old mesquite and saguaro that overlooked the yard. The one on the railing cocked its head, regarding Santana as though it understood the conversation.

Thomas sighed. Who was he kidding? It was less likely that it didn't understand.

"So spill," Santana said. "Where've you been?"

Thomas ran a hand through his hair. He looked from his sister to Auntie. "Where haven't I been?" he said.

"Yeah, that tells us a lot."

So Thomas told them everything that had happened since he'd left to join Morago and the others at the community center. As he spoke, the first crow was joined by others. By the time he was done, a whole row of them lined the railing, following his every word. Considering everything he'd been through, Thomas was surprised at how unsettled he felt by their rapt attention.

Beside Santana, Auntie stared off into the growing dawn, her mouth set in a straight line, eyes flashing. The crows, picking up on her anger, stirred and clacked their beaks, making a small chorus of rattling sounds.

"If she ever shows her face in the Painted Lands again," she finally said, "I will kill that woman."

Thomas was sure that the shocked look on his sister's face mirrored his own. "Auntie!" he said.

But Auntie was unrepentant. "She crossed the line, doing what she did to you."

"Hey, I get that you're mad. She's not exactly my favourite person either. But what happened to your telling us that the Kikimi are a peaceful people who don't go looking for trouble?"

"Did I say I would seek her out?"

A couple of days ago, Thomas would have described Auntie as frail. Right now, she looked like she could take on a mountain lion. And win.

"No," he said. "You're just acting a lot…fiercer than I thought you were."

"I wasn't always trapped in an old woman's body. There was a time I could outrun and outfight any of the dog boys."

"You were in the Warrior Society?"

"No," Auntie said. "But who says they're the only ones who can be warriors? When I was young, we all had their skills. They have a calling, but we were still of the People. We were all strong."

Thomas thought of his dead Aunt Lucy, beyond in the otherworld. Young, powerful, determined. That was what Auntie had been like when the two were girls growing up in the Painted Lands together. Formidable.

All things considered, Consuela Mara would be well advised not to show her face anywhere around these parts—not with Auntie gunning for her.

Daylight began to pink the sky behind the mountains and the crows rose up in a crowd to fly off cawing, all except for one. It might have been the bird Thomas had seen when he'd first arrived, or perhaps it was another. He had no idea.

"So are you going to study with Morago now," Santana asked, "and become a shaman?"

"No."

"But—"

"I doesn't mean I won't at some point. It's just I've never seen anything except for the rez and Santo del Vado Viejo. There's a whole world out there that I don't know anything about."

Santana nodded. "I get that."

Of course she did. The two of them had often talked about it, sprawled out on the big flat rocks behind the house, trying to imagine what lay beyond the expanse of desert they could see from that vantage point. Thomas had always thought that Santana would be the one to go, while he stayed to take care of the family. He was the oldest, and she still had a year of school, but he wanted his sister to have every opportunity she could, and if that meant him staying, he was okay with it.

But if Steve was on the level—if he really could help them out—maybe they could both go.

"Did *you* ever go away?" Santana asked Auntie.

Auntie shook her head. "Lucy was the wanderer, in this world and over in the *ma'inawo* lands. I'm like your mother. I never needed to travel because everything I've ever wanted in this life is right here in the Painted Lands."

"Red rock, dust and desert," Thomas said in a tired voice.

"That's right," Auntie told him. "But also friends, family and community."

The crow on the railing ruffled its feathers and made a hoarse chuffing sound.

Auntie laughed. "I think that would be included in all three, Jorge."

"What did he say?" Santana wanted to know.

"He wanted to know where lovers fit in."

Santana tilted her head and regarded their aunt. "Because..." Her voice trailed off and she made a small grimace. "Ew. With a bird?"

"He's not a bird when we—"

Santana put her hands over her ears. "Too much information!"

That made Auntie laugh again. "I wasn't always so old," she said. "And Jorge is still a handsome man when he's not wearing his jacket of feathers."

The crow rattled his beak and puffed out his chest.

"If a little vain," Auntie added. The bird gave a cry of mock protest and flew off to join his companions perched in the mesquite tree.

Auntie turned to Thomas, her features serious now. "Wherever you go," she said, "stay clear of the ghost roads. In life, as well as in death. She may not have intended it, but Consuela Mara led you into a curse as black as any skinwalker's. The salvagers have marked you as theirs, and they will never forget or let you go."

"I have no intention of ever going near a ghost road again," Thomas assured her.

"See that you don't." She pushed herself out of her chair. "*Ohla.* I'm glad you're home. This old woman's going to bed now."

She ruffled his hair as she went by. Santana jumped up and gave her a kiss on the cheek, then held the door open for her as she went inside.

When Santana returned to her seat, Thomas was staring off into the dawn light. "It's funny," he said. "Now that I'm no longer scared of Morago, and I'm actually interested in learning from him, another part of me wants to get away from the rez even more than I did before."

"Maybe it's not so weird," Santana told him. "You've just seen and done all kinds of crazy stuff, but in the end, it's still tied to your being trapped here, taking up shaman ways."

Thomas nodded. "I feel if I put it off for much longer, I'll never get away."

"Yeah," Santana said. "I can totally see that. First chance I get, I'm out of here too—and I love all the stuff that seems to scare you to death."

"It's not that I'm scared."

Santana smiled. "I know. It's the not having the chance to see if there's anything better out there, or at least different."

"Do you think you'll come back?" Thomas asked.

"Oh, sure. Doesn't everybody eventually drift back?"

"I suppose most do."

But Thomas wasn't sure that he'd be one of them. Back to visit? Maybe. Back to stay didn't seem as likely.

He was still thinking about that when Santana went off to bed and he remained alone on the porch watching the sunrise. Even the crows had headed back to their roost in Yellowrock Canyon.

66

STEVE

Reuben offered to drive me all the way over to Painted Cloud Canyon, but I got out at Thomas's house and hiked up to the ridge trail instead. I said I needed some time to think, and walking's how I do it best. Both are true, but I'm hoping that being out here on my own will give me a chance to talk to Calico.

I wait until I'm a mile or so down the trail from Thomas's place before I start calling her name. My voice seems to fall off the ridge trail and disappear into the desert and scrub. The only response I get is this hour before dawn, the quiet all around me. I keep on calling for a mile or so until I give it up.

Yeah, she's seriously pissed off with me.

I don't actually feel like going back to the empty trailer, but I don't have any gear with me and I'm too old to sleep rough without a bedroll. At least that's what I tell myself. But what I'm really hoping is that I'll come around the side of the trailer and she'll be lounging by the picnic table, asking, "What took you so long?"

Instead, I get Morago.

The shaman's sitting on the table, feet on the seat, staring out across the canyon while he drinks a beer he probably helped himself to from my fridge. Morago turns as I come out of the arch and walk past the trailer, but I'm sure he heard my approach while I was still up on the ridge trail.

Beside him on the table, a lit candle sitting in a puddle of hot wax in its dish tells me he's been waiting for a while. There's the faintest hint of pink on the horizon and enough light that everything is shades of grey.

"*Ohla*, Swallows Spirits," Morago says.

"That's not funny," I tell him.

"No kidding. What the hell were you thinking?"

"You say that like I knew what was going on and had a choice."

"Point."

He has a swig of his beer. "I hear you're not big in Calico's books these days."

I ignore that to get myself a bottle. I come back with three, pass one to Morago and pop the cap on one of the others. I down half of it before I sit down beside him on the table.

"How do you know all this?" I ask.

He shrugs. "Cousins talk, I keep my ear to the ground."

He doesn't mean people he's related to, he means *ma'inawo*. A few days ago I would have rolled my eyes. Now I just nod in understanding. "They've got nothing better to do than gossip about an old desert rat who only wants to keep to himself?"

"They find you interesting, always have. Some little cousin is always telling a story about something you've done."

"Until the past few days, I haven't done a damn thing except walk the desert, hang out with my girlfriend, play my guitar, eat, and sleep. What's so interesting about that?"

"You know you're different, right?"

This time I do roll my eyes. "Jesus. Now you going to tell me some bullshit story about how I've actually got a lizard or a rabbit or something living under my skin."

He smiles and shakes his head. "No. It's two things, actually. You've been living a long time in the otherworld, and that changes a man."

"Calico said something about that."

"The other thing is, you've built up a lot of goodwill—not just on the rez, but with the *ma'inawo* as well."

"Besides my girlfriend, I don't know any other..." I start, then let my voice trail off.

That was the old me. Apparently, I've met plenty of others while I was out walking in the mountains. Hell, maybe even right in town or on the rez. I just can't tell them apart from people unless they shift to their animal shapes.

"So," I say. "That and a quarter gets me what?"

"You were never about *getting* anything," Morago says. "That's what they find so intriguing. Even the most charitable person wants something. It's human nature." He smiles. "*Ma'inawo* nature, too."

"So?"

"So you never have, and they couldn't figure it out. They kept waiting for you to show your true face—you know, reveal the long con you're playing—except the face you show *is* your true face and in time, they've come to know that too."

This Mr. Nice Guy stuff is making me feel a little squirrelly. I take a swig of beer. "Do you have a point to all of this?" I ask.

He doesn't answer me. Instead, he just goes on. "You ever notice how often random people come up to you, lay out some situation, and ask you what you think? You might be a couple of days into the mountains and then there's some old man sitting on an outcrop, says howdo, gets to talking?"

I give a slow nod. "It's just being neighbourly, passing the time of day."

"That's what *you're* doing. Around here, you're known as the Arbitrator. Those random people are treating you like you're their own personal King Solomon. You've settled more disputes in the Painted Lands than Aunt Nora's gone through bingo cards."

"The Arbitrator," I repeat, rolling the unfamiliar term on my tongue.

"That's you," Morago says.

I shake my head. "Sounds like some big-ass boots that don't fit," I say. "But anyway, so what?"

"So, just like Calico, other *ma'inawo* are confused as to why you, of all people, would want to protect a man who makes a business out of killing them and destroying their homes."

"*What?*"

Morago ignores my reaction and keeps on talking. "You've been to the hunting lodge," he says. "Seen the size of it, the helipad, all the trails. You think all that crap doesn't have an impact on how the *ma'i-nawo* live? I've been talking to them since Consuela Mara showed up. They really did put out a call to Night Woman for help."

"But Consuela isn't actually Night Woman."

He waves a loose hand in the air. "It doesn't matter. If she says she is, and if she helps them the way Night Woman would, then what difference does it make?"

"Are you saying you agree with them? That we should've let Consuela kill Sammy? Or that maybe we should have just dropped him off the mountain ourselves?"

Before he can answer, I give him a quick run through of what happened when I met Si'tala—what she said about how the rez was going to need Sammy's expertise in a few years.

"I get it," Morago says. "And at the rate new housing tracts are going up on the outskirts of the city, anyone should know that water rights are going to be a problem in the near future. And though I don't doubt that the Women's Council will do a bang-up job dealing with the city's negotiators, she's right: having Sammy's help would be a big plus for our side. He's got inside connections that the rest of us don't."

I tap my beer against his and smile. "So you'd have done the same thing as me?"

Morago looks out toward the desert for a long moment before answering. "I'm not disagreeing with you," he says cautiously before meeting my gaze. "I'm explaining why Calico believes she should've had a say about how to deal with Sammy."

I breathe a sigh of frustration. "Look, she was talking about killing Sammy, and that would only have made everything worse."

"Have you ever known Calico to kill anyone? Didn't she have the right to express her anger about what's been happening? Why shouldn't she get to blow off a little steam?"

"But if Sammy's lodge is having all this impact on how they live their lives, how are they going to feel when some big-ass reservoir gets built on their lands?"

Morago wags a finger at me. "You're talking and not listening, just like you did with Calico. From what I'm hearing, the only *ma'inawo* you listened to was Consuela's ghost sister, Si'tala." He pauses and gazes out into the desert. "It seems strange that she was on such a different page than Consuela."

"Actually," I say, "her flying into me was about something else, and our conversation about Sammy was secondary." I tell him about how Si'tala asked me to make her a body—which, supposedly, will let her separate from Consuela. "I can't really blame her," I add. "Have you ever spent time around that bitch?"

Morago rubs his chin. "Okay," he says. "So let me get this straight. You pretty much disappear with this *ma'inawo* ghost woman, who has a whole other agenda, but she just happens to weigh in on the Sammy thing. And you buy her opinion to the exclusion of anyone else's, including your girlfriend's."

He looks at me and continues. "After all your years with Calico, I'm pretty sure that would rankle. Don't you think she'd want a sense that you value her opinion? That you'd at least talk it over with her first?"

"Fuck," I say. "I screwed that up."

I scratch my head, thinking back. "You know what? I didn't even let Calico argue with Consuela. I stepped right in between them. That's when Si'tala flew into me."

I drain my beer and pop open the cap on the other. "Man, I was only trying to do the right thing, but I can see how I've been a dick."

"Talk to her."

"I've been trying, but she's not making it easy. I haven't seen her since she disappeared back in the otherworld."

"You know this is still the otherworld that you're in, right here?"

I sigh. "Doesn't matter. I have no idea where to go look for her."

"Well," Morago says, "there's a reason they're called 'the hidden people' in some stories."

He sets his empty bottle on the table beside his first one. "This other thing," he says. "Providing Consuela's shadow sister with a body. You sure you want to go through with that?"

"Do you think it's a bad idea?"

He shrugged. "Does the world really need a second Consuela Mara?"

"Si'tala's not the same person. They're total opposites. It's not right that she's stuck with that evil twin."

"I guess I'll have to trust your judgment. When are you planning to do it?"

"As soon as possible. She said to just make a figure out of clay or sticks or something—it doesn't matter what size. After that, the only clue she gave was that she said my intent mattered. Does that make sense to you?"

Morago nods. "Medicine is everywhere. It sleeps inside us and fills the world. But it requires a focused will to make it anything other than aimless energy."

"So I should really concentrate on the purpose of what I'm doing."

Morago nods again. "And it will help if you do it in a sacred place." He closes his eyes for a moment, thinking. When he looks at me again he says, "The medicine wheel at Aggie's place would be best. It's got good red dirt with a thousand years of ceremonies lying deep in its memory."

"I've never seen a medicine wheel at Aggie's," I say.

"It's just back of her place, where she has the big fires."

I know the spot he's talking about. I've been out there for some of Aggie's campfires.

"But don't all medicine wheels have circles of stones?" I ask.

"They do," Morago says. "Most of the stones at Aggie's place have sunk so deep that the ground's swallowed them up."

"That would take forever."

"It's an ancient circle that predates the Kikimi," he says.

We fall silent then. The birdsong's started up in the canyon and we watch the morning light creep along its length.

"Si'tala didn't just talk to me about the future," I say after a while.

Morago gives me a questioning look.

"She talked about the past as well. Or at least, she said I have nothing to regret."

"Sounds like she's got some things right," Morago says. "I've been telling you that for years."

"Except my regrets aren't something I can just forget. I think about them all the time: Sully, Martin. And especially Steve. All their deaths are on me."

"I was there," Morago says. "You had nothing to do with Sully becoming a junkie, or Martin taking off the way he did. It's not like you were breaking up the band forever."

"Maybe. But it was my band. I was the guy in charge. I should've been looking out for them. And Steve... Don't tell me that swapping places with him didn't cause his death."

"I'm telling you exactly that. What caused his death was whatever malfunction caused that plane to go down."

"But—"

Morago cuts me off. "He made the offer. He was thrilled that you said yes. None of us ever dreamed it would play out the way it did."

"Because we were young and stupid and stoned."

"Yeah, we were all of that. But we also had free will, Steve included."

Morago leans over, blows the candle out, and looks up at the pink sky. "We're all beings of power. Some of us are strong, some weak. Every mistake that we learn something from, makes us stronger. As does every sacrifice, every good deed. That's how we learn. Our power is the sum of all we have been and all we are. When you take responsibility for somebody else's decisions, or actions, you take away their power. And when you take away somebody's power, you leave them spinning wheels when they could be moving forward."

I feel a little sick. "You think Steve's spinning wheels wherever he is because I feel responsible for what happened to him?"

"No, I think it's *your* wheels that are spinning. When you take away somebody's power, you lose some of your own as well."

I shake my head. "Well, fuck. You really believe that?"

"After all you've experienced," Morago says, "how can you still not accept that there's more to the world than what you can see?"

"I believe that. I just don't believe that it's got anything to do with me. Once I was Jackson Cole, rock star. Now I'm just his ghost."

"What you whites call ghosts, we Kikimi think of as spirit guides."

I know exactly where he's going with this: the notion that I'm some arbitrator for the *ma'inawo* around here.

"I'm too messed up to be anybody's guide," I tell him. "Everybody's way better off if I just stick to the desert and the mountains, and leave the rest of the world to carry on without my interference."

"You can't really believe that."

Before I can respond he goes on. "Without your 'interference,' as you put it, Sammy would be dead, Si'tala wouldn't be getting herself a body, and many of the cousins around here would be at odds with one another."

He shakes his head, then continues. "So long as you hide from the world and hold on to misplaced guilt, you will continue to lose the power that would allow you to become who you are meant to be."

I don't know what to say. We've skirted around these guilt issues plenty of times before, but this is the first time Morago has been so blunt about it. The thing is, intellectually, I've always known he's right. I just can't get my heart to accept it.

"There's humble," Morago says, "and then there's stupid."

I want to keep on arguing. I want to tell him that he's been wrong about me all along. But I'm tired of carrying all this weight around. I don't want to be that guy. Not anymore. Hell, I never wanted to be him. But the guilt just laid itself on me and I've never been able to shake it.

"I don't know what to do," I say, speaking aloud the words I've never been able to admit before, not even to myself. "I don't know that I ever did—not since Steve died."

Morago turns to look at me. Those blue-green eyes of his seem to swallow my gaze. It's like they're looking right inside me, all the way to my secret core. I don't know how long he studies me, and I don't know what he sees, but he finally nods as though he's come to some decision.

"Let's go sculpt a body for a raven spirit," he says.

67

LEAH

Come morning, Leah was still intent on staying. She woke up more certain than the night before. Her dreams had been full of women with the heads of dogs, and great clouds of crows that spelled out incomprehensible words in the sky, mimicking old-fashioned skywriting. The images were disquieting and she was unsure what they meant, but they didn't alter her decision.

She sat up in her bed to see that Marisa was already up, bent over the little desk under the window of their motel room working on her laptop. She glanced Leah's way and said, "Good morning," before returning her attention to her screen.

When Leah came back from her shower, drying her hair with a towel, Marisa asked, "So what did you decide?"

"I'm staying."

Marisa didn't ask if she was sure. Instead, she just studied Leah for a moment. Whatever she saw in Leah's face seemed to satisfy her more than Leah's affirmative response.

"Okay, then," she said. "I'm going to have some breakfast, stop by the hospital, and then hit the road."

"Do you want company for the first two?"

"I want company for all three, but I'll settle for whatever I can get."

TWENTY MINUTES later they were sitting in a booth at Jerry's Roadhouse, nursing coffees while they waited for Janis to bring them their breakfast. Living at the motel, this would be her new kitchen, Leah thought, with the benefit of not having to cook or clean up after herself.

"How are you going to get around?" Marisa asked.

Leah shrugged. Something else to consider. Perhaps it was finally time for her to learn how to drive.

"They must have public transportation," she said, then grinned. "Maybe I'll see about renting a mule."

Marisa laughed. "I'd pay to see a picture of that."

"If my bank account gets low enough, I might hold you to that."

"Seriously, if you need any help…"

"Don't worry," Leah told her. "I've got enough in my savings to see me through a couple of months, and that includes keeping up my apartment in Newford. After that, I'll just have to see where things stand."

"I think you're brave," Marisa told her, "leaving everything behind and just starting all over again. Crazy, but brave."

"It doesn't feel particularly brave," Leah told her.

She might have said more, but right then Janis returned with their breakfast.

"Did you hear about that kid who stabbed Aggie White Horse?" Janis said as she laid their plates on the table. "You were going out to see Aggie yesterday, weren't you?"

They nodded.

"What about the girl?" Marisa asked.

"I heard on the news that she turned herself in." Janis shook her head. "What could make anyone go after a sweet old lady like Aggie?"

"It isn't always so cut and dried," Marisa told her. "That girl had a terrible home life."

The waitress shook her head. "I don't know about that. Seems to me, people just don't take responsibility for what they do. Instead, they hide behind their liberal excuses."

Leah noted how Marisa's face went stiff.

"So you're a Republican?" she asked.

"I'm not anything. The closest I can get to a political party is the Libertarians. Everybody else just lies and cheats. And doesn't take responsibility for their crap."

"Sadie did," Marisa said. "The girl who turned herself in."

Janis gave a slow nod. "You know what? You're right."

Somebody from another booth called her for a refill, and she went back behind the counter to get the coffee pot.

"I hate that," Marisa said when the waitress left. "Troubled kids have enough problems without people saying that a horrible upbringing is no excuse—that what's done is done, so they should just suck it up and get on with their lives."

"I don't think she really meant it like that," Leah told her. "Most people speak in generalities, but at the end of the day, they come through for the individual."

"I suppose. But why do they have to immediately assume the worst?"

"Because the first thing they see is something awful—in this case, a kid knifing an old lady—and they haven't had time to process anything else. And some of the time, they never do."

"Huh," Marisa said, winking at Leah. "You should write a blog about that."

Leah smiled and turned the conversation to other topics. Soon they were gossiping about the people they knew in common back home. Their conversation gave Leah a twinge about missing her friends in Newford, but didn't change her resolve to stay.

After breakfast they walked back to the motel and loaded Marisa's luggage into the rental. "Are you going to see about keeping the room?" Marisa asked.

Leah shook her head. "It's not like this place is packed. I can wait till after we've been to the hospital and you drop me back off."

She stood for a moment, took a deep breath, then turned in a slow circle, looking at their surroundings. It was still early, but the air was already warm, the wind bringing in a wealth of unfamiliar scents from the desert behind the motel. She smiled at the big saguaro across the parking lot and got in the car.

This was so the right decision.

WHEN THEY GOT to the hospital they had no trouble getting in to see Aggie. The black-haired men from last night with their striking features and muscular frames were still on guard outside the hospital entrance, in the lobby, and in the hall outside Aggie's room. Each group seemed so grim as the two women approached that Leah was nervous that she and Marisa would never get past them. But the men simply nodded when they drew near, and smiled as they went past. Any hospital staff studiously looked away from them as they went by, which felt a little odd, but it was better than having to lie again about being Aggie's granddaughters.

They found Manny dozing by Aggie's bed, slouched in a chair. He sat up at their entrance and lifted a hand in greeting. Leah's gaze went to Aggie. Her colour was a little better, and she seemed to be sleeping soundly.

"I'm just on my way back to Vegas," Marisa whispered to Manny, "but I wanted to see how she's doing before I left."

"I'm doing just fine," Aggie said from the bed without opening her eyes. "And I'd be doing even better if people didn't treat me like an invalid."

"Can't be helped," Manny said with a smile. "You are an invalid."

Aggie opened her eyes and frowned at Manny before smiling at the women. "*Ohla*, Marisa, Leah. So you're going home?"

"I am," Marisa said. "Leah's staying on for a while."

"Still searching for the ghost of Jackson Cole?"

Leah shook her head. "I have a book to write, so I thought I might as well do it here, where I can get the chance to do some exploring when I'm not at my computer. I also want to write about the people coming across the desert from the border."

"You live so far away from our problems," Aggie said. "How did you get interested in the fate of the migrants?"

"I met this man named Ernie, who lives at the motel where we're staying. We got to talking and he started me thinking about it."

"Oh, Ernie. He's a character."

"And a good man," Manny added. "Well respected among the *ma'inawo*, though he probably doesn't realize it."

Leah took a step forward, fascinated by the turn the conversation had taken. "I'd love to learn more about them, as well," she said. "The *ma'in*— What did you call them?"

"*Ma'inawo*," Aggie said. "It just means cousins."

"I like that," Marisa said. "It makes us all feel like family."

Leah nodded in agreement and Manny smiled.

It was funny. Last night, while he and his companions were looking out for Aggie, she'd thought of him as part of this grim thuggish gang. Dangerous and unbending. Now he felt like somebody's friendly uncle.

"Where will you be staying while you're in town?" Aggie asked Leah.

"At the motel."

Manny and Aggie exchanged a glance. Leah could almost see thoughts pass between them, but the reason caught her completely by surprise.

"I have room at my house," Aggie said.

"And I'd rest easier if I knew somebody was staying there with her," Manny added.

That earned him another frown from Aggie. "I'm not some helpless old lady," she said.

"Keep talking like that," Manny told her, "and I'll make sure you don't get out of this hospital for a month."

Aggie turned to Leah. "You see what I have to put up with?"

"Are you serious?" Leah asked. "About my staying with you? I have to warn you that I can't drive."

"I can't either," Aggie told her. "But that's what the young men and women of the tribe are for—to make sure an old woman like me gets around."

Manny laughed, then nodded. "I can have one of Reuben's dog boys give you a ride out."

Now it was Leah and Marisa's turn to share a moment of silent communication. Leah could see an echo of her own excitement in her friend's eyes. She couldn't believe her luck. Having the chance to live right out in the desert, getting to know Aggie, being able to look at all those paintings at her leisure.

"That would be fantastic," Leah said.

"They're probably going to release Aggie this afternoon," Manny said. "Could you head over this morning to check out the house, maybe put together a grocery list?"

"Sure," Leah started to say until she remembered that she had an appointment. "Except I was supposed to see Ernie this afternoon. He's going to help me get a start on some of the research I want to do."

"I can get word to him," Manny said. "He'll probably be happy to come out."

"Tell him he's invited for dinner," Aggie told Manny. "I've never known him to turn down a free meal."

So that was how, an hour later, Leah found herself saying goodbye to Marisa and being taken to Aggie's house by a young man named Jack Young Tree, a nephew of Reuben Little Tree. And also one of his dog boys. After everything Leah had already experienced, she could only assume that Jack could literally turn into a dog.

She wanted to ask him about it. She had a hundred questions for anybody who'd talk to her. But after they turned off the highway onto the dirt road, Jack's old pickup seemed to hit every bump, and she thought it would be more prudent to brace herself against the dash and let him concentrate on his driving.

SHOWDOWN AT THE WHITE HORSE MEDICINE WHEEL

68

STEVE

Morago sends me over to Aggie's place to draw some water from her well. When I get back to the fire circle with a couple of pails—one full, one empty, like he asked—he's digging under one of the big red rocks on the ridge overlooking the desert and the city beyond. Beside the pile of red dirt he's made are a bunch of sticks. No, I realize, as I get closer—they're dried saguaro ribs, broken into shorter pieces. I set the pails down nearby.

"Go cut some sweetgrass," he says without turning around. "As long as you can find."

"What's that for?"

"To hold the bones together."

I look at him, waiting for further explanation, but he ignores me. Sometimes I really miss the days when I was his boss and he wasn't a shaman.

I pull out my jackknife, snap the blade out and head off to harvest some of the sweetgrass that Aggie has growing not far from the well. It's a large healthy patch—I've watered it for her from time to time. I harvest a few small bunches, remembering to send some gratitude to both the plant and Aggie.

By the time I get back, we've been joined by an audience of a half-dozen of Aggie's dogs and twice as many crows, perched in the trees or strutting around nearby. There's also a hawk making lazy circles high above us. Regular crows would be up there harassing the shit out of it, but most Yellowrock Canyon crows are *ma'inawo*, or so Morago says, and I'm not going to argue that point. Stories told around the camp-fires say that the *ma'inawo* call hawks *tío*, meaning 'uncle,' using the term as an honourific. Apparently the uncles have some big power, so the *ma'inawo* try to stay on their good side—which explains why these crows are hanging around down here rather than making a ruckus up there.

Under Morago's direction, I braid the grasses into thin ropes, tying off the ends to keep them from coming apart. Then I use the grass ropes to bind the saguaro ribs into a rough stick figure only fifteen inches or so in length, total.

Now I know what he meant by 'bones.'

Morago looks over at a bunch of the crows. "Any of you have some raven feathers stashed away somewhere?"

One lifts from its perch on a saguaro arm and flies north.

"I need four of them!" Morago calls after the bird.

"Four?" I ask.

He nods. "Sure. Sacred number."

While we wait for the crow to return, Morago has me put most of the dirt he dug out into the empty pail, then mix in some of the water. Turns out it's actually clay, powder dry when I start, turning to mud as it mixes with the liquid.

"That's too much water," he says.

I add more of the clay dust, kneading the mess with my fingers as I try to get the consistency he's looking for. While I work out in the sun, he rests in the shade of the rock, hands behind his head, watching me through half-closed eyes. The dogs have found shade too; they all seem to be asleep. The crows don't appear to mind the sun's heat, which has my shirt sticking to my back.

"We need to put something of you into the mix," Morago says as the clay begins to get stiffer. "Saliva will work, but blood's better."

"The hell?"

"It's to make the connection between you, and the raven sister, and this little clay dolly you're making."

His gaze holds mine until I spit into the clay. I'm not going to cut myself if I don't need to.

"A little more," he says.

I spit again.

"That should do."

I go back to working the clay. The crow that flew off earlier returns with four long black feathers at about the same time that Morago's satisfied with the consistency of the clay. He thanks the crow. "Okay," he says to me. "We're fast approaching the point of no return. You still sure you want to go through with this?"

"I said I'd do it."

"Yeah, you did."

I begin to press clay onto the stick-figure bones. I don't even try for realism. Morago coaches me as I work, reminding me to think of Si'tala, to imagine that each glop of clay I'm putting on the figure is a call for her.

"Looking good," Morago says.

Maybe so, but this thing is not pretty—that's for sure.

He sticks the raven feathers into the top of the head so that they stick up like a headdress. I study what I've done so far, then add a bit of clay for a nose, poke two holes for eyes and drag my thumbnail under the nose to make a smiling mouth. While I'm doing that Morago rolls a cigarette and lights it up. He offers the smoke rising from the tip to the four directions.

I sit back on my heels and look at my handiwork. The facial features have only made it weirder, so I just have to hope Si'tala was right about how the look of it doesn't really matter. This was the best I could do, so it'll have to suffice.

I look around, wondering what's next. Shade would be good; so would sleep.

"How long do we have to wait to see if it works?" I ask.

Morago shrugs. "*Ma'inawo* move to their own time. But if she still wants a body, it shouldn't be too long."

He starts to adjust one of the feathers but stops, lifting his head. A moment later, I hear it too. The sound of a truck engine. The dogs scramble up as one and lope toward the house where a pickup pulls into Aggie's yard. I recognize the truck as one of Reuben's old junkers that he lets his dog boys work on. The driver's door opens and Jack Young Tree steps out and walks around to the back of the truck, where he pulls a suitcase out of the bed. The dogs are all around him, sniffing his legs, bumping him with their shoulders.

"Looks like Aggie's home," I say.

"I don't think so. Too rough a ride. Reuben would never put her in that heap."

Morago's right. When the passenger door opens its not Aggie who gets out, but the journalist who was trapped in my head back in the otherworld. Leah Hardin. I'm happy for a moment, knowing she survived the leap off the cliff, then I wonder what she's doing here.

"That's interesting," Morago says.

I nod. "But what's she doing here?"

A couple of the crows rise into the air and fly over to the house as though they plan to get the answer for us.

69

LEAH

J udging by the worried look on her brow, Leah couldn't quite emulate Jack's casual indifference to the dogs' eager greetings.

Jack smiled as he reached into the bed of the truck. "They're cool," he said. "They won't hurt you."

Her face relaxed as she smiled back at him. "I know," she said. "I found that out the last time I was here." But as she continued to look around, the puzzled look returned. "I even kind of bonded with Ruby," she said, "but I don't see her."

Jack didn't respond. When she turned to look at him, his features had taken an unhappy cast. "Yeah, she's not with us anymore," he said.

Leah felt like she'd been punched in the chest. She'd really liked Ruby, both the dog and the woman, and had been looking forward to spending some time with her.

"What happened?" she asked.

"She got swallowed by an *hechicera*."

"A what?"

"*Hechicera*. A witch that controls spirits."

He turned quickly and carried Leah's bag to the door before she could ask what he meant. She followed after him, the dogs still swirling around her legs. Jack set the suitcase down and pulled a piece of paper from his pocket.

"This is the number for my uncle Reuben's store," he said. "If you or Aggie need anything, just call and someone will fix you up."

"Thanks. I—"

He didn't give her a chance to go on. "Everybody really appreciates your helping out like this," he said. "Aggie's kind of an institution around here."

Then he was walking briskly back to the truck.

Leah stood in front of the door, surrounded by all the dogs. Jack gave her a wave as he backed up the truck and she automatically waved back. Then he was driving away, leaving only dust in his wake. Leah looked down at the dogs.

"So," she said to them. "Any one of you want to change into a human being so you can tell me what that was all about?"

But the dogs just acted like dogs. A couple touched her leg with their noses, then they all went trotting into the desert, back toward where they'd come from earlier. From the roof above her, a pair of crows took wing, trailing after them. Leah took a few steps away from the house and shaded her eyes to follow their passage through the scrub. Their destination was a large open circle of dirt with a fire pit in the center. Off to one side, where the land rose in a jumble of red rocks, she could see a pair of figures, one kneeling, the other sitting on the ground nearby. It took her a moment to recognize them. Morago and Steve Cole.

She couldn't tell what they were doing, but clearly it had gathered them an audience of rez dogs and crows.

It wasn't any of her business, and she was about to go into the house when Steve glanced in her direction and raised a hand. Perhaps it was in greeting, perhaps to beckon her over. She decided it was the latter, if only to satisfy her curiosity.

Although she had a clear sight line to where they were working, she realized it would be easier to take the meandering path that presented itself at the end of the yard, rather than a direct route through the desert scrub where she'd have to be careful of all those cacti with their barbed thorns. When she finally circled the large fire pit and joined them, all she could do was stare at the odd thing they'd been making.

She wasn't sure if it was a sculpture, a fetish, a voodoo doll, or what. It was made of red clay, a rough human-like figure over a foot long, with black feathers stuck in the top of its head in the shape of a fan. The features were just as basic: the suggestion of a nose, two holes poked into the clay for eyes and a curved indented line for a mouth.

"Hey," Steve said, looking up. "Glad to see you made it back okay."

She nodded, but didn't really want to think about the last time she'd seen him because that had been beyond weird. Except the funny thing was, until seeing him and Morago here with their odd clay figure, the past day's events had already begun fading a little, just as Marisa had said they would. No. Not so much fading, as losing their intensity. They were beginning to feel like a story told, without the emotional resonance of having been a part of it.

"What brings you out here?" Steve asked.

It took her a moment to register that he'd spoken.

"I'm going to look after Aggie while she's recuperating."

"I would have thought you'd be on a fast track back to Newford."

"No, I like the desert."

He smiled. "Even after all you went through?"

He obviously had no trouble remembering. She could tell it wasn't the same for him as it was for her. Her being here didn't change a thing. But his presence brought her memories some uncomfortable clarity.

"That was challenging," she said, "and not something I'd want to repeat in quite the same way, but it doesn't stop me from wanting to get to know it all a little better. The landscape's so primal and the beauty is so stark, both here and in that other place."

"So you decided to stay on."

She nodded. "I was going to stay at the motel, but Manny and Aggie made the suggestion of coming here, and I couldn't refuse."

"You'll find that living here is something else. I fell in love with the area, just hearing about it from Morago."

She smiled and looked at the shaman. "Are you that eloquent?"

"I have my moments," Morago said, "though I can't string words together like He Who Rides the Wind Like a Song."

"Like who?"

Morago jerked a thumb in Steve's direction.

"Don't pay any attention to him." Steve laughed. "He's just yanking your chain. Seriously, he comes up with a new Indian name for me every time I see him."

"Someday one of them's going to stick," Morago said.

They joked with the familiarity of old friends.

Leah laughed. "So what would my Indian name be?" she asked.

Morago pretended to think, humour twinkling in his eyes. But when he spoke, his features went still, his eyes serious.

"Probably something like, Dancing With Secrets," he said.

Her eyebrows went up. "You think I've got secrets?"

Morago smiled. "Everybody does. But you're dancing with yours."

Before Leah could ask what he meant, Morago turned back to Steve. "It's time we finished up here," he said. "Refocus."

"What exactly are you doing?" Leah asked, looking down at the strange figure again.

"Nothing you could call exact," Morago replied at the same time as Steve said, "Making a body for a raven spirit."

They looked at each other and laughed.

Leah looked from one man to the other. "So which is it?" she asked.

"Bit of both," Morago replied. "Steve told the raven spirit he met in his head that he'd make her a body."

There it was again. Inside Steve's head. Where she'd been, too.

"And *that's* what you've made for her to inhabit?" she asked, unable to hide a slight grimace. "Isn't it kind of…small?" And ugly, she added to herself.

"It's symbolic," Morago explained. "Making the figure opens a passageway between spirit realms and the physical world, with Si'tala and Steve standing in for the two states of being, and the figure serving as a door. Once she is inside the figure, she'll be able to look however she wants."

"But she'll still be so small, like a child's toy."

"When she first manifests in it, I suppose," Morago said. "But after that—you've seen how crows can become men and men can become crows?"

Leah shook her head. But she *had* seen a dog become a woman. Ruby.

She'd been so full of life, it was hard to imagine she was gone.

"I understand the concept," she said, "but the physics defy me."

"It's the medicine of the *ma'inawo*. How a rabbit can become a woman, or a snake a man. These transformations should be impossible, except I don't think they actually transform, so much as shift from one form, to nothing, to the new form."

"So how does she get inside it?" Leah asked.

"I'm still trying to work that out myself," Steve told her.

Morago adjusted another of the feathers coming out of the figure's head.

"Getting in—that's the easy and hard part," the shaman said. "All the stories of what could possibly happen here are waiting for us, with each breath we take. Steve just has to reach into all those possibilities and pull out the one we need by calling the raven spirit to this sacred place."

He gave Steve an encouraging smile. "And you've been doing exactly that since you first started making the clay figure."

"Because of my intent as I was making it," Steve said, as much to explain it to Leah as to reassure himself.

Morago nodded. "Mostly. But also because you're doing it here, in one of our sacred places. The prayers we sing in a medicine circle are magnified. The older the circle, the stronger the prayers, and this is a very old circle."

"Except I haven't been praying," Steve said.

Morago smiled. "Haven't you? You're asking the thunders to allow a spirit that has never had a body to be housed in one you've made for her. What else would you call that?"

Leah thought Steve would say the first thing that came to her mind: wishful thinking.

But Steve seemed to perceive something she didn't. Or couldn't. He placed his finger on the figure's chest, brushing softly against the clay surface. His gaze went inward. He whispered something under his breath—she thought it was a name—and closed his eyes. The surrounding desert went still and the shadow of a cloud fell upon them.

Steve suddenly opened his eyes and looked up. Leah followed his gaze and realized the shadow wasn't caused by a cloud. A woman with black hair and enormous wings floated above them, her wings filling the sky.

The stranger drifted down to where they were standing, and the sunlight returned as she folded her wings gracefully behind her back. The sunshine gleamed on Morago and Steve's skin, but the woman seemed to absorb any light that fell on her. She looked even darker than she had in the sky.

Leah realized that this must be the spirit raven that Steve had been trying to call. Only why did she even need a body when she was already here, so tall and present in the moment?

"Consuela Mara," Morago said to the woman. "We did not call you, and you are not welcome in these Painted Lands."

The woman tossed her hair back from her face and glared at him. "And you, little shaman," she said. "You have no right to intrude into my life, doing your best to steal away a part of who I am. So each of us is cast in an unfavourable light. But in the days to come, when the tale of our meeting here today is told by storytellers, no one will blame me for holding on to what is mine."

Her gaze shifted to Steve and she held out a hand. "Give me the doll," she demanded.

Steve shook his head. "Not happening."

A mocking smile came over her features. "I've found it amusing when you've stood up to me in the past," she told him, "but my patience has its limits. You have no idea how easily I could end your life. You might have stolen a few extra years by walking in the dreaming lands, but I have been here since the first days. You are like an idiot child to me, and your attempts to interfere in my affairs can only be as effectual as a child trying to stay my hand, when he needs punishing."

Steve picked up the clay figure, cradling it carefully in his arms. He didn't offer it to the raven woman. Bits of dried clay fell onto the ground below it, but mostly, it remained intact.

"You're so full of shit," he said.

Consuela seemed to grow taller still. Her dark eyes went black.

Morago touched his shoulder. "Steve," he began.

Steve paid him no attention. His gaze remained fixed on Consuela as he stood up. "You don't *get* to throw something out," he said, "then demand it back when someone else takes an interest in it."

"I didn't throw her out. I put her aside for safekeeping."

Steve shook his head. "We both know that isn't true. Si'tala started out as a vessel for all the memories you didn't think worth keeping. But the problem is, you've ignored her for so long that she's become something else. And so have you. She doesn't belong to you anymore. She never did—not once you put her aside."

"You don't know what you're talking about," Consuela told him, extending both arms in his direction. "Give me that or I'll tear you in two first, and then take it."

"I've talked to her," Steve said. "I've listened to her. Have you done the same? Can you even hear her voice? It's all a one-way street with you—admit it."

"Go away," Morago added. "Steve is under the protection of the Kikimi people as well as the *ma'inawo* that live in these canyons. If you lift a hand against him, you'll awake a blood feud that you can never end."

The woman laughed derisively. "The days of big medicine are long gone. I'm not afraid of you. Your tribe has dwindled, and you are only a shadow of what your ancestors once were. And why would the cousins care about some five-fingered being whose life span is so short that he's here and then gone in the blink of an eye?"

"I don't know," Morago said. "Why don't you ask them?"

So riveted had Leah been on the argument that she hadn't realized that the four of them were no longer alone. She looked around to see dozens of beings standing in a circle around them, with more and more approaching from every direction. Some were human—they looked like Kikimi, though their skin was darker and they didn't have the Kikimi's broad features—and some were animals. Coyotes, birds, lizards, rabbits, every creature she could imagine. But the ones that held her gaze were the ones that weren't quite one or the other. They were like Aggie's paintings come to life—a bewildering array of magical creatures, part human, part animal. They all stood quietly, with their attention focused on the raven woman.

Staring wide-eyed at them, Leah took a nervous step closer to Steve and Morago.

Consuela regarded the crowd with a tired sigh. "I came to answer your call for help," she said, "yet here we are and you view me as the enemy. How can you stand by him? He's a five-fingered being who protects the five-fingered beings that hunt you and take your homes."

"He's been a good neighbour and friend to us all," someone in the crowd said.

Leah couldn't see who'd spoken.

Consuela shook her head. "A good friend doesn't let Sammy Swift Grass kill you for sport, leaving your bodies to rot in these precious canyons of yours."

A red-haired woman stepped out in front. Fox ears poked through her hair and two small antlers rose from her brow. Leah recognized her as the woman she'd seen with Steve when she'd first met him. "Steve has always been honest with us," she said. "He never came sneaking into our lives pretending to be something he's not."

"He's stealing away a part of me! How would you like to have your soul ripped in two and then half taken away?"

"You mean the half you *threw* away?" Steve said. "And I'm not taking her from you. I'm giving her the body that *she* asked for. If you don't like it, you can take it up with her. But I gave her my word that I would do this."

Consuela gave him a sneer. "Who values the word of a five-fingered being?"

"I do," Steve told her. "Si'tala gets her body. End of story."

"I'll have your heart for this," Consuela told him. "I'll cut out your tongue, and your eyes, and I'll wear your entrails as a bloody necklace."

Leah couldn't suppress a shudder, looking at all the tiny bones that adorned her hair and dress.

"You have to be alive to do that," a woman's voice said.

She stepped forward from the crowd and pointed a six-gun at Consuela, the old-fashioned kind of handgun that Leah had only ever seen in cowboy movies. The stranger seemed human, and old, but her hand was steady.

"I have no quarrel with you," Consuela told her.

"Too bad. I've got one with you."

Consuela's eyes narrowed. "You wouldn't dare. Shoot me and you'll start a blood feud with all the corbae clans."

The old woman cocked her six-gun with her thumb.

"Yeah," she said. "I don't think so."

70

THOMAS

Thomas woke late, jolted out of a dream so abruptly that it took him a moment to figure out that he was actually still in his own bed rather than the desert landscape in his dream. He'd been back at Aunt Lucy's house in the otherworld—or maybe that should be the *otherwhen*. Or both. In the dream, it didn't matter. He was just there, sitting at the old wooden table under the spreading boughs of the mesquite tree in her yard. Aunt Lucy was at the adobe oven, bowl in hand, doling out a big helping of stew. The smell of the white tepary beans, peppers and short-ribbed beef, combined with chipotle and who knew what other mysterious spices, drifted in Thomas's direction. A platter of fresh cornbread sat on a plate on the table. Beside it was a fat clay jug, condensation beading on its sides, a wet ring on the table beneath it. Beyond the shade of the tree, the sun was scorching. Heat waves shimmered among the cacti out in the desert scrub.

"Eat," Aunt Lucy said as she set a bowl of stew in front of him. "You're a young man with not nearly enough meat on your bones."

"This is a dream. What difference could my eating here possibly make?"

"A dream," she repeated, then gave a slow nod. "Yes, of course. Seeing it that way makes it easier for you."

"Are you saying I'm actually *here*?"

"Eat."

Thomas automatically obeyed her. When she used that tone, the same as his mother's or Auntie's, he knew there was no point in arguing.

The stew was perfect, better than anything his mother could make, though he'd never tell her that. The cornbread was moist but not greasy, and melted in his mouth.

Aunt Lucy sat across from him at the table. "I know you haven't decided what you want to do yet," she said, "and I don't want you to feel that I'm trying to manipulate you, as Consuela did, but I was wondering if you'd do me a favour."

She didn't play the old woman card, the way Auntie sometimes did. It wouldn't work anyway, looking as youthful as she did. Instead, she was conspiratorially sweet.

Thomas swallowed another mouthful of stew. For something eaten in a dream, it was pleasantly filling.

"What do you want me to do?" he asked.

"I'd like you to go to the White Horse medicine wheel as soon as you get back home."

Thomas sighed. "I don't hate being a Kikimi."

"I know that."

"So you don't have to send me to some ceremony for me to understand what the traditions mean."

"I know that, as well."

"Then why do you want me to go?"

"There's going to be trouble there," she said, "and I am hoping you will do what you can to stop it."

"What kind of trouble?"

She didn't answer; she just fixed him with a steady gaze.

"You don't have to be so mysterious," he said.

"It's not deliberate. It's just how things have to go sometimes. But you'll know what to do when you get there." She paused, then added in a quieter voice, "I hope."

"Okay," Thomas said. "I'll go. But you have to tell me where it is."

"It's on Aggie White Horse's land."

"I've never seen a medicine wheel there."

"It's old," Aunt Lucy said. "And it doesn't look like one anymore."

She meant the fire pit, Thomas realized. He tried to think of how Aggie could be harmed again, or rather, who would try.

"Has this got something to do with the girl that knifed her?"

"Everything's got to do with everything else," Aunt Lucy said. "We're each on our own wheel, but eventually our individual journey affects the journeys of everyone else—people we might never meet. Only the thunders can see every pattern."

"What do *you* see happening?"

"That you should go to the White Horse medicine wheel."

"Okay."

He was about to stand up, but Aunt Lucy caught his hand before he could do so. "First, finish your stew," she said. "You'll return at the same time whether you eat or not, but everything makes more sense on a full stomach."

She didn't have to ask him twice, the food was that good. She poured water from the jug into the two clay mugs on the table between them. Pushing one toward him, she drank from the other.

"You know this is weird, right?" Thomas said around another mouthful of stew.

"How strange a thing is depends on your normal."

He smiled. "You talk more like you're writing T-shirt logos than I remember."

Aunt Lucy laughed. "It's hard being a young medicine woman. Leila and I have spoken of this many times. People don't always take you seriously."

"Auntie—Aunt Leila's not young anymore. She's old now."

Aunt Lucy nodded. "I know. I remember being old, and young, and all the years in between. Here, I'm as you see me. In your time, I'm dead."

The words sent a small pang to Thomas's heart. "I wish you weren't," he said.

She shrugged. "You can always visit me here."

He wanted to ask if she was a memory, or real, but knew that even if she answered, he probably wouldn't understand. This whole business of the past, present and future all happening at the same time was beyond confusing.

"Is it true that you taught the medicine ways to Ramon Morago?" he asked instead.

"Ah, Morago. He left the Painted Lands as a colt and came back a stallion. I had little hand in his transformation, but I might have told him a thing or two after he got back."

Thomas sopped up the last of his stew with another chunk of cornbread. He drank the cool water that Aunt Lucy had poured for him. When he stood up this time, she didn't stop him.

"Any last minute advice?" he asked.

She came around the table to give him a hug. "You know the difference between right and wrong," she said as she stepped back. "Trust in that, stand up for what you believe, and it should go well."

Thomas nodded. "I told Aunt Leila about meeting you. She didn't seem too surprised."

"Why should she?"

"Because...never mind."

She said something else to him, but he couldn't make out what it was. The desert faded around him and he found himself sitting on the edge of his bed, fully dressed, feet on the floor. Sunlight poured in the window. He looked down at his high-tops to see that they were covered with a thin patina of dust—not red, like the dirt here in the Painted Lands, but a dull brown. Like the dirt in Aunt Lucy's yard.

It was disorienting, to say the least.

When he got downstairs, Santana was just about to go out the front door. She paused at the sound of his footsteps and turned to look at him.

"Where are you going?" he asked.

"After Auntie."

"Where'd she go?"

It wasn't like Auntie to go anywhere unless someone was driving her. In these later years, she appeared content to spend the better part of every day sitting on the porch with her crows.

"I haven't a clue," Santana said. "I was listening to tunes on my phone and fell asleep on the couch. I woke up a few minutes ago when she came come down the hall with that old pistol from the trunk where Mom keeps Dad's things. When I asked her what she was doing, she gave me this fierce look and then went marching off into the desert. Think she's gone hunting?" Santana smiled as though they were sharing a joke, but Thomas saw the flash of worry in her eyes.

"I know where she's gone," he said, "and I think maybe you're right."

In the dream, Aunt Lucy had told him to go to Aggie's place. Everybody knew that *ma'inawo* gathered at the fire pit from time to time. And if one of those *ma'inawo* was Consuela Mara, and Auntie's friends from Yellowrock Canyon had told her about it, then Thomas knew exactly what Auntie was planning to do.

"I am?" Santana said.

"Only one way to find out." He shooed her out the door and closed it quietly behind them.

"Where are we going?" Santana asked as she followed him across the yard and into the desert scrub.

"To Aggie's fire pit."

"What makes you think she's going there?"

Thomas hesitated before admitting, "Aunt Lucy told me to go there."

"Wait a minute. You never said anything about that before."

"That's because it just happened this morning. I thought I was dreaming, but..." He remembered the dust on his shoes, the way his stomach still felt full, how the taste of the stew remained on his lips. "I think I really went back to her place in the otherworld."

Santana stopped dead. "Are you shitting me?"

"No." Thomas gave her arm a tug and they continued weaving their way through the cacti and shrubs.

"You went back to the otherworld," Santana said. "On your own? And you hooked up with the young Aunt Lucy again?"

"Yeah."

"And she told you Auntie's going to do...what, exactly?"

"I don't know. She didn't tell me anything about Auntie. She just told me to go to the fire pit, except she called it the White Horse medicine wheel."

"It used to be a medicine wheel?"

"Apparently."

"So what does any of that have to do with Auntie?"

"I figure there are only two reasons she'd want me to go," Thomas said. "Either there's something going on there to do with tribal traditions, or the *ma'inawo* are up to something over there. But she said there's going to be trouble, and that I might be able to stop it if I can figure out the right thing to do."

"Could she be any more vague?"

Thomas laughed. "Yeah, that's pretty much what I told her."

"This still doesn't explain why Auntie's stomping off into the desert with a gun."

"I think it's a *ma'inawo* gathering, and if that's true, then maybe Consuela Mara will be there."

"Oh crap," Santana said, and she picked up her pace.

Thomas hoped he was wrong as he and Santana followed a dry wash down from the arroyo that ran alongside their house. But when they climbed up the side of the wash to look down at Aggie's property, the crowd of *ma'inawo* came into view below. None were sitting around the fire pit. Instead, they had gathered at the far side of the circle, with yet more up on the bluff beyond it.

Shading his eyes, Thomas saw what the center of attention was: Morago and Steve, and a white woman with dark hair. Facing them was the raven woman. There appeared to be an argument happening, with the *ma'inawo* standing closest joining in.

"I don't see Auntie," Santana said.

Thomas turned his attention back to the crowd, looking for Auntie. As he searched he got a feeling of *déjà vu*, as though he were back in Ancestors Canyon. The *ma'inawo* were of all shapes and sizes —human, animal and startling combinations of the two. No two were alike, and they presented a bewildering array that made it difficult to pick out one old Corn Eyes woman among them. Finally, he spotted Auntie making her way through the *ma'inawo*, on a collision course for where Steve and Consuela Mara were facing off. He pointed her out to Santana, then headed down the slope at a quick jog. Santana kept pace behind him.

When he reached the *ma'inawo*, the crowd was so thick that he couldn't help but jostle them as he pushed his way through. "Sorry, sorry," he repeated, but he never stopped moving, Santana in his wake. There were snarls and growls and angry looks until he heard one of them say, "That's the Corn Eyes kids." Thomas had no idea why that made any difference, but ahead of them, the *ma'inawo* stepped aside to let them pass.

They were still too late.

By the time they reached the front of the crowd, Auntie already had the six-gun pointed at Consuela Mara's head.

71

STEVE

I guess Thomas Corn Eyes' old aunt is the last person I'd expect to show up waving around a vintage six-gun. It looks massive in her skinny hand. The damn thing has such a kick that if she actually fires it, she stands a good chance of the recoil snapping the brittle bones of her wrist and forearm. I don't know if she realizes this herself, but even if she does, the look in her eyes says she doesn't give a damn.

I'm not sure why there's bad blood between her and Consuela, or at least I don't know the specifics. Let's face it, so far, Consuela seems to rub everybody the wrong way. Still, I don't think shooting the raven woman is any kind of answer. Crap like that's never the right solution, and having it threaten to go down here and now complicates everything.

This should have been a simple, private matter. Something just between Si'tala and me, with Morago here to give me some guidance. But first Leah came along, and now I feel like I'm back on stage, the audience growing to what looks like every *ma'inawo* in the Hierro Maderas mountains. Instead of fans screaming for the latest Rats hit, I've got Consuela telling me in graphic detail how she's about to kill me; Aunt Leila's ready to shoot Consuela; and we're surrounded by onlookers.

This whole situation has gotten way out of control, but I find that I don't give a damn any more than Auntie does. I told Si'tala I'd help her, and if her sister has a problem with that, they can take it up between themselves—saying Consuela lives long enough.

I brace myself for the big boom of Auntie's pistol, but before she can pull the trigger two things happen.

Thomas and his sister push out of the crowd of *ma'inawo* to stand on either side of Auntie.

And the unfired clay doll twitches in my arms.

I almost drop it. I must have yelled because all eyes lock on me, and next their gazes drop to what I'm holding. I look down as well.

If the past few days had never happened, I'd be stunned. Back then—and it feels like a lifetime ago—I didn't know anything about the otherworld or that the beings Morago's always talking about are real. I didn't know that Aggie's paintings weren't from her imagination. But I've been to the otherworld, and right now I'm surrounded by a crowd of those same animal people. So I'm not all that surprised that the red clay of the little statue I'm holding has become flesh, its raven feathers a mane of black hair, my naive attempt at features the face of a beautiful woman who looks like a miniature version of the one standing in front of me—the woman who wants to kill me and wear my body parts as gruesome fashion accessories.

Except the little being I'm holding isn't Consuela, not even close, though they could be taken as identical twins if you didn't know better. But I can tell them apart without even trying. I look into those tiny eyes and see Si'tala blinking and smiling back at me, not Consuela.

A murmur runs through the crowd. Beside me, Leah puts her hand over her mouth and murmurs, "Oh my god." Even Auntie seems surprised enough to hold her fire.

The warm figure in my arms keeps getting heavier, and I realize that's she's growing. I carefully lower her, feet first, to the ground, making sure that she has her balance before I let go. She's about the height of a toddler at this point. By the time I straighten up, she's up to my waist. A moment later, she's a full-sized woman standing naked in front of us all. Maybe I should have fashioned her a dress of some sort.

She makes a quick graceful movement with her hands, and a small dust devil starts up at her feet. The swirling mass of fine dust rises and hides her body for long seconds. When it clears, she's still barefoot, but wearing a pair of blue jeans and a tank top with a fringed vest over it. Her hair's in a long single braid, tied off with a strip of leather from which hang four black feathers.

"How'd she do that?" Leah says, eyes wide.

"*Ma'inawo* medicine," I tell her. "Magic."

"I need me some of that. Think of the money you could save on clothes."

I know what she's doing: trying to make light of it all, to make the impossible seem normal so that she doesn't freak out. The reason I know is because I'm feeling the same way, like I'm right on the edge of some kind of a meltdown. Making clothes out of dust isn't the biggest miracle I've run across recently, but this whole manifestation, topped by the casual efficiency with which Si'tala dealt with the problem of being naked, makes me a little unsteady. The ground feels spongy underfoot.

But even with the sensation of being unbalanced, I can't help feeling a little pleased that I managed to pull it off.

Consuela doesn't share my pleasure. "What. Have. You. Done?" she shouts.

Her booming voice seems to come from some far distance. Her gaze is fixed on Si'tala, but I know she's talking to me.

I don't answer. My own attention is fixed on Auntie and the gun she holds with a steady hand.

"He's given me my life," Si'tala says, "to do with as I please instead of being tied to you."

"You have no life," Consuela says, "except what I have given you."

"Once, maybe, but that no longer holds true. I am my own woman now, and as such," she turns her gaze to Auntie, "I offer you my apologies, Leila Corn Eyes. I was present when the salvagers were set upon the scent of your nephew, so I bear part of the blame. I understand your anger, but I ask you to consider that, because of this undertaking, Thomas has been befriended by a spirit of death, and I know that this spirit, Gordo, will do all he can to protect your young man. All will not be lost when his time to enter the afterworld comes."

Auntie gives Si'tala a confused look—I'm guessing not least because of her uncanny resemblance to Consuela. But the gun doesn't waver in her hand.

"You can blame me, too, Auntie," Morago says, taking a step forward. "I let Thomas go represent the tribe instead of going myself, which is what I should have done."

"This is ridiculous," Consuela says. "No one is to blame. The encounter with the salvagers was an unfortunate accident, that's all."

Auntie ignores both Si'tala and Morago. Instead, she gives Consuela a long piercing look. I don't know Leila Corn Eyes well, but it's easy to see that the darkness in her eyes is completely at odds with the calm tone of her voice when she finally speaks.

"The problem with some of the older *ma'inawo*," Auntie says, "is that they presume to know our needs better than we do, ourselves. They mean well, but their conceited attempts to improve the world inevitably lead into disaster. Never for them, of course. Instead, it falls upon those unlucky enough to be standing close by when they set one of their ill-considered plans in motion."

Consuela takes a step forward, reaches up a hand. "Enough of this. I'm going to take that gun and stick it where—"

She doesn't get to finish because Auntie shoots her. The sound of the six-gun is like a thunderclap. The bullet hits Consuela in the shoulder and spins her around. Blood jets from the wound. Most of it sprays over Leah. Some reaches Morago and me.

Consuela falls to the dirt, her eyes wide with shock and disbelief. Auntie takes a step forward, still pointing the gun at the raven woman. The dark circle of its muzzle is aimed at her head. Si'tala takes a step back, but otherwise remains motionless.

Though I'm vaguely aware of Reuben helping Leah wipe blood from her face, I can't look away from the tableau in front of me. There's something wet on my own cheek and I wipe it away without looking.

"Jesus," I find myself saying. I can't believe what just happened.

What also gets me is that the big handgun's recoil had no effect on Auntie. It's like she just fired a pellet pistol. I don't think she's a cousin, but like a lot of the *ma'inawo*, she's far stronger than she looks.

"Don't go feeling sorry for her," Auntie tells me. "*Ma'inawo* like her can heal their wounds just by shifting to their animal form and it's like nothing ever happened. Unless they get taken down with a shot to the head, or they get hit by a bus. Buses don't run out here, but I've got five bullets left and my aim is good, so maybe," she adds, addressing Consuela now, "it'd be best if you just lie still until our business here is finished."

"Or we could put the gun down, Auntie," Thomas says softly, holding out his hands.

I read the hard look in Auntie's eyes and think, yeah, that's not going to happen.

"Señora Corn Eyes," Si'tala says, her voice gentle. "Is this truly the best solution to your problem?"

Auntie shakes her head. "The problem can't be solved. We both know that. This is just revenge."

Something clicks in my head when she says that, and I think back to all the nights I've spent sitting around campfires on the rez and out in the canyons, listening to the storytellers spin their yarns.

People usually think of the Kikimi as a peaceful tribe, a farming community that used primitive irrigation canals to grow their corn, beans and squash on the banks of the San Pedro River until they were pushed away from the water into the mountains. First, it was by the Spanish who tried to enslave them, then by the western expansion of the fledging American States, who thought it more expedient to simply kill them. But while it's true that the Kikimi prefer peace to war, they are more than capable of fighting.

When they retreated into the mountains, they became ghost warriors like the Apache, striking hard and fast from one end of the valley to the other, some riding stolen horses, dog boys running on all fours alongside the mounted warriors. Their hunting parties attacked ranches, farms and soldier patrols in deadly waves, leaving behind a wake of destruction before disappearing back into the canyons. Troops sent after them rarely returned from the high country.

But eventually, the Women's Council saw the futility of battling the endless tide of invaders—just as, more recently, they'd seen the futility of fighting Sammy Swift Grass and the casino crowd. They made their peace with the invaders, signed the treaties, and allowed themselves to be herded onto the barren lands of the rez.

Now the old stories and the history of the tribe have been relegated to campfire tales. Some of them are lesson stories, while some are ribald or just humourous. Many are about Jimmy Cholla—part trickster, part shaman, part village clown. But he was also a spirit of vengeance, and the stories of his great victories over his foes, even after death, are told the most when there are only adults around the campfire or the story drum.

A bloodthirsty death isn't necessary. Listeners are just as satisfied with Jimmy Cholla's enemies being humiliated, preferably in a way that reflects back on their original transgression.

I'm no longer surprised by the popularity of these stories—not like I was when I first began to hear them—and now I see that their roots go deeper than a storyteller's narrative. Even under the lined features of an old woman like Leila Corn Eyes, the spirit of Jimmy Cholla lives on.

"What are the other Aunts going to say?" I ask her. "You know, the rest of your Women's Council."

"I'm no longer on the council and it's of no concern to them. This isn't tribal business—it's personal."

"Don't do this for me," Thomas says, his eyes pleading.

"Listen to your nephew," I tell her. "Don't be a Jimmy Cholla."

Her attention doesn't waver. The gun remains steady in her hand, pointed at the raven woman she's already shot once. "None of you understand," she says. "When we die in this world, we go on to another. That's how the wheel turns. Once we leave, we are safe from all the dangers and sorrows of this world. But because Thomas has been marked by the salvagers, he won't get that same safety."

"The salvagers," I repeat.

I've heard the term a couple of times now and I don't quite get it, though maybe I'm alone in that. I see a number of *ma'inawo* make warding signs with their fingers at the use of the word, as though just hearing it gives them the creeps.

Si'tala looks at me with pained features. "They travel the roads of the dead," she explains, "and collect anything that's been lost or abandoned in our world. Those roads belong to them and they can salvage anything that has found its way onto them. Sometimes it's harmless things. An old car that doesn't run anymore, a wagon with a broken axle, a box full of empty oil cans. But sometimes it's a soul that gets lost, or has taken its own life. And sometimes a very foolish person still alive stumbles upon one of those roads, and if they manage to escape, they are still marked. Once seen, once smelled, they're never forgotten."

I nod like I totally understand what she's saying. "When you say 'salvagers,' that presupposes that there's some kind of profit involved. Where do the salvagers sell what they find?"

"At a crossroads," Auntie says before Si'tala can answer. "To the spirit that lives there. And what those spirits do with what they acquire, no one knows."

Si'tala nods. "But not just any crossroads. Those spirits live where powerful roads cross each other, which makes them powerful in turn."

"Exactly," Auntie says. "What happens to Thomas if one of them gets their hands on him?"

"You still can't just kill her," Santana says. "That's not going to solve anything."

"But it's the only way for us to stay safe," Auntie says. "If we let her go now, we'll always have to be looking over our shoulders because she'll be back. And the next time, we won't see her coming. Don't believe for a moment that she will spare our lives."

Consuela tries to sit up, but Auntie brings the six-gun even closer to her head. "Uh-uh," she warns. The veins in her hands rise as she tightens her grip on the gun.

We're at an impasse. Any moment now, she's going to pull the trigger.

I look at Morago, hoping that as the shaman, he might be able to defuse this tinderbox. "Do something," I say.

"It's out of our hands," he says. "This is between the two of them now. And the thunders."

All this time, the audience of *ma'inawo* has been quiet. I've looked for Calico, but she seems to have faded back in amongst the others after speaking her piece earlier. I can't spot her. I can't get a read on the general mood of the crowd, either. Then an old man shuffles forward. Instead of hair, he's got a lizard's crest running from the top of his scalp down his back.

"We need an arbitrator," he says.

All around us, heads nod in agreement.

And then they're all looking at me. I remember the story Morago was spinning earlier—how the *ma'inawo* call me the Arbitrator.

"No," Auntie tells him before I can say the same thing. "He's already told us what he thinks."

The lizard mans shakes his head. "That doesn't matter. He's the Arbitrator. He will put aside his personal feelings and listen to both sides before he makes his decision."

"Can you do this?" Auntie asks me. "Can you give us each a fair listen?"

All I can do is tell her the truth. "I don't know," I say. "But I can try."

She studies me like Morago did before we started to make the raven sculpture. Maybe it's because they're both medicine workers, maybe it's a Kikimi thing, but under her scrutiny I feel that she can peel back the layers of any secret I might think I can hide.

"I find him acceptable," she finally says and lowers her six-gun.

"And you?" the lizard man asks Consuela.

"A moment," she says. She pushes herself up to a sitting position, then gets to her feet. She sways, catches herself. Lifting her arms she suddenly shifts into her raven shape. Just as quickly, she becomes human again, but now there's no sign that she was ever shot. The blood's gone from her clothes, as is this bullet hole. Whatever pain or weakness she was feeling a moment ago seems to have vanished.

It appears Auntie had that much right. *Ma'inawo* only need to shift their forms to be healed. So what else is Auntie right about?

"I will abide by the five-fingered being's decision," Consuela tells the lizard man. Her attention turns to me. "What is your name?"

In the fairy tales I read as a kid, one of the things you were never supposed to do was give someone your full and true name because that gave them power over you. It doesn't work like that among the Kikimi, and I'm guessing that holds true for the *ma'inawo* as well. With them, everything turns on truth, and that begins with your name.

"My parents named me Jackson Steven Cole," I tell her.

72

LEAH

"I *knew* it," Leah said as soon as the words left Steve's mouth.

She turned to Morago, but his only response was a shrug. "I didn't think you would lie," she said.

"And I didn't," the shaman said. "Everything I told you in the hospital was true. I just never clarified which Steve I was talking about."

"Semantics."

"Truth."

"But you deliberately misled me."

Morago nodded. "Because it was not my secret to tell. Especially not to…" He lets his voice trail off.

"Someone who'd broadcast it to all the world," Leah finished for him.

Morago gave her another nod.

"Steve doesn't have to worry," she said. "I'm not going to tell anybody."

It was funny. Even though she knew the truth now, she still thought of him as Steve.

"What comes out of your mouth isn't my responsibility," Morago said.

What a weird way to put it, she thought, but then she realized something had been happening while she'd been talking to the shaman. Steve, Consuela Mara and Auntie were walking away. The *ma'inawo* parted in front of them, making a corridor until they reached the fire pit in the middle of the clearing. When the three figures stood alone in the center, everyone moved back until no one was close enough to overhear their conversation.

"What's going on?" Leah asked.

Morago glanced over to the fire pit. "Steve's going to mediate the dispute."

Leah thought of the videos she'd seen of Jackson Cole, when the Rats had just broken big, rocking it out in front of a stadium of screaming fans. And then later, when the crowds were just as big but the tone was more thoughtful, how the fans were even more mesmerized by the magic that the four musicians created. Admittedly, half the fans were probably stoned—hell, half the *band* was probably stoned—and by then they'd added a couple of backup singers and Derek Fahy on keys, but the four main players were the heart of the music and they'd never been more popular.

She tried to imagine what Cole would say if she could go back and tell him what the future held. How he'd go from riding an unparalleled wave of popularity and goodwill to living alone in the desert among people who could take the shape of animals.

"This is so weird," she said.

Morago cocked an eyebrow.

"Oh come on," Leah said. "That's Jackson Cole. It's like having Elvis—the real Elvis—officiate at a hearing."

"It's just Steve. Whatever he was before doesn't matter anymore."

"Except it won't go well, this talk," Si'tala said.

Morago looked at her. "Why would you say that?"

"Because I am her memory. I know what she's done. There's a reason that Raven dissolved their marriage and no other has taken his place in her heart. She…" Si'tala sighed. "She's good at bloodshed and starting wars. Not so much at thoughtful discussions where she has to plead her case. I remember when she called herself the Morrigan, and led her armies to feast on the dead—then she was in her element."

"There'll be no more bloodshed today," Morago told her. "She is honour bound to abide by Steve's decision, even if it goes against her."

Si'tala shrugged. "Honour bound, yes. If those two were *ma'inawo*. But they are five-fingered beings, and she holds no respect for them. In the end, she'll do whatever she wants. It's what she always does."

73

STEVE

And now it's just the three of us sitting on rocks by the fire pit. I can smell the cold remains of one of Aggie's campfires, the scent of the ashes faint but still pungent. As I wait for the women to begin talking, a few turkey vultures make lazy circles up above the ridge trail and I can't help wondering if they're ordinary birds or cousins. I remember the hawk I saw earlier, but it's no longer in sight.

I lower my gaze and look over at the crowd of *ma'inawo* who watch and wait as they keep a respectful distance from the fire pit so that we have some privacy. I keep searching for Calico—her red hair should make her stand out—but if she's still here, she's keeping a low profile.

Finally, I turn to my companions. Auntie's scowling at Consuela, who makes a deliberate show of looking bored.

I'll be honest. I'm surprised that either of them agreed to this, and I'm not sure how I got to be the monkey in the middle. The *ma'inawo* might think of me as their arbitrator, but I don't feel remotely qualified for the job. I was a musician. Now I'm just another desert rat. Nothing about that past prepares me for anything like this, yet here I am all the same.

"So which of you is going to start?" I ask.

"This is pointless," Consuela says. "It's like trying to have a conversation with the birds and beasts. They hear the sound of your voice, but they're unable to comprehend what's actually being said."

I see Auntie bristle, more anger gathering in her eyes. Her fingers lightly tap the barrel of the six-gun lying in her lap.

"So tell me, why are you even sitting with us?" I ask Consuela before Auntie gets a notion to pick up the gun and fire it a second time.

"Out of respect for the *ma'inawo* who have gathered here today."

"Okay. So, out of respect for them, why don't you tell your side of the story?"

She doesn't say anything for a long moment; instead she just studies me.

"What is in this for you?" she asks.

I smile. No one ever really gets it, other than Morago, but I tell her anyway.

"I get to live here," I say. "In beauty. Away from the madding crowd."

Her dark eyes narrow. "Tell me the truth."

"It is the truth. I had everything a person could want, but I traded it for this because all that other stuff wasn't as important."

I don't bother to tell Consuela that I didn't start out knowing that. Guilt and unhappiness put me on the journey to my old pal Morago's homeland. I came here because of his stories. And because it sounded like a place where I could lose myself and the world wouldn't find me again.

It's a big land, he told me on more than one occasion. *One of those places where a man can step out of the world and live his life with no one ever seeing him again.*

At that point in my life, the appeal couldn't be denied.

"Enough about me," I say. I'm still hyper aware of the gun on Auntie's lap and her diminishing patience. "Tell us your story," I say to the raven woman. "Or maybe we should let Auntie deal with this in her own way."

Consuela glares at me until Auntie shifts on her rock, her fingers curling around the grip of the gun. The two women regard each other with equal disdain.

Finally, Consuela gives a brusque nod and begins to talk. Gazing off at some distant place between Auntie and me, she runs through everything that's happened since she first stopped in at the Little Tree Trading Post on Friday morning. She speaks in quick, clipped sentences, but it still takes a while.

I have to force myself to concentrate. I'm dog tired, the heat's oppressive, and I find myself wishing I had some water. I've heard a lot of this before—some from Thomas, some from Reuben—and I guess Auntie has too, but this time we hear what was going through Consuela's head while it was all going down.

As I listen to her story I pay as much attention to Auntie, trying to gauge her reaction. Auntie'd make a good poker player. Her face gives nothing away. But she does have one tell: as Consuela keeps speaking, Auntie's hand slides away from the six-gun on her lap. Not far, but it's better than having her point it at the raven woman, hammer cocked.

So this is good. At least she's calmed down some.

When Consuela finishes, her gaze returns from whatever distances she was looking at to settle on me.

I glance at Auntie, whose mouth remains set in a straight line. It's clear she's got no intention of commenting.

I look back at Consuela. "I don't think anyone thought you deliberately intended for this to happen," I say, "but Thomas is still in danger because of your actions."

"What am I supposed to do?" Consuela asks.

"Fix it," Auntie tells her through gritted teeth, stomping her heel on the ground and raising a little cloud of dust.

A cold look comes into Consuela's eyes. "Don't push your luck," she says. "I am not an enemy you wish to have."

Auntie's hand has returned to grip the six-gun. "Did you ever wonder," Auntie asks, "why the *ma'inawo* and the Kikimi get along as well as they do in the Painted Lands?"

Consuela blinks at the sudden switch in topic.

"Why's that, Auntie?" I jump in, hoping to reestablish some calm before Consuela can make it worse.

"A long time ago," Auntie says, "the *ma'inawo* in these mountains were just as arrogant as you, Consuela Mara. Humans, they felt, were put on this world only for their amusement. I could tell you awful tales of the things they did—how they stole away our young men and women, flooded our crops, harried our hunters—but I'm just an old woman. I don't have the stomach or stamina for such a long and unhappy story.

"What I can tell you is that then, as now, we Kikimi were a peaceful people, but as the *ma'inawo* grew more and more cruel with their tricks and their torments, we'd finally had enough. Like you, they laughed when we warned them to leave us in peace. But the next time some antelope women lured away one of our young men, the first chief of our dog soldiers went after them.

"He had studied with *los tíos*, the Toltec hawk uncles down south. They taught him how to see the difference between animals and cousins, and trained him how to fight the *ma'inawo*, compensating for their strength and speed. He was gone two days and a night, but when he returned from the mountains, the stolen boy walked at his side and three antelope had died unfortunate deaths in the canyons.

"After that, he took those young men and women who were willing, and made them into dog soldiers—what we call the dog boys today. They took the battle to the *ma'inawo*. Every time the *ma'inawo* interfered with our lives, the dog boys went hunting. They weren't always successful, but the casualties were far higher on the side of the *ma'inawo* than they were on ours.

"Finally, the *ma'inawo* sent emissaries to the Women's Council and a truce was made—here, at this very medicine wheel. That truce turned to respect, and that respect became genuine friendship until we are as you see us today: two peoples living in harmony with each other and the land."

"Who was this first chief of the dog boys?" Consuela asks.

"His name was Jimancholla."

Consuela lets out a scornful laugh. "Oh please. Do you really expect me to believe that? Jimmy Cholla is only a character from a story."

"Says one who knows nothing about my people."

"Wait," I say. "Are you saying Jimmy Cholla is *real*? That all those crazy stories are true?" It's like finding out that Paul Bunyan actually lived.

"Jimmy Cholla is a story character," Auntie says, "but he got his name from Jimancholla, and he was definitely real. Many of the families here in the Painted Lands can trace their ancestry back to him. The Corn Eyes Clan gets their Sight from his blood."

"You're serious," Consuela says, rolling her eyes.

Auntie doesn't bother to speak. Her answer is plain in the disdainful look she gives back to the raven woman.

"So, if you all live in such harmony now," Consuela asks, "why do you still need your dog boys? It's not like they do much good protecting you from the five-fingered beings that aren't part of your tribe—or even from your own members who decide to build casinos and go hunting for the very cousins you're supposed to be living in peace with."

"These days," Auntie tells her, "they play games of chase with certain *ma'inawo* who find entertainment in such things. But they will not hesitate to deal with *ma'inawo* who stray into the Painted Lands and disrespect the truce."

I'm dying to learn more about this ancestor who gave rise to the Jimmy Cholla stories, but the tension is still heating up between the two women.

"Okay," I interrupt, hoping to head off another confrontation. "We've established that Consuela didn't put Thomas in danger on purpose, but if she hadn't involved him, we wouldn't even be having this discussion. That sound about right?"

I look from one to the other. Consuela gives a reluctant nod. Auntie takes a deep breath, then follows suit, a pinched look still on her brow.

"So Auntie wants you to either fix this," I tell Consuela, "or she plans to take more drastic action. Seems to me, the best way to deal with the threat to Thomas is for you to find a way to call off the salvagers. Maybe you could get that big dog of yours to help."

"Gordo's not a dog, and he's not mine."

"But you could ask him?"

"Gordo is more loyal to Si'tala than to me, and I don't need to remind you what you've just done with her." Consuela looks so pissed that I think she's going to have a go at me. It's enough to make Auntie raise her six-gun and thumb back the hammer.

"Please, Auntie," I say.

When she lowers the gun again, I return my attention to Consuela. "Remember what you told us? You said you were speaking to us out of respect for the local *ma'inawo*. Why don't you at least try to follow through with that?"

Consuela looks out at the gathered *ma'inawo* on the periphery of the circle. As she looks from one to the next, her body seems to relax a little. "Fine," she says. "I'll try to find a way to call the salvagers off. And if I don't succeed?"

"At least you'll have tried," I say.

"But don't come back," Auntie adds.

As Consuela rises smoothly to her feet, I realize that Si'tala is standing beside her. I blink in surprise. I never even saw her walk over here. But maybe she didn't. For all I know, she's been there all along and was invisible until now. Or she instantly teleported herself from where she'd been standing with Morago and Leah. There's so much I don't know about the *ma'inawo*.

Consuela gives her sister a cold look. "What do you think *you're* doing?"

"I'm coming with you."

Consuela shakes her head. "How stupid do you think I am?"

"What is it that you think I will do?"

"Pretend to be me? Kill me in my sleep so that you can take over my life?"

"Why would I do such a thing?"

"Because you're not real. You're my memories, that's all. But you'd like to be more."

"I already am more, thanks to Steve."

Consuela takes the time to shoot a glare my way. "Which I won't forget."

"The world has colour, sister," Si'tala says. "It's never been simply black and white."

Her gaze moves to Auntie. "You'd do well to remember that as well, elder."

I think it's a good point, but Auntie doesn't bother to respond.

"Why should I trust you?" Consuela asks her sister.

Si'tala smiles. "Because I know all the terrors you have spilled into the world, but I also know the great good you have done. Raven would not have loved you otherwise. You were the first he brought into this world. I know because I remember, where you can't."

"You remember..." Consuela says softly.

I hear both longing and horror in her voice.

Si'tala nods. "And unlike before, when I was only a ghost bird, now I can share your lost memories with you when you ask."

"And what do you get out of it?"

"You are my sister. I'd like to see if we can find a new beginning."

Consuela doesn't say anything for a long moment before she finally nods. "Then come with me," she says.

Si'tala smiles. "Thank you. I haven't forgotten my promise. Call me when you're ready, and I will come."

"Sure," I tell her. I feel a deep pang of disappointment that she's made this choice, but what do I know? Maybe they need one another. There's all kinds of weird co-dependency in this world.

"And Señora Corn Eyes," Si'tala says. "I will talk with Gordo. We will do all we can to dissuade the salvagers from taking Thomas. And if we can't call them off, then we will protect him, in this world and the next."

"We will *not*," Consuela says.

Si'tala bows her head. "My pardon, Señora," she tells Auntie. "I should not speak for my sister. I meant to say that *I*, and hopefully Gordo, will protect him."

Then she turns away, and between one moment and the next, the two women are ravens flying off, side by side.

As if that's a signal, the *ma'inawo* disperse as quickly as they came. I stand up and search their ranks as they leave, looking for Calico's red hair, but if she's with them, I don't see her. There's only Auntie and me here by the cold coals of the fire pit. On the far side of the medicine wheel Morago stands with Leah, Thomas and Santana. Everyone else is gone.

When Auntie doesn't get up, I reach a hand down to her. She doesn't accept it, so I sit down beside her.

"Do you think they'll find a way to help Thomas?" I ask her.

"I doubt it," she says. "They'll do what the old spirits always do: cause mischief and bring trouble to anyone standing near them. It's not in their nature to do otherwise. You should have let me shoot her."

I follow an impulse and put my arm around her shoulders. "You know that's not the answer," I say. I think for a moment, looking in the direction that the ravens flew off, before I add, "I trust Si'tala to do the right thing."

"Then you are a fool."

"I've been called that and worse."

Auntie shrugs. "So...Calico," she says, changing the subject. She touches my cheek. "The crows told me about this rift between you."

"Yeah, not my best moment."

"Do you care about that *ma'inawo* girlfriend of yours?" she asks.

"Of course I do."

"Then perhaps you should go find her. Tell her how you feel."

"It's not that easy."

She leans in to me. "How hard can it be to open your heart to the one you love?"

"It's the finding her in the first place that's hard."

Auntie nods. "That's true. They're hard to track when they don't want to be found."

I find it a little disconcerting to be sitting here sharing affection and discussing my love life with this tribal elder. I don't really know any of the Corn Eyes Clan all that well, except for Thomas, but that's only from seeing him at the trading post when I drop by to pick something up or to shoot the breeze with Reuben. I've often seen Auntie when I pass by the Corn Eyes' house. She's usually sitting on the porch, crows lined up on the railing in front of her or perched on nearby trees and cacti. Sometimes she lifts a hand in greeting; sometimes she just ignores me.

We've hardly been confidantes.

"You should ask Morago to find her for you," she goes on. "And if it helps at all, I don't think she actually disagrees with you. What's upset her was that she didn't get to be heard."

"I *was* listening to what she said. But she wasn't there when Si'tala was telling me about the problems that are coming a few years down the road."

Auntie shakes her head. "No, from what I've been told, you went ahead and made a decision without allowing her any input."

"But the decision couldn't have gone any other way. Sure, the outcome benefits the Kikimi, but it benefits the *ma'inawo*, too."

"And now you're not listening to me. You're not a quick learner, are you?"

I stop and look at her, realizing she's right. The point isn't who's right or wrong. It's that I didn't respect her enough to talk it over first.

"I need to find her," I say.

I stand up again. This time when I offer my hand, Auntie takes it.

"But be careful," she says as we walk over to where the others are waiting. "I won't say that no good comes from being friendly with the *ma'inawo*, but remember, at the end of the day, they aren't human beings. They might look like us and feel things the way we do, but they are still other. Living as long as they do, in and out of the other-world, makes one see the world differently."

"I'll be careful, Auntie."

But we both know I'm going after Calico, no matter what it takes.

74

LEAH

"How do you think it's going?" Leah asked, looking across the sand to where Steve sat with Consuela and Auntie.

"Well, nobody's dead yet," Morago said, "so I'd say it's going pretty well."

Leah turned to look at him. "I can't tell if you're joking or not."

The shaman gave her a wry smile. "A bit of both. Look," he added, "you know how the rez is divided between the traditionalists and the casino crowd, right?"

Leah nodded.

"Well, there are other divisions. Maybe they're not as obvious, or argued as strongly, but let's just say there's a reason the Women's Council is made up of younger women at the moment. They're all in their forties and fifties now."

"I like that you think that's young," Leah told him. "Gives me hope."

Morago chuckled before continuing. "The young people on the rez, they either don't believe in the *ma'inawo*, or if they are aware of them, they're more accepting.

"The older folks are polite and friendly, but they hold on to the old prejudices that date back to when there was war between our tribes. Like Auntie Leila, most of the elders don't fully trust the *ma'inawo*."

"Our mom's always warning us about the *ma'inawo*," Santana says.

"That's because she listens too much to Auntie." Morago paused, then added, "But the elders are not completely wrong, either. The *ma'inawo* who share the Painted Lands with us aren't the same as their wilder cousins who live beyond the mountains—the ones who never made a truce with us. For some of them, it can still be amusing to walk one of us off a cliff, or have us follow them into the otherworld and leave us there for a few decades."

"So how do you tell the difference?" Thomas asked.

"Good question," Morago said.

Leah waited for him to go on, but he didn't elaborate.

"What about those two?" Santana asked nodding to the center of the medicine wheel. "Are they good or evil?"

Leah wasn't sure who she meant until she realized that Si'tala was standing behind Consuela. She'd never even seen the woman get up from where she'd been waiting beside them. Somehow, she had covered the distance without Leah noticing.

"I don't know," Morago admitted. "The older a *ma'inawo* is, the more powerful they get. Some become friendlier toward us; others grow ever more embittered. Consuela has been accused of long-forgotten kindnesses as well as terrible deeds. Si'tala is a newborn spirit with the memories of another's long life inside her. And even when they try to do good…" He sighed. "You know how it goes with Cody in the old stories."

Leah gave him a puzzled look, but Thomas and Santana nodded.

"I love Coyote stories," Santana said.

"Cody is the Coyote trickster's name?" Leah asked.

"Among others," Morago said. "He likes to cause mischief, but he also likes to help. The problem is that even with the best of intentions, he usually makes things worse for those around him. I've heard the same about Consuela. The added danger she presents is that she has a history of deliberate malevolence. It's the reason Raven turned his back on her."

"So that's a true story?" Thomas asked.

"They're all true stories, to some extent."

"And Raven is?" Leah asked.

"He made the world," Santana explained in the tone a person might take with someone who was a little dim. "He's the one who stirred his cauldron in the first darkness and ladled the world out of it, bit by bit."

Leah's gaze rested on the girl for a long moment. "You mean that literally, don't you?" she asked.

Morago smiled. "It's as valid an explanation as the one about some old white man with a big beard who lives in the sky and made the world in seven days, don't you think?"

Leah sighed. Religion. She'd gone and put her foot in it, hadn't she. "I don't believe in that, either," she said.

"Then what do you believe in?" the shaman asked her.

"I..."

She realized that she didn't know anymore. It wasn't just the sudden shift in interest from writing about pop culture to tackling issues with more meaning. And it wasn't even that she might actually be able to put Aimee's spirit to rest. Everything she thought she knew about how the world worked had changed. It felt as thought the ground was constantly shifting underfoot, leaving her more than a little unbalanced.

"I don't know what to believe anymore," she said.

"Trust what your instincts tell you," Morago said. "Listen to the voice of your heart when it speaks in your mind."

"Yeah, except that's what schizophrenics do too."

Morago gave her a look that was sad and scolding at the same time.

"Okay," she said. "I know that's not what you're talking about, but look at it from my perspective. I didn't grow up believing in all of *this*." She made a vague gesture toward the two raven women.

"Neither did I."

Leah couldn't hide her surprise.

"What?" he said. "Do you think I went on the road with the Diesel Rats because I was so comfortable with the traditions of my people? Few of us grow up fully believing."

"And if we do see things that nobody else does," Santana said, "we keep it to ourselves."

Thomas nodded. "But Leah's partly right. We might not have grown up believing, but we grew up with the stories. When we started seeing things, we had a context for them."

"I didn't get anything like that," Leah said. "I mean, I got stories as a kid, but they were European fairy tales and picture books, and Saturday morning cartoons—nothing you could think of as real, no matter how much you wanted them to be when you're that age." She paused, then looked from Thomas and Santana to Morago. "*They're not real, right?*"

The shaman shrugged, an enigmatic smile on his lips. "I don't know anything about the European mysteries," he said.

That wasn't an answer, Leah thought. She was about to call him on it when she noticed that Consuela was standing up. A moment later, she and Si'tala shifted into birds and flew away. All around them, the *ma'inawo* began to retreat back into the desert.

As Leah watched them leave, she was dying to know how Steve had managed to defuse the situation. She started toward Steve and Auntie but Morago caught her arm.

"Wait a minute," he said. "They're still talking."

75

STEVE

When we join the others, Auntie plays up her age by asking Thomas and Santana if they can "help this old woman get back to her home in one piece." She gives Thomas the six-gun, then slips her hand into the crook of Santana's arm. Thomas and Santana share a smile.

"Be careful with that thing," Morago says, pointing at the gun. "And you might want to keep it out of sight," he adds.

Thomas nods and sticks it into his belt at the small of his back. His T-shirt hangs over the gun, hiding it from a casual glance.

"Don't shoot your ass off," Morago says, shaking his head, "or you'll never get out of this place."

Auntie and Santana both bend over laughing. Thomas tries to keep a straight face, but doesn't succeed. Soon we're all having a good chuckle.

Finally the laughter dies down and they start to go. "If we're lucky," Thomas says, "maybe we can get back without Mom ever knowing where we were."

His mother's on the Women's Council. The way gossip flies around here on the rez—especially when you add the *ma'inawo* into the equation—if she doesn't know by now, she will soon.

"Yeah, good luck with that," I tell him.

We watch the two of them lead Auntie up the slope where a dry wash will take them most of the way back to their place. There's still water in the bucket I brought down from Aggie's house earlier, so I scoop a few handfuls into my mouth until my throat starts to feel a little less parched.

"So you did it," Morago says, turning to me. "Gave a spirit a body and settled a dispute that I wouldn't have wanted to try my hand at." He smiles. "I might not have figured out your Indian name yet, but the name the *ma'inawo* have for you fits like a glove."

I shake my head. "This is ridiculous. I have enough trouble figuring out my own life."

"You get the job done—that's what counts. And they're satisfied with you." His smile gets bigger. "You've done it for years even though you didn't know you were doing it."

I look at Leah. "It's a hell of a thing," I tell her. "A few days ago, my world was a whole other place."

"Welcome to the club," she says.

"Yeah, except I've been interacting with *ma'inawo* for years and never knew it. My trailer sits right smack dab in the middle of the goddamned otherworld. I've been *living* there all along and I never knew. At least you only got here a few days ago."

"It's still way beyond weird."

I nod in sympathy.

"But I'm glad I know about it now," she says. The light in her eyes as she speaks is echoed by a glow that seems to come from under her skin. "The Internet makes the planet feel like a small place, so it's exciting to know that there's still as much of the unknown in the world as there was for our grandparents, when they were our age."

"More," Morago says. "Trust me. There's much, much more."

I smile at the two of them. Since I reconnected with Morago, he's always been a true believer, but Leah's got all the enthusiasm of a new convert. They make a good pair.

"I need a favour," I tell Morago. "Auntie said you can help me track down Calico."

One eyebrow goes up.

"Don't give me that look," I tell him. "You know how ticked off she is."

"But she just spoke up for you."

"I know. But she won't speak *to* me."

Leah looks uncomfortable. "Listen, I should be going," she says. "Aggie's going to be coming home soon and I haven't done a thing to get ready."

"*Ohla,*" Morago tells her. "I'm sure I'll see you again."

"I'd like that. I've got at least a hundred questions."

Morago laughs. "Don't save them all for me. Aggie knows as much as anybody around here."

"I'll remember that." She turns, then pauses and looks back over her shoulder. "Good luck with your girlfriend, Steve," she adds before heading off to the house.

I turn back to Morago. "Will you help me?"

He scratches his chin. "I don't know," he says. "It's not such a good idea to get on the wrong side of the *ma'inawo,* and if she doesn't want to be found, and I lead you to her…"

Just before I start to argue, I catch the laughter in his eyes. "Yeah, like you care what anybody thinks," I say. "There's just as many stories about *your* meddling in people's lives as there are about Jimmy Cholla."

He taps a stiff finger against my chest. "A little respect for your elders."

"You're not my elder."

He laughs. "Let's take a walk, rock star. See what we can find."

After I drink some more water, Morago takes me up to the ridge trail. It's usually an easy climb from Aggie's fire pit, but I'm feeling the aftermath of everything that's gone down, so it's a little tougher than normal. But as soon as we're a couple of miles north, my tension starts to fall away. It's as though it broke into pebbles and they're falling off the trail, bouncing and skittering their way down the steep slopes as the land drops away on either side of us. I inhale deeply and realize it's the first real breath I've taken since Consuela and the *ma'inawo* showed up. I feel grounded with the rock underfoot, the sky above, the world spread out around us. The sun's fierce, but the wind takes away the worst of the heat. Turkey vultures fly in their slow circular patterns, but we're so high up now we're looking down on them.

I check the position of the sun. So much has happened this morning, it's hard to believe it's not even noon yet.

Morago keeps us to a slow amble instead of the steady, distance-eating pace we usually move at when we're out hiking.

"Do you have some particular place in mind," I finally ask, "or are we just randomly hoping to come across her?"

"I'm waiting to hear from the cousins."

I look around, but we're still alone on the trail.

"And you're—what?" I ask. "Communicating with them telepathically?"

He gives me a grin. "Well, I am a shaman."

Normally, I'd be ragging him at this point, but I've seen too much. He might be teasing, or he could really be having some sort of inner conversation with the *ma'inawo*.

"So what are they saying?" I ask.

"Nothing really useful yet. They're happy to help you. They say that's new for you."

"What is?"

"Accepting somebody else's help. Usually you're the one that has to fix the problem."

"Considering how this week's gone, that's a thing of the past."

"It's not a sign of weakness, you know," Morago tells me. "Just as you like to help other people, people want to be able to return the favour."

"I know." I don't really—or I didn't. But I'm beginning to understand that you can't completely disengage from the world, and when you do engage, there has to be give and take. I've just never been good at the take.

"Have you given any thought to what you'll ask Si'tala to do for you?" Morago asks.

I shake my head. "I didn't help her so that she'd owe me a favour. Giving her a body just seemed like the right thing to do." I pause. "It was the right thing to do, wasn't it?"

Morago has to think about that. "Probably," he says finally. "Consuela carries an air that says anything might happen, and if something does, it might not be good. A lot of the old *ma'inawo* are like that, even if they've given their word. Don't get me wrong—they'll keep their word, but they'll find a way to twist what they've promised, so that the end result could well be the opposite of what you wanted."

I think I get what he's saying. "But because Si'tala's so young…"

"Except she isn't," Morago breaks in. "Her body is new, but her spirit is as old as Consuela's."

"So she could cause a problem somewhere down the line."

Morago shrugs. "That could be said about anyone, including ourselves when it comes right down to it. But no, it's not that. From what I can tell, Si'tala has a purity about her, a strength of purpose that guides her along the paths of Beauty from which her sister has strayed."

"You got all that by just being around her for a few minutes?"

He points at himself. "Shaman—remember?"

"If you say so," I say with a wink, just to egg him on a little.

He doesn't take the bait. "I think you can trust her to do what you ask," he says, "without any of Cody's trickery." He studies me carefully and adds, "But it sounds as though you might not ask for any favour at all."

"Well, now that I think of it, I've got a couple of ideas," I tell him.

A crow comes drifting out of the sky, interrupting us. He lands on one of the long arms of a nearby ocotillo, his weight making it dip alarmingly. The crow doesn't make a sound. He just balances there on his perch, which continues to sway up and down from his weight and the wind.

Morago watches the crow for a moment, then turns to me. "She's near your place, in the little canyon behind the trailer where you keep your garden."

I look at the crow. "What's her mood like?" I ask. Even with all I know, I feel a little self-conscious talking to a bird. The crow seems amused, as though it knows exactly how I'm feeling.

The crow preens his feathers with his beak for a moment, then Morago says, "Apparently she just seems sad. Word is, she's going to pack up and go deep into the ghost lands."

I stare at the crow and it flaps its wings at me. The message is so clear, I don't need a translation: *You'd better run if you want to catch her before she's gone.*

I turn to Morago.

He nods. "Go," he urges. "Because once that foxy antelope girl runs off, you'll never catch up to her."

I take off at a fast trot. This is the first time I've taken the ridge trail and not paid any attention to my surroundings. All I can think of is what they said—that if I don't get to her in time I'll never see her again.

The turnoff to the hollow behind my trailer feels like it comes up sooner than I expected. I scrabble and slide down the narrow path into the hollow, then stop when I see the fox with antelope horns sitting on Possum's bench looking out through the gap that overlooks the desert valley below. The fox turns to look at me and relief floods my body.

"I'm sorry," I say.

I don't go into an explanation of why I did what I did. I don't try to explain myself at all. Possum shared this lesson with me a long time ago, but I've let the years steal it away.

No woman wants to hear the bullshit of why you did what you did, he told me. *They just want to know that you regret what you did or said, and that you'll do your damnedest not to do it again. Listen to this old desert rat. It took me a couple of divorces and a bunch of failed relationships to figure it out.*

The fox seems to be waiting for me to go on.

"I screwed up," I tell her. "I can't swear it won't ever happen again, but I can promise that I'll do my best to make sure I don't repeat it."

She cocks her head, still waiting, but I've said all I'm going to say.

A long moment passes before the fox shimmers into the red-haired woman I know so well. She sits on her haunches, head still cocked. "Do you know why I got mad?" she asks.

I nod. "I disrespected you."

"And do you know why you did that?"

I shake my head. "Wasn't thinking, I guess."

"Come here," she says and pats the bench beside her.

When I sit down, she scoots a little distance down the bench and turns, so that she's facing me. I do the same.

"I get that things have been confusing," she says. "You've had to take in a lot over the past few days. How are you feeling now?"

"Embarrassed."

Her eyes widen a little. "Why do you feel embarrassed?"

"I've spent years living half in the otherworld and half out of it. I can't tell you how many of the people I thought I knew are actually *ma'inawo*. Hell, remember when I didn't even believe *you* were real? I mean, back then I was actually pretty impressed with myself, being able to dream up a hallucination as fine as you were. Are. Oh, you know what I mean."

She smiles and lets me continue: "So all the while the *ma'inawo* and everybody on the rez have been having a good laugh at my expense. I'm not particularly thin-skinned, but I can't pretend it makes me feel all that smart."

She shakes her head. "They're not laughing at you, they're laughing with you."

"Except I'm not laughing."

"The *ma'inawo* wouldn't mock you. They think of you as their arbitrator."

"And how weird is that?" I say, picking at a splinter on the bench.

"They wouldn't come to you for advice if they thought of you as a joke. The cousins and Kikimi are as bad as each other when it comes to teasing. That's all that's happening."

I look at her, knowing she's trying to make me feel better. "Okay," I finally say, but I'm not really buying it.

She shakes her head. "You'll have to trust me on this."

I pick at the bench some more. "I trust you."

"But you're still going to feel self-conscious."

I shrug. Sometimes I think she knows me better than I know myself.

"So…embarrassment," she says. "That's all you're feeling?"

"What do you mean?"

"I was wondering if you might be feeling a little resentment, as well."

"Resentment? Directed at what?"

"Me."

I look at her. "Why would you ever think that?"

"Well, you just said that back in the day, when you thought I was a part of a flashback or whatever, you were proud of yourself for dreaming me up. Maybe you wish you'd been right, so you could make me agree with you."

I smile and shake my head. "Oh, darlin'. Even when I thought you were a dream you were strong-willed, and I wouldn't want you any other way. I may be a lot of things, but I'll never be the guy who thinks that everybody around him should just do as he says. That's why this whole arbitrator business has me so freaked out."

"There's nothing wrong with being an arbitrator. That's the person who listens to both sides, then gives the advice that will give the most benefit to everybody."

I don't say what I think next aloud, but she reads something on my face.

"What?" she says.

"Well...that's kind of what I was doing with Sammy. Trying to find a nonviolent way that would benefit everybody."

She doesn't say anything for a long moment. Then she sighs.

"You know what?" she says. "You're right. I let my anger get the better of me." She looks down and adds, "And I was a bit jealous of Miss Ravenhair."

I reach out and lift her chin so that she's looking at me. "I should have listened to what you had to say."

She smiles and moves a little closer. "Yeah, you should have."

"I've missed you."

Her smile turns coy, sexy. "You should. You never had it so good."

"I think that was where you were supposed to say you missed me, too."

I'm sitting cross-legged on the bench. She moves closer until she's in my lap, her face inches from my own.

"Maybe we should start over," she murmurs.

Her gaze is locked on my own. I can feel her breath on my skin. She smells wild and beautiful.

"I'd love to rediscover you," I say, slipping my hands around her hips.

"Yeah." She puts her arms around my neck. "I'm game if you are."

She pulls me into a kiss before I can answer.

AFTER

76

LEAH

Leah fell into a comfortable routine so readily, it surprised her. There was no need to adjust to the unfamiliar landscape, to the wide expanse of the desert sky with its crisp air, or to her new life, which was so dramatically different from her old one. Not that she was living *la vida loca*. If anything, her life was more contained than it had ever been. But the routines immediately felt familiar rather than new.

Mornings, she got up before light and sat at the little table on the front porch, watching the sunrise while she did her daily journaling as recommended in *The Artist's Way*. She hadn't followed this exercise in ages, but she took it up again on her first morning. She wrote down whatever came to mind without trying to censor herself or edit, and without reading it back immediately.

She covered a lot of ground in those entries, from her guilt—and yes, anger—about Aimee, to the convoluted feelings she had about the Diesel Rats, especially now that she knew that it really was Jackson Cole living the life of a hermit out here in the Hierro Maderas.

Aimee still mattered. She tried to write past the guilt and resentment, to before her friend had died. Before Aimee's mother had given her that damned journal to read. It still didn't make sense. Not how

Aimee could put on a cheerful and fearless face to the outside world while hiding so much pain inside. Not how she'd never come to Leah to share that pain. And especially not how Leah herself had remained oblivious to it while Aimee fell into an ever-darker spiral of depression.

She wanted to remember the best of her friend, but she didn't know where to start, because the truth was, she'd never known the real Aimee.

If all of that wasn't enough, she also had to struggle with the reality of magic. The otherworld. Animal people. It all seemed so preposterous, but as day followed day, this whole supernatural view of the world seemed more real than her old life back in Newford. Where—sidebar —according to Marisa, there were just as many magical goings on, but she'd been oblivious to those as well.

By the time she finished writing in her journal, she would hear Aggie stirring. She'd put the kettle on and have fresh tea and breakfast ready by the time the older woman came into the kitchen.

The rest of the morning she'd spend with Aggie, soaking up the old woman's knowledge of the area, her tribe, and the neighbouring *ma'i-nawo*. Sometimes Aggie would have Leah flip through her paintings until they found the one that illustrated some point or other.

After lunch, Aggie would rest and Leah would work on research, on one of her blogs, or simply catch up with her friends back in Newford. She talked to Marisa on the phone at least every day and they texted regularly. It was hard explaining her sudden absence to her other friends, but most were supportive. Jilly was positively giddy with excitement and extracted the promise of an invitation to visit as soon as Leah had her own place.

"I won't be in the way," she'd assured Leah on the phone one day. "I'll just be off painting." Short pause. "And hanging out with animal people!"

Her voice had gone steadily up in pitch with that last bit.

That was so Jilly. Give her a hint of magic and she was off and running.

"I hate to break this to you," Leah said, "but they're not all just waiting around with bated breath for you to show up. You know that, right?"

"Oh, don't be a spoilsport. I'll be on my best behaviour. I'll walk around all humble and without a smidgeon of prodding and prying."

Leah could only respond with a laugh.

When she had to go online, she used the hotspot on her cell phone to connect her laptop to the Internet since cell reception was decent out here and all Aggie had was a land line. Her data plan was good, but she still kept her online presence to a minimum.

Dinner, they ate out on the front porch watching the sunset. That was when visitors usually came by, including Reuben or Thomas, who dropped off groceries every other day. Leah wasn't sure if all the evening visitors were human, but they all looked human. A few she recognized from Aggie's paintings, minus their long rabbit ears, pronged horns, forked snake tongues, or whatever other elements of their animal selves that Aggie had put into the paintings.

And of course there were always dogs, mostly outside, but from time to time one would wander into the house, and then Leah would get a pang and remember what Reuben's nephew had told her: that Ruby had been eaten by a witch.

Morago and Steve were the most frequent visitors. Sometimes they showed up on the same evening, sometimes on their own. Calico accompanied Steve whenever he came, and that made Leah happy. It was one thing for him to disappear from the outside world. She could understand his reasons because she was doing pretty much the same thing herself. But exiling himself didn't mean he had to be alone.

She was grateful for how everyone made her feel so welcome. No, that wasn't quite it. Normally, amidst a group of old friends, it would be easy to feel like the odd woman out. Not because anyone would deliberately exclude her, but because it would have been so easy for them to fall into old habits, talking about unfamiliar people or long-past incidents. She would have been happy enough to sit quietly in a corner of the porch and listen to them talk, but one or another of them always included her, explaining who or what they were talking about.

The first evening that Steve, Calico and Morago dropped by, they later fell into a companionable silence until Steve shifted in his chair. "Where's Ruby?" he asked Aggie. "I haven't seen her around."

Aggie sighed. "She offered herself to an *hechicera*."

Morago sat up straighter and gave her a sharp look.

"What's that supposed to mean?" Steve asked.

"It means," Aggie said, "that when Sadie got into more trouble after that business in the police station, Ruby traded her own freedom for Sadie's."

"So, when Reuben's nephew told me she was eaten," Leah said, "he wasn't being literal, right?"

"He might as well have been," Aggie said. "The witch owns her soul. Ruby will never be free of her."

"Is this true?" Steve asked Morago.

"I need to know more," the shaman said. "What *hechicera* are we talking about?"

"Manny can explain it all," Aggie told them. "He was there when it happened."

Steve glanced at Calico, then got up from his chair. The dogs all stirred, lifting their heads at the movement before settling down again. "I need to talk to Manny," he said.

Calico nodded. "I liked Ruby." Her lips curled up for a moment and showed far too many pointed teeth, then became a humourless smile. "And I've never eaten an *hechicera*'s heart before."

"Be careful," Morago said.

"I know, I know. You don't want any blowback on the tribe. But you don't have to worry about that. This is a *ma'inawo* problem, and we'll handle it our way."

"What I meant," Morago said, "is that kind of a witch can be formidable."

Calico smiled. "That's sweet," she told him as she rose and joined Steve.

Leah watched the pair go off into the darkness.

"So," she overheard Steve say they walked away. "I know how you want to go about this. Do you feel like hearing my take?"

Calico's laughter trailed off as the two moved out of Leah's hearing. She turned back to Morago and Aggie.

"Was she serious about that?" she asked. "Eating somebody's heart?"

Morago shrugged.

"The thing people forget," Aggie said, "is that the *ma'inawo* can be formidable, too."

Leah sighed and settled back into her seat. "So witches are real," she said almost to herself, "and horrible. I don't know why that should be a surprise."

"There are witches and then there are witches," Morago said. "Among the tribes—the Navajo, the Kikimi, the Hopi—witches are creatures of pure evil. They're the main reason we have Reuben's dog boys as part of the Warrior Society. They protect the tribe against all manner of threats. But outside the tribes, the question becomes trickier. The Wiccan witches are earth worshippers, more like hippies—you get on their bad side by not sorting your recycling properly."

"Morago," Aggie said.

"So I exaggerate. The point is they aren't evil. Nor is a *bruja*, at least not necessarily."

"Which type is the old woman in the barrio that people call Abuela?" Aggie asked.

Morago turned to her, thoughtful. "If she's an *hechicera* it means she's bad medicine. They're more like a sorceress than a witch. A *bruja* would never mess around trying to control spirits."

"So how do we stop her?" Leah asks.

Morago shakes his head. "Damned if I know, but something needs to be done about Ruby's situation."

BY THE SECOND WEEK, Aggie had returned to working afternoons in her studio. Leah would join her, sitting out of the way with her laptop open, but more often than not, she watched Aggie painting and didn't do much writing.

When she did write, she divided her time between the book she'd promised Alan and her new blog about the plight of undocumented migrants in this part of the country. Ernie had come by one afternoon and they'd talked for so long that she was late getting dinner on the table. Since then, they'd exchanged a flurry of emails until Leah finally put up her new blog post. There was some good feedback, but a dismaying amount of racism and hate mail in the comments. Ernie assured her that the intense response showed she was doing something right, and he offered to introduce her to some people who could help her better understand the situation.

The book was easier to work on than she'd anticipated. Her morning journaling brought it all back: her friendship with Aimee, along with the part that the Diesel Rats played in her life both before and after Aimee's death. But while it wasn't hard to get the words down, the writing was so raw that she wasn't sure she could ever show it to anyone. The idea of Alan and Marisa reading it was hard enough. Even more terrifying was the notion of complete strangers having an intimate look at her private life and innermost thoughts.

One afternoon, she looked up from her computer screen while rereading a particularly hard section. She'd been writing about the time just after Aimee's mother had given her Aimee's journal. From across the room, she saw that Aggie had turned from her canvas and was regarding her with worried eyes.

"Sometimes," Aggie said, "I see you writing and you seem filled with so much pride at what you're accomplishing. But then there are times such as this, when it appears that every word is a cholla thorn digging its barb deeper under your skin."

That was exactly what it felt like, Leah thought, having brushed up against those tenacious thorns a few times during her walks in the surrounding desert—except these barbs were in her heart.

"Do you want to talk about it?" Aggie asked.

"Not really."

But she found herself telling the old woman the whole story all the same. There was something about Aggie that made her a natural confidante. Leah wasn't sure what it was, but she'd felt comfortable in the older woman's presence from the moment she'd first met her.

She waited now for Aggie to say something, but the older woman sat quietly after Leah was done. Aggie looked out the window before she finally nodded to herself and looked at Leah again. "Everything's a story," she said. "Not just our memories. Every part of our lives—how we interact with each other, how all the Wheels turn in our lives. Have you thought of telling this as a story in another way, rather than as a personal memoir?"

"You mean, like fiction? I should make it up?"

Aggie shook her head. "No, tell the same story, but pretend it belongs to someone else just to give yourself some distance from how it affects you."

"Isn't that side-stepping the issue? It doesn't seem honest."

Aggie didn't argue the point. She let her hand trail down to muss the fur of the dog sleeping beside her chair.

"Let me tell you a story," she said. "A long time ago, there was a woman of the People who fell in love with a man who was not a man."

"He was a *ma'inawo?*"

Aggie nodded. "But he was like Steve's Calico. His mother was a Gila monster and his sire was a wolf."

"How does that even work?"

"They met and mated as five-fingered beings. Now be quiet, and listen to the story."

She smiled to take any possible sting out of the words.

THIS HAPPENED *in the days before the Europeans came to us from across the mountains in the east, even before the Spaniards came up from the south. The desert people lived on the banks of the San Pedro River, which they called Sand River, and there wasn't much interaction between them and the* ma'inawo. *They traded with other tribes. Sometimes war parties raided another tribe's camp. But mostly, it was a peaceful existence.*

The woman in this story—let's call her Running Deer—was the youngest of three daughters. She was what we would call a tomboy today, but back then she was considered a wild girl. Every chance she got, she went off into the desert—exploring, walking, searching for she didn't know what. She was fearless until the day she got her foot trapped in a crevice over by Yellowrock Canyon.

I told you that there wasn't much interaction between the ma'i-nawo *and the desert people, but some of the* ma'inawo *clans held more*

animosity toward us than others. In those days the crows were the
worst, and there she was, her foot ensnared in a crevice, and those
crow boys gathering around, mocking her, poking at her with sticks,
building up their courage to do who knows what.

It could have gone very bad for her if he hadn't come upon the
scene. Let's call him Walks Alone, a ma'inawo of two clans, but she saw
only a handsome boy her own age who could have come from any of
the villages along the banks of Sand River.

He drove off the crow boys. He extracted her foot from that
crevice with a gentleness she didn't think was possible. Then, because
her ankle hurt so much, he carried her home, where he was welcomed
by her family and the tribe.

He didn't stay, but he returned from time to time. That wasn't so
strange in those days. Even then, there were restless youth who had to
see what lay beyond the next mountain before they could settle back
on the land where they were born, and the desert people simply
assumed he was one of them.

What Running Deer's family didn't know was that their daughter
and Walks Alone saw each other much more frequently that anyone
else might imagine. Once her ankle was healed, Running Deer
continued her desert rambles, but now when she was out of sight of
the village, Walks Alone would appear as if out of nowhere and fall
into step beside her.

It was months before he told her what he was, and by then she
didn't care. She was as much in love with him as he was with her. And
once she knew and accepted him, their rambles went farther afield
than any of the other desert people who had travelled before her.

He began to take her into the ghost lands, deep into the
otherworld.

A little known facet of this other place that exists so close to our
own, is that the more time humans spend there, the more they are
changed. Some go a little crazy, some go a lot, but others thrive. Those
that do well live longer and healthier lives than if they had never
ventured.

This is where the Europeans got their ideas about their Faerieland,
only it's all the same place. Puck's just Coyote in a different guise.

Oberon and Titania are our elder thunders. Their gnomes and hobs are our prickly pear boys and crows.

Time moves differently on the other side. The otherworld is actually an onion of worlds, each skin peeling back a different layer to reveal yet another world. In some places, years pass in what are only minutes here. In others, a few days can be a decade.

Sometimes, after months of travelling, they would return to that village on the dry banks of the Sand River to find that only a few days had passed. Other times, they would cross over for a few minutes and lose a month. But although Running Deer worried about losing the best years of her family's lives, she worried more about not being with Walks Alone.

Such places they explored; such beings they encountered. Ma'inawo clans Running Deer had never imagined. Tribes of five-fingered beings that lived a hundred years ago, or would not begin their lives for another hundred years. They met thunders, tall and unfathomable, and spirits so tiny that a dozen could caper on the flat palm of Running Deer's hand.

It was a time of wonder and beauty. Running Deer was no longer the dark-haired girl of the desert people that she had been when first she met Walks Alone. She was changed. Not quite a ma'inawo herself, but like the animal people, her life was long and sickness had become a stranger. A hundred years old and she still looked much the same as that girl she had been.

The Wheel of her life had grown so tall that she could no longer see the beginning or the end of it anymore. But she was content. It didn't matter that sometimes the journey was hard, and sometimes easy. That sometimes the weather was foul, and sometimes it was fair. That sometimes they had too little to eat, and sometimes too much. All that mattered was that they were together.

But then...oh then. Disaster.

Ma'inawo live long and can heal themselves from many grievous wounds, but they were never immortal. Walks Alone was surefooted, but this day, he misjudged his step on a narrow ghost of a trail up in the mountains. Running Deer was behind him and reached out, but he was too far ahead. She watched him fall. She seemed to watch him for a very long time. Her mouth was open, but no sound came out. It felt as though it took a hundred years for him to fall, a hundred more for the terrible sound of the impact his body made to echo back up to her.

She stood there, balanced precariously on the path. She might have cast herself off as well, but she couldn't resist the thought that he might have survived. He was a ma'inawo. They were strong. They healed as the desert people didn't.

She descended at a reckless speed to reach his side, far far below. But when she finally got close to him, she saw she was too late. She could never have been there in time. A part of her had known this all along. The fall was long, the rocks unforgiving. Ma'inawo can heal, but from some wounds, not even the thunders can return.

Sinking to her knees, she cradled his broken body in her arms and knelt there, rocking back and forth, keening, her heart as broken as the man she held.

It was a long time before she could rouse herself to bury her lost love. She dragged stones from nearby gullies and arroyos, one by one, piling them up until the cairn was as tall as her own waist.

And then she walked away.

She wandered through the otherworld for years, seeing through a grey haze, keeping to herself, trying to find something to fill the bleak expanse in her chest that had once been filled with her love for Walks Alone. She searched for him on the ghost roads. She asked every man, woman and ma'inawo that she met if they had seen his spirit. She begged favour from the thunders and even tried to bargain with the fearsome spirits of the crossroads. But it was all to no avail.

The Wheel that Walks Alone had travelled ended under a cairn of stones. Fate had stolen him from her and she was alone.

When she finally accepted that, she knew she had to find another purpose to her life. So she returned to the village of her people on the banks of Sand River, but her family was long gone. The people—the village itself—was gone. Now, the desert people lived in the canyons of the Painted Lands and were called the canyon people. None of them remembered Running Deer, the girl who went away into the other-world to be seen no more. She wasn't even remembered as a story.

She took her lover's name, calling herself Walks Alone. She made herself a home near those canyons, close to the tribe that only knew her as a stranger who'd come down from the mountains. And where the Women's Council and the tribal shaman guided the tribe in their relationships with the ma'inawo, she, in turn, became a guide for the animal people, helping them traverse the ways of the five-fingered beings.

But she was a protector of the canyon people, as well. While she was no Jimmy Cholla, she befriended the pack of dog soldiers who defended the tribe from spiritual attacks, teaching them the difference between those who meant real harm, and those who were only mischief-makers and tricksters, like the crows of Yellowrock Canyon. Teaching them the medicines and mysteries that Walks Alone had taught her.

So she had purpose, but her life was very long. Generations came and went, and still she endured, growing older at a pace that was different from the tribe, as their life spans were to that of a fly. She changed her name every few decades until she no longer needed to because she'd become such a fixture in her little adobe house on the edge of the tribal lands, that no one ever wondered how it was that the same woman lived there, while the rest of the canyon people were born, had their turn on their Wheel, and then went on to walk the ghost roads to the other place where their spirits begin their next journey.

You might ask why she didn't simply step from some cliff and join Walks Alone, meet with him again in whatever place it was that his new Wheel had taken him. But she understood that life is a gift, and it is not up to us to decide when our Wheel ends. Only the thunders know when lives begin and end, and even they answer to a greater Spirit.

But one day, she thought she was given permission to finally follow her lost love. Her body lay on its sick bed and her spirit floated in the skies above otherworldly mountains. All she had to do was let go, and this she did, only to be returned to her body once more while it healed.

She understood then that her purpose had not yet run its course.

Her Wheel, so tall, so tall, was still turning. She still had years she must endure.

LEAH DIDN'T SAY anything for a long time. She sat there in Aggie's studio, her laptop forgotten, hugging herself against the chill that the story had put under her skin. One of the dogs sleeping on the floor by her feet shifted its position and she started at the movement.

"Are you—are you telling me that was you?" she finally said.

Aggie's gaze held hers. "I'm telling you that our stories are easier to relate when we take a step back from them and tell them as though they belong to another."

Leah gave a slow nod. "Part of my problem is that I feel like I'm writing this all down for closure, but instead it's just bringing everything back."

"You mean your guilt."

Leah gave her another nod.

"I could tell you it wasn't your fault," Aggie said, "but you're not ready to hear that, although a part of you already knows it. So let me tell you this instead. You can plan the best tale in your head—the perfect way things should go—but the people in your life don't have your insight, and even if they did, they probably wouldn't follow your plan anyway. In the end, we are each of us alone. We can offer comfort and companionship to each other—do our best to help our friends onto the road that might lead them to hope. But we can't think or feel for them. We can't be inside them and change the way they see the world, no matter how much it breaks our heart to watch them fall."

Leah sighed. She thought again of the story Aggie had told her, of this immortal woman who had to live forever without her partner.

"So how do you get over it?" she asked. "The survivor's guilt."

"It's never really about that. People put their traumas into little boxes in their heads. They try not to think of the bad times, or tell themselves that they're not supposed to think about them, but it never works. You don't get strong from ignoring what happened. You get strong through finding the mechanisms to cope."

Aggie's gaze grew distant for a long moment.

"Everybody deals with it differently," she said, when she focused on Leah once more. "The one thing I'm sure of is that guilt doesn't make you strong. You only get strong from talking, living, loving. With other people, yes, but with yourself most of all. That's what makes you strong."

"But how could I not have seen the bad place she was in?"

"I don't know," Aggie told her. "I do know that even if you had known what was happening to your friend, you couldn't have stopped it. Only she could do that."

"So we just let people spiral down to a place from which they can't return?"

"Of course not," Aggie said, a flash of annoyance in her eyes. "We do everything we can to help them. But if they hide their pain so well that we can't see it, the fault doesn't lie with us. And if we do see what they're going through, we can only give them all the love and support we can muster."

Her voice softened. "We can't *make* them better. We can only stand by them.

"That is the hard part of having a friend," she added.

She looked at her painting, then picked up the brushes from her palette and put them in a jar of turpentine. When she stood up, the three dogs in the little studio all scrambled to their feet.

"Do you want to take a walk before dinner?" she asked.

Leah nodded and closed her laptop.

"Have you ever done a sweat?" Aggie asked as they wandered out of the yard in the direction of the hidden medicine wheel.

Leah shook her head. The little pack of three dogs that had left the studio with them grew to twice that many. They ranged ahead and followed from behind, panting happily.

"The world is full of poisons," Aggie said. "All sorts of bad medicines cloud the air, even here in these canyons, and not even the purest of heart can shield themselves from all of it. A sweat draws the poison from our bodies and lets us walk in beauty again."

"Sounds good to me."

Aggie smiled. "It is. I was planning a sweat before the whole business with that girl got in the way."

She stopped at the foot of a tall saguaro with a half-dozen arms, which Leah had learned meant it was an old one. A pair of crows perched on the lowest arm.

"I think we should have another," she said, her head tilted so that she was looking at the crows. "We'll need a good-sized lodge, a pile of stones and lots of firewood. Water, too."

The crows lifted from the saguaro and flew north. The dogs scattered into the scrub.

"How can I help?" Leah asked.

"There's little for us to do," Aggie told her. "The crows and dogs will see to it that everything's prepared."

Leah shaded her eyes to watch the two specks that were crows flying off. There was no sign of the dogs anymore.

"Really?" she said. "Are they all *ma'inawo*?"

Aggie slipped her hand into the crook of Leah's arm and headed back to the house.

"Some are," she said. "The ones that aren't will pass the word along. By tomorrow morning, there will be plenty of helping hands." She paused to give Leah a glance. "Remember when you first arrived and I said that I didn't sense you and Marisa coming?"

Leah nodded.

"These friends of mine," Aggie said, "are my eyes and ears beyond my home."

"Why didn't *they* sense our arrival?"

"You'll have to ask the thunders. But I think it's because you were instrumental in saving my life, back in the otherworld. The spirits like to keep that kind of thing away from us. I gather it's to stop us from becoming too cocky."

Leah tried to imagine what her old self—the person she'd been before she'd ever come to the Painted Lands—would have thought of this conversation. She'd have thought she was being put on, she decided.

"So you're an immortal," she said to Aggie.

Aggie smiled. "No one's immortal, except for maybe Cody."

"That's Coyote, right?"

"It is. But I've lived awhile. Stay on here, and the years will stretch out for you."

"Because the rez is in the otherworld?"

"No, but my home is."

By the time they got back to the house, a few of the dogs had returned. There was also a handful of tall men waiting for them, all dark-skinned with lean faces and long black hair except for a pair with hair the colour of a yellow rez dog's fur.

"I think we'll need the big pot for dinner tonight," Aggie said.

77

SADIE

S olitary suited Sadie just fine. Her cell had cement walls and floor, a sink, a toilet, and a bed that was simply a metal platform bolted to the wall. There was no window. The door was a huge steel affair with a slot through which food could be passed. Once a day, she was taken out by two guards into what looked like a glorified dog run and allowed to walk back and forth along its length for an hour.

She'd lost track of time, but was pretty sure her court date was coming up soon. Her court-appointed lawyer assured her she wouldn't get much time, and the days she'd already spent here in the Kikimi County Young Offenders Correction Facility would be counted against her sentence. Whoop-de-do.

With the constant fluorescent light turned on overhead, and no window, the only way she could tell time was by the regular routine of breakfast, lunch, walk in the dog run, and dinner. She'd taken up an exercise regime because expending energy on push-ups and sit-ups eased her cravings for her knife and distracted her from wanting to bash her head against the wall until it bled.

She already hurt all over. Her orange jumpsuit hid a patchwork of bruises, and every time she stretched a muscle she could feel the pain in her cracked ribs. Sometimes it hurt just to breathe.

The jumpsuit didn't hide the cut on her temple, her swollen lips, or the blue-black bruises that raccooned her eyes. Those bruises might be going yellow by now, but there was no way to tell. There were no mirrors in solitary.

There *was* plenty of time to think.

Too much time.

Breakfast was watery lukewarm porridge with maybe three raisins, but no milk or sugar; lunch was stale white bread, usually with a wetish slice of bologna or some other mystery meat, plus an apple or another fruit past its prime; and dinner, a congealed mess of instant potatoes, some sort of flaccid, overcooked vegetable and another gross meat, along with some lumpy pudding-type thing for "dessert." Sadie had yet to recognize what kind of dinner meat since they all tasted the same, even if they vaguely resembled chicken, beef or pork.

Tonight's meat had looked mostly like chicken. It had come served with the usual potato paste and a watery green purée, which she decided had once been broccoli. Her dessert might have been rice pudding, but it looked more like maggot pudding, so it remained untouched.

After dinner, she'd spent her time lying on the bed staring at the ceiling and then doing a series of sit-ups. She finished her count of fifty before she got on the floor to do a bunch of push-ups.

Her ribs throbbed with a sharp ache that helped her get past the need to cut herself. There was nothing in her cell that could be used for cutting.

She got up, and was about to pull down her coveralls to have a pee, when she realized that there was someone sitting on the bed.

"What the hell?" she said.

She banged up against the wall beside the toilet, trying to put some distance between herself and the intruder.

"Don't worry. I'm not here to hurt you."

"Manny?" she said, suddenly recognizing him.

His words didn't register. All she could think was, fuck, the old woman died and now he's here to kill me. Just when she was actually trying to get her life on track.

He stood up and seemed taller than ever in the confines of her cell.

"Who did that to you?" he demanded.

"What?"

"Who hurt you?"

His voice was hard and cold.

Why should you care? almost popped out of her mouth, but she remembered what Aggie had told her about which spirit a person should feed if they want to be a better person, so she stopped herself and took a deep breath instead.

"Some girls," she said. "They were 66Hers."

"I don't understand."

"66 Hermanas," Sadie said. "The *putas* that run with the 66 Bandas." She spat into the toilet bowl. "Turns out the spell the witch put on me had a best-before date. They jumped me in the can after I got into a fight with one of them in the exercise yard."

"That's the problem with an *hechicera*. Their spells wear off unless you keep them topped up."

"Whatever."

Manny sighed. "What were you fighting about?"

"Hey, don't sigh at me. I was minding my own business. The wannabe 'banger was just testing the new girl. Plus I'm white—not a popular skin colour when most of the kids in here are brown, black or Indians."

"Tell me their names."

"And you'll do what?"

"Teach them some manners."

Sadie almost smiled. "Yeah, it doesn't really work like that in here."

"So they can beat you, but *you* get punished? And that's okay with you?"

"Pretty much. I told the guards I started it. I kind of like being in solitary. I'm not really a people person, as you've probably noticed."

Manny shook his head and sat down again. Sadie perched on the toilet.

"So why are you here?" she asked. "Is Aggie okay?"

"I'm not here at her behest. Steve asked me to see you."

Oh crap. She remembered the disappointment and anger in Steve's eyes the last time she'd seen him. "If he wants to tear a piece off of me," she said, "he's going to have to wait in line."

Manny didn't respond. He sat there on the bed, staring at her. Waiting.

"Okay," Sadie said. "Why did Steve ask you to come see me?"

"One of the *ma'inawo* owes him a favour. She has a medicine that could fast track you out of this place."

"You mean some kind of magic?"

Manny nodded. "Something like that."

"So what's the catch?"

"There's somebody else he knows who's also in trouble, and it could help them."

Sadie cocked her head. "Why are you telling me this?" she asked.

"He wants you to decide which of you gets the benefit of the *ma'inawo*'s medicine."

"You're serious? Why would he want *me* to decide? I think I'd be the last person he'd pick."

Manny's stoic features gave none of his own opinions away. "I don't have an answer for that," he said.

"Well, my answer's easy. Have him help the other person."

"Why do you say that?"

"Because, a—" She managed to clip the "asshole" that wanted to spring from her lips. "—I'm trying to fix my life, and busting out of here is not going to be a big help."

"But you'd be free."

"Maybe. But Aggie wouldn't help me."

Manny didn't say anything for another long moment. Sadie thought she saw a hint of a smile in his dark eyes.

"Is that it?" she asked. "Are we done?"

"We are. And you just won me five bucks."

"What? This was all some stupid game?"

"No, Morago said that you'd jump at the chance to get out of here."

"And you didn't think I would?"

He nodded. "Steve and I both said you wouldn't." He smiled. "Morago's down ten dollars."

Sadie scanned his face. "Steve said that too? After everything I put him through?"

Manny nodded. "He sees the best in people."

"No shit. Now I feel even worse for what I did to him."

Manny shrugged.

They sat in silence for a few moments. Sadie found herself wishing he'd stay for a while, keep the sudden loneliness at bay.

"So, five bucks?" she finally said. "That's a pretty cheap bet."

"It's all I had in my pocket." He paused, then added, "Tell me the names of the girls who beat you up."

But all Sadie would say was, "Tell Steve I'm sorry."

Manny tried to wait her out. Finally, he stood up. "I will," he said.

And then he was gone.

Sadie had the pee she'd been holding, then went and lay down on her bed, her arm across her eyes.

That was weird, she thought, but she was proud of herself for doing the right thing. It was kind of a first for her.

Maybe Aggie was right. Maybe you got to be a better person by doing better things.

As she fell asleep, she wondered who was going to get the benefit of the help she'd turned down.

78

RUBY

Like most *ma'inawo*, Ruby was as comfortable in her animal shape as she was in her human skin. But where most *ma'inawo* flitted regularly between the two, dog cousins were used to spending long periods of time in their four-legged shape. Ruby was no different, so it was no hardship for her when, after she'd made her bargain with the witch, she switched to the shape of a red-furred dog and held to it through the weeks that followed.

She did whatever Abuela told her to do, all except for shifting back to human form.

It was a small rebellion but it was all she had, so she savoured it.

She hadn't expected to still be alive. She'd expected the witch to kill her and harvest her soul as soon as Manny and Xande had taken Sadie away. But apparently Abuela didn't need a death to fuel her magic.

"You don't have to worry," she'd told Ruby when the door closed behind the corbae and Sadie. "I'm not planning to hurt you. My *brujería* isn't like that of the Kikimi witches. I'm as much a *curandera* as a *bruja*."

Ruby sniffed her disdain. "Healer or witch, your medicine has still been stolen from the thunders. Is that what you plan to do with me? Steal what medicine you can draw out of my soul?"

"I told you before: I've taken nothing from your thunders. Do you think the only medicine in the world comes from your spirit elders?"

"Yes."

"You are naive if you think that."

Ruby waved a dismissive hand. "We were here long before you five-fingered beings. The thunders came to our elders and shared their medicine. They didn't come to you. You don't even know their names."

"We have other gods."

"It doesn't matter what you believe," Ruby said. "I made this bargain and I will keep my word. Do what you want with me. But I warn you: if what you take from me to work your magic does harm to the land, my pack, or any cousin, there will be consequences. That pair of crow boys who just left will be the least of your worries."

"I won't hurt you."

"Says the rattler, mesmerizing her prey before she strikes."

Abuela frowned at her. "What do you take me for?"

"A thief and a monster."

"Because I am a *bruja*?"

"You're no *bruja*. Only an *hechicera* controls spirits."

Abuela's gaze darkened. "You know nothing about me."

"I know you are a five-fingered being and your kind have no magic of your own."

"Are you so certain of that?"

"Where do *you* think your medicine comes from?" Ruby asked her.

Abuela laid a hand upon her chest. "From my heart."

Ruby shook her head. "It comes from *ma'inawo* blood, but that blood runs so thin in you five-fingered beings that you have to draw power from the land and true *ma'inawo* to give it any potency."

"True *ma'inawo*? Are you such a pure and perfect race?"

"We were untouched by evil spirits until the desert people came to share our land. Then they took it from us, just as the Spanish took it from them, and the Anglos stole it again, in turn. You might think that I should have sympathy for you, relegated to this barrio while the Anglos live high on their spoils, but in my eyes you are all thieves. You enslave; you kill at random."

"Some humans do, but not all of us."

Ruby held her gaze. "This land wasn't always desert. You made it so. And you, in particular, continue to squeeze the medicine from it, giving no thought to replenishing what you take."

"So you hate all humans, do you?"

"Only witches. Most five-fingered beings aren't worth considering."

"Yet you offered up your soul for that despicable girl."

Ruby shrugged.

"And you live with Abigail White Horse. She's as human as I am."

"If you think that, you truly know nothing."

"I know she's no *ma'inawo*," Abuela said. "Is she a witch?"

Ruby smiled. "If she was a witch, the dog boys would have killed her and eaten her heart."

"A Kikimi witch, you mean."

"Witches are all the same," Ruby said. "The dog boys just don't bother with the ones outside their tribe."

"Yet they leave the Women's Council untouched."

"They are medicine women, not witches."

"As am I."

Ruby fell silent. It was a pointless argument, she realized.

"So what do you need from me," she asked, "to harness *my* medicine?"

Abuela shook her head. "I need only to lay a hand on your shoulder or arm while I set the enchantments for my charms and *milagros.*"

"Then this is the last conversation we will have," Ruby told her.

That was when she took her dog shape.

In the days that followed, Abuela tried to get her to change back, but Ruby would have nothing to do with her. She let the witch touch her while making her spells, but any attempt to treat Ruby as a pet made her growl low in her chest. If Abuela persisted, Ruby would snarl, baring her teeth.

When the witch didn't have need for her, Ruby would spend her time outside. She'd lie in the dirt, moving around the house with the sun so that she was always in the shade. From there, she watched what she could see of the neighbourhood, which consisted mostly of the goings on next door around the clubhouse of the 66 Bandas. They worked on their cars and bikes. People would come and go. At night there were parties, the deep bass of the *narcocorridos* they favoured, the thumping sound resounding throughout the neighbourhood.

Nobody complained.

The witch didn't either, but her house was soundproofed with some kind of spell so the music couldn't make it inside. When the noise in the yard got to be too much, Ruby would come in and lie by the door.

She was also inside when the witch's customers came, and then she was surprised to find that Abuela had apparently spoken the truth. None of her charms appeared to be evil. There were *milagros* and votive candles that the buyers would take to nearby Santa Margarita Maria to increase the potency of their prayers. Charms for health. Charms for love or prosperity. Charms for finding lost things or people. Charms of protection.

And always, before she gave the finished product to a customer, Abuela would call Ruby to her. She'd lay a hand on the red dog's shoulder and Ruby would feel a shiver of something travel from her to the witch's hand, and from there to the charm.

If the witch worked evil, she didn't do so in front of Ruby. Ruby might have regretted the harsh words she'd delivered to the witch when they first met, except that she could see how, with every charm she made, Abuela drew a sliver of vitality from the land along with what she took from Ruby herself, unlike Morago and the medicine women in the Painted Lands who always gave thanks for what they used.

Ruby was sometimes tempted to shift to her human form to point this out, but she didn't bother. She already knew what the witch's answer would be. She would say that she did this for herself and her own people, and had no concern as to how it might affect others. It was merely how most five-fingered beings dealt with the world around them.

The first Sunday that Ruby was with her, she followed Abuela when she left the house. Now her darker ways would be revealed, Ruby thought. But Abuela only went to Santa Margarita Maria for Mass, and came home afterward.

Whenever the witch left the house Ruby kept her in sight. She followed her to market, where Abuela bought groceries, and to the desert, where she collected plants. Unlike Aggie, she didn't thank the plants for their sacrifice, but that was as evil as she got.

Although Ruby always stayed close to the house, she explored the dry wash that ran behind the property. Sometimes she lay on the border between the Bandas' yard and Abuela's, head resting on her paws while she watched the gangbangers.

She knew her presence bothered them. She also knew they feared the witch and would leave her alone. The nervous looks they cast her way was one of her few sources of amusement.

One afternoon as she lay near the dry wash, her attention was on a ground squirrel but she was also vaguely aware of a crow in the branches of the mesquite tree above. She paid it no attention until it fluttered down to the ground and became a man.

"So she hasn't killed you yet," Xande said.

Ruby cast a quick glance in the direction of the witch's house before she slipped down into the wash. Xande followed, then Ruby took her own human shape and sat on the bank of the wash.

"I don't think she means to," she told the crow man. "But not even the mountain can withstand an endless trickle of water."

Xande sat down beside her. "What's that supposed to mean?"

"Every charm she makes, she fuels with a whisper of my spirit."

Xande frowned. "That can't be good."

"My point, exactly." She turned to look at him. "How's Aggie?"

"She's doing well. One of the women who came to see her from Newford is staying with her."

"And the girl?"

"She's in jail."

Ruby's eyebrows went up. "So she got caught."

"No, she turned herself in. Manny says she's actually trying to fix the mess of her life."

Ruby smiled. "So my being here is doing some good."

"I suppose that's one way of looking at it."

He picked up a pebble and sent it skittering down the wash, where it startled a half-dozen quail under some brush.

"Sorry, cousins," Xande murmured. "Didn't see you in there."

Ruby's sharp ears caught the sound of the witch's door opening. She rose to her feet before Abuela could call for her.

"I have to go," she said.

"Don't give up hope," Xande said.

Ruby shook her head. "What do I have to hope for, beyond a quick end?"

"You know Steve—lives in that old Airstream that belonged to Possum?"

"Sure. He comes by Aggie's place all the time, visits, gives her a hand in the garden and such."

"Manny says he's got some plan to help you."

"Steve?" Ruby was confused. Steve was a kind man, but what could he possibly do to help her?

Xande nodded. "Word is, this big-time cousin owes him a favour. Steve's just waiting for her to show up."

"It doesn't matter. Whatever he thinks he can do, won't change anything. I gave my word."

She heard the witch call for her. "Now I really have to go. Thanks for stopping by," she added before she shifted back into dog shape.

She went up out of the wash and through the brush that had hidden them from the witch's house. Behind her, she heard wings lift into the air, but she didn't look back.

AFTER THAT, she was visited from time to time by various *ma'inawo*. Old pack members would find her in the dry wash and bring her pack-rats and other small game. The Yellowrock Canyon crows perched companionably in the trees above, sometimes taking human form so that they could pass the time with conversation. There was no more talk about Steve, or Ruby's fate at the hands of the witch, though her pack members would talk of revenge if Ruby were to die. Ruby tried to make them promise not to avenge her, explaining how Abuela wasn't an evil witch, but they refused.

After a while she gave up because she knew if the situation were reversed, she wouldn't have made that promise either.

One evening, almost two weeks after she'd first come to live with Abuela, the noise from the 66 Bandas' clubhouse drove her inside once more. She lay by the door watching Abuela fill jars with the finely ground herbs and other plants that she hung from the rafters to dry.

It was getting late when Ruby suddenly lifted her head. Something —some *presence*—was approaching the house. At first she didn't recognize who or even what it was. All she knew for certain was that it was old and powerful.

Before she could bark a warning, the witch's front door suddenly blew open and a tall black-haired woman filled the door. Ruby had the impression of huge black wings disappearing into her back, but that might have been just the play of light on the darkness behind the stranger.

Ruby rose to her feet, hackles raised. A growl rumbled deep in her chest. Her warning wasn't so much to protect the witch or her house, as a reaction to having been startled.

Abuela didn't move from the table where she was working, except to lift her gaze. "You're either very stupid or very brave," she told the stranger. "Do you know whose house this is? Do you know who *I* am?"

The woman smiled mockingly. "Will I be suitably impressed when you tell me?"

Ruby backed away so that she no longer stood between the stranger and the witch. She lay down once more, thinking, this could be interesting. She smelled corbae on the stranger—not crow, but raven. She'd already heard the story of an old corbae who called herself Night Woman having recently visited the Painted Lands.

Abuela stood up from the table. "You can't come in, so you might as well go away before I decide to teach you a little respect for your elders."

Was she blind? Ruby wondered. This woman's aura was so ageless and powerful, she might well have been here when the world was first born.

The woman snorted at Abuela's use of the word "elder."

"I can't come in?" she said. "Do you have something to guard your house besides this little ward you've cast upon it?" She ran a long finger through the air in the doorway. There was sudden flash of light and a sharp electric smell, as though a wall socket had overloaded. Then she stepped inside, followed by the thump of bass and drums drifting over from the 66 Bandas' clubhouse.

Ruby grinned at the look of shock on Abuela's face.

"You shouldn't be so unfriendly," the stranger told the witch. "I'm actually here to help you."

Suspicion lay in Abuela's eyes. "Help me…how?" she asked.

Ruby could also detect…not so much fear, as nervousness. Which was probably why Abuela said nothing when the woman made herself comfortable in one of the room's armchairs. The stranger crossed her long legs at the ankles, then cocked her head to study the witch over her steepled fingertips.

"I want you to think about what you're doing with Ruby," the stranger finally said. "Think of it as a head's up."

Abuela gave her a puzzled look.

The stranger smiled. "You do know that when you've used her all up, you'll have every canid within a hundred miles out for your blood."

Abuela scoffed. "I'm not afraid of a few mangy dogs."

"You should be. You're starting a blood feud here, and surely you realize that among the *ma'inawo* there's only one way to stop a feud: when the guilty party is dead."

Ruby knew the exaggeration was deliberate, to scare Abuela, but the witch chose only to defend herself.

"I'm not guilty of anything but making a bargain that Ruby agreed to of her own free will."

The stranger tapped one foot against the other. "That would be a good argument," she said, "except she was in an untenable situation, which you used to your advantage such that she had no choice but to agree to your disgusting bargain."

"I didn't seek that child out. She came to me."

"And you took advantage of her."

"She entered my house uninvited. There is a cost for everything."

"As you will find out."

The witch's eyes narrowed. "I don't know who you are, but you have just done the same, and I won't have you come into my home to disrespect me."

The woman regarded Abuela with a steady gaze. "Understandable. You should remove me."

Ruby smiled to herself. She could already see that, while Abuela had no idea who the stranger was, the witch knew that the woman would only leave when she was ready and there was nothing she could do about it.

"And then you took further advantage of Ruby, an innocent," the stranger went on. "You're familiar with how loyalty works in the canid clans, even when it's as misplaced as it was here. You know their belief that the strong must protect the weak."

"You're too late. The bargain has been struck."

The dark-haired woman nodded. "On the basis of treachery, which makes its validity questionable. Even if it holds, it will only last until you've used her up, and then they will come after you—by the hundreds."

The witch let out a derisive laugh. "There aren't that many *ma'i-nawo* dogs."

"Are you so sure of that? Not on the rez, perhaps, but there are dogs everywhere. I haven't counted how many live in this area, even just in your own barrio, but I'll wager there are more than enough to extract their revenge."

"Not many are *ma'inawo*," Abuela tried again.

The stranger shrugged, ignoring the comment. "Of course, the other way to conclude the bargain is for you to die."

"You can try your worst—" Abuela began.

The stranger cut her off with a lazy wave of her hand. "Oh, it wouldn't be me. I don't really see violence as the best solution to anything. My sister, however, has no such scruples. And, I should warn you, rather a heavy hand. She's as likely to lay waste to your entire barrio, simply to deal with you. The trouble with the *ma'inawo* in this area is that we despise witches. We find it hard to differentiate between what you think you are, and the evil of the Kikimi witches."

Ruby had been taking some pleasure in Abuela's discomfort, but this was going too far. She shifted to her human form so that she could speak.

The stranger turned to look at her with a radiant smile. "*Ohla*, Ruby," she said. "I've come to take you home."

Ruby shook her head. "No matter how bad the bargain was, I still gave my word."

The smile faded and was replaced by a world of sadness in the woman's eyes. "But you know it's true," she said. "Your kin will have vengeance when the witch is done with you."

"I've asked them not to."

The woman reached out and touched Ruby's arm. "And will they listen to you?"

Ruby gave a slow shake of her head.

"So you see," the stranger told Abuela, "your only hope to survive this is to set Ruby free."

"What's to stop the canids from still attacking me?"

"I give you my word."

Abuela wasn't foolish enough to question the word of this elder *ma'inawo*, but Ruby couldn't see how the woman could speak for the canid clans. Whoever she might be, the stranger had no hold over them.

But apparently Abuela wasn't taking that into consideration. "Very well," she said. "Ruby can go. But now the debt returns to the girl."

The stranger sat up straight, feet on the floor, eyes flashing with dangerous light.

"Now you're just pissing me off," she told Abuela, all pretense at polite talk gone.

Abuela glared back at her. "You can't expect me to come out of this empty-handed."

The stranger stood up. She seemed even taller than she'd been when she entered. Black wings unfolded behind her, spreading out from wall to wall, ceiling to floor.

"You're right," she said. If frost and ice were given a voice, it would sound like hers. "I came with such absurd expectations," she went on. "I should have realized that you five-fingered beings are all the same.

It's never how you can help those around you, but what's in it for yourself."

Abuela bristled. "I help my community," she said. "If that comes at the cost of some foolish white girl, why should it bother me?"

"No reason. As always, you five-fingered beings always come up with some ill-reasoned justification that you presume will kill any argument."

Her voice had lost some of its coldness, but Ruby couldn't help feeling that her anger had grown even more. But that appeared to be lost on Abuela as well.

The witch reached behind her and picked up a staff that had been leaning against the wall. Ruby couldn't quite make out the symbols carved on it. They seemed to swim in her vision when she tried to focus on them. Her nostrils twitched. The staff reeked of magic.

A sly smile came over Abuela's face. "You won't be the first of your kind to underestimate me," she told the stranger, fingering the engravings.

Her gaze went to Ruby. "Come to me," she said.

Ruby didn't move.

"She's no longer yours," the stranger said, "You renounced your hold on her."

Abuela had been holding the staff upright. Now she tipped it until its top was pointed at the stranger. "I do whatever I wish in my own house," she said through gritted teeth.

Her eyes closed as she murmured something inaudible under her breath.

A tight band of flame sprang from the staff's tip, engulfing the stranger in a fire that didn't burn anything but her. The air filled with the stench of burning flesh and feathers. For a long moment, the stranger was outlined in the flames, then she seemed to collapse in on herself.

With the bright flare still raising spots in front of her eyes, Ruby couldn't see precisely what had happened, and despite the smell, she wasn't sure that the woman had actually been consumed by the fire. It seemed more as if she'd simply vanished.

She heard the sound of wings and looked back at Abuela to see a raven appear behind the witch.

Abuela heard it too. She turned, but she was too slow. Bird became woman, and the stranger plucked the staff from Abuela's hands as though the old witch had no more strength than that of a child. The stranger snapped the staff in two as easily as if it were a twig. She cast the pieces aside, then one hand caught Abuela by the throat and lifted her so high that her feet dangled well above the floor.

"The only reason you're not dead yet," the stranger said, looking up at her captive, "is that I meant what I said about violence. It solves nothing."

Abuela tried to fight the other woman's grip. She gagged, her feet kicking the stranger, but she might as well have been trying to hurt a stone wall. The stranger held her a moment longer before finally setting her back hard on the floor.

Abuela staggered, catching her balance by grabbing the table. She held her throat and gasped for air while the stranger regarded her without expression. The dark-haired woman waited until Abuela could breathe again before she spoke.

"There are no more bargains to be made tonight," she told Abuela. "You will renounce your hold on Ruby and the girl. And you will never touch another *ma'inawo* again."

"Or…or what?" Abuela croaked.

"Or I'll send my sister to visit you. She makes me seem like kindness incarnate."

"And if the dogs come after me?"

The stranger shrugged. "You'll have to charm them into leaving you unharmed."

She draped an arm over Ruby's shoulder. "Are you ready to go now?" she asked.

Ruby glanced at Abuela, still stroking her throat, then back to the woman. "She won't harm Sadie?"

"I don't think so." The stranger regarded Abuela. "What do you say, witch? Is the life of 'some foolish white girl' worth your own and that of everyone else in the barrio that you claim to protect?"

Abuela shook her head.

"You see?" the stranger said, her smile returned. "A peaceful outcome."

She started for the door again, arm still over Ruby's shoulder. Halfway there, Ruby felt a shift underfoot as they stepped into the otherworld. She inhaled a deep breath of clean air and shook herself as though she were in her dog shape.

"How can I thank you?" she said.

The stranger smiled. "Save your thanks for Steve—and Sadie. It was their decision that my debt to Steve be repaid with your rescue."

"*Sadie* had a hand in this?" Ruby said.

The woman's smile widened. "Sometimes when you think the best of someone, you bring out that best."

Then she shifted and a raven rose into the air. Ruby watched it fly away into the darkness until even her *ma'inawo* sight could no longer see it. After a moment, she shifted as well. She rolled in the dust of the otherworld until she wore it like a coat. Shaking herself again—a much more satisfying action in this shape—she trotted off into the otherworld night.

79

STEVE

I've never been to a sweat before. I've just never felt that I should attend a Kikimi spiritual ceremony, but Morago told me it will be disrespectful to Aggie if I don't show up. This is her comeback party, he said, after having been so close to death.

So the day of the sweat Calico and I come down off the ridge trail to find a small village has sprung up around the fire pit. I've never thought of it as a large space, not even a couple of weeks ago when all those *ma'inawo* came down out of the mountains for the confrontation with Consuela Mara. But right now, there seems to be more room around the fire pit than I remember. It's probably got something to do with being so close to the otherworld here, or maybe we're even in the otherworld. I don't ask.

A large tent erected on the outer edge of the circle acts as a change-room. A sweat lodge covered with heavy blankets has been built about twenty feet from the fire pit, where flames are already crackling, heating stones that men are carrying into the lodge using pitchforks. Still others carry pails of water inside.

Nearby, women are cooking on a large portable grill set up under an awning, and young men and women walk the periphery of the circle waving smudge sticks. The air is rich with the smell of wood smoke, sage, cedar and fry bread.

People and dogs are everywhere. And crows. They're perched on the red rocks, saguaro arms, and branches of the mesquite and palo verde trees. Some of the people, I recognize from the rez. Reuben and his nephew Jack and some of the other dog boys. Morago, of course. As shaman, he goes to almost every gathering on the rez, from powwows to some little potluck up in the mountains. Thomas and his family. Petey Jojoba. There are lots of familiar faces. I assume the unfamiliar ones are *ma'inawo* in their human forms, although I suppose that could be said of many of the people gathered here today.

I spot Aggie sitting in a plastic lawn chair near the fire, with Leah perched on a rock beside her. Leah and I are the only white faces in the whole crowd, but I don't feel unwelcome or out of place the way I've always expected to at something like this. Leah glances in our direction, pushes away from the stone and comes up the slope to meet us, a big smile warming her face.

"Aggie said she doubted that you guys would come," she says when we draw near. "I'm glad she was wrong."

"*Ohla*," Calico says as she gives Leah a quick hug. "This feels like a party."

"And Calico's always in the mood for a party," I add.

Calico laughs and we walk hand in hand as we follow Leah back over to Aggie. The old woman smiles at our approach.

"*Ohla*, Steve, Calico." Her gaze fixes on me. "So have you finally figured out your place in the world?" she asks me.

"I don't know about that. But I am getting more comfortable with all of this." I release Calico's hand and gesture vaguely at the gathering. I'm not sure if I mean the sweat, or magic, or what, exactly.

That puts me on the receiving end of another of Aggie's smiles, as though she gets what I mean, even if I don't.

Aggie reaches up for my hands. "Don't be afraid of community," she says as I take both of her leathery hands in mine. "Solitude can strengthen the spirit, but community strengthens the heart. We all need our tribes, even if we have to make our own, but I hope you finally understand that you are always welcome in ours."

"I do," I tell her. "Thank you." The warmth in her eyes is genuine.

Somebody else comes up to pay their respects, so I let Aggie go, and Calico and I head off into the crowd, greeting the people we know, which, between the two of us, is pretty much everybody.

We find Morago at a portable table with some old aunties, his hands and jeans coated with flour as he shapes fry bread with them.

"*Ohla*, Speaks Justice, Calico," he says.

"I still prefer Beans for Brains," Calico says, which makes the aunties chuckle.

I lay a palm on my heart and give her a hurt look, but she only elbows me in the ribs. The aunties chuckle harder.

"Are you going to participate in the sweat?" Morago asks me.

I shake my head. "Baby steps," I tell him. "I'm here, right? You got me this far."

"It's never been about me," he says.

"I know."

One of the aunties says something in rapid-fire Kikimi.

"Gotta go," Morago says. "Aunt Judy tells me that fry bread doesn't make itself."

Calico and I fade back into the crowd before Aunt Judy can decide that we should be helping them too.

We wander through the crowd some more, talking with people we know, introducing each other to those we don't.

"You see?" Calico says later when we're sitting up on a rock overlooking the fire pit. "It's not so bad."

"I never thought it would be bad. It's just..." I search for the words. "I don't want to pretend I'm one of the tribe. Taking part in a sacred ceremony feels inappropriate."

"Even when you're invited?"

"Even then."

Calico smiles. "So don't think of it as the tribe. Think of it as a community, like Aggie said. It's how we cousins get along with you five-fingered beings."

I nod. "Like neighbours."

She leans against me. "Or more than neighbours." Then she pokes me with a finger. "But don't you go trying that with any of those pretty Kikimi girls. I see how they look at you."

I have to laugh. "Right. What they see is an old man, worn down by the desert."

"Not so worn down," Calico says. "I think there's still some life left in—"

She breaks off as first one dog, another, then all of them get up from where they've been lazing around in the dirt. They gather, facing us, on the slope below the rock where we're sitting.

"What the hell?" I say.

Calico glances over her shoulder. "It's got nothing to do with us."

I turn as well to see a dusty red dog higher up on the slope behind us. She makes her way down to us, slowing long enough to brush her head against the side of my leg before she goes bounding the rest of the way down. When she reaches the crowd of dogs there's a sudden mad frenzy of barking, sniffing and happy running around.

"Looks like Si'tala actually came through for you," Calico says.

Down below, I hear Leah calling Ruby's name and the red dog bounds over to where she's sitting with Aggie. Leah drops to her knees and enfolds the dog in her arms, burying her face in Ruby's dusty fur. Ruby lets Leah fuss with her for a few moments before she turns her attention to Aggie. She lays her chin on the old woman's knees and looks up into her face. Even from where we are, it's easy to see the mutual affection shining in their eyes. It's an image that I take a snapshot of in my mind so that I can pull it out whenever I think there isn't enough love left in the world.

Aggie ruffles the red dog's fur then gives her a little push. That's all it takes for Ruby to go racing off with the other dogs, a stream of crows following in their wake like a string of jet beads.

"What would you have done if Sadie hadn't made the right choice?" Calico asks.

I turn to her. "Honestly? I don't know. I was counting a hundred percent on it not coming to that."

Calico smiles. "You're such a big softie. It's one of the things I like about you."

"One of the things?" I tease.

She puts a languid finger under my chin and looks into my eyes. "Well, besides a few *other* first-rate skills you have—and then there's your music."

That catches me off guard. "I didn't know you'd ever even heard the old band."

"I don't mean that music. I mean the music you play now. You should let Leah hear some of it." She puts her hand on top of mine. "Comes to that, you should let more than the walls of the canyon hear it."

"Performing," I say, "That's not me anymore."

Her lips form a little pout. I can't tell if she's still playacting or serious, but she presses her case. "Is it still performing when you're playing for your friends?" she asks, "or your community? Don't you think Morago would love to hear what you do with those Kikimi powwow songs?"

I cringe inside. "I just play around with those on my own because I like them," I tell her. "I'd never perform them in public—it would feel disrespectful. There's no way that Morago would appreciate that."

Like speaking his name is a cue, we see Morago approaching the changing tent. It's almost time for the sweat to start. Morago has removed the T-shirt he was wearing earlier and there's not a trace of flour on his jeans. He stands beside the flaps of the tent's opening wearing a buckskin jacket, beaded and fringed. Looking at him in that jacket, it could be forty years ago, backstage at a Diesel Rats concert. No wonder the groupies adored him as much as they did the band.

A drumbeat starts up and the participants move toward the lodge. Most wear shorts and T-shirts; a few of the women are in loose dresses.

"Are you going in?" Calico asks.

I shake my head. "Baby steps, remember?"

"Except you're not a baby. You're only acting like one."

"I don't see you joining them," I start, but I don't get to finish.

Like everybody else, I turn to look at Aggie's house, where three SUVs have pulled into the yard. When Sammy Swift Grass steps out of the first one, a murmur ripples through the crowd. Beside me, Calico growls under her breath.

I slip my fingers lightly around her wrist. "Will you let me try to handle this?" I ask, keeping my voice calm and low.

She gives me a slow nod, her gaze never leaving Sammy. The drumming stops. The doors of the other SUVs all open and now Sammy's got a dozen of his boys standing behind him. They move in a wedge toward the fire pit, Sammy out front.

Morago starts walking to meet him, but I call out for him to stop. This is on me. I'm the one who insisted we give Sammy another chance, so I'm the one that has to deal with him. I just can't believe Sammy would bring it here. Even with all his men, he's seriously outnumbered.

Morago studies me for a moment, then nods.

People are giving way to let Sammy and his boys pass. He gets grim looks as they approach, but Sammy doesn't pay them any attention. He doesn't pay attention to Reuben either, or the sudden influx of dogs behind them, or the young men and women who are standing with Reuben in the crowd. His dog boys.

I realize that Sammy's heading straight for Aggie, so I jog down the hill and cut him off before he can reach her. He finally stops, but only because I'm standing in his way.

He looks like anybody on the rez, except everything leans to the one percent, if one of those CEO types were dressing down. A crisp, tailored white shirt rounds his belly and tucks into a pair of dark blue jeans with a sharp crease. His tooled-leather boots gleam and a matching belt is fronted by a large buckle of a rearing horse. It looks like it's made of gold. Hell, knowing Sammy, it could be gold. He isn't carrying any weapons, but that doesn't mean his crew is unarmed. Most of them are wearing loose, cotton hunting shirts with the casino logo on the pockets, which could easily hide weapons.

The tension in the air makes me wish Jerry Five Hawks were here. A badge and a gun can keep a lid on a lot of situations. But he pissed off his boss too much with how he handled that sorry business with Sadie and her sleazeball old man. Reuben told me Jerry's been assigned to a desk for the past couple of weeks and won't be out on patrol anytime soon. That's harsh, but apparently he's devoting all his attention to substantiating every charge they've got against Higgins to make sure the jerk gets his comeuppance when his court date rolls around. I just hope I don't get called in to testify. To his credit, he's also refuted Sadie's claim that I'm anything more than the famous Jackson Cole's cousin, so I don't have to worry about Higgins trying to cash in where Sadie failed.

"I gave you a chance," I tell Sammy. "I stuck out my damn neck for you. Why do you have to go and prove me wrong?"

"How am I proving you wrong?" he asks.

I nod toward his crew. "Showing up here with your bully boys in tow."

Sammy shakes his head. "I don't know why you've got that chip on your shoulder, but I'm not here to knock it off. I've come to pay my respects to Aunt Abigail and to take part in the sweat." He looks over my shoulder to where I know Morago's standing, then adds, "If that's all right."

When he looks back at me I hold his gaze, trying to read behind the bland expression he's giving me back.

"You're on the level?" I ask.

He nods.

"And the entourage?"

He shrugs. "I wasn't sure what kind of a welcome I might get, if any." He doesn't look over his shoulder when he calls back to his crew, "It's all good here. You can wait over by the cars, unless you want to join us."

And just like that, they head back toward the cars, all except for Dave Running Dog and another guy that I don't know.

"Hey, Steve," Dave says reaching out to shake my hand.

"Welcome home," I tell him, accepting his handshake. Then I step aside.

Sammy walks up to Aggie and goes down on one knee to bring his head level with hers, those fancy jeans of his getting a coating of dust where he's kneeling. "*Ohla*, Aunt Abigail," he says. "I brought you a little something." He takes a package of rolling tobacco out of his back pocket and offers it to her.

Aggie smiles as she accepts it. "*Ohla*, Sammy. It's good to see you. You don't have to make your boys wait by their cars. They can sit out here with us while you're inside."

Sammy sends Dave back to get them.

"Thank you, Auntie," he says to Aggie.

He stands up and looks in my direction. "I *was* listening to you," he says. "You made a convincing argument." Then he walks over to where Morago and the other guy wait by the teepee.

When Dave returns, all four of them enter the changing tent, strip down to their shorts and follow the others inside the sweat lodge. Morago's the last to enter. He closes the flaps behind him. A few moments later, a chorus of voices rises up in song inside the sweat lodge.

"What the fuck," Reuben says, stepping up beside me. "Did hell freeze over?"

Calico comes up on my other side and slips her arm around my waist. She grins at me and then at Reuben. "Never underestimate the sweet-talking charm of an old rock star," she tells him.

HOURS LATER, we're sitting in the moonlight with just the coals of the fire glimmering in the pit. Most everybody's gone. Reuben lies in the sand with his legs crossed, his head resting on a log, eyes closed. I'm sitting beside him with Calico's head on my lap. Her breathing's even. I don't think she's asleep, but she hasn't moved in half an hour. Thomas took his family home, leaving only Santana drowsing on the other side of me. When he tried to get her to go with them she shook her head. Thomas would only leave after extracting a promise from Reuben to see her safely home. Aggie's gone back to the house, but Leah's still here. Several dogs are sprawled around us, with Ruby lying on top of Leah's feet. Ever since Ruby's mad run with the rest of the pack, she's been sticking close to her.

Morago's been telling us stories. Some are traditional Kikimi and Jimmy Cholla tales, but he's also been talking about his various adventures after he left the rez all those years ago and then hooked up with the Rats and came on tour with us. He mixes the stories up and runs them into each other, so that sometimes it's hard to tell whether he's talking about himself, or if it's some old folktale. I've heard most of them before, but I never tire of them.

The sky's big tonight, like it is most nights in the desert. The spread of stars wheeling above us is humbling. I stare up into that forever dark, my fingers playing lightly with Calico's hair as I listen to the murmur of Morago's voice. When he finally falls silent, we listen to the stories of the night instead. After a while, Santana gets up and walks toward Aggie's house.

"Do any of those old trucks you've been working on forever actually run?" I ask Reuben when she's gone.

He opens his eyes to look at me. "Sure. We've just finished a rebuild on the engine of a nice old Ford."

"What kind of shape's it in?"

Reuben purses his lips. "It just needs bodywork now. Why do you ask?"

"I want to buy it."

"What the hell do you need a truck for?"

"It's not for me. It's for Thomas."

"Oh."

"I don't get it," Leah says. "Everyone's been saying that Thomas has so much potential to be a shaman. Why are you making it easy for him to leave?"

It's Morago who answers. "Because he needs to find himself," he says.

Leah turns to the shaman. "What does that even mean?"

"Right now," Morago says, "his spirit is bigger than the rez. He needs to go out and see the world. Maybe he'll come back. Maybe he'll like it better out there. Or maybe he'll do well enough that he'll find himself wanting to return to help make it better here."

She studies him for a moment. "Is that what happened with you? Touring with the Diesel Rats made you see the world in a new light?"

Morago shakes his head. "No—being friends with Steve did."

Leah gives a thoughtful nod.

Suddenly the dogs all lift their heads, but it's only Santana returning with a small wool blanket under her arm.

"Too bad we don't have a guitar here," she says to me as she settles back down, pulling the blanket around herself. "I'd love to hear you play again."

That raises a murmur of agreement all around, but I just groan.

"You play for her," Morago says, "when you don't for us?"

I shrug. What am I supposed to say?

"It's not like that," I tell him when I see they're not going to let it go. "Santana and Thomas showed up with my propane tank while I happened to be running over some tunes."

"What kind of music do you play now?" Leah asks, unable to hide her interest.

"Nothing serious. It's not even that good."

"Are you kidding me?" Santana says. "He was playing all the parts of a round dance on one guitar. It was amazing." She says it like she doesn't give a damn that it was based on their tribal music. In fact, she's grinning ear to ear.

"It wasn't all that—"

Santana talks over me. "If you play, I'll dance."

Calico jumps to her feet. "I'll dance too," she says and disappears.

A moment later she reappears with a guitar case in hand. My guitar case. She sets it down in front of me.

"Baby steps," she says before I can argue with her. "You're just here with your friends. What's the worst that can happen? You play a bum note and none of us notice?"

I don't have a response to that. She's right. I can't say why I don't play for anybody anymore. Except for Calico and the wildlife around my trailer, nobody else has heard me since Possum died—that I know of, anyway. Then Santana and Thomas snuck up on me, but so far as I can tell, no one else has been eavesdropping.

I sit up and crack open my guitar case. There are all kinds of great guitars out there on the market, new luthiers making incredible instruments, but I never felt I needed more than what this old Martin can deliver. I bought it with my first songwriting royalty cheque—yeah, even back then I never gave up my publishing rights and that royalty money is what keeps projects like the one Morago and I have going here afloat.

I pick up my guitar and check the tuning, aware of everyone

watching me. I've played for thousands and I've played for a lot fewer, but the pre-gig jitters are always the same. That moment just before you start in on a song and you don't know if you've won your listeners over or not.

Always open with something you know backwards, sideways and forwards, my cousin Steve once told me when we first started gigging with our high school band, so I start by playing the opening bars of "Stars Are Falling."

It's a song I woke up with one morning just as we were putting the finishing touches on the third album. It came to me complete, all of a piece. I wrote and recorded it on piano, and we added it to the end of the album—just voice and piano with Sully on harmonies, the whole thing sweetened with some tasteful strings. It cracked the top ten at number two—I think it was the Beatles that kept us out of the number one spot. But it's had a long shelf life. Before I left my old world behind, someone told me that there were almost three hundred covers of it—everybody from Elvis, Sinatra and Streisand, to Joe Cocker and Linda Ronstadt. Who knows how many there are now?

Leah's head jerks up as soon as she hears me fingerpick the familiar piano riffs on the guitar. When I start the first verse she closes her eyes and begins to sway, a blissful smile on her lips. I take a verse break at the end, gather my courage, and move right into a Kikimi jingle dress dance, the ball of my hand waking the song's heartbeat rhythm as it bounces on the strings.

Santana throws off the blanket and gets on her feet. She pulls Calico up beside her and the two of them step their way through a silent version of that old traditional dance. I play a few more Kikimi dances, then switch to another Diesel Rats song before finishing off with an instrumental cover of "What a Wonderful World" because it's pretty much my favourite song ever written.

Santana and Calico clap enthusiastically and sink to the ground as I put my guitar back in its case. The pair lean against each other, grinning.

"That wasn't so hard now, was it?" Calico says.

I shake my head.

"I can see why you don't play out anymore," Leah says. "A couple of bars of you singing and you'd blow your whole cover."

"Except nobody cares on the rez," Reuben tells her. "Steve can even go into town and nobody bats an eye."

"How can nobody have ever noticed?" Leah says. "You're older than you were in your heyday, but you don't look that much older. You'd think someone would have twigged. For that matter," she adds, "I can't believe some tabloid didn't get a forensic accountant to look into where the money from your royalties go."

"Jackson left everything to Steve," Morago says. "He was the only surviving family member."

I nod. "That part all worked out okay."

Reuben comes over and claps a hand on my shoulder. "Great playing, man."

He looks at Leah, his features serious. "Most of us don't know who Jackson Cole is," he says. "We just know Steve, and all of us would like things to stay that way."

Leah looks at Reuben, then her eyes meet mine. "I respect that and will honour it. The Diesel Rats' heyday was a long time ago. They still have a devoted fan base, but if I have anything to do with it, our dearly departed Jackson will still rest in peace."

She smiles at Reuben. "Just make sure that no one ever records Steve's music. The last thing he needs is to go on YouTube."

That raises a chuckle all around, but she's got a point. The world has changed with all the cell phones out there, so I take her warning to heart.

"Can we change the subject?" I ask before anyone can explore the topic further.

"I can do better than that," Morago says. "I can call it a night—at least for myself. I've got a storytelling session with the kids at eight o'clock tomorrow morning…this morning? Doesn't matter. It's still going to come too soon."

He stands up, brushes the dirt from his jeans.

"*Ohla*, my friends," he says.

He adds something in Kikimi that I've heard before. I don't know the exact translation, but it runs along the lines of a blessing.

Stay strong. Dream true. Walk tall.

That, I can try to do.

The dogs all get up when he walks off. Except for Ruby. She waits for Leah to say goodnight, then they both follow Morago back to Aggie's house. I hear the sound of wings in the sky above the desert as the crows leave as well.

"That's our cue," Reuben tells Santana. "Time to take you home."

"You don't have to do that," she says. "I've walked home from here a thousand times."

"Maybe so. But I told your brother I'd bring you home, and that's what I plan to do."

Finally, it's just the two of us. I stand up and pull Calico to her feet. Picking up my guitar case with my free hand, I lead the way back up to the ridge. Calico's noticeably quiet.

"Are we good?" I finally ask. "You're not mad about me taking the lead on talking with Sammy?"

She squeezes my hand. "Of course we're good. That could've gone a whole other way if you had jumped to conclusions, like I was inclined to do."

I shrug. "I was going there too, but I wanted to hear him out."

She smiles. "And that's why you're a good arbitrator."

I shake my head. "I'm not so sure about that, especially since all of this is so new to me."

"How are you feeling about everything that's gone down in the past couple of weeks?"

"Confused. A little freaked out," I admit.

She puts her arm around my waist and we continue to walk toward the ridge trail. "I have just the thing to relax you," she says, pressing her face into my neck and giving it a little kiss.

The whole way back to the trailer she keeps flirting, and I'm glad of the distraction. Just before we start down from the ridge trail she pulls me to a stop.

"Just remember," she says, her voice serious. "You don't have to deal with any of this on your own. You've got Morago and the aunties and Reuben. They'll talk you through any confusion you might have."

"And I've got you."

She rises on her tiptoes to kiss me.

80

LEAH

fter seeing Morago, and then Reuben and Santana off, Leah walked around to the front of the house and sat in the chair where, every morning, she watched the sun rise. The dogs had all vanished to wherever they spent their nights. Even Ruby was gone. Or at least Ruby the dog. As Leah leaned back in the chair, staring out at the starry desert night, she heard a creak on the porch. She turned to find Ruby the human being approaching. The red-haired woman settled in the chair beside Leah, drawing her legs up under her.

"So this isn't weird," Leah said.

Ruby looked at her. "What isn't?"

"I'm sitting with the same...being that I was patting on the head earlier."

"I liked it," Ruby said. "It was comforting."

"Still weird."

Ruby shrugged.

"I know," Leah said. "I'll get over it." She glanced at her companion. "Reuben's nephew said that a witch had eaten you, but you seem okay."

"It was true in its way. She was stealing my medicine, little by little every day. More quickly than it could be replenished."

"That's awful."

Ruby nodded. "Except the witch, Abuela, doesn't seem to be evil."

"How can you say that?"

"She steals medicine from the land, and she stole it from me while I was with her, but she used it for the betterment of her people."

"Her people? What people?"

"The people that live in her barrio."

"But she kept you prisoner," Leah said. "How did you manage to escape? Did she keep you in a cage, or were you chained up?"

Ruby shook her head. "It wasn't like that. I was free to wander around within earshot. I just had to be ready to come back to her house whenever she needed my medicine for one of her spells or charms."

"I would have just run away and not looked back."

"That's not something I could do. I gave Abuela my word that I would stay."

"But now you're here. What changed?"

"Steve sent Si'tala," Ruby said, "and she convinced Abuela to let me go." She paused before adding, "I'm still not really comfortable with how she did it."

Leah waited. Ruby was looking out into the darkness, her gaze thoughtful.

"What did she do?" Leah finally asked.

Ruby sighed. "Si'tala explained to Abuela that if I died, the bargain we had would no longer exist. That's true, but she also said she'd set her sister upon the witch, and not only would Abuela die, but her sister would probably burn the barrio to the ground while she was at it."

Leah grimaced. "Would her sister actually do that?"

Ruby nodded. "Given her reputation, I think she would."

"Seems unnecessarily harsh."

Ruby didn't say anything, but Leah could tell she agreed. Leah shifted in her seat and watched as a pale light started to creep across the desert in front of them, shadows resolving into various cacti and shrubs.

"I'd like to know more about the barrio," Leah said after a bit. "I'm guessing that's where a lot of the migrants end up, if they don't move on.

"Don't even think of going to the witch. I can find someone safer for you to talk to. I have friends in the packs that live there."

"Thanks. My friend Ernie's been trying to find somebody, but nobody wants to talk to the *gringa*."

"Why are you so interested in the migrants?"

"I'm not sure. It's weird. I've been sitting on the story of the century. I could name my own price if I were to let the world know that Jackson Cole is still alive. But even though I've spent the better part of my life writing about him and the band, I now realize that it's his story to tell, not mine. And however he wants to live, I respect that."

"I'm glad to hear you say that," Ruby told her. "Steve does a lot of good around here. People understand that many of the dogs on the rez are *ma'inawo*, but they forget that we understand everything they're saying. I know from listening to Morago and Steve that the whole turnaround we're starting to get on the rez is partly because of him, though of course the casino payments help a lot too. But Steve doesn't just provide money to help keep the school and community center running. There's a trust that he's set up to make sure that any kid who wants a decent education can get a scholarship."

Leah nodded slowly. "And that might fall apart," she said, "if people knew where the money was coming from—who it's been coming from. The rez would be flooded with reporters and people trying to get a piece of the action."

"Probably. But what I like about Steve is that he doesn't just give money. He loves this land and the people, and he's always lending a helping hand to whoever needs it. But at the same time, he keeps a respectful distance. He doesn't want things done his way. He just wants to quietly help preserve the Kikimi culture." She smiled. "He'd make a good dog."

Leah laughed. "And a talented one," she said.

The morning bird chorus started up around them. Leah loved this sound.

"Anyway," she said, "the reason I want to write about migrant people is that their story interests me." She paused, then shook her head. "No, that sounds too clinical. Their story moves me. I want to know more and to share what I learn, so that when some ugly reporter or politican accuses them of stealing jobs or ruining the country, I can help show that they're not scary aliens. They're people, just like us, who don't deserve to be hunted down or dying in the desert."

She turned to Ruby, her gaze earnest. "I love stories, both reading and writing them. But they have to be true. Fiction doesn't interest me. It never has. Why would I want to read some made-up story when the world is full of real people with genuine riveting stories? So many, that no one could ever have the time to absorb them all. It's not that I don't love language, but for the play of words, I read poetry."

"But don't people's stories become...repetitive after a while? Not everybody lives a full life."

Leah nodded. "I suppose. But those people don't tend to tell their story. It's the people with tremendous passion, or those who find impossible strength in extraordinary circumstances. Or endure and rise above great hardships. You can often tell, just looking at them. They have a glow."

"Like you."

Leah laughed. "I doubt that."

"No, you do, and you could use it to help others," Ruby told her. "You should talk to Morago. He can help you better understand other-worldly matters, and in exchange, you could help out at the school."

"I don't know that I'm cut out to be a teacher."

"Only one way to find out. The kids could use the help of someone like you. You don't have to teach. You could just advise them on things like passing their SATs, and the value of their own stories."

"I suppose I could try. I've enjoyed doing some volunteer work with kids back in Newford."

The morning had fully arrived while they spoke. Leah thought she should be tired. She hadn't pulled an all-nighter in years. But she felt full of energy. "I need to get Aggie's breakfast ready," she said. "You should join us. Do you eat people food when you're, you know, in human shape?"

Ruby laughed. "Dogs eat almost anything in whatever shape they happen to be wearing."

"Yeah, but do they help prepare it?"

Humour continued to bubble in Ruby's eyes. "I can certainly try."

81

SADIE

Sadie found it weird being in Newford. It was so different from how it was back home in the barrio. For one thing, it was way colder, which she hated, but apparently a shopping trip for warmer clothes was planned a couple of days from now. It was also a much bigger city. The traffic was crazy; it never seemed to stop. She'd lie awake in her room in the middle of the night and hear cars on the street, groups of people wandering by, talking in too-loud drunken voices. Sirens all the time. Really. Sometimes it felt like they never fucking stopped.

She had no idea how long she'd be staying—it all depended on how she did in "the program."

She was living in an apartment provided by some organization called Angel Outreach. The place had two bedrooms, a kitchen, bathroom and living room. Everything was kind of shabby, but at least it was clean. Candice, the adult supervisor, had one small bedroom. The larger room where Sadie slept was set up dorm-style, with four beds. At the moment there were only two other girls: Willow, who was from North Carolina, and Jennifer, from Alaska.

Alaska. Wasn't it always ten feet of snow and forty below or something there? Jennifer probably thought she was on a Caribbean vacation with the fall weather here. She'd be totally used to it being way colder.

Sadie thought she should probably look that up when she finally got computer privileges. She could just ask Jennifer right now, but a simple question would be like starting a conversation, and who the hell knew where that could go?

Sadie wasn't ready for conversations yet. It was hard enough to "share" with her counselor.

She knew she should feel grateful—she *was* grateful—but a part of her was still pissed off because her being here was just more people deciding on how she was supposed to live her life. Yeah, sure, she was trying to change, but she kind of wanted to do it on her own terms. That was when a little voice in the back of her head would pipe up: "Yeah, because that's worked so well before."

Sometimes the voice was enough to get her back on track.

Sometimes it was only when she started to go too far down that road, with the urge to sneak into Candice's room where the knives and other sharp objects were locked up, that she'd go someplace nobody was and do sit-ups and push-ups until she was trembling with exhaustion. But at least it worked and nobody got hurt.

Afterward, she'd sit on her bed and stare out the window at the brick wall of the building next door. She'd think about how all these people got together to help her. People she hardly knew. Hell, people she'd screwed over.

Apparently, the cop whose pickup she'd stolen had gotten together with Aggie, and Leah and Marisa—those women who showed up at Aggie's place right before all hell broke loose—to set it up. Steve was involved too. Or at least she'd been told that he'd paid for the flight and was her sponsor in the program. Whatever. She didn't know where he got that kind of money. Maybe his famous cousin left him a shit-load of dough that he kept stashed away somewhere in the mountains. He sure as hell didn't spend it on himself.

She couldn't believe she'd ever actually thought he was Jackson Cole.

One minute, she'd been in solitary, the next, she was released into the custody of that cop and Leah's friend Marisa, who'd returned from Newford to bring Leah some of her clothes and stuff. The three of them, along with Aggie, testified on her behalf to a juvie judge in Santo VV. Somehow, they convinced the judge to release her into this rehab program for screwed up kids run by a woman called the Grasso Street Angel.

The cop actually drove them all the way to the Vegas airport.

Sadie had never imagined that she'd ever get on a plane. It was so far from living in a crap house in the barrio and nowhere near as cool as she'd expected. As the plane started down the runway, she had to do some serious deep breathing when all she really wanted was to have a knife in her hand and do a little cutting to release the pressure.

The counselors were trying to help her with that. They'd even gotten her reading a book called *Scars* by a Canadian writer named Cheryl Rainfield. So far, it was a pretty good story. The writer's sliced up arms were on the cover. Sadie would stare at the cover. Who'd think that someone as messed up as herself could ever become a writer?

Today Angel called over to tell them that a friend of hers, an artist named Jilly, was going to pick them up and bring them to this drop-in center called the Katharine Mully Memorial Arts Court to show them around. Sadie tried to look interested, but all she could think was: great, the messed up loser kids in the program get to meet other loser kids and do fingerpainting or some other therapeutic art.

Sadie was told that the Arts Court was right downtown. She figured she could probably disappear pretty easy in a city this size, but if she did take off and then get caught, she'd be tossed right back in the slammer where she'd either find herself back in solitary or have those 66Hers *putas* in her face again. That got old fast.

She hated to think it, because she didn't want to jinx it, but the program was okay so far. Nobody was ever really in her face here and the food was heaven compared to the crap they served in jail.

So when Candice came in the bedroom to tell them their ride was here, Sadie was determined to try something different. Maybe she'd make some loser art, maybe she wouldn't, but anything was better than the crap that had been going down back home. Whatever came up, she'd try to follow Aggie's "do better things to become a better person" master plan.

It was worth a shot.

82

THOMAS

Thomas pulled over to the shoulder at the top of a rise on Zahra Road. In his side mirror he could see the highway wind its way as it returned to the rez. He got out of the pickup and stood there with one hand on the door frame, shading his eyes with the other.

It was hard to believe this was actually happening, how everything had just fallen into place.

Reuben had given him this old truck and two weeks' pay, and gave Santana his part-time job at the trading post. He'd also given Thomas the name and address of a friend in LA who had a job for him in construction if he wanted it.

When Thomas had tried to protest, Reuben just waved a hand. "When you're out there in the world," he said, "pay it forward."

"That's it?"

"Just be careful out there. Come back in one piece or your mama'll have a piece of my hide."

"What makes you think I'm coming back?"

"We always come back. This red dust is in our blood."

Mom had been pissed. She'd tried not to show it, but Thomas had lived his whole life with her. He didn't bother trying to explain himself because he knew she didn't want to hear it. So he'd just told her that he loved her.

Auntie had seemed amused, but maybe she was like her sister Lucy. Maybe she lived past, present and future all at the same time, and already knew how everything was going to turn out.

He didn't try to explain his reasons for leaving to William and Naya, either. But he told them he loved them, the same as he'd told Mom, and assured them that he'd come back.

"You shouldn't make promises like that," Santana said, following him out to the truck as he got ready to leave. "Not unless you're sure you can keep them."

"I can't tell them why I'm going. I don't want to put ideas in their head. Right now they're happy living here."

"I guess." She stood back and looked at the truck. "This thing's pretty much a piece of junk."

Thomas shrugged. "It's just the body that needs work. Reuben says it's mechanically sound." He grinned. "Plus it was free."

"Can't argue with that."

He reached out and touched her shoulder. "Are you going to be okay?"

"Hey, I've got a job now. I might even join up with the dog boys."

Thomas raised an eyebrow.

"They look like they have a lot of fun," she said.

"Except they're soldiers."

"Yeah, but they get to wear dog skins—and don't tell me you never wished you could go running with them up in the canyons."

"If I was going to wear a cousin skin, I'd want something that flies."

Santana smiled. "Yeah, that'd be sweet."

"You know, when school's finished and I get settled, you can come stay with me if you still want to get away from here."

Her eyes filled. "There you go, making promises again."

"You know I'd never turn my back on—"

He didn't get a chance to finish. Santana hugged him, squeezing him so hard it took his breath away. "I'm going to miss you," she whispered. Then she ran back to the house.

Thomas stood there for a long time after the screen door closed. Auntie sat in her chair on the porch, a pair of crows on the railing beside her. He couldn't read the look in her eyes. He wanted to comfort his sister, but he didn't see how he could. In the end, he was still leaving her behind. But it was hard.

Finally, he lifted a hand to Auntie and got in the truck, driving away before he could change his mind.

And now here he was, looking back once more, wondering all over again if he was doing the right thing. He wouldn't know until he actually left. And as Reuben had said to him—one of the last things he'd told Thomas before they said goodbye—"You can always change your mind at any time and come back."

As he turned to get back in the pickup, a raven landed on the roof of the cab. The big bird cocked its head and studied him. Thomas sighed.

"So which one are you?" he asked. "Si'tala or Consuela?"

The raven didn't answer.

"I'll tell you right now, I'm not going on any road trips with either one of you."

The raven just continued to look at him. Maybe it wasn't one of the raven women. Maybe it was just an ordinary bird, but nothing seemed ordinary around here anymore.

The ma'inawo no longer hid from him and Thomas wasn't sure if that was a good thing or not. It was disconcerting to have birds share gossip with him from their perches in the cacti and trees he walked by. He would see faces appear in the prickly pears and saguaros, passing along messages he didn't understand. Lizards whispered to him, lolling in the sun, and spiders, too, dangling from long silken threads. A dog sprawled out on the floor of the trading post would keep up a running commentary of everyone who came in.

He heard their voices in his mind—a questionable "gift" of his being a shaman, even an untrained one such as he was.

Even more disconcertingly, he caught himself studying his surroundings all the time, looking for some telltale hint that everything around him was a prop, just images painted on wood. If he thought about it for too long, the dirt started to feel spongy underfoot and the air would shimmer like heat waves for drawn out moments.

"You know," Thomas told the raven, "the Corn Eyes Clan only ever have crows for spirit guides. Yellowrock Canyon crows. We've never had much of a soft spot for ravens, even less so these days. So go follow somebody else."

The raven lifted a wing and began to preen its feathers. Like it couldn't care less.

"Just so we're clear," Thomas said.

He gave a last look down the highway before getting back in the pickup. The raven took off when he started the engine, following him down Zahra Road as he drove. He considered stopping in to say goodbye to Steve as he came up on the mouth of Painted Cloud Canyon, but only lifted a hand in passing to the red rocks as he went by.

He leaned forward, looking skyward. The raven was still up there, keeping pace.

Damn bird.

He turned on the radio, punching through the stations until he paused at an oldies station because they were playing "Gimme, Gimme, Gimme," one of the Diesel Rats' first hits. It had probably been a lot of fun back in the day, long before his time. In the current musical climate it sounded as corny as the Beatles' "She Loves You," but Thomas turned the sound up anyway and sang along, the miles unwinding under his tires.

∽

In the Dreamtime, all things are true,
Whether or not they are real.
—Sandra Kasturi,
from "Speaking Crow"

AFTERWORD

First, thanks to my readers who've waited patiently (I hope) for eight years for a new adult novel from me. Big changes happened in the publishing industry over that time, and my agent wisely advised me to focus on juvenile fiction for a bit while things sorted themselves out.

I enjoyed writing *The Cats of Tanglewood Forest* and my three *Wildlings* novels, but after that I felt a strong pull to return to my first love in this field, adult fantasy. I dove right in, but quickly rediscovered an old lesson: even with a wealth of experience, one has to learn how to write each new book, and *The Wind in His Heart* was a complex novel to write. It took me over three years to get it to the point where I could put it into my wife MaryAnn's hands, and as always, I owe her much gratitude for her editorial work, which improved the book significantly.

Although the novel has a fictional setting in the American Southwest, and several of the characters are from a purely fictional Native American tribe, I've done my utmost to treat *all* of my characters with respect, as fully rounded people with a rich culture. Beyond that, I want to send up a cheer for this particular time when more indigenous writers are coming to the fore in the literary world. I've been reading their work and talking about it for years, and once again, I encourage all of my readers to seek out these writers, whose voices can only enrich our cross-cultural understanding and empathy for one another. They deserve our attention and support.

I'm grateful to our eagle-eyed beta readers—Julie Bartel, Sean Costello, Lynn Harris, Lizz Huerta, River Lark Madison, and Kim (AKD) Welsh—for astute feedback and suggestions. Thanks as well to Alex Bledsoe, Janis Ian, Seanan McGuire, Melissa F. Olson, and Charles Vess for taking the time to read the novel and responding with such glowing comments.

Thanks also to Mark Lefebvre of Kobo Writing Life for his generous advice and encouragement, and to Rodger Turner, my stalwart pal of over 30 years, who also generously hosts my website on the SF Site.

I remain grateful to my agent, Russ Galen, who has taken care of us and patiently put up with my indie publishing ventures. Plus he got us a nice audiobook deal with a topnotch company, Recorded Books, and a hardcover contract with PS Publishing whose books I've admired for many years. Russ is the best in the biz.

It may be weird to thank my dog, but our little Johnny Cash has made my past ten years that much richer for his beautiful soul. Johnny's the one who gets us away from our computers, out into the sunshine, and under the moon and stars.

Most of you know that I value kindness and loyalty more than just about anything in life, and I've been rewarded with a wealth of readers who've stuck with me since the beginning, or discovered me midway through my career. Thanks to each of you. Dream large and true, and remember to take care of one another.

—Ottawa, Summer, 2017

ABOUT THE AUTHOR

Charles de Lint is a full-time writer and musician who makes his home in Ottawa, Canada. This author of more than seventy adult, young adult, and children's books has won the World Fantasy, Aurora, Sunburst, and White Pine awards, among others. Modern Library's Top 100 Books of the 20th Century poll, voted on by readers, put eight of de Lint's books among the top 100. De Lint is also a poet, artist, songwriter, performer and folklorist, and he writes a monthly book-review column for *The Magazine of Fantasy & Science Fiction*. For more information, visit his website at www.charlesdelint.com.

CPSIA information can be obtained
at www.ICGtesting.com
Printed in the USA
LVHW03s1230010818
585593LV00002B/384/P